Women in Nepali Politics

Looking Through Feminist Perspective

Women in Nepali Politics

Looking Through Feminist Perspective

Binda Pandey
PhD

ADARSH BOOKS

Book design by Limited Colors, Delhi

Women in Nepali Politics:
Looking Through Feminist Perspective

ISBN 10: 81-83631-44-4
ISBN 13: 978-81-83631-44-0

Published by
Adarsh Book 2019

Distributed by
Adarsh Enterprises
4393/4 Tulsidas Street, Ansari Road,
Daryaganj, New Delhi 110 002
Phone: 011-23245131-32, 41009940
Fax: 91-11-23246130
email: adarshbooks@vsnl.com

Printed at:

Visit us at: www.adarshbooks.com

Contents

Preface

Considering politics as the centre of the change process and women as contributors to it, I attempted to explore the nature and process of women empowerment in Nepali political movement from a feminist perspective.

In this process, I analyzed women's role in Nepali democratic movement focusing on the CPN-UML policies and practices in different levels. Being myself as part of this, I used personal reflexivity in interpreting the findings from the field. Similarly, I did interview some of the participants, organised focus group discussions with local cadres of CPN-UML, and interacted with several other people to get their insight into women empowerment process in the political movement.

From the study, I found that women empowerment appeared as: (a) familial participation; (b) agitating against oppression; (c) street action for human rights; (d) movement for workers' rights; and (e) activism as party-politics. I entered CPN-UML to scrutinise its gender policy and practice of empowering women in different phases. I found that CPN-UML's policy on women was based on Marxism in the beginning, which was shifted to Marxist feminism in between, and later to the socialist feminism.

Five major gender agendas of CPN-UML after 1990 anticipated the equal rights: (a) descent; (b) ancient property; (c) participation; (d) end of violence against women; and (e) affirmative action which increased the women empowerment in party politics as outcome of a triangular combination of Marxism, Socialist Feminism, and

International Communist movements. However, I found wide gaps between policies and practice as a major challenge of stereotypic mindset and women subordination, which debar women's leadership within the movement, and rampantly prevailing as patriarchal norms and values in society.

In conclusion, I understand that political parties need to: (a) make their policy known to members with motivation to enforce effectively; (b) translate gender policy and programme into action plan strategically with allocation of relevant resources; (c) timely monitoring to note out of the gaps between policy and practice; (d) periodic revisiting the policy and improve it; and (e) listen to the grassroots voices and the choices respecting their need, knowledge and experience in a systematic manner, while implementing its mission of social transformation towards an egalitarian society.

This book is based on my PhD thesis, which cover the period until 2016. Some major changes have been happened in regard to women participation in the state politics after completion of three tiers of election in 2017. That changes have been added as postcript at the end.

Binda Pandey

Acknowledgements

I would sincerely like to express my gratitude to all those who contributed in the process of the completion of *Women in Nepali Politics*, including all those scholars, friends, and well-wishers who provided kind support, encouragement, and invaluable suggestions. I am grateful to all the informants for their time, information, and commitment. I appreciate all of them, to whom I communicated in person for their experiences and who provided information as well as personnel in the CPN-UML offices for sharing and providing available information and materials. I also acknowledge the participants of the group discussions from district to ward committees of CPN-UML for sharing their works, problems, and the way of tackling local crises. I have used their pseudo-name in the book for the cause of their privacy.

I sincerely express my heartfelt thanks to Professor (Dr.) Bidya Nath Koirala, for his invaluable guidance, supervision, and continuous academic inputs to finalize this research report in a homely environment. I owe my gratitude to Dr. Mahesh Nath Parajuli, Dr. Bal Chandra Luintel, (Dr.) Mana Prasad Wagley, and Dr. Megh Raj Dangal for their continuous guidance and input from the beginning of the course to the conclusion of this research work. And, I would like to extend my sincere gratitude to Dr. Meena Acharya, Dr. Kyoko Kusakabe, AIT, Bangkok, Dr. Jai Raj Awasthi, Dr. Bhim Prasad Subedi, and Dr. Laxman Gnawali for their timely and creative comments to enrich my study.

I am indebted to Dr. Kailash Nath Pyakurel for his invaluable contribution to inspire me to continue this work. I would like to sincerely thank all my brothers, sisters, sisters-in-law, and nieces and nephews for their consistent support and insistence to complete the work. Among them, my special thanks go to nieces Liberty, Monica, Subigya, nephew Wisdom and friends Purusottam Neupane, Dr. Suresh Gautam, Dr. Prakash Chandra Bhattarai, Dr. Hem Raj Kafle, and Prem Raj Adhikari for their technical support for faultlessness. My sincere acknowledgements go to Dr. Khadga K.C. and Madhab Dai from Mandala Books for showing me the way to make this book more useful and accessible.

I am also grateful to trade union colleagues such as Sister Elizabeth Cotton from the UK and Brother Phee Jung-sun from Korea (while they were working with ICEM) and all the colleagues of GEFONT for their encouragement and support. Last but not the least, I express my sincere thanks to all my friends, colleagues and relatives, who encouraged and supported me mentally, psychologically, and physically with good intention and inspiration.

Binda Pandey

List of Tables

List of Figures

Abbreviations

ANWA	All Nepal Women Association
BPA	Beijing Plan of Action
CA	Constituent Assembly
CBS	Central Bureau of Statistics
CC	Central Committee
CCM	Central Committee Member
CEDAW	Convention on the Elimination of all Forms of Discrimination Against Women
CoCe	Coordination Centre
CPN	Communist Party of Nepal
CPN-M	Communist Party of Nepal (Marxist)
CPN-ML	Communist Party of Nepal (Marxist-Leninist)
CPN-UML	Communist Party of Nepal- Unified Marxist-Leninist
CWD	Central Women Department
ECN	Election Commission of Nepal
ESCR	Economic, Social, Cultural Rights
EU	European Union
GAD	Gender and Development
GoN	Government of Nepal
IIQM	International Institute for Qualitative Methodology
IPC	Inter-Parliamentary Conference

IPU	Inter Parliamentary Union
IPWA	Inter Party Women Alliance
IWD	International Women Day
MPs	Member of Parliaments
NAN	Nursing Association of Nepal
NC	Nepali Congress
NFE	Non-Formal Education
NLFS	National Labour Force Survey
NPC	National Planning Commission
NWO	Nepal Women Organisation
PMO	Prime Minister Office
PMPD	People's Multi-Party Democracy
PO	People's Organisation
PS	Parliamentarian Secretariat
RH	Reproductive Health
SLC	School Leaving Certificate
SPD	German Social Democratic Party
UG	Under Ground
UK	United Kingdom
UML	Unified Marxist-Leninist
UN	United Nations
USA	United States of America
VAW	Violence Against Women
VDC	Village Development Committee
WAD	Women and Development
WID	Women in Development
WT	Whole Timer

Introduction

Through my engagement in the progressive movement since 1980, I feel that democracy is the base of human dignity. I have developed a firm belief that gender equality makes the democratic system more practical. Because women are an integral part of the human society, their participation in every aspect of the human activities provides basic measures of equality. Empowerment of both men and women is necessary to make their meaningful participation not only in the party politics but also in social spheres. Keeping these basic premises in mind, I have chosen 'women's empowerment in politics' as topics to go through in-depth study. And, taking political party as the main vehicle to deliver democratic values and equality as norms, I have chosen CPN-UML as the institution for a case study.

As a woman, I believe that women's role is significant in all spheres of the society. Their contribution is crucial in economic, social, cultural, and a number of other sectors. In the process of social upliftment, women's participation is indispensable. Making their participation more effective, enhancement of their knowledge, skill, and experiences through changing attitude and behaviour is named empowerment. Consequently, their political participation becomes the most essential, where they can play and get an important role in the decision-making process as well as enforcement of the policy in practical level. In this regard, women play an active role to make the society equitable. Achieving the equitable society is not only what they deserve, but is inseparable from their lives and careers. Thus, to accelerate their involvement in decision-making bodies is also a must for realising their empowerment in all levels and spheres of the society.

Empowerment is an important issue of public concern; it can have an immense and intense impact, especially on women's lives and, in general, on the society as a whole. It would also be unjust to keep such a large section of the population away from decision-making and operational processes. It is not only the issue of being a larger population but essentially of having a vital role in every walk of life, including being the key agent to transfer culture and tradition to the new generation.

The Government of Nepal (GoN) ensures women's participation in all spheres of life, which is manifested in the agendas of political parties as well (GoN, 2015). Some of the gender-related issues have been included in the policy and programmes of the government. These include the right to property, participation and ending violence against women (VAW), etc. Terms, conditions, and commitments are spelled out consciously, but we see problems in their implementation. Being a part of women's movement in Nepal, I have closely experienced that patriarchal mindset and male chauvinism in the leadership of the state and political parties have subjected women to the state of voicelessness. Women are consistently trying to be audible in their political parties, communities, and even in their families. They are trying to have the opportunity at every level and field to play decisive roles for the purpose of social transformation that enhances justice and equality. This study attempts to probe into the same issue. How are these issues reflected in the policies, programmes, and decisions? Are they implemented and practiced in line with institutional commitment or not? If not, what are the causes and effects of non-implementation? Answering these questions has been the central objective of selecting the issue of women's empowerment for the purpose of this research.

Motivating Factors

Date 18 May 2006 was the historical day in Nepal. It has been more important and memorable for people like me, who were the part of the unprecedented people's movement. On the very day, the Parliament which was restored through People's Movement declared a historical document that curtailed powers and privileges of the monarchy, suspended the kingship, and later uprooted it and brought the state sovereignty completely under the Nepali citizens. The country was declared a secular state, the then His Majesty's Government became Nepal Government, Royal Nepali Army was converted into Nepal Army and came under Nepal government from the palace. In short, the declaration was called 'The Magna Carta of Nepal' (GoN, 2006).

Though the Movement had tremendous consequences, I was a little confused and frustrated. The Declaration did not include any of the gender-related issues, which were committed by political parties prior to the People's Movement.

My engagement in the transformation of society dates back to the 1980s when I took part in student movement with the demand of fundamental democratic rights including gender equality. This was while I was studying in the high school. I had seen and experienced various types of discriminations against women from the very days of my childhood. While the student movement was getting momentum in 1979 and spreading all over the country, I came to know that one of the missions of progressive movement was 'no discrimination between men and women'. In fact, this was the very statement that deeply motivated me to join the Movement. In the succeeding years, I was very much confused and puzzled seeing the gap between the spirit of the slogan and the practice. So, I made a determination to end it and decided to devote myself to the leftist interchangeably progressive movement. I became a full-fledged activist for it to narrow down the gulf of words and actions to end the discriminations against women.

At the prime times of the successful People's Movement in 2006, political parties and leaders were pondering and listening to various concerned stakeholders including trade unions, professionals, etc. While they were preparing the draft of declaration, we as women had collectively requested to the political leaders to include at least three points that were seriously concerned with women, viz., citizenship certificate to their children in mother's name, one-third portion of women's participation (in whole) in all organs of the state mechanism, and eliminate all kinds of gender discriminatory laws. It's a pity that none of these issues were included in the 18 May, Declaration (Appendix I). I myself with other women colleagues felt it as a humiliating discrimination against all women. The seven-party alliance had made nine points commitment on 8 March 2006, including the earlier-mentioned issues (Appendix II). But the leaders, obsessed with the pre-occupied mindset, ignored all these issues and forgot their commitment. Then, I felt that we as women should do something collectively, and requested Bidhya Devi Bhandari (incumbent President of the country and) one of the then parliamentarians to submit a motion of public concern in the Parliament. She heartily welcomed the idea and tabled it in the Parliament next day. Ignoring the discouragement and humiliating behaviour of some of the senior male leaders in the Parliament, she proved herself as an iron lady and a visionary leader and her bold, courageous, and dauntless spirit and attitude kept her firm on the issue. Then, the women's movement that had started in the cities, towns, and villages also created pressure in the Parliament and influenced parliamentarians.

In the end, the motion was adopted unanimously on 30 May 2006 (Appendix III). It was a landmark declaration of the Parliament in terms of gender concern. As a result, women's one-third participation have been insured in all the elected body of the state including equal property right, stronger provision on VAW special provision to mainstream women in all sectors.

Contextualising Women's World Scenario

As equally important members of the society, women and men are complementing each other to build the society rather competing from family units to the nation. But, it is a bitter truth that women are not getting equal access to handle the leadership positions of making decision and policy that affect them as well. Its impact is negative on social progress and prosperity. Realising this, gender sphere is getting central space in social change movements.

Gender discrimination against women is a worldwide phenomenon even today. To narrow down the gapping, their presence as critical mass in the process is a pre-condition, and without quality for them, intervention cannot make intended impact. In the viewpoint of women's participation, we can see extreme imbalances. For instance, Inter-parliamentary Union (IPU)'s (2014) report says women's representation in Parliament is only about one-fifth and 6 per cent as head of the state in the world record. Keeping this in mind gender participation has been taken in two ways—the quantitative presence of women as numerical values and qualitative intervention in the process of decision-making, such as setting the agenda, making the opinion, and taking the decision. And then, women activists realised that their participation meant being part of the policy enactment and monitoring to capitalise the achievement, so that they could learn from shortcomings and work improvement. The next reason is that taking part in all these processes itself is the opportunity of educating oneself, forming leadership personality and developing knowledge, and competing in quality. As a whole, it is the stepping-up as the process of political empowerment.

The 1995 Beijing Plan of Action (BPA) set a target of achieving 30 per cent of parliamentary seats for women by 2005, but as of 1999, only eight countries in Scandinavia had met the goal (Freedman, 2002). Now, 48 countries have achieved the target. Among them, Nepal has been placed in 34th position having 33.5 per cent women in federal parliament (IPU, 2017). However, it is limited in the numerical values of women participation in Nepal. Even today only thirty-five countries have achieved this target (IPU, 2014). Nepal is just on the border ranking 36th position, having 29.9 per cent women in the Parliament. Keeping eyes and mind on this stark reality, the United Nations (UN) has passed the Convention on the Elimination of all Forms of Discrimination

Against Women in 1979, in which all the member states of UN have committed to ensuring equal rights to women and men (UN, 1979). Yet, several forms of discriminations are prevailing in Nepal. The UN passed the Universal Declaration of Human Rights in 1948, in which, Article 21 mentioned that 'Equal access to power, decision-making, and leadership at all levels is a necessary condition for the proper functioning of democracy.'

The Beijing Declaration and Platform for Action was adopted by the Fourth International Women's Conference in 1995. It has stated that the empowerment and autonomy of women and the improvement of women's social, economic, and political status are essential for the achievement of transparent and accountable government that works for the benefit of both women and men (UN, 1996). It recognises that women's empowerment and full participation on an equal basis with men in all spheres of life, including participation in the decision-making process and access to power, are fundamental to the achievement of equality, development, and peace.

In addition to setting government commitments, the Beijing Platform of Action (BPA) has urged a range of actors to take measures in support of women's participation at all levels. The political parties, the private sector, trade unions, national, regional and sub-regional bodies, employers' organisations, research and academic institutions, non-governmental organisations, etc., are the concerned actors who can accelerate the women's participation in all spheres. Almost all the states of the world including Nepal are party to these international instruments and have made a commitment to implement it. Because of these initiatives, women's participation in the political sphere is improving slowly, but still is much less than the UN Declaration of 30 per cent by 1999 and proportionate in 2005 (UN, 1990).

Nepal is not the exception in this regard. The population ratio in Nepal is 94.4 males against 100 females (CBS, 2011). It is crucial to have women's proper participation in the process of social transformation. For the purpose, women's equal access and control in the decision-making process is necessary. But the reality is still far behind. So far, little improvement has been seen in comparison to last decades, but this process may take centuries to achieve the commitment without taking bold steps for affirmative actions.

Understanding Women Empowerment

Economic self-reliance is one of the main pillars of women empowerment. It is one of the important elements to improve women's participation in social and political activities. But in the Nepali context, women's participation in informal economic activities is very high. It is seen that only 26.2 per cent women employees are in formal employment and earning only 59.3 per cent of men's average earning (GoN, 2008). The updated data in this regard is in the process of analysis. The Central Bureau of Statistics (CBS) shows that female ownership in the fixed asset as house and land is 19.71 per cent, which was 9.11 per cent in 2001 (CBS, 2011). The CBS data also suggest that women play leading role as labourers in agriculture and informal economy. But they have little right to decide anything like using the input as well as trading the product and participating in technical training to build skills and capacity (CBS, 2011). Poor access to the resources and decision-making processes has been seen as a negative impact as their low participation in political works and activities.

Likewise, Seager (1997) found in mapping that education and awareness are important elements to obtain the position, making voice and influence with clear perspectives, which can create knowledge as well. The author also mentioned that economic status is another indicator to facilitate the process. The same author further reported that people being economically empowered and self-dependent can play a more active role in the decision-making process in private as well as in the public sphere as family, community, institution, and the state mechanism.

Education also contributes to the human capital formation as enhancing the quality of knowledge, understanding, skill, and perception to analyze the things and situation with clear vision and empirical logic. For example, Myriad's (2006) studies in the US shows that education is linked with democratic behaviour and attitudes, which contribute to increase political participation.

Looking back ourselves in Nepal, the literacy rate of male is 75.1 per cent and 57.4 per cent of the female in 2011. While the education level moves upward, women's participation seems in a reverse way as three-fourth in completing school leaving certificate (SLC) level, almost half in graduate, and one-third in post-graduate level in comparison to male students (CBS, 2011). But, the present scenario is changing. For instance, boys' enrolment is 98 in lower secondary and 93 in secondary level in compare with every 100 girls' enrolment (CBS, 2017). It means women's participation in education is changing as well as the space of the feminist intervention is also being expanded. Freedman (2002) argues that one of the most important contributions of the twentieth-century feminist theory is redefining the politics to include both public and private realms, both male and female concerns. And, the feminist movement seeks to restructure society to end legal discrimination and expand economic, reproductive, and political rights.

Based on all these statements, we can draw the conclusion that education, awareness, economic self-reliance, and political participation are important integral ingredients of the women's empowerment.

Less opportunity in education might be one of the major hindrances for women remaining behind than men in the political process. This suggests that as a corrective way, practical measure to achieve 'education for all' should be reviewed with a gender perspective. It also suggests that to strengthen women's access and control over resources, the policy and practice of property right and employment opportunity should be adequately defined. Provision to balance numerical participation and package programme to enhance capacity needs to accompany the policy. In our context, VAW and recognition as a citizen of equal identity are fundamental issues restricting women's empowerment. To create a conducive environment for women's empowerment, patriarchy-based social values, attitude, and behaviour need to be changed and establish such understanding that men and women are citizens of equal status having different biological capacities.

Women in Parties' Policy and People Multi-party Democracy

Nepal Praja Parisad (1937) is one of the oldest political parties in Nepal. It aimed to provide civic rights to all people (Gautam, 1990). Yet, this Party had not spelled out any specific statement on gender.

Then Nepali Rastriya Congress (NC) established and conducted its first congress during 25-26 January 1947 in Kolkata, India (Basnet, 2009). NC demonstrated its resolution recognising the oppression of women and adopted a resolution to fight for equal rights for women (Basnet, 2009). At the same time, the NC included a provision in the constitution that women can be qualified to apply for party membership at the age of 16 years, while male should be 18 years of age (Adhikari, 2003). The Party had given priority to women's education as one of its goals.

The Communist Party of Nepal (CPN) was established in 1949. It has mentioned the issues of gender equality in its founding Manifesto (CPN, 1949). Its leader Puspalal (1996) mentions 'equal right for women in all spheres of the national lives'. As a continuation of CPN's political journey, the Communist Party of Nepal-Unified Marxist Leninist (CPN-UML) carries forward the issue, with the commitment of achieving gender equality through the political process and ultimately transforms the society toward gender balance and justice. By adopting the new programme called the People's Multi-Party Democracy (PMPD) through its Fifth National Convention in 1993, CPN-UML has included five points programme on women such as that: (1) all kinds of exploitation and suppression including abduction, trafficking, prostitution, and other social evils, perpetrated against women will be brought to an end; (2) equal rights of all children to the patrimony and equal pay for equal value of work will be brought into effect; (3) complete equality between men and women in national and social walks of life will be guaranteed; (4) special campaign of eradicating illiteracy and providing social security will be guaranteed; and (5) women's active participation in political, economic, and social fields will be constantly encouraged and increased (CPN-UML, 1993a).

From this point, UML has realised that the policy of equity needs to be followed to achieve gender equality. Reflecting the policy into practice, the Convention elected two women in the central committee, first ever in the UML history. UML has further mentioned in its election Manifesto (1994) that:

> *Removing all the age-old discrimination and prejudiced treatment between male and female in all fields–political, social, cultural, and economic—our party is committed to guarantee[ing] equal rights to women in all fields as men.*

Arriving at the second National Council Meeting in 1995, UML started to set quota to ensure women participation and decided to have at least one woman in its every committee (CPN-UML, 1995). Progressing the quota within a decade, UML Central Committee adopted to ensure at least 33 per cent of women's participation in all state mechanisms including its own structure (CPN-UML, 2005). It decided to develop a special package programme to empower and enable women to take equal responsibilities.

Keeping these provisions in mind, to empower women by creating opportunity and proper space in decision-making in all spheres and level, UML took initiatives to bring the resolution forward in the Parliament in 2006. This included women's right, mentioning at least one-third women participation in all spheres of the state mechanism so as to eliminate all discriminatory laws through amendment. This indeed was a historical step at the state level (GoN, 2006a).

Arriving in the constituent assembly in 2008, UML added more issues in its Manifesto (2008) as reflected in these statements:

> *Women would have the progressive right to reproductive health and divorce and get special priority in relation to education and health. A special plan would be adopted for women's employment in the labour sector, where women's participation is low.*

Similarly, accepting the effort, UML made constitutional provision, the first time in the history to include not less than one-third women participation in its internal structure (CPN-UML, 2009a). In order to crosscheck the earlier mentioned provisions in action, I calculated the percentage of women in UML and found that it is having 18.7 per cent women (50,530 out of 2,70,520 in total) members and 23.8 per cent in average in district committees. Similarly, much fewer women are in the central leadership than commitment as 16.3 per cent (30 out of 184) in central committee and 8.4 per cent (2 out of 24) in standing committee (as per data available in department of organization of UML, December 2014), which was much lower during the previous period than this.

Reports of UML organisational department show that 78 district level committees (including three special committees beyond geography) are functioning. Among them, there is one woman as Chair (in Makawanpur) and three Secretaries (in Tanahu, Chitwan, and Rupandehi). Less than a 5 per cent of those committees have a woman as either Vice-Chairperson or Joint-Secretary, as assisting positions rather than major decision-making posts (in October 2016).

The People's Multi-Party Democracy has also mentioned that economic right is one of the essential factors for gender equality. Addressing it, the fifteenth meeting of Central Committee in 2007 decided and directed the district members through circular to provide equal inheritance property rights for all children regardless of gender and marital status (CPN-UML, 2007a). But the Party Headquarter neither has any information about it nor record of its implementation in any rank and file and at the cadre level.

The Unified Marxist Leninist discussed the code of conduct regarding VAW in the 15th meeting of Central Committee in 2007 and forwarded for next meeting to take a final decision on it (CPN-UML, 2007a). But, the UML was not able to take action against the culprits as some of its members were found involved in VAW. For example, as reported in the *Kantipur* daily (19 November 2012), one of its cadres, Devbahadur Bista from Rukum broke his wife's leg beating her up brutally. The case was brought to the Party. But, no serious action was taken against him. Since many such cases piled up unaddressed, women members raised the issue continuously and tabled a draft of a code of conduct on VAW collectively with all sister organisations, in the ninth convention of UML in 2014. Finally, it was adopted.

Going through all these policies, decisions and practices, it would be relevant to study the matter in depth and probe the reality about the status of women and their issues within the party structure.

Shaping the Study

The issue of gender parity is much linked with women empowerment and is part of the policy-making mechanism and process in the party politics of Nepal. Political parties are considered the main vehicles in a democracy to gear up the state policy through institutionalising the issues and processes leading toward social changes. Defining democracy, Chilean women movement has coined the slogan 'democracy without women is not [a] democracy' (Freedman, 2002). An important logic behind this statement is that women are half of the population, without their full participation democracy cannot function well. It is yet to be fully realised in our context.

It is also believed that political party as an institution could play a vital role to change social norms, attitude and practice, responding to the demand of the era by developing contemporary policies. The political parties attempted to translate policies into action within the parties and played a leading role as necessary to influence change in the society as a whole. Connecting the issue with local experiences, the issues of private and public are being blurred. For example, contextualizing domestic violence and marital rape in our society, these issues were considered the very private matter until the last decade but now these have become public and are covered by state laws. Many issues like citizen identity, reproductive right, right to marriage and divorce, culture-based discrimination against women, counting the domestic work, etc., used to be private matters but now they are the matters of public concern. These changes have been very much based on the ideology of 'the personal is political', which is the leading statement of the second wave feminists in the world (Hanisch, 2006).

The earlier mentioned provisions have been discussed on the public spheres of the Nepali society. The information presented earlier shows gradual progress in policy, programme, and participation but in practice, the process and achievement are quite slow. Many decisions have been taken but they are not implemented properly in practice. Owing to such a despairing situation, women's participation in the apex decision-making bodies is negligible in Nepal and elsewhere. According to IPU (2014), there are 6.6 per cent women heads of the state, 15.8 per cent speakers, and 22 per cent in parliaments. In Nepal, too, the data presented earlier suggest that UML as one of the leading institutionalised parties has not yet been effective enough to respect and implement its own policy and decision to improve gender justice within its internal structure. In this context, this is important to see women's position and status with the critical approach in its organographies and figure out possible measures to promote gender role and create a conducive environment for gender equality and justice for women emancipation.

Nepal has started periodic development plan from 1956, named Five-year Plan. It had mentioned women's issues as part of the periodic plans when the UN declared the year 1975 as the 'Women's International Year' and 1975-85 as the 'Women's Decade'. But, the provisions mentioned in it were hazy in terms of the perspective and approach. It was only after the restoration of multiparty democracy in 1990, the National Planning Commission began to think on women's issues a bit more systematically. For the first time in the history, the Ninth Five-year Plan (1998) included gender equality through affirmative action and other programmes (Acharya, 1999). From then on, the state has taken some steps to promote gender empowerment by establishing women ministry, national women commission as a mechanism, 20 per cent women participation in the local body, amendment of civil code popularly known as the Eleventh Amendment in 2002, etc. But most of them have been popular in paperwork rather making a meaningful impact in women's lives and society.

The gap between the principles and actions of women was wider and the activists continued voicing their needs and demands. Finally, after the success of people's movement in 2006, the state declared commitment in the Parliament on 30 May 2006, to eradicate all kinds of gender discrimination in law and policy and move forward to achieve women's proportional participation in all the state mechanism through ensuring at least one-third critical masses (Appendix III). But, the public impression and facts that I received from the different walk of the lives are not very inspiring. The commitments have not been taken into account in practice.

The Communist Party of Nepal-Unified Marxist Leninist was the first party to adopt Eight-point Gender Agenda of Women's Empowerment in 2005 including one-third women's participation, equal right to descent and property, ending VAW, reproductive right, etc. Later, in 2006, based on the previous commitment, UML forwarded four-point motion in the Parliament, which was unanimously adopted. But, even then it did not show enough empathy to execute this declaration within own party as well as the state mechanism. For instance, while its' senior leaders were leading the cabinet three times in 2009, 2011 and in 2016, the report from the Prime Minister's Office (PMO) said in regard to nominate people in state mechanism that very few women had been picked up (GoN, 2009, 2011, & 2015). What were the obstacles for UML from nominating enough women in the state mechanism? It is an unanswered question, yet. Within the party structure as well, UML's commitment on gender agendas has not been fully respected, though much progress has been made. What are the elements contributing to making these changes? What are the constraints behind for full enforcement of those commitments? And, what can be done in the day to come to gear up the empowerment process? These are key questions for me to conduct this research.

The main purpose of this study is to explore the nature and process of women empowerment within CPN-UML. Specifically, it is focused to identify the UML's contribution to promoting women leadership; its policies, programmes, and practices of empowering women to attain gender equality as ultimate goals.

Women in Nepali Politics aims to explore women's empowerment in the context of policy, programme, decision, and practice in the CPN-UML, which has been observed closely from the feminist perspective.

The research findings might help to promote gender parity within the UML. It might contribute to making tangible changes in reality in the process of women's empowerment within in terms of gender mainstreaming and its impact with visible policies could be replicated in the society as well for socio-cultural transformation. Similarly, the research findings may contribute to promoting democracy in terms of making it more inclusive, representative, functional, and sustainable.

As one of the members of the research institution, the process of study has broadened my experiences as a participant observer. Besides this, the outcome of the study might give more factual ground to raise the issue inside to promote participation in the process to develop appropriate policies, strategies, and action plans accompanied with equity measures and to enforce them to achieve the set goals of substantive equality.

This study is focusing on gender policy of CPN-UML. Prior to doing so, in connection with getting historical aspect, has been reviewed Nepali women's movement and mentioned some of the information beyond UML. But, for the purpose of getting gender policy and programme to analyze, other parties have not been included. I selected interviewees and participants of the group discussion for the primary data, only among the leaders and cadres within UML, having diverse experiences as of senior, leaders, and some of them junior as well.

Connecting with the History

Feminism as the Theoretical Principle of Study

The feminist inquiry has been characterised as oppositional research because it challenges the rights of the powerful across these diverse disciplines to define realities (Devault, 1999). Frye (1993) illuminates the enormity of the task of feminist inquiry as being related to developing an account of the world that places women's lives, experiences, and perspectives at the centre of analysis. Thayer-Bacon and Turner (2007) say that feminist inquiry has made a significant contribution to contemporary philosophy and that the philosophy of education is standpoint epistemology. They have further argued about various ways of taking women's perspectives such as black, outsiders, marginalised, etc., where women share histories and experiences based on their positions in relation to power, different than the dominant culture. It is associated with the third wave feminism approach to diversity among women.

Digging out the deep-rooted problem and shortcomings in the society, critical theory have been employed. The roots of critical thought have a long tradition of intellectual rebellion in which rigorous examinations of ideas and discourses constituted a political challenge. International Institute for Qualitative Methodology (IIQM) explains that critical thinking implies freedom by recognising that social existence including our knowledge of it (Saldana, 2014).

Having this understanding in the background, this study has been done with the feminist inquiry and critical view based on Marxism, Feminism, and PMPD to probe into the issue of women empowerment within the UML. There are different perspectives of feminism in the context of the political process. To analyze the trend of Nepali women's movement, this study has been done with the standpoint of socialist feminist principle.

Education: The Cornerstone of Women's Empowerment

Education plays a vital role in the human capital formation and has been considered one of the key elements of human development index. In almost all democratic systems, education has become an integral element of fundamental human rights, which has been mentioned in the Constitution as well (GoN, 2015). Duke II (2010) says that the relatively high level of illiteracy serves as an instrument of disempowerment for women. With the limited access to education, in comparison to men, women remain marginalised in their inspiration to attain a higher level of education, which is reflected in their advancement in politics, economy, and other spheres of societal life.

Michelle (2006) describes the direct and indirect effects of education on political participation. Similarly, Fink (1992) notes in regard to non-formal education (NFE) in Latin America and says that non-formal and popular education programme often becomes a key for women to have meeting, create mutual support, and a sense of community. Western (1994) observes that the literacy education programme following the welfare approach social participation and integration in community activities is promoted in order to improve the welfare of the family and the community and for the women to acquire more self-esteem as mothers, wives, and citizens.

All the aforesaid statements confer education as a vital input contributing to empowering women and increasing the probability of their participation in politics, in the community activity and leadership at any level. But quality leadership in policy-making and empowerment to be accepted as a political representative in the democratic process are two different things. For example, when Dr. Meena Acharya, one of the prominent women of Nepal contested the parliamentary election in 1999, she could secure only few hundred votes (ECN, 2008). But, my argument is that wherever she got opportunities to show her leadership in public, she could present herself as a good leader as logical and influential and play a vital role in policy and law-making process better than other less educated ones. It is where I realised that exposing the personal quality of general people and win their trust is one of the challenges in regard to empowering women in different dimensions. Education is one of the factors in this regard.

Recalling the experiences working as a Constituent Assembly Member from 2008 to 2012 women having better education played an active role using empirical facts, figures and logic and made intervention more effectively in comparison to the less educated members. Even the cross-national comparative work on the features of political engagement shows that the political participation is more likely to be more closely related to women's educational levels than is the number of legislative seats won by women (Goetz, 2003).

Claassen and Highton (2009) say that the political significance of the low and unequal distributions of political awareness, knowledge, sophistication and engagement in the mass, the public remains one of the central questions for public opinion scholars. On the other hand, Edward, Giacomo, and Shleifer (2007) quote Martin Luther King's argument from his essay 'Students' role in Democracy' that 'education is key to raise the benefits of political participation'. In our context, one woman in each unit in the election of the local body, more than 40,000 women were elected promptly in 1999. Some of them even could not read and write. After being elected, they felt embarrassed to put thumbprint as a signature in meeting minutes. Some other felt uncomfortable while they could not read the written text in the minutes and other related documents. Then, they realised the importance of education to take part in politics and to make better intervention in their day-to-day work as well. It encouraged many of them to take initiative to run literacy and non-formal classes among women as part of local government activities, in which they themselves participated. One of the examples of this process is Khadga Kumari, the elected woman representative from my own native place in Nuwakot, who became literate in this process (Personal Communication with Khadga Kumari, 2013).

Education creates multiple impacts on human beings, which is directly connected with the empowerment of people to participate in the process of policy-making. In this regard, Wu (2003) gives several reasons to explain the relationship between educational attainment and political participation. Among the males, an individual with higher education is more likely to have higher incomes, occupy a higher social status, interact with others in social and political groups, possess more information about government and politics and, therefore, participate in politics. She notes that increasing education and income level is positively associated with the increasing level of political efficacy, and is directly linked with empowerment.

This aspect is reflected in the Nepali context as well. Nepali history shows that those women who took part in political rallies in 1947 with the demand of civic and political rights were motivated by education to fight for equality, rights, and democracy even in the era of oligarchy (Pandey, 2002). Education builds the capacity to understand social realities and analyze them objectively. In this sense, to be the part of politics as a higher level of social work, education is one of the essential ingredients for political activism and to motivate people with strategic views. Connecting with women empowerment, education in any form—as formal, non-formal, and informal—is necessary to grasp the matter properly, analyze it, and then communicate to others effectively. It is linked to knowledge, skill, attitude, experiences, quality participation, etc., which are unavoidable elements of the empowerment. But, I hold the knowledge that education alone cannot make much influence in politics. It needs to be accompanied by awareness of other kinds of sensitivity including gender to make social transformation effective and efficient toward social justice.

Defining Empowerment

Empowerment is the process to move forward progressively to establish an egalitarian society, which includes both representation and intervention. Women empowerment is an active multi-dimensional process to enable them to realise their identity and power in all spheres of life through greater self-reliance and internal strength (Narang, 2012).

The governments of the world made their commitment to the women empowerment in the International Conference on Population and Development in Cairo 1994 and reiterated in Beijing Conference in 1995 (UN, 1996).

Empowerment is the process by which women gain power and control over their own lives and acquire the ability to make strategic choices. It can be defined in different levels as an individual, group, and societal or community. The individual level empowerment deals with individual woman's abilities; the group level deals with the collective action as a sense of agency of woman experience together; and the societal level deals with the permissiveness of the political and social climate in connection of societal norms and the public discourse, too. The empowerment processes in the different levels are interconnected and mutually reinforcing (Megharaja, 2014).

The UN has defined empowerment with the inclusion of five components. These are as follows: (1) Women's sense of self-worth; (2) Their right to have and to determine choices; (3) Their right to have access to opportunities and resources; (4) Their right to have power to control their own lives, both within and outside the home; and (5) Their ability to influence the direction of social change to create a more just social and economic order, nationally and internationally (UN, 2012).

Empowerment is multi-dimensional in nature (Figure 2.1). With regard to empowering women through the political process, having their appropriate representation in the different mechanism with a capacity of self-determination, standing with self-esteem, ability to make self-opinion and express them independently and confidently. It helps women make proper intervention setting agenda in the decision-making process and being involved in the enforcement process.

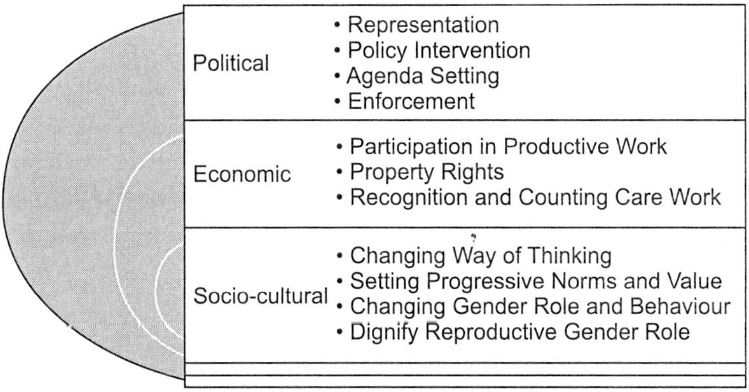

Figure 2.1 Multi-dimensions of Empowerment.

Economic empowerment is linked with equal access and control over the private and public resources (Kabeer, 2001). Participation in the productive work and equal right to property is one of its parts. Recognition and counting of the care work is another essential aspect, where women are dominant. Shifting the culture to share household work among all members of the family is another aspect to empower women in public lives.

A third aspect of the empowerment is a socio-cultural aspect. Education is one of the decisive aspects of the socio-cultural dimension, which empower people to widen their awareness and deepen the understanding. Linking with women empowerment, education creates the space to be part of a public sphere and intervene in the process of decision-making, which plays a key role to change gender stereotype. At the same time, changing the socio-cultural aspect creates self-image free from any kinds of systemic and structural discrimination. Oppression and subordination as different sex are one of the fundamental aspects. For the cause, social stigma based on gendered attitude, norms, values, and practices under the name of 'culture' need to be dispelled. And, reproductive role (as domestic care work) requires to be dignified.

Dimensions of Participation

The ultimate goal of the empowerment process is to expand choices of life. In regard to women empowerment, gender balance participation in all spheres of lives without any differences is the foundation to ensure such move. In the process of historical development, participation has been loaded with ideological, social, and political thoughts giving rise to a wide scope of interpretations (Lawrence, 2006). Stoker (1997) defines participation as a representative of the public taking part in any of the processes of formulation, passage, and implementation of public policies.

The first theoretical work attempting to classify different levels of participation is Arnstein's (1969) famous 'ladder of citizen participation'. The framework describes a continuum of increasing stakeholder involvement from weak to strong forms of participation (Figure 2.2).

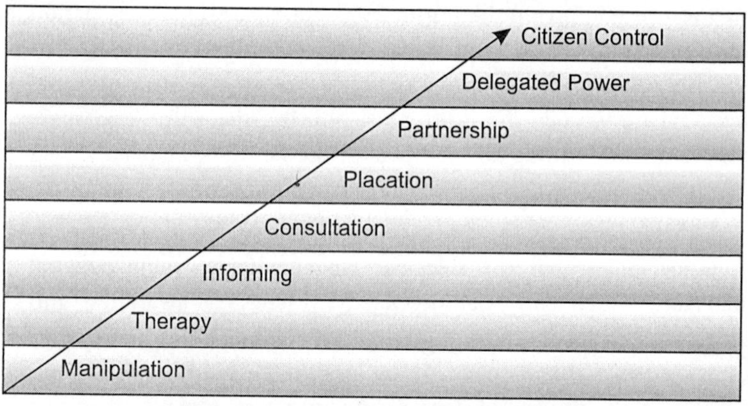

Figure 2.2 Ladder of Citizen Participation.
(Level of Participation adopted from Arnstein, 1969, p. 216.)

The participation ladder features eight levels of participation with indirect 'manipulation' or pseudo-participation at the bottom, and real power controlled by stakeholders is shown on the top three notches—partnership, delegated power, and citizen control. This model was developed in the process of developmental work and is based on it. It can be defined in connection with political participation as well.

The higher the participation of citizens, the more visible is the impact of policy-making and operational intervention. It is applicable to the empowerment of women as well. Empowered gender participation is expected in the upper level with unambiguous ideology to achieve the final goal of the political journey. In our context, the participation of women in larger number lies just at manipulation level. Increasing women's participation in upward position is still a big challenge. Empowering the women with clear ideology accompanied with required technique to upgrade the participation to citizen's control level is a must to accelerate the process of the redistribution of power.

Basically, the political participation can be categorised into two spheres based on dimensions of participation as quantitative and qualitative, which can be measured in breadth and depth. Quantitative participation shows numerical presence. The UN (1990) had declared 30 per cent critical mass of women participation to achieve by member states by 1995 and go for proportional representation after 2005 in all policy-making mechanisms. Emphasising the UN declaration, the BPA has also declared to achieve 30 per cent women in all structures of the state including political parties.

As a member state, respecting the declaration of UN and BPA, the interim constitution of Nepal guaranteed 33 per cent women candidate for the Constituent Assembly in 2007 and guaranteeing in the result by the Constitution 2015 (GoN, 2007 and 2015). Similarly, UML has also included this provision in its own constitution (CPN-UML, 2009a and 2014a).

According to the constitutional commitment, one-third women's participation was reflected in the Constituent Assembly in 2008 and 29.5 per cent in 2013. Rest of the structures including executive, judiciary, constitutional bodies, etc., are still far from achieving the said target.

The qualitative dimension of participation includes intervention, argument, logic, intellectual influence, etc., which is closely linked with strategic achievement including the change in attitude, mindset, and behaviour. Since one of the objectives of this research is to see the gap between the policy and practice from a feminist standpoint, the consideration of quality intervention in the process of policy-making is crucial. Where and how is space and role given to gender in terms of setting agenda? How is the tendency of attending the meeting, making an argument in the process of opinion building through discussion on set agenda and decision-making? These are some basic areas of qualitative dimension.

Another level of qualitative participation is women's presence, which plays role in decision enforcement, and its monitoring and evaluation process. Initiation to change the attitude and the way of thinking and doing of both male and female, mainstreaming the gender agenda in the institution, gearing up the changing stereotype in gender perspective and role, developing affirmative action based on present context are important sectors for quality intervention. These are the ingredients of the women empowerment.

Roberto (2009) says that effective leaders direct the process to marshal the collective intellect of the organisation, rather come up with all the answers themselves. He further adds that great leaders ask good questions and empower the group member to ask good questions with one another. Taking this statement in account, EU (2005) has adopted a women's charter as:

> *Gender balance in decision-making, in political and economic life and in the public and private sectors, with belief that this provision would help Europe to shape more effective policies, develop a gender-aware knowledge-based society, and create a stronger and more prosperous democracy.*

Uncovering the problem, Derbyshire (2002) mentioned that too often gender-mainstreaming policies 'evaporate' before implementation and remain as paper commitments only. She says, 'policies must include strategies and action plans with clear procedures and targets as well as designated roles and responsibilities for promotion, implementation, and monitoring.' Addressing the challenges, it is needed to question oneself that why the decision and work are not being effective enough in terms of balancing gender participation and promotion.

Emphasises the difference between strategic and operational decisions. Strategic power involves the ability to set targets, allocate priorities, and determine policies. Operational power has the ability to decide how these tasks are carried out. Focusing on factors to account for political activity, mention that people may be inactive because of three factors, such as lacking resources, lacking psychological engagement with politics, and being outside the recruitment networks that bring people into politics. Resources, on the other hand, have been defined here as 'time, money and civic skills' that the participants hold. All of these are necessary elements for the effectiveness of empowerment.

Lesson learning from the earlier-mentioned experience, together with the proper allocation of resources and creation of enabling environment, should have contextualised matching strategic and operational decisions to motivate people to make a higher level of participation.

The previous discussion implies that while analyzing women's situation in leadership, making them more effective and efficient, additional emphasis on escalating skills and knowledge and making them resourceful should be taken into account. It also implies that there is a need for managing women's time in public activities by preparing male counterparts to share reproductive responsibility at home. It also indicates that leadership in politics, as well as social sectors, should be prepared to change the gender roles in the process of social transformation.

Women's Agenda in the Change Process

Considering women's presence as half of the society and realising the importance of their participation to have justice-based social change, they must be the part of every sphere of the society. Reflecting the basic principle of democracy as the rule of majority, it is not possible to claim the society as democratic enough without having gender-balanced participation within the party and the state mechanism. In this context, Freedman (2002) can be quoted as follows:

> *Today, as in the world before feminism, women continue to resist patriarchal dominance by affirming their authority within families as mothers. At the same time, feminist movement continues to demand full citizenship right, independence from family relations, and international agencies and transnational feminist organization is promoting the issues such as equal education, property rights, marital choice, and suffrage.*

The logic behind this is that wherever women have exercised political rights, they have been able to initiate changes in powerful public institutions, like legislatures, courts, and the military. These multiple feminist challenges to male dominance have irrevocably infiltrated world politics. Elaborating the agendas, Freedman said, 'Women's politics have strong links to broader social justice concerns, such as environmentalism, pacifism and democratic government as well.'

Taking Freedman's view into account, it is argued that Nepali women's movement is still struggling for the cause of equality in citizen identity, inheritance property rights, and reproductive right based on the principle of 'our body- ourselves'. Women's participation in the state structure for real democracy is a mainstream agenda, which, nobody dares to deny overtly though it is not being practiced enough. It is argued that the domestic domain is still very much gendered and even for those people who believe in Marxism and socialism. The quote here Marx's saying that 'for their own liberation, women should enter into productive sphere' (Marx, 1978). But, the practice has taught us that without men's participation in the reproductive role in the domestic matters, only women being part of the productive sphere cannot liberate them rather it burdens them with additional responsibility.

Realising this fact, PMPD (1993) has addressed this question mentioning that 'complete equality between men and women in national and social walks of life will be guaranteed.' It means men should be an equal partner in the social (domestic) walk of life and women should join public sphere to blur the gender role.

Though the political statement is clear in the document, it has not been sufficiently elaborated on how to achieve it in practice. This suggests a need to elaborate it into an action plan and then translate into practice through the process of socio-cultural transformation accompanied with a feminist perspective.

Feminism: An Empowerment Journey

Feminism has a direct relation with the power structure. The feminist movement was started from the middle of the nineteenth century and is deep-rooted into the issues of women's liberation to achieving gender equality in all spheres of life (Rampton, 2015). In the process, feminist theory revealed how gender roles are socially constructed, how they vary across time and cultures, and how they continue to adapt and change. This shows that feminism is concerned with the forms and functions of power, in particular, which is against girls and women. Feminist movements also seek to restructure society to end legal discrimination and expand economic, reproductive, and political rights, to achieve long-term goals as 'strategic gender interest in contrast to the practical gender interests of materialists (Monteux, as cited in Freedman, 2002). It is where Franke (1987) referred Rubin (1984) and mused that feminism was best equipped to analyze and address gender-based subordination.

Feminism has been divided into three waves (Dorey-Stein, 2015). The 'first wave' feminist movement was influential from the mid-nineteenth to the early twentieth century until the end of the First World War (1848-1920s) representing women's efforts to get the right to vote, property, divorce and receive alimony and child support, and manage their own bodies. The 'second wave' feminist movement corresponds to the 1960s to 1970s and women's efforts to obtain equal access to higher education in all fields and freedom from any kinds of discrimination in their workplace. And, they continued the fighting for the right to manage their own bodies. In the early 1990s, a 'third wave' of the feminist movement began with an explosion of multiple, diverse perspectives.

Like feminism, post-structuralism also says that intellectual faculties are not determined by biological essentialism but are the results of socialisation. The subject is decentralised and occupies various sites, which are determined by cultural and physical practices (Acker, 1995). Even though feminists resist the notion that biology determines identity, the underlying discourse posits that feminine and masculine genders would be expressed in male and female bodies. Butler (1990) rightly suggested that gender is not a fixed characteristic but a flexible variable that changes with context and time.

Riley (1999) says that feminist theoretical approaches vary greatly in their focuses, starting points, political grounding, and many other aspects. Recognising the variety, they incorporate at least three common ideas as central to most feminist theoretical perspectives that gender is an organising principle, a social construction, and engages in the politics of inequality.

Back in Nepal, we can hear the story of very brave women, fighting in Nalapani war against the British imperialist army during 1814-16, which has not been supported with empirical data yet (Kunwar, 2008). Those women fought with patriotic perspective with the feeling of no difference between men and women. They were fighting for the nation. Kamala was one of the leading women in that battle. During the Shah dynasty before the rise of Rana oligarchy in 1846, some of the queens including Rajyalaxmi Devi Shah became a de-facto ruler (Nepal, 1995). But they were in power not to improve the livelihood of people or women's situation but as the agent of retrofitting traditional power structure. Power-mongering by the top level women did not make any positive impact in general, neither on women's right nor people's right by and large.

The next scenario of women's involvement in politics in Nepal was initiated by Yogmaya Neupane. She fought against taboos. She had faced widowhood in her childhood and she married challenging the social taboos and obstacles. She not only rose against social evils but also revolted against Rana oligarchy and social injustices and discrimination against women, representing poor and lower class people. Her movement was launched a century ago, emerged in the remote village from the people's level. This is one of the landmarks in Nepali women's movement (Basnet, 1996). Around the same time, Mahila Samiti (Women Committee) was established in Siraha which asked a Rana queen to chair it. But, it could not sustain for a long time (Tumbahangfe, 2009). Moving forward, Chandrakanta Mathema opened women's school in the decade of the 1940s. Following that Sahana, Sadhana, Snehalata, and Kanaklata were arrested for demanding civic rights in 1947. After few months, Nepal Women's Organisation (NWO) was established under the leadership of Mangaladevi Singh. And, on behalf of NWO, a delegation visited Rana Prime Minister Padma Shamsher demanding voting right and education for women, which were achieved immediately (Singh, 1994). If we analyze the issues raised in those movements, it is argued that they match the first wave of the world feminist movement.

After the abolition of the Rana regime, the Movement was continued with further vigour. The major issues of the Movement were education, employment, political participation, etc., which are the burning slogans until now. The level of gender sensitivity in society, organising culture among women, and readiness to take different roles and responsibilities has been enhancing gradually (ANWA, 1985). This process is fostering the space for the feminist movement and mainstreaming the issues even in the political movement and state power. At this point, it is realised that all these issues and perspectives are close to the second wave of feminism. But arriving in People's Movement II in 2006, Nepali women movement shifted to third wave feminist movement with voicing out that women are not a single community rather a diverse group situated at the intersection of the class, ethnicity, caste, and region.

Feminism: Not a Single Idea

The feminist movement was started in the middle of the nineteenth century (Dorey-Stein, 2015). In the beginning, it was dominated by the issues of suffrage and equal opportunity in education and employment. Based on changing time and issues, feminism has also been divided into different waves and categories.

The first wave of the feminist movement was started with liberal feminist perspective. Later in the process, while Clara Zetkin took the lead of the working women's movement, Marxist perspective entered the equality movement. The second wave of feminism was started as well with the dominance of liberal feminist principle focusing much on formal equality based on individual rights. But, a fraction of women emerged as radical feminist group viewing that men are the primary cause of women's oppression. It contributed to establish some of the agendas in the Movement. By 1980, Marxist feminists had come in the scene with the class-based collective perspective and participation in productive work outside the home for earning as the basis for women's liberation.

Later, a group of feminists realised that women's subordination is deep-rooted not only in economic power but also in socio-cultural values, which have a strong influence in politics as well. Identifying this main feature of the cause and effect, women's movement theorizes that both men and women should be changed holistically to achieve gender equality in the society as a whole. This has been named as Socialist Feminism.

In the 1990s, the third wave of the feminism started focusing on the issues of sexuality and diversity within women. Women are being 'othered' not only on the basis of biological gender. There are various elements to maintain social status in the society such as class, colour, caste, ethnicity, etc., based on local context.

Though the feminist movement can be divided into different waves and categories based on its specific characters, the issues raised in different stages are interconnected and complementing each other in the process of attaining the goals of the feminist movement.

Comparing and contrasting with different waves of feminism, I infer that Nepali women movement at present is blurring different waves and categories of feminism, focusing on equality in law and policy. But, the literature that I came across (National Women Commission [NWC], 2011) made me deeply realise that Nepali society needs to move forward for economic and socio-cultural transformation rather than just legal reforms in the state. And, the feminist movement following the popular People's Movement in 2006 has carried the aspiration of third wave feminism. In this ground, with the aspiration of third wave feminism, the socialist feminist approach is relevant to empower women with the perspective of social transformation toward an egalitarian society. Internalising this reality, third wave feminism with socialist perspective has been used as the ideological base for this study.

It suggests that feminists too are contextual and do not subscribe to a single idea. Some take a definite stand and advocate for equality and justice and others go for a fusion of two or more feminist trends creating their own. These puritan versus fusionist approach to feminism also helped people to have different thoughts under the same umbrella. Nepali feminists, it is argued that belong to the fusionist category. UML is not an exception to it.

Socialist Feminism: The Better Path Toward an Egalitarian Society

There are two ideological poles, representing the prevailing tendencies within the feminist movement—one directs toward new lifestyles within women's culture, emphasizing personal liberation and growth. Another direction emphasizes on a structural analysis of the society and its economic base, focusing on the ways in which productive relations are organised (Booth, Creamer, Davis, Dobbin, Kaufman, and Klass, 1972). These authors further mention that feminist movement has grown with an understanding of common oppression of an institutionalised system of oppression based on the domination of men over women, in which women have no control over their lives, which could only be regained if they acted collectively. For this reason, reaching to most women, organising them, and developing collective actions are the key priorities to weaken the power of the ruling class, give women a sense of their own power and improve their lives.

Mao (1955) opines that genuine equality between the sexes could only be realised in the process of the transformation of the society as a whole. He advocates that the socialist vision of a

Table 2.1 World Trend in Feminism as Waves and Categories

	Waves	*First Wave*	*Second Wave*	*Third Wave*	*Remarks*
Types	Basic elements	Collectivist, defining women as a single group. Limited issues.	Collectivist. Define women as a single group. The main slogan is 'Personal is Political'	Multiple recognition of gender identity. Focus on 'our-body-our-self'	Nepali women movement started at the end of the first wave and now as well much dominated by the second wave.
Liberal	• Major issues–suffrage, access to education, and property. • Movement dominated by the middle class, educated white women. • Emphasis on legal equality and individual right.	• Started from the mid-nineteenth century to end of the First World War, in industrialised countries. • Named after the 1950 decade. • Major issues suffrage, education, and property right	• Major time-frame 1960 to 1980 • Equality in all sectors including education, health, employment, property, participation, etc., both in private and public place. • Emphasis on a legislative measure	• Similar issues continue with some new features such as the right to abortion, adultery, multiple gender identity.	• First wave's issues marked in 1947 with the demand of women education and voting right • After this, the second wave liberal feminism remains much dominated by issues and perspective focusing on equality in law and policy.

(*Contd.*)

Table 2.1 World Trend in Feminism as Waves and Categories (*Contd.*)

	Waves	*First Wave*	*Second Wave*	*Third Wave*	*Remarks*
Radical	• Patriarchy as the main problem of women's subordination • Power is based on sexuality • Man as an enemy	Since the beginning, some of the activists were raising radical voice for women's liberation	• Came in a debate during the 1960s • Attempted to have a new theory with the positive value of womanhood.	• Man as the root cause of women's subordination and hetero-sexual relation causes male power. • Women's right to sexuality	Some individual followers of radical feminist have been seen one after another but not organised and recognised as movement
Marxist	• Main issue, class-based society • Power lies in the ownership of means of production. • Focus on collective liberation	The decade of 1870 already Marxist, especially Labour Movement was following it, which was led by Clara Zetkin.	• Came into discussion after 1970. • Technology supported domestic work and equality through participation in work outside the home. • Women's liberation through class struggle.	• Realise class struggle alone cannot liberate women. • But still economy considered as the decisive factor.	• During the period of the 1990s, Marxist approach emerged as dominant through the Left Movement • Still some groups believe in this as ideology, but in practice, liberal one is much influential.

(*Contd.*)

Table 2.1 World Trend in Feminism as Waves and Categories (*Contd.*)

	Waves	*First Wave*	*Second Wave*	*Third Wave*	*Remarks*
Socialist	• Inequality based on class and deep-rooted in patriarchy • Grassroots mobilisation for equality and justice • Men and women should work together for change. • Focus on collective action as class and gender.	In the process of Socialist Movement, Socialist Feminism Movement was expanded from the beginning of the 1920s, because of the VAW during the First World War.	• Came into debate after 1990. • Gender inequality based on economic class and patriarchal value. • Economic, social, and cultural transformation is the way of liberation • Women and men both are equal actors for change.	• Believe in both class and gender equally as important phenomena. • Equal identity, economic, social, and cultural rights • Reproductive rights as abortion, divorce, crèche for all children, etc., and sharing domestic work	• Socialist feminist approach fostered after 1990. • Issues are getting popular but practice dominated by liberals, and male participation is still not enough • Mainstreaming the agendas adopted by the third wave feminism

(Dorey-Stein (2015) and *Feminism: Basic Principles*, 2005.)

humanist world can be made possible through a redistribution of wealth and an end to the distinction between the ruling class and those who are ruled. In this way, the socialist feminist movement combines both visions as the personal and the structural analysis and its strategy grows from an understanding of the dynamics of power.

Hochschild (2003) says socialist feminists emphasize the economic, social, and cultural importance of women as people who give birth, socialise children, care for the sick, and provide the emotional labour that creates the realm of the home as a retreat for men from the realities of the workplace and the public arena. Socialist feminists see this as important labour that is overlooked and denigrated.

Feminism is collective and organised against men's vested interests. But, women and men are united in class position against powerlessness. In that regard, both of them having socialist ideology are the co-partners of the feminist movement. Having all these sayings in the course of changing society, UML's shifted paradigm to promote social change through peaceful mass mobilisation and policy on women's liberation.

It is notable that when the second wave of feminism was expanding in the world, it questioned on the process of promoting women's dependency and vulnerability by the modernisation and argued in favour of responding to their needs (Boserup, 1970). Then, the approach 'Women in Development (WID)' came into discussion, which defined women as the passive recipient and focused to improve women's condition. But, it did not question the social structure. After few years, the new approach 'Women and Development (WAD)' came in vogue with little attention on women's subordination caused by the division of public-private sphere and gendered roles (Table 2.2). It defined women as a part of productive work, but could not acknowledge the reproductive role defined as the responsibility assigned solely to women (Rathgeber, 1989).

Both these WID/WAD approaches were initiated by the first world middle class, educated women, which could not properly respond to the diversity of women by race, colour, class, etc. Then,

Gender and Development (GAD) approach came in discussion recognising diversity among women and subordination not only caused by economic class, but also socio-cultural practices. Rathgeber (1989) further says that the GAD approach has been taken as third world women's approach, which has included most of the elements of socialist feminism with defining both men and women as change agents and emphasising on men's participation to change women's condition and status from the family up to the state. Recognising economic as well as socio-cultural values as the cause of women's subordination, it has recommended affirmative action as equity measures to bring women in equal status as men.

Keeping the concepts of WID to gender mainstreaming in mind, state policy of Nepal did not recognise women's needs, condition, and position until the beginning of the 1980s. After participation in the International Women's Year (1975), the government started to respond to women's needs and included some elements in the national plan with the WID approach (GoN, 1980). While multi-party democracy was restored in 1990, national policy recognised the WAD approach, with an objective to include women in productive activities (GoN, 1997). This was the departure point from the conventional way towards gender mainstreaming, to eliminate gender inequality in all laws and empowerment of women through affirmative action programmes. This strategy was continued in the Ninth Five-year Plan (1997-2002) as well.

Setting the millennium goals, the Tenth Plan/poverty reduction strategic programme (PRSP) clearly emphasised women's empowerment as enhancing the capabilities through increasing their access to resources and decision-making positions to mainstream women in the development and governance process and state structures (GoN, 2002).

Moving ahead, in 2006, the importance of the GAD approach has been recognised, with the agendas of changing socio-cultural values, equal rights on identity, property, participation and ending all kinds of VAW. But, it is yet to be realised in real life, owing to no appropriate follow-up of the policy in the process of implementation.

Table 2.2 WID, WAD, and GAD Approaches in Nepali Context

Women in Development (WID)	WID concept came in the early 1970s, influenced by Ester Boserup's *Women's Role in Economic Development*, with liberal feminist focus on practical need and trickle-down theory. It recognises different experiences of women and men defining women as a homogenous group and passive recipients of developmental activities. It is grounded on traditional modernisation theory; expecting improvement within existing social structure rather changing power relation.	In the Nepali context, after the International Women's Year 1975, this perspective was included in the Fifth Five-year National Plan (1975-80) with recognition of women's role in the economy and was continued until the Seventh Plan.
Women and Development (WAD)	The WAD concept emerged in the second half of the 1980s and gave attention to women's subordination, was promoted by UN through first World Women's Conference and women's decade. It believes that integrating women into the development process as an actor can reduce economic dependency with the expectation of women to participate in the public sphere, seem close link to Marxist feminist view. It is critical to women's subordinated position and assumes improvement while outside structures become more equitable but unable to address the reproductive role and changing social structure.	The Eighth five-year national plan (1992-97) recognised the WAD approach, which is much in practice until now influencing our state plan and activities.

(*Contd.*)

Table 2.2: WID, WAD, and GAD Approaches in Nepali Context (*Contd.*)

Gender and Development (GAD)	The GAD concept emerged in the early 1990s as an alternative idea focusing on patriarchy-based power relations. Kate Young contributed remarkably, considering women as a change agent; focus on shared productive and reproductive role, dismantling the public-private separation, stressing on collective voice of the oppressed gender to make effective changes politically. It explores both the connection and contradiction of gender, class, race etc., with focus on strengthening women's rights including inheritance, customary and statutory provisions with emphasis on changing social, political and economic status with balanced gender participation. It underlines both strategic and practical needs of men and women with full integration of the socialist feminist ideology.	The state recognized its appropriateness after 2006. But it has not been integrated into the national plan in the proper way yet. The new constitution has incorporated most of these issues.

{Rathgeber (1989); GoN (1997; 2002)}

It is the argument that women movement is raising these issues on socialist feminist grounds and demanding the pursuit of GAD approach in developmental policies. The state institutions, on the other hand, are responding with liberal perspectives based on the WAD approach. This is the major gap between Nepali gender equality movement and state's responses. Furthermore, is that political parties including UML do not seem clear on the approach of addressing the matters in the proper way though PMPD (1993) has carried socialist feminist perspectives in approach to women related policy and agreed on the GAD approach in regards to action.

Relevance of the Feminist Standpoint Epistemology

Standpoint theory is a post-modern method for analyzing inter-subjective discourse. Standpoints always involve more than one factor. Harding (1993) says that standpoint theories argue for starting off thought from the lives of marginalised people; beginning in those determinate, objective locations in any social order will generate illuminating critical questions. Harding called it strong objectivity, or the notion that the perspectives of marginalised and/or oppressed individuals can help to create more objective accounts of the world.

Brooks (2006) says feminist standpoint scholars call 'double vision' or 'double consciousness'. This is to say that they argue about women as members of an oppressed group, who have cultivated a double consciousness, a heightened awareness not only of their own lives but of the lives of the dominant group (men) as well.

Brooks (2006) explains in his book with reference to Nielsen (1990) that if a woman is in an oppressed position, it is often to her advantage to be attuned and attentive to the male perspective as well as to her own. To survive socially and sometimes even physically, women must familiarise with men's worldviews and be able to 'read, predict, and understand the interests, motivations, expectations, and attitudes of men'.

Nielsen further says that women are tuned into men's activities, attitudes, and behaviours and to their own. This feminist standpoint concept, sometimes called as 'strong objectivity', teaches us that women are more capable of producing an accurate, comprehensive, and objective interpretation of social reality than men (Brooks, 2006).

Friedan's (1963) study on American housewives in the 1950s and the 1960s provides another example of how women's subordinate status in society places them in an advantageous position from which to build knowledge–to construct a more accurate picture of social reality. But the feminist standpoint epistemology is an innovative and dynamic approach to knowledge building that breaks down the boundaries between academia and activism, as well as between theory and practice. Feminist standpoint researchers also seek to give voice to women as oppressed groups and uncover the knowledge cultivated from life on the margins. This epistemology also takes women seriously as knowers and translates their knowledge into practice. That knowledge learned from women's experiences would be used toward social change and elimination of the oppression of all marginalised groups (Brooks, 2006).

Feminist standpoint theorists recognise instead that women hail from a diverse range of class; cultural and racial backgrounds inhabit many different social realities and endure oppression and exploitation in many different shapes and forms (Brooks, 2006). Observing all these statements and ideas, I realise that the feminist standpoint epistemology can be used relevantly in this study. The research as well focuses on why women are being marginalised in the political process and, how can their knowledge and experiences be blurred in the process of social transformation for social justice? Though women are taking part in the political process since the beginning, why are their contribution and knowledge positioned in the periphery?

Learning Experiences From Others

The capacity to reason, argue, and draw decision is the basis of the political activism, and acquiring these elements is the foundation of women's empowerment especially in the political participation. To strengthen the women's capacity in this area, talking to Lenin (1921) says as follows:

> *Everywhere there is evidence of a sincere wish to put this equality into practice. We are bringing the women into the spheres of economy, legislation, and government. All educational institutions are open to them, so that they can increase their professional and social capacities.*

Trotsky (1923) states that 'in order to change the conditions of life, we must learn to see them through the eyes of women', which can be regarded as an excellent expression of the Marxist tradition.

Laws and policies are important for social change but are not sufficient. If the proper implementation of them is not achieved in time, change might track back after sometime. For instance, between 1917 and 1927, the Soviet government passed a series of new laws providing women legal equality as men, first ever in the Soviet history (Lund, 1970). But it was not fully realised in the process of action. As a result, a complete reversal occurred by the 1930s and many gains achieved by women just after the revolution were eliminated slowly. Lund has summarised the situation, saying that 'genuine emancipation of women is inconceivable without [the] general rise of economy and culture.'

Millet (1970) argues in *Sexual Politics* that the major reason for the counter-revolution in family life and the status of woman was that Marxist theory had failed to supply a sufficient ideological base for a sexual revolution and was remarkably naive as to the historical and psychological strength of patriarchy. In addition, there was no realisation while every practical effort made to implement a sexual revolution, the real test would be in changing attitude. In line with Millet and Lund (1970) also draws one great lesson to be learned from the Soviet experiences, both positive and negative, which is the need for women to organise as women before the Socialist Revolution and during the Socialist Revolution. In that case, Lund believed that women would be able to play a maximum role in the Revolution to ensure their needs and aspirations are satisfied and not subordinated. Trotsky (1923) says that for women's emancipation, both material resources and strength of will, knowledge, and effort are necessary for the process of transformation of family life. Pointing out women's role in the social change, he mentions that every awakened woman should devote a major part of her strength and attention to the task of transforming our everyday life. Trotsky (1925) also advocates altering the position of women at the root, which is possible only if all the conditions of social, family and domestic existence are altered. He views socialism, as the emancipation of women and most important capital is the people. Recommending the way-out, he says that changing this, the conservative mentality and attitude toward women is basic and enabling women's participation in public life, which is equally important.

Learning from Russian experiences can be very useful in our context. After a long struggle, Nepali women have achieved equality (except few issues) in policy and laws including equity measures in many aspects. But if we did not give enough attention to action, this may evaporate after sometime. It is the big challenge in front of social and political movement with the aim of building on an egalitarian society.

China, the close neighbour of Nepal, has gone through a revolution in 1949 and has changed women's social status remarkably. According to Mike (2008), during the Cultural Revolution women made substantial gains. Many broke into higher-paying jobs in industries, developed as political leaders, challenged ideas of women's inferiority, and began to dig up the Confucian-patriarchal roots of women's oppression in China. Mike has further mentioned that 10 years after liberation, Chinese women had made great progress, as a direct result of the socialist transformation of Chinese society and the full participation of women in the labour-force was the key ingredient for attaining equality between women and men. As a special measure to promote women's status, 'Iron Girls Brigades' of young women was formed. They took part in the most demanding and difficult tasks in many enterprises. Those women were given national publicity for breaking into all-male jobs such as oil drilling, repairing high-voltage lines, and building bridges. This helped to increase the number of women workers in heavy industry. This kind of action also helped to break the stereotypical of thinking and seeing women as a weaker sex. Nevertheless, at higher levels of leadership, women's representation was not satisfactory. The reason behind this was that they were following the Marxist way of action, which sees women's liberation only as taking part in productive works. But, they did not have a holistic approach and feminist standpoint to make a change in women's daily lives.

Cuban experiences in regard to gender participation and perspective are mentionable here. Sarmiento (2003) says that at the political level, the rectification process, which expanded from late 1984 until 1988-89, was aimed at correcting sexual discrimination. In 1986, the Communist Party of Cuba declared the need to promote women, non white and youth to decision-making positions. Sarmiento further mentions that Cuban scholars see the gender perspective as a Marxist way, for it implies a feminist commitment to pursue social justice for all, which has a direct relation with politics and power. It helps to understand the structures of inequalities between men and women by revealing sex as traits in political decision-making, along with social and legal policy-making and their actualisation in everyday life.

The women in America conducted a National Women's Conference in 1848 and adopted the nation's first women's rights resolution, popularly known as Seneca Falls Declaration (Rampton, 2015). This Conference claimed natural equality of women and outlined the political strategy of equal access and opportunity. But the Conference was not much successful. Responding to this situation, women were agitating radically. For instance, on 23 October 1918, women demonstrated outside the White House with the banner as reading 'Germany has established equal, universal, secret direct franchise, but the Senate has denied equal universal suffrage to America. Which country is more of a Democracy, Germany or America?' After series of these kinds of activities, they achieved the voting rights in 1920.

The earlier discussion indicates that democracy on its own does not create a path for women's empowerment unless political leadership opens broader eyes to see the marginalised community and follows a strategy to bring their knowledge cultivated from the margin into the centre. Ideally, women are equal as men in terms of law and policy in many countries and have equal access to education and economic field. But because of continuation of stereotypical mindset to see women as a subordinated community, is an obstacle in the change process of changing gender inequality.

It gives the sense that formal equality in policies and laws and equal access to education and economy alone do not create a conducive environment to achieve substantive gender equality. Internalising the biological differences as a natural fact, realising the different gender needs based on biology, addressing them differently with equity measures based on local contexts can be the proper way to achieve equality.

Changing Patriarchy Fostering Way to Women's Empowerment

Socio-cultural factors play a very important role in women's empowerment. Realising this fact organisations need to create enabling culture and environment to include more women within the structure and process. Lamsal and Sintonen (2001) emphasizes the idea that the number of women leaders should be increased because women hold such new qualities as networking skills, ability to motivate others, social skills and so on, as the need of contemporary organisations. The reason behind it is that patriarchal values are a big challenge for women's emancipation and participation in the public domain. Referencing research in the Shaanxi province of China, even after almost 50 years of revolution, Coleman et al. (1998) indicated, the 'underlying patriarchal values made it very difficult for women'. Chowdhary (1994) also suggests that the culture of the stereotyped role of women which limits them in the family domain should be changed by initiating appropriate culture, educating and informal policies, and discrimination against women clearly should make unacceptable.

Sharing the experiences from Bangladesh, Panday (2008) identifies education, mobility, structural deficiencies, religion, culture, and patriarchy as major factors affecting women's involvement in politics, which are deep-rooted in the socio-cultural ground. And, as part of its remedy to ensure gender equality in every sphere, Panday (2008) suggests that constitutional and legal reforms should be done and additional legal measures adopted in order to enact legislation effectively.

But, mentoring is more relevant in terms of socio-cultural changes, in addition to policy and laws. In fact, changing the way of thinking and doing is not so easy as making changes in the policy documents. Socio-cultural values are not changed only by external activities, as talks, demonstration, etc. To make a change in this aspect, every individual needs to change his/her mind as a way of thinking and doing. They should change as well their attitude toward women as beings equal to men. Women, too, need to come forward collectively to challenge patriarchy for their purpose.

Localising the Context

Roza (2011) reiterate that one of the strategic objectives for achieving women's empowerment through equality included in the BPA is 'measures to ensure women's equal access to full participation in power structures and decision-making' (UN, 1995). To ensure this BPA has also urged political parties to establish initiatives for women to participate in all decision-making structures, including the party leadership, appointment, and election processes. Localising the BPA commitment, 24 governments of Latin America and the Caribbeans conducted regional conference on women in 2007 and adopted the 'Quito Consensus', where they agreed to develop permanent policies to mainstream gender in party policies, activities and statutes, and ensure equitable participation, empowerment, and leadership to achieve gender parity as a state policy. Political parties were asked to take positive steps and implement strategies (Roza et al., 2011).

Looking back into the Nepali politics, Malla (2011) says that Nepali political parties have been fully recognised only after the restoration of multi-party democracy in 1990 and people have become aware of their rights. Nepali women have started to demand their due rights in abolishing social evils, inequality, injustice, illiteracy, ignorance, and violence. Just before the people's movement in 2006, on the occasion of International Working-women's Day (IWD) on 8 March, women set 9-point common gender agenda including full citizenship identity, one-third participation, end to VAW, guarantee of social security, non-discriminatory laws, equal access in education and employment, etc., which are closely linked with women's empowerment (IPWA, 2006). The representatives of political parties have publicly expressed their commitment on it to fulfil after the restoration of democracy. But, a decade of the restoration of democracy and achieving republican system; women are still pushing the agendas to political leadership for enforcement.

Lovenduski and Norris (1993) classify the localising strategies for promoting women's participation in parties and in elections into three categories—rhetorical strategies as declarations made in party rules and procedures to promote women's inclusion, positive action strategies to develop leadership quality as party members and activists, and strategy of positive discrimination includes measures such as gender quotas for party structures, candidate lists, etc., are still valid in regard to empowering not only women but also all marginalised community.

Back home again contextualising the specific strategy, the Constitution of Nepal has insured one-third women participation in result in federal and state parliament and 40 per cent in local government and inclusive participation in a political party (GoN, 2015). But, the provision of inclusiveness in a political party is not sufficiently assertive to guarantee women's participation. In the case of UML, its constitutional provision of one-third women's participation in internal structure has not been reflected in practice, though it is progressing.

Here, the argument is that the localising strategies have some difficulties as well. For instance, referring only 18.6 per cent women members, there is an argument that when the women members will be increased, participation in structure will automatically be increased. But, Roza et al. (2011) mention different experience such that Latin American parties have had more than 50 per cent women members on average. But, women are still occupying only 16 per cent as senior leadership position as chair and general secretary. This experience teaches us that without changing the patriarchal mindset and behaviour and readiness of men to leave the position and women to take the senior position with the vital role of decision-making, only increasing membership at the base level does not make a change in power structure.

Referring to the former UN General Secretary Kofi Annan saying 'the significance of women's representation and socialisation in political parties for the success of democracy', Malla (2011) writes that women participation in political parties is important because it provides a path to power and political decision-making. These experiences tell us that circumstances are changing internally and externally. Women are getting ready to take responsibility. This environment demands the change in political power structure with transformative strategy, and the male counterpart needs to be ready to accept women's leadership and leave the space for women to facilitate the process of power redistribution. And, women need to challenge the situation politically and socio-culturally with fact, evidence, and logic to widen the space and deepen the impression.

Many researches and studies have been already conducted in the area regarding women's empowerment in different areas around the world. Among them, most are connected with the developmental field in one way or another. Very little academic research has focused on gender in politics, in fact, which is core to influence all other sectors. I feel this gap needs to be responded and taken into account.

Also, how politics embedded in different political ideologies is taking up the issues of women emancipation in contemporary situation is researchable. But not enough work has been done yet.

People Multi-Party Democracy as a new dimension in the communist movement has been adopted by UML in 1993. It has given special emphasis on women's agenda as empowering through increasing participation, raising awareness and leadership quality, ending discrimination and exploitation to ensure equality. But, what efforts have been made to translate them into reality to empower women, and what has been achieved is not explored yet. Since it is already completing more than two decades of adaptation of PMPD, how has it been internalised to enact and what are the achievements and shortcoming in the area of women's empowerment? It has not been studied through a feminist perspective, yet.

Finally, the issue of gender parity is not only women's issue but is rather a social issue. And, to it, male and female both as an equal part of society need to have specific role and responsibility. What would be the roles of men and women in the process of social transformation? Standing on the socialist feminist perspective, the opinions of both sides have not been studied categorically. Contributing to narrow down these gaps is the central objective of this study. The intention here is to open the window for further study on enhancement of intervention and enactment of policy from different angles and perspectives on women empowerment as compulsory agenda of the social change and development.

Mind Mapping of the Study

The intent to study women empowerment process within CPN-UML. The conceptual framework as shown in Figure 2.3 has been followed.

Structuring the Study

The thematic framework of the study is depicted in Figure 2.4, which focuses on the two main themes as dimensions of gender participation and policy and action on women empowerment. As the thematic area of participation, three main categorical dimensions as qualitative and quantitative participation as well as activities in this regard have been studied. As part of policy and action, women in different political ideas, their linkage with democratic movement, and women's participation in those processes for their own empowerment

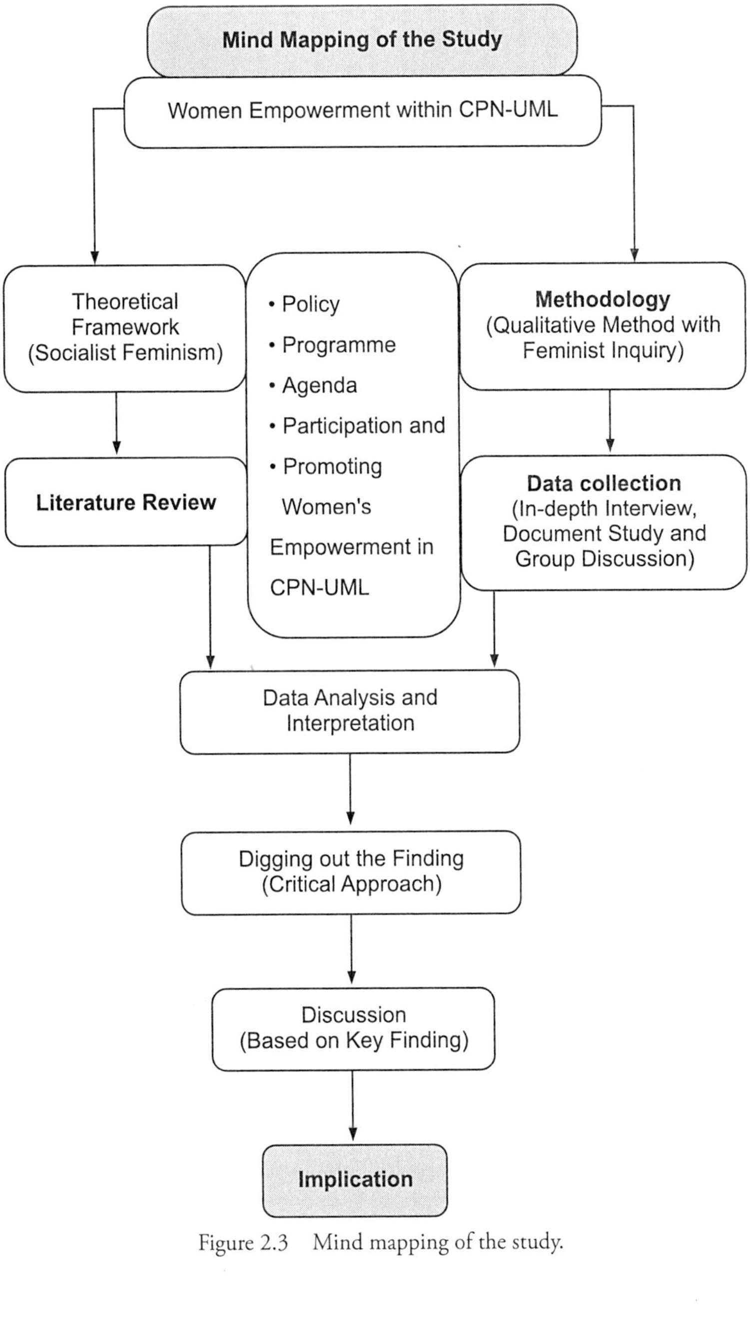

Figure 2.3 Mind mapping of the study.

and affirmative measure as policy and practice have been researched and analyzed to draw conclusion and implications.

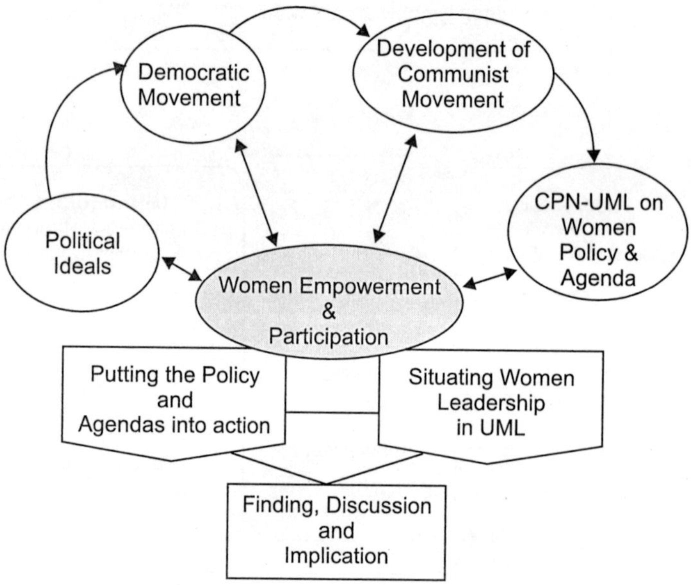

Figure 2.4 Structuring the study.

Women Empowerment Through Democratic Ideals

An ideal is the basis of democracy. Equality is one of the basic components of democracy in its principle. But, the question is how those principles have been perceived and policies formulated to achieve it in real practice. This chapter, has analyzed the evolution of democracy and the ways to posit women within it. It has also tried to show the connection among evolvement of democracy, communist ideal, and People's Multi-Party Democracy (PMPD) on women.

Political Ideals

Every person in the world is more or less a political thinker, whether s/he is aware of politics or not. The simple reason is that they talk about the rights, freedom, justice, equalities, etc., which are the elements of politics (IPC, 1997). In this sense, political ideology is the set of ethical ideals, principles and concepts, which are linked with power structure within a party as well as the state.

There are many terms, viz., *Wad, Chintan, Siddhanta, Darshan* in the East, which carry the meaning of the word 'ideology' in the West (*Nepali Brihat Shabdakosh*, 2010). But the term 'ideology' was coined in 1796 by the French Philosopher Destutt de Tracy, referring to a new science of ideas (Marx, 1848). Marx further opined that ideology is a most controversial concept encountered in political analysis. The term 'ideology' has been interpreted in the several ways as the Neo Marxist. It would be serving a certain section of the society, which can never be neutral in reality.

There are several categories of ideologies based on their principles and concepts. But, widely it has been defined as Left, Right and Moderate, based on their worldviews of using power structure and ways of its use. Ideology has been categorised as Communist, Conservative and Liberal—form of government Democratic and Autocratic, economic system Socialist and Capitalist. Here, I focus on women's position in different political ideals broadly on the Vedic era as eastern history and Communism and Liberal democracy in the later-day politics.

Women in Political Construct

In the Vedic era, there were chiefdoms, kings, and emperors, according to the size of the country. The chiefdoms and kings were elected by the assembly of the people. The conquerors of the kingdoms and chiefdoms used to be emperors. The chief of the society or the clan-based tribe used to form *Vis* and the chief of the administrative body was called as *Visapati* and comprised mainly of males. Women were invisible in governance in those days.

Women used to hold a high position in the early Vedic society. But, in the later days, it was slowly reversed. According to Priyadarshini (n.a.), women influenced domestic affairs and enjoyed an equal place with men in religious ceremonies and festivals. This shows that early Vedic society represented human equality and simplicity. Women were classified as *Sadhyobadini* and *Brahmabadini* in those days (Dikshit, 2010). The first type of women used to get a domestic education through rites, rituals, and socio-cultural orientations. The second type used to go for Gurukul to get enlightenment through study and meditation. Women like *Viswavara, Apala*, and *Ghosa* who composed Vedic mantras and attained the rank of rishis belonged to the second group (Kaudinyannyayan, 2006). In the later days, the *Sadhyobadins* were also classified into two types. The first types were regarded as *Swechhacharini* (free) and the second as domesticated. These domesticated *Sadhyobadins* were protected by males (father and/or husband). In this sense, they were dependent on males. These gendered notions of societal mindset promoted child marriage, mandated polygamy, restricted widow marriage, and kept women inside the house in the post-Vedic era (Priyadarshini, n.d.). Therefore, *Sadhyobadini* women needed democracy to be able to come out of the yoke of domestication. This was the way slowly women became domesticated and subordinated.

Prakriti Ranjanat (happiness of the people) of the Vedic age equates to democracy of these days which is a terminology used to express the political system, which defines people's rights in an individual as well as a collective form. According to Moghadam (2008), the different definitions and understandings of democracy focus mostly on qualities, procedures, and institutions. Democracy in this new era is defined as a universally recognised ideal and a goal of the community, irrespective of cultural, political, social, and economic differences. This definition reflects the diversity of experiences and cultural particularities without derogating from internationally recognised principles, norms, and standards (IPC, 1997). IPC has also mentioned that internationally accepted elements of the democracy are such factors as the holding of free and fair elections at regular intervals, ensuring the enjoyment of civil, cultural, economic, political and social rights of its citizens, public accountability, ethics and transparency, independent judicial institutions, and an active civil society.

This suggests that a sustained state of democracy requires a democratic climate and culture constantly nurtured and reinforced by education and other vehicles of culture and information, which ensures full integration of the most disadvantaged groups in the democratic process. This further safeguards diversity, pluralism, and the right to be different in a climate of tolerance, decentralises local and regional government and administration, etc., which has been respected for a long time. But from the women's perspectives, democratising the democracy means engendering the whole structure and process, which has not been the inclusive part of the IPC (Cornwall and Goetz, 2005).

It is difficult to demarcate the values of democracy differently in today's world. But historically, the Vedic culture was practiced more in the eastern world and the concept of modern democracy emerged from the western part of the world. Now, the values are blurred in common ground as one has difficulty to separate, which one is the Vedic value and which one is the western value.

Waves of Democracy

Huntington (1991) categorizes democracy of the West into three different waves based on the processes and timelines. The first 'long' wave of democratisation began in the 1820s, with the widening of the suffrage to a large proportion of males in the United States. This continued for almost a century until 1926. During this time only 29 countries followed the democratic process. The Second World War initiated a second wave of democratisation, which reached its zenith in 1962 with 36 countries governed democratically. Lastly, the current era of democratic transitions after 1990 constitutes the third wave of democratisation in the history of the modern world.

Huntington further mentioned that democratic waves did not move in a linear path forward but rather took reverses as the first 'reverse wave' in 1922-42 and the second reverse wave in 1960-75, which reduced the number of democratic countries. During the first wave of the democracy, he said women were not treated as equal citizens. They were not even part of the popular voting system, where male achieved that right. Women in many countries, including those who had 'so-called' democracy, were initiating collective movements with demands of suffrage, property, and opportunity for education and employment. Only at the later part of the first wave democracy, some countries like New Zealand in 1892 and USA in 1920 provided rights to suffrage for women. Economically, in general, women were dependent on men though most of them were working as informal workers. Culturally, women were deprived as domesticated beings. Liberal feminists in those days were initiating activities at national levels.

Socialist women were moving one step further by developing an international network of women's movement (as mentioned in the resolution of Second International Socialist Conference of Women in 1910).

Arriving in the second wave, women in many countries were allowed to vote and work in formal sectors of work like industries. Despite this, the majority of women were still informal workers. Responding to the situation, the United Nations and International Labour Organization (ILO) adopted many conventions regarding equality, which are available on the sites like un.org and ilo.org. More and more women from democratic countries joined education and work in public sectors. Many countries went through a revolution during that period, changed their policies and laws based on equality. There the women were provided formal equality.

The third wave of the democracy moved further into recognising women as equal citizens having different human qualities, which should be respected and regarded differently to achieve substantive equality. This process still continues.

Women's empowerment process has grown differently in the different waves of democracy, while women were demanding integration of their issues within. Women in the first wave democracy were demanding recognition as citizens of equal status. During the time of the second wave, women had already entered into formal employment and came up with collective voice with the demand of equal opportunity and rights. And, arriving into the third wave, they were demanding for substantive equality with recognition of differences in quality and needs as women's agenda.

New Democracy

Mao Tse Tung (1940) defines democracy differently during the course of the Chinese revolution. He said that the historical character of the Chinese revolution involved two stages, democracy and socialism. The democratic stage, according to Mao, was no longer a conventional one. According to him, the democracy of the Chinese type, a new and special type, named 'New Democracy' was defined in two steps. The first step was to change the colonial/ semi-colonial and semi-feudal form of society into an independent and democratic society and second, to carry the revolution forward to build a socialist society.

Recognising the numerous types of state systems in the world, Mao reduced it into three basic kinds according to the class character of the political power as republics under a bourgeois dictatorship, the dictatorship of the proletariat, and the joint dictatorship of several revolutionary classes. Mao (1940) further explains that Europe and America represented the first category and the Soviet Union represented the second. The third was the transitional form of state adopted in the revolutions of the colonial and semi-colonial countries. Mao named the third one as the 'New Democracy', which was established in China through a revolution in 1949.

The expression of the politics of the 'New Democracy' is the governing system of democratic centralism as the joint dictatorship of all revolutionaries. In terms of the economic system, basic infrastructure and backbone of the economy such as big banks, the big industrial and commercial enterprises, shall be operated and administered by the state so that private capital cannot dominate the livelihoods. He opined that a given culture is the ideological reflection of the politics and economics of a given society, and the new democratic culture is the anti-imperialist and anti-feudal dimension of the broad masses.

The programme of new democracy defined women as reserve forces for nation's economic development, which should be mobilised with additional policies and programmes (Mao, 1940). The concept of 'Iron Lady' after the Revolution in 1949 was one of the key initiatives to promote women in non-traditional sectors of work. Similarly, laws regarding marriage were changed denying arranged marriages to promote self-selection. All these initiatives were taken to promote women's decisive capacities and facilitate the transition from private to public life, as part of implementing New Democracy.

Though the ideal of New Democracy surfaced the patriarchy as one of the aspects to subordinate women, it did not consider care work as productive, which is one of the agenda of the feminist movement. Caring is a compulsory aspect of human lives and it adds values to make public work more efficient, effective, decent, and dignified. But, the approach of New Democracy was more justice based than care.

Women in Different Democratic Settings

Women have been portrayed as holding different positions in the history of Nepal. Table 3.1 shows comparative picture portraying women in the Vedic era, after the Cairo Conference and in New Democracy. Women were equally respected during the Rig Vedic era. But, in the post Rig Vedic era, they were pushed in subordinated positions through rites and rituals mentioned in the *Smritis*. Manusmriti (Manusmriti, n.d.), Yajnyavalkyasmriti (Ramanujachari, n.d.) and *Puranas* (The Purans, 2002) highlighted such subordination.

By the time of the Cairo era, formally, women were considered equal citizens. Legally, women were allowed to compete in all sphere of human life, which was reflected in Nepalese politics too (IPC, 1997). Modernised economy allowed women to be part of the economy. But, the majority of them became cheaper working masses in informal sectors. Moral and social values characterised by patriarchal norms as invisible social bindings restricted them from being an equal part of public decision-making.

New Democracy in China tried to break the traditional social constructs and abolish all forms of legal and policy discriminations against women. They opened all spheres of life equally for women (Mao, 1940). State-owned economy enrolled many women in the workforce. Politically, women were presented as change agents. Affirmative action plans were adopted to promote women in different sectors.

Yet, social stigmas rooted in the feudal system played the role of an obstacle to stand on equal footing in the decision-making. Following next is the list of projected women's status in different periods.

Table 3.1 Comparative Status of Women in Democratic Ideals

Timeline	*Vedic Era*	*Cairo Conference*	*New Democracy*
Ideology	Pre-Feudal, in which women were having a dual position	Democracy, in which women were considered part of the process	Communism, in which women are promoted based on the principle of equality
Political system	Clan system called *Vis*, in which Sadhyobadini women were subordinated	Liberal Democracy, in which women were included formally.	Democratic centralism, in which women were promoted with affirmative action.
Policy	Visapati ruled in accompaniment of representative council. Women were invisible	Ruled by elected representatives. Women were included in the process.	Ruled by the Communist party in cooperation with other fringe parties. Women were presented as change agents.
Economy	The agro-based production system in which women were assisting force	Industrial production and trade based economic system in which women are cheaper labour-force	State-led economy accompanied by the state-owned production system in which women were promoted to be part of the production process.
Socio-cultural system	Consideration of men-women as better-half of each other especially in religious activities	Subordination of women to men, as considering him/them breadwinner	Promoting women as equal status as men.
Legal system	Religious law composed by Rishis subordinated women	Formal equality in front of the law	A special provision of affirmative action to empower women

Source: Kaudinnyanya, 2006; IPC, 1997; Mao, 1940.

Table 3.1 indicates that there is no explicit discrimination against women in policy. But, the differences in practices were observed. It shows that only having policy, laws, and activities to empower women to be part of the public domain is not enough to promote women in the equal status. As Yingyi (2009) mentions:

> *Unless given enough attention on the social matter based on biological quality, role and the gender needs based on that it is not possible to achieve intended equality in [a] substantive manner.*
>
> *Addressing the social gender construct is the way to empower both women and men to achieve gender justice.*

Women in Different Political Ideals in Nepal

Unified Nepal was founded under the leadership of late King Prithvi Narayan Shah in 1768. While the monarchy was getting weak, taking its advantage, Rana oligarchy became the country's *de facto* ruler from 1846 until 1951. Since those days, Nepal and India shared open borders and people from both sides used this access for crossing the borders. In this regard, Nepali went to India for education, trade, and employment in the British-ruled Indian subcontinent from 1757 to 1947 (Iyer, 2004). Indian people's movement against British colony got high momentum in 1942-47, under the slogan of 'Quit India' (Reddy, 2010). That liberation movement influenced Nepali people living in India in those days and many of them became part of that. Some of those Nepali including Bishweswar Prasad Koirala and Manamohan Adhikari were imprisoned (Basnet, 1996). In that course, dozens of Nepali living in India realised the importance of democracy and basic human rights. Then, they returned to Nepal and started collective action to end Rana oligarchy for democracy in Nepal.

Praja Parisad, as the first political party presided by Tanka Prasad Acharya, was formed in 1937 with the main aim to end the Rana regime and establish democracy in the country (Gautam, 1990). Great martyrs of Nepal such as Dharmabhakta Mathema, Sukraraj Shastri, Dasarath Chand, and Gangalal Shrestha, were also among them who returned from India with a democratic spirit and joined hand with Praja Parisad for a democratic fight (Personal communication with Govinda Gyawali, January 2016). Unfortunately, many of them were arrested in late 1941 and the four activists received a death sentence in February 1942.

Since the main aim of Praja Parisad was to replace the Rana regime, sectoral issues such as women's concern were not in Praja Parisad's priority in those days. As a result, there were no women-related issues mentioned in their policies clearly. But, the female relatives of those political actors and some young women were involved in their political activities.

After a decade, Nepali Congress (NC) party was formed in Kolkata, India, in early 1947 with the main objective to establish multi-party democracy in the country. Influential women like Dibya Koirala were in touch since the conceptualising to the formation of the Party. That might have helped NC to internalise the vulnerability of women in the society and mention in their documents that women were marginalised, discriminated, oppressed, and needed to change their condition. As a policy response, NC had adopted a resolution that women should have equality in all spheres of human life, with the aspiration of equality in front of the law (Basnet, 2009). Some women including Kumari Laxmi Devi were present in the first congress held on 27 January 1947, in Kolkata (Basnet, 1996). Rawanta Kumari Acharya took part in that meeting as representative of Tanka Prasad Acharya.

The Communist Party of Nepal (CPN) was also founded in Kolkata, India on 22 April 1949 under the leadership of Puspalal, with the aim of launching a revolution in the country. Motidevi Shrestha was one the five founding members of CPN (K.C., 2005). CPN had mentioned in its founding manifesto that women were vulnerable and subordinated in society and the communist party should fight for their equal rights in all spheres of national lives (Puspalal, 1996). However, Motidevi was not included when its working committee was formalised on 15 September 1949. The historical documents of CPN have mentioned that women were present in all the conventions, conferences, and activities. But none of the women was included in the central committee until 1992. According to traditional communist ideal, CPN believed that class-based leadership could lead the revolution and liberate all oppressed people including women, instead of promoting them to be part of the decision-making body.

Later in 1960, late King Mahendra imposed party-less Panchayat system, banning all the existing political parties and people's organisations. Panchayat also agreed on the marginalised situation of women and Nepal Women Organisation was established as its sister organisation. The Panchayat system implemented some welfare programmes for women. The *Muluki Ain-2020* (Civil Code, 1963)

Table 3.2 Gender Provisions of Different Political Parties/Systems in Nepal

Political Parties/ Systems	*Women as Understood*	*General Provision for Women's Equality*	*Special Provision for Women's Equality*
Nepal Praja Parisad (1937)	Not Clearly Mentioned.	Not Clearly Mentioned.	Not Clearly Mentioned
Nepali Congress (NC 1947)	Subordinated, Marginalised and Discriminated.	Should be Equal to Men.	Legal Equality for Women in Every Sphere of Life.
Nepal Communist Party (CPN, 1949)	Subordinated, Discriminated and Oppressed.	Political, Economic, and Social Aspect Need be Changed to Achieve Equality.	Equal Opportunity for Girls and Women in Education, Remuneration, and Equal Right in all Spheres of Lives.
Panchayat (1960)	Backward, Subordinated and Marginalised.	Educate and Organise Women.	Welfare Activities for Women Aiming to Address Their Condition.

(Basnet, 2009; K.C., 2005; Gautam, 1990; Puspalal, 1996.)

regulated the marriage system with restricting polygamy in general (Article 12), some property right to daughter (Article 13), women's property (Article 14), etc. Thus, to some extent, these provisions were progressive in regard to women's right. Some articles in the Civil Code such as Article 15 on adopted child, Article 16 on a childless property right, etc., were still discriminating women.

The Panchayat system was replaced by Multi-party Democracy in 1990 through the popular People's Movement I. Newly established Multi-party Democracy adopted new constitution in 1990 and took initiatives to include many provisions regarding women's rights such as equal property right, equal wage for equal work, apart from delineating that all citizens shall be equal before law and no person shall be denied the equal protection of law.

Table 3.2 shows women's position, provisions, and programmes of different political parties/system, while they were founded.

But it could not provide full justice to women as equal citizens as men with mentioning 'The persons whose father has obtained the citizenship of Nepal are qualified to obtain descent citizenship of Nepal.' (GoN, 1990, Article 9-1). In this way, the state subordinated children to father (avoiding mother's identity), which is the root of limiting women's identity, dignity, and self-esteem even in the democracy'.

Communist Ideals in Different Waves

Communism is the science of the conditions for the emancipation of the proletariat as the working class people (Bedacht, 1925). The proletariat was originated in the latter half of the eighteenth century in England and later on, this term was popularised in all other countries as well. Even before popularising the words communism and proletariat, there were communal practices that can be loosely called s 'communist practices' in the world. Some of the people have given name the 'Vedic communism' for the Vedic era. Prabhupad is one of them. He has mentioned that socialist idea says no one should starve and everyone must have food. The Vedic concept of *Grihastha* (householder) has recommended that not only human being, every living creature should not starve. Modern society takes the people as a whole as the proprietor of a certain state. But, the Vedic conception is everything and is owned by the supreme controller (Prabhupad, 1971). So, there are some similarities between them. Anthropologists such as Malinowki (1927) also figured out the communal practice of communism in the ancient society (as cited in Conley and O'Barr, 2002).

This suggests that the values of communist movement were already in practice here and there by different groups. But, it was named formally as a communist movement in the world in 1848, when Karl Marx and Frederick Engels jointly brought up the document called the 'Communist Manifesto'. Based on that document, they started to organise people individually in different countries as well as collectively at the global level. The Movement continues to move forward passing through different eras and waves.

The communist movement was divided into three waves. The first wave of communism covered 1848 to 1917. The second wave was from 1949 to 1970. And, the third wave started in the late 1990s. At the end of the First Wave Communist Movement, proletariat revolution had taken place in the Soviet Union in 1917. Unlike what Marx had predicted that revolution would take place in the industrialised country, it took place in an under-developed Zarist Russia. The joint movement of workers and farmers made the revolution possible (Lenin, 1921). Women like Clara Zetkin, Rosa Luxemburg, Nadezda Krupskaya, Alexandra Kollontai were in leading positions at that time. Consequently, women's participation increased in leading positions. Their issues were included in the communist internationals of 1866 and 1889 (The Minutes of the Communist International). For instance, as the inspiration of first international, Clara led the organising work to empower working women through a separate mechanism to develop leadership quality first, and then include them in mainstream organisations as comrades-in-arm together with male counterparts in political party and trade unions (The Minute Book of the First International, 1864-1966). And, she raised the issues of equality at the workplace for the first time ever in the international forum in 1889, which was unanimously adopted (The Minute of the Second International, 1889-1914).

Under the leadership of Clara Zetkin, two international socialist women's conferences were conducted in 1907 and 1910 to identify and mainstream women's concerns. In memory of the historical women's liberation movement, the second conference in 1910 declared 8 March, the Commemoration Day of the women's struggles and successes (Chitrakar, 1980). These historical footsteps inspired Nepali women as well to move forward. In this regard, Astha Shakya (pseudo name) says:

> *We took inspiration from international communist movement. As a result, after having women's first meeting in Hatauda in 1980, UML set up All Nepal Women Association (ANWA) as separate women organisation to work among women. Internalising the inspiration of International Working-Women's Day (IWD), we started to celebrate it among working-class women, which was spread over the country in the later years. Now even the government has recognised it and has declared a holiday for working women to celebrate it.*

Class-based approach regarding women's liberation movement was dominant in those days and the revolutionaries of that era used to believe that women's problems were a part of class-based society and proletariat revolution could solve all these problems (Lenin, 1922). However, women's physical presence in decision-making was not considered mandatory to formulate policies to address these issues.

The second wave of the Communist Movement took a paradigm shift in the principle of the communist revolution. Mao led this wave establishing new principles in China that semi-colonial and semi-feudal society could go through revolution and establish new democracy to develop national capital as preparation of the path to socialism (Mao, 1940). This era was continued until 1970 when the Vietnamese revolution took place. Women's mass participation in revolution became possible in these countries.

They believed that joint authority of revolutionaries' class under the leadership of proletariats could make revolution possible and it would liberate all the exploited groups (Mao, 1940). They defined women as reserved forces to develop state's economy as agents of social change. Based on this principle, different activities under the name of a special programme to mainstream women in public life and productive field were conducted. Iron lady was one of the examples in China, where young women were regarded as role models in male-dominated sectors. All these activities were happening under the Marxist feminist approach as a theoretical base. Following this approach, UML also encouraged women to be part of the economic production. In this regard, Chudaraj Joshi (pseudo name) says as follows:

> *Learning from the Marxist principle, Nepali communist movement as well encouraged women activists to join the productive field. Many qualified woman activists of UML joined the economic activities, specially after 1990. But, joining the economic activities, most of them were limited in profession and taking care of family. This limited them in political activism, which impacted negatively in terms of women's participation in policy-making bodies of the communist movement, particularly in UML.*

The third wave Communist Movement started after 1990, when the first socialist country, Soviet Union collapsed. Communist movement worldwide fell in crisis and started to revisit their policies and programmes. Those communist regimes, even having stable political systems like China and Vietnam, were changing their social and economic policies as a remedy and those being part of the competitive process in a parliamentary democracy, like communist parties in India were also revisiting their functioning. This wave considered women as necessary participants of social transformation and advocated socialist feminist approach. They emphasised on women empowerment to develop competent and confident leadership as an integral part of the structure. But, the values of the human society never move in the linear form rather back and forth in the process. It applies to the communist movements as well. The women empowerment process in the Soviet Union within first two decades of the Revolution (1917-37) can be taken as one of the examples in this regard. Table 3.3 shows that all three waves of communist movement promoted a revolutionary class to take a lead in the society with some ingredients of the similarities and differences. But the communists changed their political ideology, i.e. from revolutionary authoritative dictatorships to representative democracy. It also shows that women were involved in the movement for the political change, and now, the system has accepted them as the agents of social transformation. Because of these changes, communist movement is following women empowerment strategy to achieve gender equality based on social justice, which was not possible within the traditional communist principle.

Table 3.3 Different Waves of the Communist Movement

Specifications	*Wave 1*	*Wave 2*	*Wave 3*
Revolutionary Class	Revolution Through Joint Effort of Workers and Peasants.	Revolution in the Countries Having Semi-feudal, Semi-colonial System Under the Leadership Proletariat Class	Revolution With Popular Support of People.
Political System	Proletarian Authority	Joint Authority of Revolutionary Class	Elected Representative by Popular Vote
Women's Status	Revolution can Liberate Women Together with Working-class People	Women as Reserved Force for the Revolution and Economic Production	Women as Essential Force for Social Transformation, Need to Empower Them for Equality and Justice

(CPN-UML, 1991; Mao, 1940.)

Connecting these changes in different waves of communist movement, UML has adopted the third wave principle through PMPD. It has been putting emphasis on women empowerment as a necessary component to achieve socio-economic transformation as its prime agenda. It has also carried some of the elements from the history of the world communist movement, such as participation in economic activities to avoid male dependency, collective action to liberate them from subordination, shifting domestic domain to end stereotypic and gendered way of living, etc.

Women in Nepali Communist Ideals

In the process of establishing CPN in 1949, Puspalal described Nepali society as semi-colonial and semi-feudal in characteristics (CPN, 1949). Based on this analysis, CPN developed its policy and programme as 'New Democracy' following the line of Mao-Tse Tung in China. Under the semi-colonial and semi-feudal society, women were portrayed as marginalised, oppressed, and subordinated beings in the society and needed to be organised to come on the front lines to change their statuses as equal citizens (Puspalal, 1949). There were several branches and offshoots within the broad CPN in the process. The Communist Party of Nepal-Marxist Leninist (CPN-ML) was formed in 1978. It also adopted New Democracy as its programme, having basic political characters as democratic centralism with the dictatorship of the proletariat as the collective move of the revolutionary classes as the CPN ideals regarding women (CPN-ML, 1978).

The international communist movement was facing a crisis in the 1990s, which was basically caused by the financial situation (Stoner-Weiss and McFaul, 2009). It also resulted due to the collapse of the 70 years long Soviet Union. This compelled Nepali communist movement as well to rethink its new democratic ideals. So the CPN-ML, while conducting its fourth national convention in 1989, initiated the debate of whether the policy and programme of 'New Democracy' should be revisited and redefined in the context of the shifting paradigm of the world communist movement. Women's policy was also reviewed and new policies proposed to address them more concretely (CPN-ML, 1989). Astalaxmi was one of the delegates to the convention, who was Chair of the All

Nepal Women Association (ANWA) as well. Sharing her experiences, she says, 'Whatever policy issues were adopted by ANWA's first conference in May 1989, we pushed to make it part of the party document, as part of UML's gender policy.'

After the successful people's movement in 1990, two communist branches CPN-ML and Communist Party of Nepal-Marxist (CPN-M) were unified under the name of CPN-UML (Unified Marxist Leninist) currently known as UML and, for the first time, mainstream communist movement included women in the decision-making positions. Sahana Pradhan, the Chair of the Left Front during the 1990s movement became a politburo member of the unified party. CPN-UML conducted its fifth convention in 1993 and adopted programme as PMPD, which reaffirmed the gender policy adopted in 1989 (CPN-UML, 1993a). Thus, PMPD set up the clear programme for women.

As a legacy of the women policy since the foundation of CPN up to people's movement in 1990, issues such as fundamental human rights and women's education, participation, violence against women, affirmative action to mainstream them, etc., became part of the state constitution of 1990. However, it was not completely based on equality. Women's agendas in the course of the journey from CPN to CPN-UML were also progressing in their levels of understanding. In the initial stages, the issues were mostly mentioned as principles, which was nice to hear. However, there was no concrete policy and programme to interpret these into actions. Arriving in the CPN-ML time, the coverage of these issues was widened and the principle was elaborated into policies. Still, there was a lack of programmes and targets. In the era of CPN-UML, most of the issues had been defined concretely as programmes with the target, which could be realised in tangible ways and measured whether it is achieved in reality. It is still in the process of proper enforcement. In this connection, Astha Shakya (AS after this) says as follows:

> *While the party was working underground before 1990, we women were fully confident on party leadership in regard to making an action plan to achieve gender equality. But, the situation was changed after*

> *having a multi-party system in 1990. Most of the issues needed to be enforced even within the Party. For that, we were also not fully prepared at the initial stage.*

Table 3.4 shows the path of progress on women's issues from principle to action within the communist movement of Nepal.

Communist ideals in Nepal have taken a dramatic shift within a short period. When it was started in 1949, CPN was totally based on class ideology and struggle under the party mechanism. But, when it was banned, it then took the turn to mobilise people based on the peasant's movement (Upadhyaya, 1997). At the beginning of the formation, CPN-ML also followed the programme of 'New Democracy'. But, when mass movement led by students was spread over the country in 1979, it took a policy turn to form mass organisations in different sectors and politically mobilised them as change agents. Women's sector was identified as one of the important sectors in this process and ANWA was established on 28 February 1981 under the full guidance of Party as part of its internal organ. Sharing her experiences in this regard, Astalaxmi Shakya says:

> *Until 1991, male leaders of the party used to be in-charge of ANWA to guide for decision-making in the central committee as well as in local branches. Only after the second conference of ANWA in 1992 and fifth convention of UML in 1993, women became ANWA's in-charge. Then, ANWA started to conduct their meeting and make a decision on their own.*

But, my argument here is that UML was not clear itself whether the women mainstreaming policy should be class and/or gender-based? And, it could not make clear to its cadres on this matter. This resulted in the lack of clear vision on the issues and way forward.

Paradigm Shift in Nepali Communist Ideals

The fifth national convention of UML in 1993 adopted PMPD as the new policy and programme. Madan Kumar Bhandari, the architect of the PMPD, added 14-point democratising elements in

Table 3.4 Development of Gender Policy and Programme in the Communist Movement

Issues Under Women's Rights	*CPN (1949)*	*CPN-ML (1978)*	*CPN-UML (1991)*	*Remarks*
Citizen Identity	No Discrimination	Citizenship with Mother's Name	Elimination of Gender Discrimination	No Unanimous Understanding on it.
Property Right	Equal Property Right	Equal Property Right	Equality in Inheritance of Property	Constitution Guaranteed as Fundamental Right
Education	Women Education in Priority	Women's Equal Access to Education	Special Provision for Women's Education	Mentioned as Affirmative Action in Constitution
Reproductive Health/ Right	Equal Right on Children	Equal Rights on Children	Maternal and Reproductive Right to Women	Constitution Guaranteed Women's Rights
Participation	Right to Participate	Equal Participation	Equal Participation as Critical Mass of not Less than one-third Women	Constitution Guaranteed, but not Enforced yet, Properly.
Violence Against Women (VAW)	Eliminate VAW	Campaign to Eliminate VAW	Take Special Measures to Eliminate VAW	Constitutional Commitment and Code of Conduct in the Party

(CPN, 1949; CPN-ML, 1989b; CPN-UML, 1993a and 2014b.)

the communist politics, which replaced the traditional communist understanding of the dictatorship of the proletariat (CPN-UML, 1993a). The following is the list of original communist ideals and the added ideals of CPN-UML:

As indicated in Table 3.5, the 14-point additional political characteristics of PMPD were (1) periodic election; (2) government of majority; (3) opposition of minority; (4) separation of power; (5) independent judiciary; (6) respect of universal human rights; (7) rule of law; (8) selective foreign investment and technology; (9) open society with multiplicity; (10) multiparty democratic system; (11) strengthening people's democratic system; (12) foreign policy based on equidistance; (13) compensation in the process of

Table 3.5 Paradigm Shift in Nepali Communistic Ideals

Areas	*Traditional Communistic Ideals*	*CPN-UML's Ideals*
Governance	Governed by the Revolutionary Proletariat	Governed by Periodically Elected Government
Parliamentary Process	Parliamentarian Selection Through Party Mechanism	Parliament Election by General People
Judiciary System	Party Directed	Independent
Women's Position	Pulled up Through Affirmative Action Programme	Develop Capability to Make Them Competent and Confident Through Emancipation and Participation
Power Structure	Power Control by Communist Party	Power Separation Among Different Authority
Foreign Investment	Restricted	Selective in Favour of Nation's Interest
Foreign Policy	Selective	Equidistance
Land Reform	Captured by State	Compensatory
Party System	Cooperation Among Different Parties	Competition Among Parties

(CPN-UML, 1993a; Mao, 1940; Puspalal, 1949.)

land reform; (14) people's state-power; and (15) people's multi-party democracy (CPN-UML, 1993a). These 14 points show that in comparison to the traditional communist ideals with that of a new democracy, PMPD had taken a major shift. For example, the new democracy of the communist party always propagated for the dictatorship of the revolutionary groups. But, PMPD gave up the ideals of dictatorship and followed the ideals of the democratically elected government. History shows that the political assassination of Madan Bhandari kept the aforesaid ideals unelaborated. However, in a political report adopted by the convention, he had insisted on democratising the governance system from three corners of the human lives as a party, society, and the state mechanism (CPN-UML, 1998). As defined later by his co-comrades, the first corner was the democratisation of the internal structure of the UML. Because of this democratisation process, it has created more space for marginalised groups including women from local to the national level (CPN-UML, 2009a; 2014a, Article 66-4). Commenting on this policy, another informant PA says, 'UML's policy on women is good. But, the weakness is the lack of an operational action plan to translate policy into practice for women's empowerment.'

The second cornerstone of the democratising process is the society through collective initiation. Its purpose is to form a community-based organisation. Community-based forestry as a wider network, having 50 per cent women, the formation of *Aama Samuha* (mother's group), single-women network, and saving-credit cooperatives are some examples. Some of these organisations were already existent while some were new. But, UML emphasized organising activities based in the community, with the intention of bringing women from private sphere to public. PA adds in this regard 'Those women in the community organisations play [a] vital role to empower women as community leaders changing social gender attitude positively.'

And, the third corner of the process is democratising the state mechanism making it more inclusive, effective, and efficient. For this to happen, UML played an effective role in the process of changing policy and law regarding women participation. For instance, in 1997, while UML was leading local development ministry, it proposed at least 20 per cent women's compulsory inclusion in the local elected body, which made it possible to bring 40,000 women at once as local political leaders (GoN, 1997, Article 7). Similarly, the Eleventh Amendment of the Civil Code (2002) with establishing new milestone in regard of right to property, abortion, divorce, etc., ensuring one-third women participation in state mechanism (formally adopted as demand by ANWA in 1998) are some examples of strengthening women's position as part of empowering them through state mechanism. While I was working together with them in ANWA, UML's parliamentarian, namely, Astalaxmi Shakya, Bidya Bhandari, Lila Shreshtha, etc., led these changes in the Parliament with the aspiration to empower women in the local level.

Based on the policy decision women's participation was increased in the different field of the public sphere. But, my argument is that without changing social attitude and behaviour toward women and recognition as equal identity rights by the state, it is not possible to stand on equal footing in social status as sovereign citizens. That is why the subordinated position of women in the family to state and marginalisation of their views based on peripheral knowledge and experiences in process of decision-making has not been changed notably.

Reflecting the Matter

Though there are some globally accepted characteristics, the word democracy carries contextual meaning in the political world. As a process it is dynamic. The dynamic nature of democracy responds to the global concerns and local realities. Development status, political awareness, economic status as well as socio-cultural realities of a given country shape its democratic practices.

It is also understood that women's status differs from era-to-era and place-to-place. Discrimination against women started in the post-Vedic era when they were divided into different categories according to the rulers' decisions. Such categories were observed based on the characteristics of the rulers. Later in the process of changing the social system from feudal, capitalist, and the socialist rules each treated them differently. But, the common status of the women in the industrialised process was to use them as cheap labourers. On the flip side, it also provided them a space to come together and create a collective voice for their equal rights. However, it did not liberate women from their domesticated and marginalised status. Therefore, the communist system that started in the early twentieth century defined women as an exploited group and encouraged them to join productive work in the public sphere. This new role added more responsibility to women, instead of liberating them fully, though their self-stand was changed. This was because women were already gendered in their work in the private sphere. The new work that they got in the public domain also confined them in a socially constructed gender role.

It is known that both the capitalist and the communist worlds introduced an affirmative action plan to ease the public life of working women. Mao termed patriarchy as an additional burden on women in Marx's view of three burdens, viz., political, social, and economic (Zhou, 2013). He implemented Marxist feminist philosophy to give equal value to women. But, he too failed to address the reproductive role of women.

It is realised that PMPD makes an effort to introduce universal democratic values within the communist movement in Nepal. In order to implement it into practice, PMPD set its gender policy to make women as a part of the productive sphere. This policy tried to instil the value that males should also be an equal part of the reproductive role, which was culturally understood as that of the women's. This aspiration of the socialist feminist perspective became the philosophical instrument of women's liberation recognising them as equal human beings with different capacities and needs. Beijing Conference in 1995 coined another slogan, 'Look at the world through women's eyes' which added new value to the PMPD to gear women towards their liberation. But, it has not been very successful in converting the policy properly into programmes and practice. It caused many qualified women activists to leave politics and shrink back to private arena shouldering family responsibility.

Finally, from the point of view of women's empowerment, it is realised that communist ideology empowered women by recognising them as citizens of equal status at the political level. Socially, it empowered women by helping to achieve substantive equality with recognition of their different capacity. Economically, it empowered women by providing them equal space and treatment in productive sphere. In the same vein, the UML has also set empowering gender policies. In other words, UML has adopted a policy to empower women politically through policies based on the socialist feminist perspective that men and women are equal citizens and they should be an equal part of the democratic process to blur the gendered division of power. Socially, UML policy has encouraged males to take part in reproductive activities and promote substantive equality through easing women work burden and enable them to take part in the public domain. And, economically, it empowers women by providing equal property right as well as opportunity and treatment in a productive role. The deficit in the UML policy is that it has not considered care work within the private sphere as productive work and that it lacks monitoring and evaluation process to see the policy impact in practice. In this regard, UML may need to review its policy and make a clear action plan to implement the set of policies and programmes with effective monitoring and evaluation.

Empowerment of Women Through Political Agitation

History shows that Nepali women started their movement for national sovereignty and democracy from Nalapani war, where Nepali fought against the British colonial force. A century later, Yogmaya pioneered the women's movement, who voiced against social oppression. Gradually other issues such as politics, education, civil rights, and workers' right were added. In this chapter, I have reviewed literature on women's movement in Nepal throughout the political struggle for democracy.

Women Movement in Nepal

Nepali women took part in the different movements for centuries. History says that along with the military battalion, a group of women took part in Nalapani war in 1814 for the sake of national sovereignty (Kunwar, 2014). After almost a century of Nalapani war, women started their movement focusing on socio-political issues. The movements can be categorised into phases such as Rana Regime, Post-Rana era, Panchayat era, Democratic era, and Republican Nepal.

The Rana Regime

Dibya Koirala (member of the Nepali Congress in later days) tried to form women committee in 1917 under the presidency of Rana queen (wife of Chandra Shamsher) keeping herself in the Secretary position (Pokhrel, 1984). But it could not be materialised, because her family was exiled after 6 months.

Yogmaya Neupane took another initiation to organise men and women in Bhojpur, which turned into rebellion action against Rana regime (Dhungana, 1998). It was the first collective action led by women in the Nepali history. Under Josmani Saint Tradition, Yogmaya organised hundreds of agitating women and men against the then regime (Personal communication with Govinda Gyawali on 7 February 2016). The issues mostly relating with women oppression such as stopping child marriage, allowing widow marriage, ending *Sati Pratha* (a practice of immolating widow at the death of her husband), etc., were raised as part of changing the social paradigm to humanise the society. In addition, she raised the issues of working peoples such as the abolition of *Dass Pratha* (slavery system) and the caste system. She continued the action for more than two decades. Instead of listening to her and other people's voices for social justice, Rana regime put four political prisoners (Dharmabhakta Mathema, Sukraraj Shastri, Dasarath Chand, and Gangalal Shrestha) on the death sentence in 1943. Then, Yogmaya got frustrated and finally took *Jal Samadhi* (self-sacrifice by drowning in water) in Arun river with her 67 disciples by saying that to die is better than to tolerate the political tyranny of the then Rana rulers (Nepal, 1995). Recalling the difficult task to change social attitude and practices, one of my informants, AS says as follows:

> *The issues of child marriage, widow marriage, etc. are being raised for a century. But, it has not been resolved yet. It was interpreted as the social awareness and attitude to see daughter as donating commodity (Dan Garne Bastu) and women's purity of linking with sexuality.*

In the decade of the 1940s, politically aware people started organising work and conducting activities with attention to gender concerns. As a result, women became part of the movement from the very beginning. In connection with Nepal *Praja-Parisad*, founded on 3 June 1934 to shake the century-long Rana oligarchy (1846-1951), women like Rawanta Kumari Acharya, Seeta Sharma, Ram Maya

Pode, etc., were supporting the agitation differently than their male counterparts such as passing the information outside (Upadhyaya, 1997; Sharma, 1965; Gautam, 2001). For example, Rawanta Kumari passed the camera into prison keeping inside the rice box. After taking photos, political prisoners threw the camera in the backyard vegetable plot and Seeta collected it and passed to other leaders outside. Then, the photos were posted to Banaras. But, Rana regime captured it from the post office. Finally, they came to the conclusion that only women could bring the photo to Banaras. It was because the police would not search a woman's body while they crossed the border. Then, Rawanta Kumari brought the negative of the photo-roll to Banaras (Gautam, 2001; Upadhyaya, 1997). Ram Maya Pode as sanitary worker became a messenger between the jailed leaders and the leaders working outside (Pandey, 2002). After declaring the death sentence in 1943, Dasarath Chand told to Ram Maya that he had nobody to weep on his death and whether she could weep for him (Gautam, 2001). This dialogue showed how closely Ram Maya was helping prisoners while working there as a sanitary worker. In this way, the women braved to take a risk in favour of democracy. Recalling the history of women's movement, my informant, Padma Acharya (pseudo name) says as follows:

> *While people started to fight against the Rana regime, women closely related with activists and working-class women from their community were also influenced and motivated by them to take [a] risk in favour of democracy. This inspiring history motivated us to be more committed to take [a] risk in the struggle.*

Kamari Laxmi Devi attended the Nepali Congress (NC) first conference in 1947 and raised women's issues. Later on, Mayadevi, Lakkhi, and Shusila Chalise became active in the Party activities (Basnet, 1996). But, they were not included in the formal structure. That Conference decided to fight against Rana regime within the country and many of the NC leaders came back to Nepal with the aspiration of creating movement. As a start, they launched first trade union strike in Biratnagar in March 1947. Many male leaders including Bishweswar Prasad Koirala, Tarini Prasad Koirala,

Girija Prasad Koirala, Manmohan Adhikari, etc., were arrested. Then, women braved to come on the street under the leadership of Dibya Koirala. From this agitation, women including Dibya Koirala, Nona Koirala, Indira Acharya, and Nalini Upadhyaya were arrested and brought to Dhankuta jail on barefoot (Basnet, 1996; Sharma, 1965).

After a couple of months, in May 1947, many women joined the first street demonstration with the demand of civic rights. Dozens of demonstrators including Sahana, Sadhana, Snehalata, and Kanaklata were arrested and kept in custody for 2 weeks (Pandey, 2002; Upadhyaya, 1997). After release from custody, they realised the need of a political organisation to bring more women together and formed Nepal Women's Organization (NWO) in July 1947, which was presided by Mangaladevi with Snehalata as the secretary (Singh, 1994). In the Nepali history, this was the foundation of women's political movement.

While the Communist Party of Nepal (CPN) started to organise women, Sahana, Sadhana, Snehalata, Kanaklata, Srimaya, etc., from Kathmandu and few other including Silkumari from Tanahu together with hundreds of women all over the country, whose names are missing in the history, took part in the anti-Rana movement during 1950-51.

The jute mill in Biratnagar was closed in 1951 and workers started agitation with the demand to reopen and re-operate it. But, the management did not respond positively. Finally, three women including Nanda Nepal, Rukmani Acharya, and Radhadevi Paudel staged a fast-unto-death strike. After 27 days of fasting, management agreed to open the factory for operation (Pandey, 2002). Then, the agitation was ended.

Most of these working women, who participated in those movements, were not much educated, but they were highly committed having tremendous courage to fight against the Rana oligarchy. Nanda Nepal in 2001, sharing her experiences on how she got political motivation, she had mentioned that she was working as a cook in Krishna Prasad Koirala's family. While Koirala family was engaged against Rana oligarchy, she learned politics there. Later, she joined jute company as a worker and led the workers' movement from the forefront.

With all this information in the background, we can say that women have been active in the political process since the beginning, whether it is street movement, or institutionalising the politics, raising a collective voice to make it heard and so on. These are some of the examples to illustrate the reality that women were not passive recipients of the democracy but rather forefront actors of the political movement since the beginning. In fact, they were the ones to take a risk and make things happen at the time of crisis. In this sense, women were politically empowered. But, the other forms of empowerment such as economic and social empowerment were not followed according to the need of women.

Post-Rana Era (1951-60)

After a long fight, Rana regime was overthrown in 1951 with tripartite negotiation among Rana, Monarch, and NC in Delhi. The CPN opposed that negotiation and launched series of agitating activities. When the then Indian Prime-Minister Jawaharlal Nehru visited Nepal in later part of 1951, a dozen of young women demonstrated against that visit at the airport with a black flag. Eight women including Srimaya Shrestha, Bishnu Kesari Shrestha, Sabitri Shrestha, Shilbandi Shah, Janaki Shrestha, Renuka Shrestha, Kanchhi, and Sabitri Paudel were arrested, tortured, and jailed for a week (Basnet, 1996). Mangaladevi, the Chairperson of Nepal Women Organisation (NWO) supported the Delhi agreement. This led to split of NWO. Mangaladevi Singh, as a leader of NC continued leading NWO. Many other women disagreed with her ideologically, started a new organization named All Nepal Women's Association (ANWA) on 8 March 1952, presided by Kamakshadevi (Dhungana, 1998).

After the establishment of democracy, political parties formed the government. But, women's participation was ignored again. Then, women started pressurising with demands for their inclusion in the state mechanism. As a result, four women including Mangaladevi

Singh were included in the advisory committee, when it was reshuffled in 1953 (Dhungana, 1998; Singh, 1994).

The NC led government banned CPN from 24 January 1952. Then, it started organising activities under the name of peasant movement. Women participated very actively in that from 1953 to 1959. For instance, Dati Bhoteni in Solukhumbu was a brave woman, who fought with local feudal, against capturing peasants' land illegally (personal communication with S. Shrestha, August 2016). While she was returning home from Kathmandu after complaining about the incident to the palace, she was killed on the way (Usha, 1989). Usha further mentioned that while the Movement was gearing up, a Chaudhari woman in Saptari led 500-600 people's rally against the landlord of the village. As part of the peasant movement, women from Rautahat joined the agitation aggressively and vandalised the administrator's vehicle. Later, the Indian police entered into Nepal and suppressed them. Sharing her field experiences, my informant AS says:

> *Dulalni Bajai in Ilam took very brave action against [the] male landlord of the village in 1957. She pulled down the landlord Basnet from riding-horse, while he was showing very oppressive behaviour to the villagers. Dulalni Bajai was one of the inspirations for the women from eastern Nepal to fight against injustice.*

In 1953, the Government changed the law and allowed police to arrest people without a warrant. People came on the street against that step, which is known as the Movement Against Violation of 'Court Right'. Many women including Punyaprabha Devi Dhunaga and Shanti Devi were arrested and imprisoned (Usha, 1989).

The ban against CPN was lifted in April 1957. After few months a joint front including NC and Praja Parisad launched *Bhadra Avagya Andolan* (non-violent movement) in 1957 with the demand of declaration of general election. CPN supported it unconditionally. Many women became part of it. In this connection, a mass rally was organised from Bhugol Park, Kathmandu on 7 December 1957, where the then leftist student leaders Shusila Shrestha, Indu Regmi, and Madhu Sharma took part very actively

(K.C., 1999). This Movement concluded only after declaring the general election date as 18 February 1958. Recalling the women's participation in that movement, AS says, 'The women who were following leftist ideology and part of the CPN, under the name of ANWA, actively took part in *Bhadra Abhagya* (non-violence) movement in 1957.'

Though CPN was banned, its members took part in the municipal election in 1953. Including Sadhana Pradhan as the mayor, six candidates of CPN won the election. Sadhana became the first elected woman representative of the country (Pandey, 2002). Janaklal Shrestha informed me in 2001 that Sadhana, as the first Mayor of the municipality, was overwhelmingly loved and supported by women of the time.

The long-awaited general election took place on 18 February 1958. Six women candidates contested in that election including Dwarikadevi Thakurani (Dadeldhura) the single woman party candidate from NC. Remaining five candidates, Shusila Thapa (Khadpu), Rani Sharada (Bhaktapur), Kamala Shakya (Lalitpur), Taradevei Sharma (Kalaiya), and Mayadevi (Narayanghad) contested as an independent candidate (Basnet, 1996). Dwarikadevi was only one elected woman parliamentarian, who later became the first woman minister of the country as well.

But, the then King Mahendra did military coup on 16 December 1960. He dissolved the Parliament and Cabinet, banned all the political organisations, and snatched absolute power back to the palace. Women's movement as well was banned together with political parties and party-less Panchayat system was imposed, which was sustained for three decades.

It was the first decade of the democracy. Women's participation in education and formal employment was almost negligible that time. The society was much traditional and conservative toward women. But, women's participation in every front including street agitation to ballet was occurring both as a collective effort and at the individual level. It shows the reality that women's participation in those days was not weak. They were politically empowered to take collective action for the cause of democracy, inclusion in the formal structure of the political parties in which they had faith and in the state mechanism.

Panchayat Era

All the democratic forces opposed Panchayat system, since the very day of the military coup. Many male leaders from NC were arrested and put in jail (Basnet, 1996). Most of the communist leaders went either underground or escaped to India. Women stayed in the country and conducted some of the protests. Shailaja Acharya, one of the NC leaders, started to distribute hand-written pamphlets with help of some other members. On the day of 18 February 1961, a group of women led by Shailaja Acharya conducted action against military coup with a black flag in the army stadium, while the celebration of democracy day was taking place. The army arrested and jailed many of them including Shailaja Acharya, Umadevi, Bijaya Baral, Kundan Sharma, and Gauri Rana, who were the members of NC. Shailaja was kept in prison for more than 3 years (Basnet, 1996; Pandey, 2002). After the release, she joined other exiled leaders in India and came back to Nepal, while BP, the NC leader, came back with the policy of *Rashtriya Melmilap* (national reconciliation) in 1976.

Mangaladevi, another NC leader was arrested in August 1961. She was charged with being one of the agitators at Jana-sewa (Kathmandu) incident in which a pedestrian touched upon the car of the royal family. While they were arguing, Mangaladevi reached nearby. She stood by the side of pedestrian and said that it was not the fault of the pedestrian. Then, the police accused her of the incident and imprisoned her for one and half years with her baby girl (Singh, 1994). Sadhana Pradhan and Sahana Pradhan of CPN kept quiet, as they were still under security surveillance as their husbands were either exiled in India and/or in prison. Reasoning different condition of women's continuation in activism after imposition of Panchayat, AS says:

> *Since Sadhana's husband was in prison and Sahana's husband was exiled, both of them were taking care of their children, for which it was not possible for them to continue activism at that time. But, for a single woman like Shailaja, it was easy to be determined and be part of the agitation against the royal coup and to continue activism.*

It shows that though many male leaders disappeared from the scene after smelling the difficult situation, women braved to lead the protest on the street taking risk of any danger. These are the evidence that women are not weaker sex, but can take the risk even in the difficult situation.

After a decade-long silence of the militant coup of 1960, a militant group of communists known as 'Jhapali Group' arose in Jhapa in 1972. Naxalite movement in India influenced them. That group started the armed action in Jhapa from May 1973 and continued until 1975. During that period, they conducted 14 actions and killed more than a dozen local landlords. Also, many of their leaders were killed and arrested by the state. The final action in 1975 in Dhanusa and Sarlahi did not succeed. Then, the armed agitators started rethinking about the ways of their action and analyzed whether taking personal revenge against landlord could make any revolution. The good thing is that they came with the conclusion that personal revenge is not the right way to make a revolution. They took to the way of fighting through organising and mobilising people in mass.

Three women named Gaura Prasain, Lila Kattel, and Seeta Khadka were directly involved in those actions. Later, when the police started to search and arrest many of the members of the group, they were also arrested. Those women were imprisoned for 3 to 5 years. Other members of the Group who remained outside switched from arm-struggle and started to systematise the Party ideology and structure with formation of All Nepal Communist Revolutionary Coordination Centre in 1975. Having 3 years' discussion in the Coordination Centre, they arrived at the conclusion to form a party named Communist Party of Nepal Marxist-Leninist (CPN-ML). That founding event of CPN-ML was started on 26 December 1978 on the occasion of Mao's birthday and continued until 1 January 1979 in Itahara, Morang. Out of 25 leading attendees of this event, Lila Kattel and Seeta Khadka were present. Gaura Prasain was still in prison.

Regardless of any kinds of crisis, women have been the part of Nepali communist movement. Whether it is the foundation of CPN or Jhapa Movement or formation of Coordination Centre or CPN-ML, they have been equally confident to be part of its activities. But in the process of institutionalising the movement, women are always kept at the margin instead of being promoted to the centre for decision-making.

Student Movement as Catalyst

Students organised agitations against Panchayat system, especially in the early 1970s. They raised different educational issues in the country in 1973. They demonstrated against India's invasion of Sikkim in 1975. Students' Movement was heightened in 1979 when the military regime of Pakistan assassinated Zulfikar Ali Bhutto. Nepali students having anti-Panchayat spirit stood against this assassination and conducted a procession to Pakistani Embassy with a petition letter. The police intervened in the rally before reaching the Embassy and battered them. Then, the rally started to clash with the police. Finally, the agitation changed into an anti-Panchayat movement. Hundreds of women as well took part in this Movement. Many of them were arrested and jailed. The common people including women were supporting the struggling students on the street differently. Finally, it was ended with the declaration of a referendum on giving people choice whether they preferred 'Improved Panchayat or Multi-party System'.

Taking referendum as an opportunity in the background of widespread anti-Panchayat sentiment among general people, more and more women and men were mobilised in the campaign. Female students were mobilised in the campaign to approach women labourers of the industrial area and general public and convincing them to stand in favour of Multi-party System. Meanwhile, ANWA was founded on 28 February 1981 as the sister organisation of CPN-ML.

In 1910, at the Second International Conference of socialist women in Copenhagen, as honours and commemoration of the working women's struggle taking place in the industrialised countries, Clara Zetkin had proposed the day of 8 March, to be marked as the International Working-women's Day (IWD). Kollointai (1920) mentions that the Conference unanimously adopted the proposal and decided to celebrate the DAY under the slogan 'The vote for women will unite our strength in the struggle for socialism'. It was the day of international solidarity and a day for reviewing the strength and organisation of proletarian women. In Europe, the first International Woman's Day was held on 18 March 1911, on the fortieth anniversary of the Paris Commune (Kaplan, 1985).

In Nepal, ANWA started to celebrate IWD (8 March) from Jhapa in 1981, which then spread all over the country from the next year (ANWA, 1982). Nepal Women Organisation (NWO) was not active in those days. Sharing the experiences, AS says that Pabitra Niraula was the one to lead the first IWD (8 March) in Jhapa, who was arrested and jailed. It caused to spread the news over the country and popularised the history of IWD. Explaining the ANWA's activities in the initial days, AS adds as follows:

> *Two girls named 'Namita' and 'Sunita' were raped and murdered in April 1981, while they were having [a] holiday in Pokhara. Their dead body was found in the Seti riverside. Connecting with this incident, recently founded ANWA took the issues of women's security and staged [a] demonstration on the streets with [the] demand of punishment to the culprit and strong law to end violence against women. Thousands of women and men including youths, students, professionals, workers, and peasants joined that protest. This was the first ever-biggest rally led by women after imposition of Panchayat system in 1960. It increased [the] level of anger over Panchayat system among general people including men and women.*

In January 1982, while people in Piskar, Sindhupalchock, were celebrating Maghesankranti (a festival) with progressive (communistic) cultural programme, the police intervened at the midnight and opened fire. Many people including Palkamaya Thami, Sabitri Bohara, Betrawati Paudel, Ranu Thami, Sang Dolma,

Srimaya Tamang, Jagat Bahadur Bohara, Naina Bahadur Paudel, Bhim Bahadur, and Min Bahadur were arrested and five people including Lalman Thami and Kanchhi Thami (with 15 days baby), were killed on the spot (Himali Prakashan Pariwar, 1984). This oppression was continued for 2 years where more than 83 people were arrested and tortured (K.C., 2005). It was one of the cruel actions taken by Panchayat, news on which spread all over the country and grew up as anti-Panchayat sentiment.

Just after the Piskar incident, anti-Panchayat anger among general people was spread. Capitalising the anger, IWD of 1982 was celebrated over the country voicing against that oppression. Goma Timsina and Bishnu Ojha were leading the rally in Hetauda industrial area together with their female colleagues, namely, Juneli Shrestha, Lalita Khatiwada, Indramaya Shrestha, etc., with demand of equal pay and benefit at work, maternity protection, etc., which clashed with the police (personal communication with Goma Timsina on 5 March 2016). Many women in different parts of the country including Butawal, Kathmandu, Biratnagar, Jhapa, and Pokhara were arrested. Then, IWD became an annual event of women, which police tried to suppress, until 1990 (Paudel, 2016).

Teej, the cultural event of Nepali women, was another day when progressive women used to conduct awareness-raising campaign. Traditionally, on that day women used to express their hardship through songs. But, the progressive women started to compose and sing songs to empower women to stand and fight against oppression. The police intervened in the cultural event in 1986 and onward almost every year until 1989 and arrested many women including Kabita Paudel, Maiya Bhattarai, and many more in Rupandehi (Paudel, 2016). This kind of police attempt and action made more women anti-Panchayat as part of the movement for justice.

By 1990, progressive women's alliance had become a bit stronger as a cross-sector national network. When the Joint Left Front and NC were programming to overthrow Panchayat regime, Sahana Pradhan led left front and Shailaja Acharya became a team member of NC in the task force. I actively participated in that Movement from the student front. I was one of the contact points to collect and disseminate the information about the agitating activities on the streets over the country. In this Movement, Laxmi Karki, a student leader of ANNFSU in Pokhara and Meena Paudel, the President of Nursing Association of Nepal (NAN) in Kathmandu demonstrated the courageous role, which motivated many more to join the street action.

Maximising the IWD of 1990, all the women's having anti-Panchayat ideology came together and organised joint programme as part of the democratic movement. Thousands of women throughout the country joined the event and hundreds of them were arrested. However, the state repression accelerated, the participation of women in the movement increased. Finally, the party-less Panchayat system was ended and the Multi-party System was declared on 8 April 1990. Thousands of people including men and women gathered in the open theatre in Kathmandu and different parts of the country to celebrate the victory on 9 April 1990. Because of their earlier struggles, with or without men, women got the freedom to be organised and to set their own gender agenda and share it widely.

Being an active part of the different movements and activities, women were quite aware of their rights and fights. Based on that, after the declaration of the Multi-party System, we the women were expecting equal rights and treatment as men. Unfortunately, it did not happen. Women reminded the political parties collectively about their previous commitment to equality and pushed to include those agenda in the new Constitution. But, it did not succeed according to expectation and commitment. Then, we realised that unless we reached the decision-making position ourselves, the system would not work. It was the departure point of the women's movement including within UML to start demanding women's participation in the decision-making body.

Women Struggle During Democratic Era

Though the Panchayat was replaced by Multi-party System and monarchy became constitutional, women's issues still remained marginalised. While the Constitution was under drafting process, women submitted their demands to the drafting commission regarding rights to descent, property, and ending violence. Their voice was not heard and addressed properly. But, the wide enough space to raise the voice and for lobbying and campaigning was achieved. Maximising this opportunity, women continued raising voice.

As part of the campaign, ANWA organised Teej programme in August 1990 in Pashupati area. An unfortunate incident did happen later in the evening, while the then queen visited the temple. Somebody from the crowd threw a stone over her car. With the false charge of that stoning, Binda Pandey, Laxmi Karki, Pamfa Bhusal, and Hisila Yami were served warrant notice and we were under police surveillance for almost 4 months, until the Government dismissed the case.

After 6 years of Multi-party System, CPN (Maoist) started arm-struggle, which lasted for a decade. Thousands of women joined the battlefield. Onsari Gharti (the present Speaker of the Parliament), Kamala Naharki, and Kamala Rokka were the combatants to open the fire on the very first day of the arm-struggle. Hisila Yami and Pamfa Bhusal were holding senior positions as decision-makers of the war. Many more joined the movement and contributed from the different levels and sectors including mass mobilisation and arms struggle.

Back to the open society, women were fighting to improve the condition and position in the state and in the society through organising and mobilising under party structure, mass organisation, and non-governmental organisations as civil society. One of my participants Padma Acharya (PA) says as follows:

> *After having democratic circumstances, women started to be involved in different sectors. Coordination among women activists having diverse background and experiences nurtured the movement differently to enrich the perspectives, issues, and demands.*

As a result, the state established a Women Ministry and a National Women Commission as state mechanism in this period to tackle women's issues. The Parliament adopted the Eleventh Amendment of the Civil Code widening the women's right in regard to property, right to abortion of unwanted pregnancy, strengthening provision regarding rape case, etc. Recruitment of women in armed-force as armed-police and military was initiated under the state structure. These are some tangible achievements of those movements. But, still major gender agenda such as the equal right to descent, participation, property, and ending violence against women (VAW) were not guaranteed. Arriving at this point, women realised the need to have unity in diverse movements, sectors, and ideologies to push common gender agenda through a common umbrella.

Last Struggle for Republican Nepal

After a decade of multi-party democracy, the royal assassination took place on 1 June 2001, where the then King Birendra's family was killed. Then, Gyanendra, the younger brother of Late King Birendra, already having a disputable image, became the King. After a year the Parliament was dissolved in May 2002, and mid-term election declared, which could not happen in the set time. Finally, the King dissolved the party-led government and declared himself Chair of the council of ministers. Mass media were badly under surveillance and controlled. All the security forces including civil and armed police and the intelligence agency were mobilised to make the situation fearful.

All Nepal National Free Student Union (ANNFSU), the leading student organisation, came on the street immediately and sought the slogan of 'Republican Nepal'. Then Nepal Student Union (NSU) also joined the street from the next day. Both the leaders, Ramkumari Jhakri of ANNFSU and Gagan Thapa of NSU, became an icon of the street agitation against the monarchy. Chhaya Devi Parajuli was another inspiration of the Movement, who was actively participating in the street protest in Kathmandu regardless of her old age. She was locally associated with NC and one of the elected women in the local body in 1997.

Slowly, all the major political parties set the agenda of republic Nepal. NC, which was in favour of the constitutional monarchy since its establishment, also decided to join the agenda of republican in 2005. The Maoists, who had launched armed insurgency for a decade, agreed to support the anti-monarchy street movement. Finally, the seven-party alliance (Appendix IV) and the Maoists signed a 12-point agreement (Appendix V) in November 2005 and decided to launch 'fight to finish monarchy'.

Women leaders from the seven political parties were also in consultation and preparing for the fight not only against the monarchy but also against patriarchy. For the cause, they decided to set up a mechanism named Inter-Party Women's Alliance (IPWA) and listed nine points of gender agenda to put on the table of the seven-party alliances. Finally, on the day of 8 March 2006, IPWA formalised itself and declared its Nine-points common gender agendas (Appendix II), which was supported by the seven-party alliance and expressed their commitment to enforcing them after the restoration of democracy.

On the very day of 10 April 2006, the anti-monarchy movement was staged formally, which was continued as a general strike for 19 days. Almost equal number of women as men poured on the street, not only in the city, even in the remote village. I was in Kathmandu, participating in Koteswar Morcha. The inspiring scene was that many women, especially from working class, were carrying their children on the back, flag in the hand, and shouting slogan of *Inclab-Jindabad*. Finally, monarchy bowed down in front of people's power and returned the power back to people with a declaration for resuming the dissolved Parliament. It was the greatest achievement in the Nepalese political history.

The resumed Parliament made a historical declaration on 18 May 2006. We, 16 organisations including women movements and women department of students, youth, and trade union movements prepared four-points women's demand including the equal right to descent, property, participation, and repealing discriminatory laws and handed it to all seven-parties requesting them to insert them as part of the declaration. But, none of the issues were addressed by that Declaration, which made us feel humiliated. We realised the need to be bold enough to take an extra step. As a result, Bidyadevi Bhandari registered a motion in parliament having all those issues as one-third women's participation, citizenship with mother's name, nullifying discriminatory laws and strong law to end VAW. It was adopted unanimously on 30 May 2006, which was one of the landmark achievements of the collective action of women among different sectors.

Women in New Constitution

Nepal turned into a republic from monarchy after the success of 2006 people's movement. The interim constitution adopted in January 2007, guaranteed women's rights including one-third women candidacy in the constituent assembly (CA) election, equal inheritance right, and stated all kinds of violence against women as a punishable action. Those provisions in interim constitution created a space to discuss agenda of gender equality and social justice more comfortably in the process of drafting the new Constitution. As a result, the new Constitution of Nepal (2015) has reaffirmed all those provisions, as women's rights (Article 38) included the issues of the right to decent, proportional participation, reproductive right, the strong law regarding VAW. Going beyond the equality, as part of the remedial measures of existing inequality, special measures to empower women in regard to education, health, employment, and social security have been stated. To encourage equal duty and right to a family matter, the Constitution has included the provision of equal right of both spouses in property and family matter'. In addition, under the article of the right to equality, the equal right of all the siblings to ancestral property (Article 18-5) has been guaranteed. All these provisions were drafted after having a broader discussion among diverse stakeholders already in CA-I. And, it has been declared as part of the Constitution by CA-II on 20 September 2015.

Similarly, women's participation has been guaranteed in different articles which stated at least one-third women's participation in national parliament (Article 84-8), state parliament (Article 176-9) and 40 per cent women in local government (Articles 220-3, 222-3, and 223-3) is a must. There is also a provision that woman should be in one of the positions of the two as a speaker or deputy speaker in both federal (Articles 92-1 and 92-2) and provincial parliaments (Article 182-2).

In the institutional level, the status of National Women's Commission has been raised as the constitutional body (Article 252) and other commissions as well should be inclusive. It is also ensured that political parties as most important institutions in a democracy should have inclusive composition at the executive level (Article 269-4). Similarly, in relation to nomination such as that of ambassador, and representatives from different bodies, women shall be taken into account (Articles 282 and 283).

In this way, the issues of gender equality have been constitutionalised. The political change has been institutionalised. The level of women's awareness and readiness to be part of diverse sectors in the public sphere has been geared up. The enforcement of the constitutional provisions demand changes in stereotypic attitude and to see women and men as equal human being. That is why the struggle for gender equality and justice is still continued.

Reflecting the Content

The history of Nepali women's movement was the result of four things together. One, women gave their hands to the work of their husbands and other male members of the family. There they learnt to agitate against the then autocratic government as 'situated learner' (the term coined by Lave and Etienne Wenger in the early 1990s, followed by Dewey, Vygotsky, and others later) (Clancey, 1995). Two, their growing awareness as keen observers and servers to their male folks encouraged them to be the leaders of women's movements. Three, religious women who realised the unequal role of men and women raised the social issue in their own ways. Four, women committed politically to fight for their equal right in along with men. Women in the Nalapani Fort belonged to the first category. Dibya Koirala, Rammaya Pode, and Rawanta Kumari Acharya belonged to the second category. Yogmaya comes to the third category. Sahana and Bidya in the later days come to the fourth category. These women, no matter in which category they fall, worked for the liberation of men and women together.

The Constitution of Nepal 2015 introduced the long-awaited civil and political rights of women. Provisions regarding Economic, Social and Cultural Rights (ESCR) of women and right to participate in decision-making, equal inheritance property right, criminalisation of violence against women, etc., are enshrined in the Constitution of Nepal 2015. Both parts of the documents try to go against the patriarchal legacies that dis-empowered women for years. The challenge ahead is to implement the constitutional provisions and ESCR policies as equity measures to eliminate culturally rooted norms and values and enable women to be equal to their men-folk in the sense of human dignity.

It is understood that politics of today has not been dealing enough with the private matters connecting with family lives—the life that debars women from crossing the social barrier. Males' support at home as an equal partner and taking/giving dowry or following *chhaupadi* practices (dos and don'ts during menstruation) or matrimonial at the community are some of these obstacles.

These obstacles to need to be addressed to liberalise women as equal partners with men. In other words, equal sharing of domestic work by men at home, gender-responsive public workplace for women, and equal rights of women in politics are the agenda of women's current movement. Some of these agenda came explicitly and others were put implicitly.

From women's empowerment perspective, there are four founding pillars of Nepali women's movement. First, torture and fear of losing family members motivated them to join politics and later become ideologically empowered activists to be part of the Movement. Mangala and Chandrakanta stood on this pillar while fighting against the Rana regime. Second, the middle-class, educated women were politically empowered to fight for civil right and involved to motivate and mobilise women masses. Motidevi and Snehalata represented this pillar.

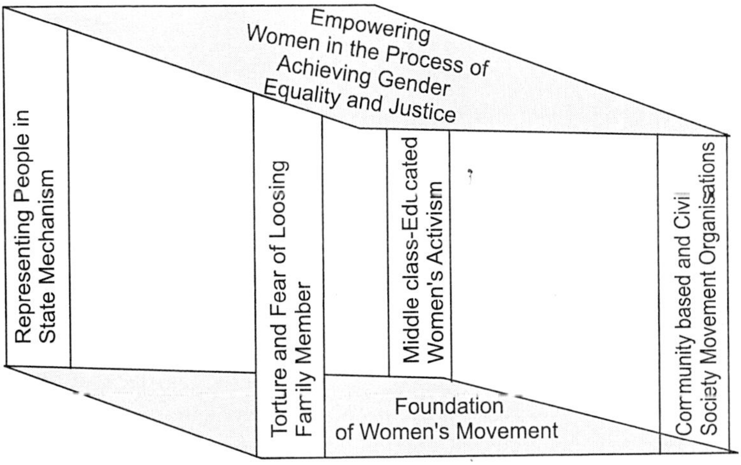

Figure 4.1 Pillars of Women's Empowerment in Nepal.

Third, representing people in state mechanism empowered themselves and others through their performances. Sadhana and Dwarikadevi founded this pillar, which has grown fast vertically and horizontally. Fourth, grassroots level empowerment activities created movement through community and civil society organisations, which stands as a final pillar, which widely emerged after 1990. This pillar contributed to building common agenda and brought women from different walks of life.

One of the motivating reflections of this chapter is that networking and collective action are important to mainstream the marginalised groups and their issues. The achievement of women's action in 1947, 1990, 2006, and 2015 are the explicit examples in this regard.

Women Empowerment Process in The Communist Party of Nepal-Unified Marxist Leninist

In this Chapter, the Communist Party of Nepal-Unified Marxist Leninist (CPN-UML)'s policy, programme, and their implementation status related to women empowerment has been examined. In doing so, it has been also analyzed gender perspective of the international communist movement. Finally, it has been tried to examine its relation with Nepali communist movement.

International Context

The Communist Manifesto gave importance to women's issue with the formal establishment of the political party in 1848. The Manifesto said that the bourgeois sees his wife as a mere instrument of production, who are exploited in common (Marx and Engels, 1848). This argumentative writing provoked women of the world to be organised and raise their voices for equal rights in the industrialised countries in those days. As a result, women from the cotton factories in USA conducted mass mobilisation, demanding definite working hours and higher salaries in the decade of 1860.

In 1865, women from Langham Place in Britain organised a petition for women suffrage bill to be presented in the Parliament. John Stuart Mill presented this Bill in the Parliament as the first-ever equality Bill in the history of the world in 1866, with 1,499 signatures collected by campaigners (Parliamentary Archives, 1866). This step was considered as the formal start of the 'first wave' of the feminist movement in the West, which aimed to end all forms of patriarchal oppression by seeking equality between men and women.

The First International gathering in 1866, under the leadership of Marx, conducted a survey on working conditions of women at the workplaces. As a result, he drew a conclusion that there should be a separate organisational mechanism to organise a big number of working women and mobilise in the communist movement. According to Munoz and Woods (2000), Marx gave three logics in this regard. First, women are biologically different from men and they may have different needs and demands. These differences should be listed out separately. Second, being marginalised for centuries, they may feel comfortable to express themselves to women only. Third, women may need additional activities to develop leadership capacity among themselves. Marx insisted that a separate mechanism among women might help to achieve these objectives. Interpreting these policies into action, Clara Zetkin took the lead to organise women all around Europe. In 1869, Mills published *The Subjection of Women*, which helped to motivate women to be organised for equal rights.

Fernandez Lassalle, the German socialist leader led the 'proletarian anti-feminists' opposing votes for women. He opined that women as inferior sex should not be allowed to work in public domain and urged male workers to strike against women's entry into the industrial labour market (Simon, 2005). He further added that instead of equality, their husbands should be given higher salary and that the kitchen is a better place for women. Marx and Engels opposed Lassalle through an argument that women's work was a step forward and a pre-condition for liberation. Women and socialists men argued against Lassalle's view. August, Bebel wrote *Women and Socialism* in 1878. Frederick Engels wrote another famous book titled *Family, Private Property and Origin of State*. Both of these books had an enormous impact, awakening both women and men to the potential of working-class women. By 1889, in the forum of second International Conference, Clara Zetkin, member of the German Women's Working Association and the Social Democratic Party in Germany, proposed a 'resolution opposing the prohibition of women in paid employment, including working-class women in the working-class movement, and calling for equal pay for equal work for both sexes', which was unanimously accepted by the Conference (Gurmai, 2010). Finally, the German Social Democratic Party (SPD) adopted the policy of gender equality in 1892. After this, Lassalle's view on women was completely rejected from the debate among socialists. This movement of the West expanded to other industrialised countries as well, demanding suffrage, equal educational opportunities, and property rights. When the Soviet revolution succeeded in 1917, the Marxist feminist perspective also expanded. But, with the end of the Second World War, many women lost the employment opportunities they had, which led them to be frustrated. As a result, Simon de Bouvier wrote *The Second Sex* in 1949, which gave a new perspective on women's movement in the industrialised world. This book was translated into many languages and widely circulated across Europe.

The footprint of international context has been manifested in women's right and empowerment in the Nepali context too. In this regard, my participants AS says as follows:

> *While I was visiting Chinese library during [the] 1970s, I came to know more about the women empowerment activities of [the] Chinese Communist Party to end the gender discrimination. That motivated us to go to [the] village and organise general people to make [a] revolution. Then, we started to approach working-class people and learn[ed] more about the reality of their lives.*

Those young people's activities helped peasants around the nearby villages of Kathmandu and they became a supporter of the communist movement. Later, they became good shelter providers during the Communist Party of Nepal-Marxist Leninist (CPN-ML) period.

Women Empowerment in Nepali Context

Yogmaya who was schooled under Joshmani sect is credited for the creation of Nepali women's movement (personal communication with Govinda Gyawali in January 2016). In her Movement, Yogmaya raised the voice against social mistreatment and mis-behaviour towards women. That Movement continued for almost two and half decades. By the time, the influence of democratic and communist ideologies had already started among Nepali youths. Govinda Gyawali further said that those Nepali who were studying in India and were involved in the Second World War came back to Nepal with political awareness and democratic perspectives and played the catalytic role to motivate people for democracy in the country.

International instruments to promote gender empowerment have also contributed to motivate Nepali politics as external factors. As a member of the UN, Nepal has adopted UN Convention on Elimination of all forms of Discrimination Against Women on 5 February 1991, immediately after getting democracy in 1990. Similarly, the Convention of International Labor Organisation (ILO) as Equal Remuneration Convention 100 (ratified on 10 June 1976) and Discrimination (Employment and Occupation) Convention 111 (ratified on 19 September 1974) have also been ratified. In 1995, the government of democratic Nepal took part in the World Women Conference in Beijing and became state part of the Beijing Platform of Action. These are the important instruments and can be taken as a reference in terms of women's empowerment. All Nepal Women Association (ANWA) makes reference of those to pressurise UML and government both to adopt better gender policy. These factors did better work even in the Constituent Assembly-I and -II, in the process of inclusion of gender issues and women's rights during the drafting of the new Constitution.

Setting Gender Agenda in the Communist Party of Nepal

Puspalal played an instrumental role to form the Communist Party of Nepal (CPN). When CPN developed its manifesto, it borrowed the basic idea of Communist Manifesto from 1848 and mentioned the economic, political, and social burden on women. According to the Communist Manifesto on women, Mao (1940) mentions, patriarchal exploitation of women is an additional burden over women in the Chinese context (Zhou, 2013). Following Mao's understanding, CPN also mentioned patriarchy as an additional burden borne by women in Nepal context. CPN's Manifesto further mentioned that women themselves should be organised and mobilised for their liberation from these burdens (Puspalal, 1949). In other words, CPN's Manifesto included the issues such as women's equality in all national spheres of life, equal pay for equal work, maternity benefit for women, crèche and free education for children, and people's democracy for independent Nepal. These provisions in CPN documents motivated women to be part of a left movement with the inspiration of revolution. In this regard, AS shares:

> *After completing the school level education (SLC), I together with many other youths, used to go to Chinese Study Centre in Kathmandu to learn the Chinese language. Soon we started to study Chinese literature and magazines. Red Book, a collection of Mao's quotes, impressed and motivated us to be part of the communist movement for social change in favour of the working-class men and women. Dr. Mahesh Man Maskey, who became our mentor, supported us to form a revolutionary youth group and encouraged us to go to the villages and help villagers in their work, talk to them and then organise to form a movement. Following his advice, some two dozen youths used to go to the villages every weekend to spend time with the villagers and motivate them to follow the communist ideology and be part of the change process.*

Following the intent of CPN Manifesto, women were recruited as members of the Communist Party since its establishment. Party structures were expanded to the local level as Jhapa district was the first ever district committee of CPN formed in 1951 (K.C., 1999). CPN conducted its first conference in 1951, which was attended by only one woman out of 50 delegates (Shreshtha, 2013).

The Communist Party of Nepal held its first convention in Lalitpur from 26 to 30 January 1954. Women party members increased in number. As a result, 3 women out of 78 delegates, Sahana Pradhan, Sadhana Pradhan, and Tarulata Rayamajhi took part in the Convention (Shrestha, 2013). Similarly, the second convention was conducted on 28 May 1957 in Kathmandu, which was participated by 200 delegates including few women (personal communication with Laxmibhakta Upadhyaya on 11 February 2016). But, this Convention as well did not include any woman in the central committees as the decision-making body.

Reflecting on the situation of women in the decision-making role, there might be two possible reasons behind this. First, CPN thought that there was a separate space for women leadership through ANWA. Second, according to the Marxist way of organising, ideology was considered more important than the presence of people from a particular group, community, and class in its organography. After the second convention, with the demand to declare the general election date, *Bhadra-Abagya-Andolan* (non-violence movement) was launched with organising a mass rally from Bhugol park in Kathmandu on 7 December 1957. A significant number of women took part in this Movement.

On the day of 11 December 1957, a petition was filed in the Supreme Court. Keshar Jung Rayamajhi, the then General Secretary of CPN, led that Movement which was joined by Laxmi, an activist of ANWA and dozens of her colleagues. After a week-long mass mobilisation, the government declared the election date for 18 February 1958 and the Movement was ended. But, almost a hundred communist cadres were imprisoned during the Movement, released only after a month (K.C., 1999).

Out of 109 constituencies, 47 candidates contested from CPN in the first general election held on 18 February 1958. Four of them including Kamalraj Regmi from Palpa, Tulsi Lal Amatya from Lalitpur, and Sheikh Farman and Hardayal Mahato from Rautahat won the election (Singh, 1994). CPN secured 1,29,042 popular votes, which was 7.20 per cent of the total valid votes.

All these facts and information indicated that women were active in organising and taking an active part in every movement in the frontline. Many of them bravely faced jail and tortures. But, their contribution was not well-counted and respected after the success of the Movement. Women were neither included in the decision-making body of the party structure nor provided opportunity to contest in the general election. It reflects that class concept was prevailing dominantly within CPN politics rather than gender participation.

Communist Party of Nepal After Introducing Panchayat Regime

The then King Mahendra imposed party-less Panchayat system on 6 January 1961. The CPN leaders started to re-organise the party from exile in India. They conducted a meeting in March 1961, famously known as 'Darvanga Plenum', which was attended by all politburo members including 54 delegates from 24 districts. This meeting was continued for a month. Finally, they decided to conduct Third National Convention of CPN, which was held during 16-27 April 1962, in Banaras, India. Tulsi Lal Amatya was elected the General Secretary. But, the Party became totally functionless during his tenure. Rayamajhi, the former General Secretary of CPN, who supported King's coup to establish the panchayat system, formed his own political party named CPN (Rayamajhi Group) in 1966. Then, Puspalal reformed the party committee in Banaras under his own leadership in September 1967 and claimed that one as authorised CPN. Unfortunately, his efforts could not unify most of the communist cadres. As a result, the fragmentation of Nepali communist movement continued (K.C., 1999). The fragmentation of the communist parties and their leaders served a blow to the women cadres. Almost all the women of the communist movement were sanctioned out during those days. None of the women attended the Darvanga Plenum in 1961 and the Third Convention in 1962. None of the women were part of any activities of the Party during those days. In my opinion, there were two reasons behind this non-participation. First, most of the women, who were in the country, were taking care of their children and family. It was not possible for them to leave home. Second, all of the Party activities had taken place beyond the border. It was not easy to travel in those days and take part in Party activities. Though the women were politically empowered, without congenial circumstances, it was not possible to be active. Only a few women including Omkumari Adhikari were active through student front (Pandey, 2006).

Jhapali Movement

While the established communist leaders were running their own fringe party, young leftists were coming together locally and acting among themselves in different parts of the country. As a part of this, a group of militant young communists started arm action in 1971 from Jhapa, which was motivated by Charu Majumdar's Naxalite Movement of India. They gave the name of this action as *Barga-Shatru Khatam Gara* (fight to finish the class enemy). They killed almost 15 'feudal' in seven actions (K.C., 2009).

Many communist women came forward by supporting Jhapali activists taking high risk. Some of them took part in the armed action too. Many of others were providing the shelter, food, and security from state surveillance to the rebellion. Pabitra Niraula, one of the prominent activists of UML from Jhapa, who is actively involved even today, gave a list of women shelter providers as Lata Prasain, Jivan Ghimire, Bhaktimaya Kharel, Harimaya Kunwar, Laxmidevei Bhurtel, Rekha Kunwar, Shila Bhattarai, Suryamaya Shrestha, Sabitra Paudel, Soma Adhikari, Shanta Bhattarai, Devi Shrestha, Tika Guragain, Ganga Shiwakoti, Renu Adhikari, Krishanamaya Kharel, Harimaya Chimariya, Muna Sitaula, Sudha Kunwar, etc., who took great risks during the Jhapa Movement. If the police had sniffed that they were supporters of the Jhapali group, they could have been brutally punished by the state. But, they braved to take that risk (personal communication with Pabitra Niraula on 9 June 2016).

Within 2 years of the Jhapali action, many cadres were killed by the state. Five leaders, Krishna Kuinkel, Ramnath Dahal, Netra Ghimire, Biren Rajbanshi, and Narayan Shrestha were killed in Sukhani on 4 March 1973. Almost 200 cadres were arrested, 500 nagged with arrest warrants, and 100s removed from the area. Out of the arrested people, 97 were jailed for 3 months to 5 years, 10 persons for 5-10 years, and 15 were jailed with lifelong sentences (K.C., 1999).

Among the women in action, Lila Kattel and Sita Khadka were arrested on 3 August 1973 from Garamuni together with many other male comrades and imprisoned for 3 years and one and a half year, respectively (Mainali, 2016; Wagle, 2016). Gaura was arrested on 30 January 1976 and jailed longest among the three of them. She was released on 15 April 1980. Shova Kunwar was working as a cadre since the beginning and she was arrested and released time and again. Then, she went underground from 1975 until 1980. She became the Secretary of the Jhapa Committee after the arrest of all other senior leaders and continued party activities in the time of crisis.

Formation of Coordination Centre

After 4 years of armed struggle, the Jhapali group arrived on the stage to review its strategy. For that reason, they gathered in Biratnagar during 6-7 June 1975. It was joined by few other activists who were not part of Jhapa Movement directly but worked under different names as the starting of the unification process by forming All Nepal Communist Revolutionary Coordination Centre popularly called the Coordination Centre (CPN-ML, 1989; K.C., 1999). That meeting divided the country into seven clusters for their organisational purpose and expanded party activities accordingly (personal communication with S. Shrestha in August 2016).

While the people outside were taking organisational moves, the prisoners of the Jhapa incident dug a 65-feet long tunnel in Nakkhu Jail in Lalitpur and 15 of them including supreme leader of the coordination centre. Chandra Prakash (CP) Mainali escaped on 25 March 1977. Five of them were arrested again and heavily tortured. The rest disappeared as underground activists and remained engaged in party work (K.C., 1999). Within 3 years, their organisational structure and relation with people, both men and women, expanded. Some of them had joined the Party as full-time activists. But, the majority were playing supportive roles, rather than being part of the formal structure.

In 1975, while Shova Kunwar was the Secretary of Jhapa, by her influence, Devaki Kharel also became an underground cadre and transferred to Siraha-Saptari for Party work. She got arrested from a shelter in Siraha and imprisoned in Rajbiraj for 5 years. Shanta Manavi, who returned from Banaras and got involved in political work in Rupandehi, had already joined the Coordinator Centre as part of the Muktimorcha (personal communication with Shanta Manavi in October 2015).

> *Ishwari Acharya, Bijaya Ghimire, Nirmala Devkota, and Jaya Ghimire joined the underground movement and spent most of their time organising oppressed communities like Chamar, Musahar, etc., in Siraha, Saptari and Udayapur districts (personal communication with Jaya Ghimire on 15 May 2016).*

In August 1978, when they were gathered for the district level programme in Siraha, Jaya, Ishwari, and Bijaya were arrested together with four other men. But, on the way to the police station, all men ran away and only the women were taken into custody and jailed for one and half years. In 1979, Radha Timalsina also became an underground activist in Siraha and was arrested after some time. Including Devaki, five of the women cadres were together in prison for some time encouraging each other to be more committed to the communist movement (personal communication with Ishwari Acharya on 25 October 2016). Later, all other prisoners except Devaki were released under the care of their family. Unfortunately, Deveki lost contact with her family and Party. Then, one policeman supported her for the daily matter. Finally, they married and now live a normal life in Chandragadi, Jhapa (personal communication with Devaki Kharel on 22 February 2017). Though Devaki has gone through the political crisis, she sticks to her political beliefs and continues her involvement in UML locally. She is one of the good examples of how politically empowered person tolerates the crisis and continues her beliefs and involvement.

Setting-up of the Communist Party of Nepal-Marxist Leninist

The revolutionaries organised under the name of Coordination Centre were still discussing whether Charu Majumdar's Naxalite line way of the revolution was correct or should they take a policy shift. Amidst this discussion, the Coordination Centre conducted its third meeting in Dhanusa in July 1978 and decided to gear up the unification process with other communist groups. As a result, many of the groups such as Muktimorcha, Purbako Rato Jhanda, Pashchimko Rato Jhanda, etc., came under a single umbrella.

In November 1978, they decided to form a new dynamic and unified party. According to the decision, the Coordination Center started the meeting on Mao Day 1978 in Biratnagar, Diphu village of Itahara and founded the CPN-ML. Among 25 participants of the meeting, Lila Kattel and Sita Khadka were also present there (K.C., 1999). This meeting elected nine-member central committee comprising exclusively of men. The discussion regarding party orientation and the line was continued.

Finally, at the end of 1979, CPN-ML decided to shift the paradigm from 'Armed Struggle' to people's mobilisation by organising them under the name of different fronts as students, workers, women, peasants, etc. (CPN-ML, 1980a). This was a big shift in the communist movement of the country, which led the people's agitational movement against Panchayat system by giving up the armed struggle, which was started from Jhapa 9 years ago. It decided to give special attention to women to organise and mobilise separately.

Women-Focused Activities

After the formation of Coordination Centre, many women one after another started to join the Party activities. Some of them became underground as whole-timers and others as part-time activists. Many of them were working in mass organisations. Sita, Lila, Gaura, Shanta, Shova, Jaya, Ishwari, Bijaya, and Nirmala were already part of the underground movement. Astalaxmi Shakya became full-time underground activist from December 1979, who was already involved as part of the *Ati-Gopya Samuha* (one of the communist factions led by Shyam Prasad). Shushila Adhikari from Dang left school while she was studying in middle school and joined underground activism the same year. Shushila Shrestha left her university and became underground activist from February 1980.

Ravilaxmi Chitrakar, Sulochana Manandhar, Mira Dwaju, Laxmi Manandhar, Sumitra Joshi, Purnashova Chitrakar, Sharada Lama, Jamuna Khatri, Kamala Amatya, etc., were already in contact with the left movement in Kathmandu. Goma Timalsina and Balkumari Thapa in Hetauda, Sabita Khatiwada in Bara, Kamala Rai in Udayapur, Pabitra Nuraula in Jhapa, Kabita Paudel, Radha Gyawali and Maiya Bhattarai in Rupandehi, etc., stayed in touch with the left movement in many ways.

The Student Movement of 1979-80 compelled the Panchayat regime to go for the referendum. The then King Birendra declared the referendum on 23 May 1979, and fixed the referendum day for 2 May 1980. CPN-ML maximised that referendum campaigning for multi-party system against 'Improved Panchayat', as a wider opportunity to reach people openly and popularise the issues of democratic rights, freedom and equality as envisioned in its political document. AS, who had already become an underground whole-timer activist, says that engaging in the activities of the referendum, they could identify many men and women to enroll in the Party activities through the Student Movement as well as ANWA.

Revolutionary Women Group

Though there were no women in the central leadership of CPN-ML, many women had already become part of it as activists. Based on the Party line, revolutionary women's groups were formed in different places. In 1979, women activists available in Kathmandu valley gathered in Narayani Rana's house in Lagankhel and formed revolutionary women group. Among them were Shusila Shrestha, Rabilaxmi Chitrakar, and Narayani Rana in the presence of Sita

Khadka as a senior leader from CPN-ML (personal communication with Shusila Shreshtha on 3 June 2016). Pabitra Niraula and Bimala Dahal were part of revolutionary women's group in Jhapa (personal communication with Pabitra Niraula on 7 June 2016). The main task of these women's groups was to contact more and more women and motivate them to join CPN-ML for the cause of women's liberation and revolution in the country. Such kinds of groups were formed in other parts of the country as well.

Women Gathering

Considering women as half of the population of the country and realising no movement would succeed without women's mobilisation in an organised way, CPN-ML came to the conclusion to conduct women's meeting and discuss on further strategies to expand work in women's sector. Based on that realisation, the first national gathering among women activists was conducted during 18-19 April 1980 in Hetauda. Almost all the central leadership of CPN-ML and core women activists including Astalaxmi Shakya, Shanta Manavi, Shusila Shreshtha, Sanjita Giri, Shova Kunwar, Swasti Bajracharya, Balkumari Thapa, Seeta Khadka, Gaura Prasain, Ishwari Acharya, etc., participated in that meeting. They discussed women's issues and gave feedback to the Party collectively for the first time ever in the CPN-ML history. Astalaxmi Shakya, one of the participants of the meeting, says as follows:

> *Based on the experiences and understanding, women expressed their problems, opinions and the way forward to gear up movement very openly in the meeting. Male leaders listened to them carefully and took women's opinion into consideration as party decision later on. One of the tangible impacts was the re-establishment of ANWA.*

Listening to the women in the meeting, CPN-ML decided to form women's wing by setting three-point objectives to: (1) raise women's problem with special attention; (2) join hand with people's movement demanding equal fundamental rights; and (3) maintain sovereignty of the nation by uplifting the progressive, scientific, and patriotic culture to end patriarchy (CPN-ML, 1980b). CPN-ML also decided that to achieve the said objectives, the entire party mechanism should keep women in the forefront and provide them support to run campaigns. After 6 months of women's gathering, the Party realised that only having women's wing within the Party was not sufficient to mobilise women in mass level and decided to set-up independent women's organisation (CPN-ML, 1980c).

Re-established All Nepal Women Association

Based on the experiences of Party work among women, ANWA was re-formed on 28 February 1981 in Puranchaur Pokhara under the convener-ship of Shanta Manavi. Rest of the members were Swasti Bajracharya, Radha Gyawali, Jaya Ghimire, Kamala Rai, Sanjita Giri, and Shova Kunwar (personal communication with Shanta Manavi on 15 October 2015). It was recognised as a continuation of ANWA established on 8 March 1951 under the leadership of Kamakshadevi (ANWA, 1991, 1998).

Being a mass organisation, ANWA developed a policy not only to conduct political activities, but also maximise different occasions such as *Deusi-Bhailo, Dashain-Tihar, Teej,* etc., as cultural events as an organising tool to reach out general women and men to let them know about ANWA's objectives and expand organisational activities (ANWA, 1991). During the *Dashain-Tihar* (the festivals), women used to visit political prisoners in-group, conduct short formal programmes outside the gate, and communicate the political messages as well.

Along with its re-establishment, ANWA started to celebrate the International Women's Day (IWD) with different activities such as speech competition, essay writing, cultural programme, and mass rallies every year. Women from other sectors such as students, workers, etc., also used to join those activities. Even on the charge of conducting those programme women faced police repression and torture in custody time and again. But, it never discouraged them. I was part of these activities in Kathmandu since 1983.

Piskar Incident: A Milestone

In 1983, people in Piskar, Sindhupalchok, were celebrating the *Maghesakranti* (one of the festivals). Suspecting the communist's penetration in the festival, the police surrounded the venue and brutally attacked the people in the middle of the night. Many people were bulleted and many more injured and arrested. It was one of the brutal actions taken under Panchayat rule. People raised their voices against it all over the country. Many women like one of my informants PA, joined the Movement after knowing this kind of brutality. Talking about engagement with movement, PA says as follows:

> *After hearing the Piskar incident, we organized [a] protest rally in our school. I delivered first ever speech in the mass. Then, ANNFSU cadres came, organized and inspired me to join the anti-Panchayat movement. At its motivation, I left school in 1987 and became an underground activist until 1990.*

Progressive people all over the country were denouncing the Piskar incident. In fact, after Piskar, many more women became whole-timer activists. Many of them raised their voices against government's action from the student front. Then, they faced arrest warrants and disappeared as under-ground organisers. My informants AS and PA listed underground activists as Laxmi Gyawali and Menaka Pokhrel in Dang, Padma Aryal and Deepa Basnet in Syangja, Sita Giri in Kaski, Pabitra Niraula in Ilam, Menaka Kafle and Dharmakala Chudal in Jhapa, Bishnu Khadka in Taplejung as the women activists, who joined underground movement after 1985. All of them appeared in public as general citizen after the success of people's movement in 1990.

Taking Piskar incident as an example, Panchayat itself was contributing to increasing full-time organisers by repressing people's voice for justice. As Marx and Engels (1848) say in the Communist Manifesto, 'Bourgeoisie develop their own grave diggers and proletariat are forced to dig graves for this erstwhile master'. Panchayat was digging its own grave by repressing people demanding democracy and their livelihood. And, passing warrants against activists who voiced against the state oppression compelled them to become whole-time activists.

Use of the Panchayat System

While CPN-ML shifted its policy from armed struggle to mass mobilisation, it was looking for every loophole in the Panchayat system to use that as an opportunity to reach people at the mass level. Implementing the policy, CPN-ML set new strategy to take part in the Panchayati election under the name of *Panchayatko-Upayog* (utilising Panchayat) in 1985. The main aim of the shift in strategy was to raise anti-Panchayat voice within its mechanism and expand anti-Panchayat influences (CPN-ML, 1985). The Rashtriya-Panchayat (national assembly) election was scheduled for 1985. CPN-ML decided to take part in this election. Implementing this decision, 38 candidates including 32 candidates of CPN-ML's own and 6 others supported by it were contesting the election under the name of *Janapakshiya-ummedwar* (pro-people candidates) (Appendix VI). Women were widely involved in the election campaign propagating their own agendas. But the unfortunate thing was that none of the women was a contestant.

Five candidates including Padmaratna Tuladhar from Kathmandu, Somnath Adhikari-Pyasi from Kaski, Nobalkemi Rai from Ilam, Jagritprasad Bhetuwal from Chitawan, and Dronprasad Acharya from Jhapa won the election and became members of parliament (MPs) as CPN-ML's candidates. Pro-people candidates secured 4,80,054 votes as 9.2 per cent of total valid votes, which was better than the votes they received in the general election in 1958, which was about 7.2 per cent (CPN-ML, 1985; K.C., 2014). Those elected members raised a strong voice in the favour of people rights in Rashtriya Panchayat meeting, an apex body of the system, and protested its autocratic move. Although all of them were men, they were feminist in spirit and raised contemporary women's issues strongly. For instance, the issue of Bhurjung Khola gang rape was raised in the Parliament as one of the major agenda demanding to take action against culprits and setting strong security systems and enacting laws for women's protection (personal communication with Somnath Adhikari Pyasi on 18 January 2016).

Evaluating the positive impact of *Janapakshiya* MPs, CPN-ML decided to take part in the local election held in 1987. It had to elect almost 1,90,000 representatives from 4,015 village panchayats and 33 municipalities. CPN-ML supported about 20,000 candidates from 54 districts (CPN-ML, 1987; K.C., 2014). Some of them were women like Prava Koirala and Basundhara Baral in Kaski, Ganga Dangi in Morang, Bhanu Rijal in Kathmandu, etc. Out of them thousands of candidates won the election and worked in favour of people and motivated them to fight for democracy. Rajendra Pandey was elected as the only district president in Dhading. Deputy president in 9 districts and 37 chair and vice-chair of local Panchayat were elected in the country altogether (Appendix V). Among them, some were women like Ganga Dangi from Itahara, Morang, Bhanu Rijal from Champadevi, Kathmandu, etc. These steps of utilising the Panchayat's election helped CPN-ML to expand its policy and structure widely and make people aware of the importance of democracy. In the personal communication (in June 2016), sharing her experiences Ganga Dangi says as follows:

> *When I won the election, we organised a rally to celebrate the victory. All the progressive people and women eagerly joined that. While I started to act in favor of people, panchayat supporters reported to the palace differently. While King Birendra was visiting Dhankuta in 1988, a team of police came to my house in the evening and asked to go with them. We were not clear for what they had arrested me. I and my husband both came to the conclusion that that might be the last night in my life and I may not be back alive. Then, I asked to call woman police to go with me. They were not in a position to listen to me. Therefore, I complied and went with them without a policewoman. After arriving in Dhankuta and having a meeting with the King and Queen, they asked me whether I was a leftist and was acting against the Panchayat system. I denied and told I was doing my work in favor of people as their representative. If there was any proof doing different than that*

> *I was ready to face any action. They warned me to work carefully as per my position. Then, they returned me back home before dawn. This time, a female police together with a male police accompanied me. My presence in Panchayat helped me to reach out and motivate people in favor of democracy.*

Sharing her experiences, she further says that having women in state positions can help to change social attitudes toward women in general and women can feel comfortable to approach them. And, if women are promoted to positions with enough confidence, they can face and act under any circumstances. Biological gender does not make much difference if social gender perspective is in favour of equality.

In the process of reviewing women's role in the local election in 1987, CPN-ML came to the conclusion that ANWA should work as an open organisation to reach broader range of women and try to get a legal status, like free student unions (students' elected representative union at college/campus and university) among the student movement, which could organise women up to local level a possibility. CPN-ML also decided to re-allocate women activists into two-categories as under-ground cadres to act fully for Party, and open organisers to work among mass organisations (CPN-ML, 1987).

Based on the changed policy, ANWA started to organise students in colleges and working women in the factories and farmers in the villages. Many of us as student activists working with All Nepal National Free Student Union (ANNFSU) also became part of ANWA and mobilised to organise women from nearby villages of their colleges. From this time onward, CPN-ML stopped to compel women activists to become an underground worker and rather encouraged them to work as mass organisers through open forums (ANWA, 1996).

As a result of all of these strategies and activities, a big number of women and men having anti-panchayat thought took part in the 1990 movement, which succeeded to end the 3-decade long party-less Panchayat system.

All Nepal Women Association's First Conference in 1989

After the policy setting to make ANWA as an open organisation, the need to set-up proper policy was realised and therefore its first national conference was conducted secretly during 12-13 June, 1989 in Kirtipur, Kathmandu. The Conference adopted the policy to fight for gender equality in all spheres of human life. A new committee was elected under the leadership of Astalaxmi Shakya, who was in Ilam jail at that time. Altogether 62 delegates from 11 zones representing different sectors as women, workers, students, peasants, and others participated in the Conference (ANWA, 1991). The Conference adopted the policy to reach out all sectors of women and suggested CPN-ML too, to give more attention to women's problems and develop quality within women cadres to organise a wider range of them.

After 3 months of the ANWA conference, CPN-ML conducted its Fourth National Convention in Siraha from 25 to 30 August 1989. The Convention adopted specific policy on women as: (1) abolition of all kinds of patriarchal exploitation over women; (2) equal right on paternal property and equal remuneration for men and women at work; (3) full equality in national and social life of all sectors; (4) special programme to make women aware, guaranteeing the social security to victims and strong punishment to the culprit of violence; (5) increased active participation of women in political field; and (6) run female education and adult literacy programme in a planned way to eradicate backwardness among women. As one of the delegates of the Convention and the then Chair of ANWA, Astalaxmi mentions as follows:

> *Out of the 84 delegates in the convention, three of us were women: Sushila Shrestha, Laxmi Gyawali, and myself. Party leadership was more sensitive to women's agenda at that time. As [a] reflection, party's convention document had already included the policy and agenda adopted by ANWA, which became part of party policy then rather than only women's movement.*

This Convention was significantly important in terms of a political shift by adopting the policy to develop unified action among anti-Panchayat forces to achieve multi-party democracy through people's mobilisation. This Policy created the space among left-wing parties to form left front and then joint action with Nepali Congress for the cause of restoring multi-party democracy. The tangible result of the Policy shift was the multi-party system, declared on 8 April 1990, which was equally important in relation to women's empowerment.

Democratic Movement in 1990 and All Nepal Women Association

As an impact of CPN-ML's policy to organise and mobilise women in mass scale, they took an active part in 1990 people's movement. Dozens of them including Astalaxmi Shakya were arrested and tortured. But they tolerated everything for the sake of democracy. Laxmi Karki, one of the icons of that movement was brutally tortured. Meena Paudel, Chief of the Nursing Association of Nepal (NAN) became popular in Kathmandu when she spoke of how the monarchy was misusing national property as the property palaces. Hundreds of women over the country bore repression and torture for the sake of democracy. Then, the Constitution-making process was started after the success of the movement. Women demanded to be included in the drafting commission. But, it did not happen.

In regards to increase women's participation, Mackay, Myers, and Brown (2003) have mentioned that the Scotts used their own strategy as forming 'a coalition of women's organizations, grassroots activists, female trade unionists, party women, key insiders and gender experts' and lobbied for a role in shaping a 'women-friendly' parliamentarian. That would 'counteract the traditional masculinity biases of political institutions'. Coming together for the collective betterment of women, regardless of ideology and sectors, was one of the good examples, which can be replicated in the local context as well.

As mentioned by Mackay, Myers and Brown, ANWA had already gone through that process in 1990. Together with women from trade unions, the student movement, professional and legal sectors, ANWA conducted a workshop and prepared a list of 16-issues to include in the new constitution (Appendix VIII). But, despite drafting commission, parties' male leaders ignored most of them in the process of adoption of Constitution. Reacting on it, one of the former leaders of ANWA says 'party leadership was susceptive on women's issues earlier, when fighting against Panchayat but, once when parties came into power, even CPN-ML started to ignore women's voices and issues'.

Scott and Squires (2003) assessed the practices of women's involvement in the decision-making positions in many countries. They found that quotas have had a significant and positive impact on the number of women's representation in national legislatures around the world, which has been helpfully understood as a form of positive action in the context of three strategies for equality as equal treatment, positive action, and mainstreaming. Following the finding like this, many countries introduced a quota system. Nepal is not an exception to it. However, there were two issues, ensuring women's participation in the state mechanism and responding on the provision of 5 per cent women candidacy for general election in the Constitution of Nepal 1990 and 3 seats out of 60 reserved for women in national assembly (GoN, 1990, Article 114 and 46-1-b). But, there was no provision to include women within Party structure.

Looking back to the decade of CPN-ML, I realise that the idea that 'women as the half of the sky', worked well to encourage women for political empowerment. But, while it reached the position of state to integrate the issues of gender equality in the policy documents like the Constitution, it took back a step and forgot its commitment and ignored women's agendas. Women also realised that without making collective noise and taking joint action against patriarchal attitude even within Party, women's rights could not be secured. Then, they started to strengthen women's voice collectively within the Party.

Formation of the Communist Party of Nepal-Unified Marxist Leninist and Women

The Communist Party of Nepal-Marxist Lenin and CPN-M were already engaged in the unification process, after the success of the people's movement in 1990. When the new Constitution was promulgated, two parties were unified under the name of the CPN-UML with the acronym CPN-UML, lately known as UML. Sahana Pradhan, who was Chair of the left front in the 1990 Movement earlier, became politburo member, first ever in the Nepali history of the mainstream communist party and inclusion of a woman in the apex body ever.

Globally, after 70 years of socialist rule in the Soviet Union, the international communist movement was facing an ideological crisis in 1989, which was basically caused by the financial situation. Stoner-Weiss and McFaul (2009) mentions that in the 1970s annual growth dipped to below 3 per cent on the average. And, it further declined to 1.6 per cent in 1985 and continued in the later years. It created problems in the political system as well resulting in the collapse of 70 years long Soviet Union. This incident compelled world communist movement to review their entire policy.

The Communist Party of Nepal-Marxist Lenin, while conducting its fourth-national convention in 1989, had already begun the political debate among ranks and files about the collapse of Soviet Union. While UML conducted its Fifth National Convention in early 1993, it came up with the new political dimension with programme named as 'People's Multi-Party Democracy (PMPD)' replacing old programme named 'New Democracy'. Heading toward the multi-party democracy was a big step or paradigm shift in the communist movement. The traditional communist ideology which campaigned for a one-party system of proletarian dictatorship turned to the multi-party competition with democratic values as a new adjustment to it.

This Convention was attended by 799 delegates. Among them, 69 were women. The Convention elected two women, Sahana Pradhan and Astalaxmi Shakya, in the central committee. Many more women in Party's rank and file actively took part in the policy debate, though they were not much influential in position. Amidst this situation, UML adopted gender policy in its Fourth Convention and reaffirmed it for further implementation. Regarding the inclusion of women in the leadership, AS says as follows:

> *Though the party had agreed on the importance of woman's inclusion in the leadership principally, to translate this into action was not that easy. The committee elected by [the] fifth convention had included only Sahanajee. When women took aggressive step immediately, then the central committee meeting nominated another woman as a committee member.*

This experience shows that adopting policy is the first step in the process of change. But, to enact policy into practice, women need to come up with additional strategy with action. The fact is that it challenges the traditional way of thinking and replaces patriarchal norms and values by progressive ones, leading further to re-structuring the position and re-distribution of power.

Gender in People's Multi-Party Democracy

The political report adopted by the Fifth National Convention of UML included the gender policy as separate points and said that to liberate women from subordinated position to promote as citizen of equal footing, they should have the following: (1) equal inheritance rights; (2) equality in all sphere of life; (3) preference for education to eradicate women's backwardness; and (4) participation of women in the politics. It has further mentioned that: (5) the mal-treatment against women under the name of culture, women and girl trafficking, and prostitution should be stopped; and (6) the culprits that engage in such activities should be heavily punished through promulgation of strong laws and their enforcement (CPN-ML, 1989b; CPN-UML, 1993b).

The argument here is that the policy and perspective of the PMPD are close to the third wave of world communist movement and socialist feminist perspective. In the course of its development in two decades, PMPD has been defined, elaborated and adopted as UML's principle in 2014. In 1990, when the Constitution of Nepal (1990) was promulgated, UML had critically accepted it noting 27-point differences (Appendix VII). Some of them directly/indirectly linked with agenda of gender equality as well. Those points were inserted in interim Constitution of 2007 (CPN-UML, 2009b; GoN, 2007). Many other issues regarding economic, social, and cultural rights were included in the draft report of the first constituent assembly, which has finally been integrated part in the new Constitution of Nepal 2015 (CPN-UML, 2014b; GoN, 2015).

Regarding gender justice, UML has reaffirmed socialist-feminist perspective (CPN-UML, 2014b). It believes that biological differences between women and men create differences in gender needs. To respond to those differences, demands related with gender equality as access and control over resources, equal citizenship identity, physical presence in policy-making bodies, property rights, etc., have been included in the political report. It has also mentioned requiring one-third women in the apex body and 50 per cent in local elected bodies of the state. In terms of implementing it, PA states as follows:

> *Parties need to start preparing/training women in advance to be candidates for the executive position. Otherwise, at the time of the candidacy, there may not be enough number of qualified and confident women to stand for [an] executive position and to be elected winning the voters' confidence.*

The UML document has further said that in essence males and females are citizens of equal status. Regarding participation, it set up the policy of requiring one-third women in its internal structure from top to bottom (CPN-UML, 2009b). Politically, it has agreed that besides participation, women should have an equal right to descent, property, reproductive health, and enabling environment to have substantive access and control over decision-making powers (CPN-UML, 2014b). And, to fulfil the gender gap created in the historical course, UML believes that affirmative action programme should be employed in certain sectors such as education, health, employment, and social security. It has also mentioned that additional activities for the empowerment of leadership should be conducted to promote quality intervention in the decision-making process within the Party and in the state programmes.

If we just go through the policy documents, they are well expressive on gender issues including remedial provisions of social justice. But, to make a change in real live policies need to be translated into practice.

Adoption of Gender Agenda

Since the set policies were not accompanied by programmes and action plans, the Central Women Department (CWD) was set-up inside UML in 2004 for policy feedback on the gender issue. In the course of CWD's close cooperation with ANWA, eight points gender agenda were prepared in 2005 and submitted to the central committee to adopt as policy. In this regard, one of the informants, AS says:

> *It caused for the first time in the UML history, party's supreme leadership to spend almost a day in the formal meeting to discuss on gender matter. And, finally the agenda were adopted unanimously.*

One of the agenda was one-third women's participation in state structure including political party (CPN-UML, 2005b). Women leaders of UML continued this campaign. As a next step, when the Parliament was re-instated after successful people's movement in 2006, Bidyadevi Bhandari, a central member of UML and parliamentarian proposed four-points motion in the Parliament including one-third participation in state mechanism, with support of Kamala Pant and NP Saud from NC and Nawaraj Subedi from Sanyukta Janamorcha (Joint Peoples' Forum). It was adopted by the Parliament unanimously on 30 May 2006 (GoN, 2006). And, the issue of one-third women's participation including equality in the right to descent, property, and in laws became a state agenda.

Participation of one-third critical mass of women in politics is an internationally adopted agenda in the Beijing Platform of Action (BPA) with the commitment of all member states. To achieve the target, many countries have already set targets and are working on it. True, Niner, and Parashar (2014) studied the impact of quota and came to the conclusion that, gender quotas and reservations have significantly improved women's political representation at national and local levels, as notable result in Mongolia, Nepal, Timor-Leste, Afghanistan, New Caledonia, and the non-independent territories of French Polynesia.

Studying Chinese society in depth, Zeng (2011) also said proactive policy in women's political participation would only work well when it is not only focusing on the middle level of structure but also dealing with the grassroots level. Zeng's statement supported the demand of Nepali women's movement that securing women participation only in apex body does not help to strengthen women's participation as a whole. This also paved the way to the realisation that women's executive position in the local level politics helps towards the transformation of existing imbalanced society into a more equitable and sustainable in terms of gender parity and social justice.

The Unified Marxist Leninist Policy seems close to the conclusion of Zeng's study. Through the Eighth National Convention in 2009, UML adopted the resolution of having one-third women in its internal structure, which became part of its constitution (CPN-UML, 2009a, 2014a, Article 66-4). As a reflection of this provision, women's participation in district level has increased from 5 per cent in 2009 to 20 per cent in 2014 and 23.8 per cent in 2016, (data collected from central department of organisation).

Lately, from the Ninth National Convention in 2014, UML has adopted the policy to have at least 50 per cent women in the locally elected body of the state (CPN-UML, 2014b). This Policy has been reiterated by the Sixth Session of Ninth Central Committee held during 9 to 18 April 2016, with the addition that either chief or deputy chief of the local body should be a woman (CPN-UML, 2016). Lately, this provision has been a part of the state law, which mentioned that one of the candidates, either chief or deputy chief in the election of the local government, should be a woman (GoN, 2017).

The major points of the decision taken by UML after 2005 has been summarised in Table 5.1.

At the state level, the Constitution has guaranteed one-third women participation in elected bodies such as federal and provincial legislative bodies (GoN, 2015, Article 84-8 and 176-9) and almost 40 per cent in locally elected bodies (Articles 222 and 223). As a policy-making position, the Constitution of Federal Nepal has the provision that either the speaker or deputy speaker of both

Table 5.1 UML Decision on Gender Issue From 2005 Onwards

Date	*Decision*
2005 August	Decided 8 points gender agenda through the Ninth Session of the Seventh Central Committee including the right to descent, property, one-third participation, to end VAW and guarantee of reproductive health (Apani-12, 2005b & Apani-20, 2007a).
2008 May	Equal inheritance property to both son and daughter, by a member of central to district committee, special package to promote women membership and leadership, action against culprits and campaign for ending VAW, etc. (CPN-UML, 2008).
2009 February	The Eighth National Convention constitutionally insured one-third women participation in the internal structure. If women having constitutional criteria are not available, those seats should be kept vacant (Constitution, 2009a).
2012	Equal right on descent, citizenship, property, one-third participation in all state mechanism (Position Paper of UML for new Constitution)
2014 July	Right to descent, property, one-third participation and code of conduct on VAW (documents adopted by the Ninth National Convention).
2016 April	Enforcement of one-third women in party executive and rank and files, 50 per cent women candidacy including executive posts in a local election, enforcement of the code of conduct on VAW (Resolution of Central Committee, 2016)

(CPN-UML 2005b, 2007a, 2009a, 2014b, 2016.)

federal and state level legislation should be a woman. Only the problem is that the Constitution does not speak about guaranteed quota for executive, judiciary, and other constitutional bodies including a political party. Regarding the effective implementation of this policy, one of the informants, Parsu Gurung (PA) says as follows:

> *Having women in the upper mechanisms, as national and state parliaments is not difficult. But, to promote women as key leaders in the local level, men and women both require more energy and resources to develop necessary quality and skills among women and changing the men's behaviour and public attitude. [The] local body would have more power to act as legislative, executive, and even to some extent of [the] judiciary in the process of implementing newly adopted federal structure. Having disqualified women in the post may cause [the] problem to fulfil the responsibility.*

Ideally speaking, to have sustainable and effective results, the structure of the gender participation needs to be in pyramidal in structure. Since a new system has been introduced by the Constitution, both men and women need to learn and accommodate its aspiration accordingly. A bigger challenge now is to change their attitude and upgrade the skill of both men and women for proper enforcement of the constitutional aspirations.

Proper implementation of these decisions would solve the major parts of the gender problems. It demands sincerely letting rank an files to know and encourage them to put them into priority while translating them into operational action plans, which seem deficit. Reviewing the status of all these, it is realised that setting the policy is one thing, but without enough effort towards implementation, policies become meaningless. And, finally, women as the concerned community need to challenge power structure with a clear gender perspective and political boldness.

Women in the State Position

State mechanism is one of the important areas to create an opportunity to empower under-privileged groups and enhance their quality and develop role modelling. UML has led four governments in between 1995 and 2015. In 1995, it formed 15-member cabinet led by late Manmohan (MM) Adhikari, having no woman. Later three governments were formed in 2009, 2011 and 2015, under the premiership of Madhav Kumar (MK) Nepal, Jhalanath (JN) Khanal and Khadga Prasad (KP) Oli, respectively. All those cabinets included only one woman as a cabinet minister. Table 5.2 gives the picture of women in UML-led government.

Unlikely an executive, UML is the first party to nominate women, Lila Shrestha Subba in the position of deputy speaker in 1995. It became almost a tradition, later on, to allocate deputy speaker post for women until 2015, regardless of whichever party's representative occupied that position. In 2015, Onsari Gharti became the first woman speaker from CPN (Centre) and a man as her deputy. CPN-UML had nominated a woman as a whip in the constituent assembly in 2009, in assisting position of chief-whip, which was followed by other parties as well. But, up to now, none of the major parties have elected a woman as leader and chief-whip as leading position in the parliamentary floor.

It explicitly shows that UML does not seem very eager to promote women in the executive position and share state power with them though it is the one initiating to promote women in the upward position up to the second position as assistance. But

Table 5.2 Women in UML Led Cabinet

Year	*PM*	*Cabinet Size*		*No. of Ministers From UML*	
		Total	*Women*	*Total*	*Women*
1995	MM Adhikari	15	0	UML (Single Party Government)	
2010	MK Nepal	27	2(7.4%)	7	1(14.3%)
2011	JN Khanal	26	2(7.7%)	10	1(10%)
2015	KP Oli	28	2(7.1%)	9	1(11%)
	Total	81	6(7.4%)	51	3(5.8%)

[GoN, 1995, 2010, 2011 and 2016 (Report of the PMO).]

the need is not only providing executive roles but the opportunity to enable them to show their leadership quality at executive posts.

Reflecting the History

The dictatorship of the proletarian class was the initial orientation of the Nepali Communist Movement with the adoption of 'New Democracy' as its programme. But PMPD changed the course by introducing universal democratic values such as individual freedom, universal human rights, property rights, and multi-party political system in place of classic communistic ideas such as the state controlled economy, party-led democracy, commune farming, collective living, etc. This changed political orientation of the UML and demanded ideological reorientation of its own party leaders and the cadres, anti-patriarchy movement for proportionate representation of women, social transformation through special package to enhance women's capacity in terms of their knowledge to understand, skills to act, and a package of affirmative action plans for both men and women change their attitudes in the home, workplace, and the society at large. This is the notable political shift of UML.

It is also realised that UML is yet to develop an appropriate strategy to translate the policy into a plan, and a structure to translate plan into action, for tangible benefits to women in their real life. In other words, social transformation is not possible without an action to achieve equality as part of life. This means changing patriarchy based attitude and behaviour of both males and females from a gender perspective and to create the women-friendly political environment. It is where PMPD requires to implement strategies such as: (1) declarations and decisions made in the party to promote women's inclusion; (2) strategy of positive discrimination including measures such as gender quotas for party structures, candidate lists, etc.; and (3) positive strategies and action to develop leadership quality as party members.

The analysis reveals that the first strategy has been followed, the second partially implemented, and the third is yet to be accomplished in UML. This suggests that UML has done enough intellectual and academic exercise and set good policy. Problems remain in the 'no matching' between perspective and action. It also suggests that women have not acted enough as intellectual rebels arguing logically. Therefore, they need to learn to come up collectively with an alternative package of action plans to push for policy enforcement and ensuring equal share to women and men in every walk of life respecting the social diversity as well.

Finally, from the women's empowerment, point of view of conclusion, shows that the international practice as well as the UML practice at home. Some of these practices are similar to each other and others differ in their nature.

For instance, Marx brought the idea of women's empowerment into discussion through the Communist Manifesto in 1848. The Manifesto suggests that women as an oppressed group in the society need to participate in economic activities to be self-reliant and be organised to be liberated from labour exploitation. It empowered women to come out from the home and be organised for collective actions.

In the process, Lenin led the revolution in Soviet Russia in 1917, where a countable number of women took part in the front line. Then they adopted an equality-based policy and programme and also empowered women to be part of politics, economy as well as social activities to liberate them from all forms of exploitation and discrimination. But it could not deconstruct the socially constructed women's role and social attitude.

Mao came with the programme of 'New Democracy' in 1940 and defined women as half of the sky and termed patriarchy as one of the additional exploitative measures over women. He set the Party policy to empower women with an additional effort such as affirmative action to expand women's domain. For instance, the Chinese communist party followed the strategy to form 'Iron Girls' brigade to promote women in non-traditional sectors. But, it also failed to address the reproductive gender role shouldered by women.

When CPN was founded in 1949, it followed Mao's policy defining four areas of women's oppression. During CPN-ML time, the Party borrowed the CPN's founding policy, defining women as half of the sky and it empowered them to be the part of public domain. But, the Marxist feminist way of empowering women was failed to define care work in private sphere as economic activities. While late leader Madan Kumar Bhandari came up with PMPD replacing 'New Democracy' defining women differently in Nepali context, he set the gender policy to empower women in the public domain calling men to be an equal part of the private domain to share reproductive gender role equally (Figure 5.1). In addition, it was said that affirmative action plans should be a factor to

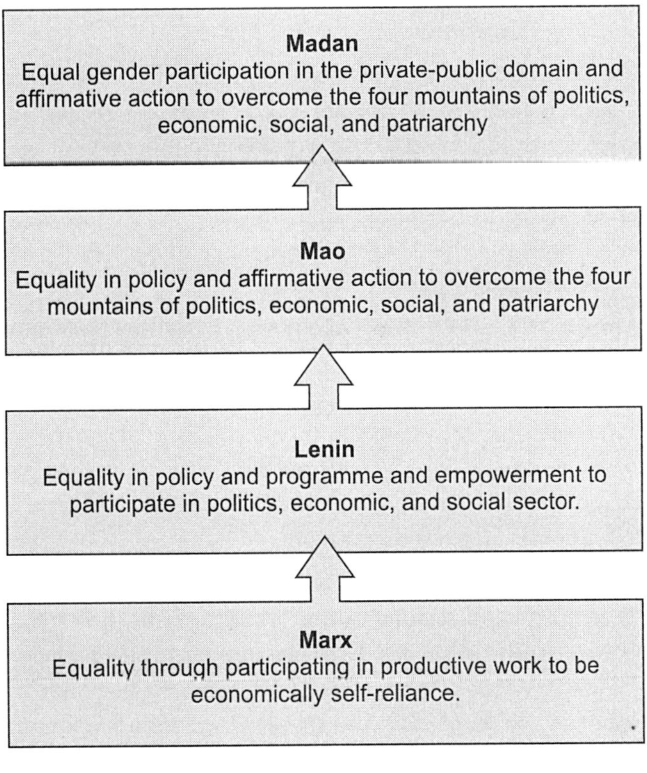

Figure 5.1 Evolution of Women Empowerment in Communist Movement.

promote women's participation and change the patriarchal norms and values being influential in the society to liberate women from the subordinated position. As a policy, PMPD has well repeated the problem of not considering household work as economically productive activities.

Under the PMPD policy, UML has empowered women politically through a quota system and increased numerical participation by multiple folds. Their performance is relatively better at the central level. Their role in lower level subordinating structure is limited to headcount rather than intervening in the process to make an action plan based on the party decision. No specific package programme to enhance the political quality of those women, who became insider through a quota system, is one of the major shortcomings of the PMPD.

The Communist Party of Nepal-Unified Marxist Leninist has encouraged women to be part of the economic activities on the public sphere and guaranteed equal property right, which has played role in economic empowerment. But, it impacted differently many women involved in economic activities have been sidelined from the mainstream politics, causing the absence of competent women in the decision-making bodies.

Women's self-esteem, confidence and awareness level has been boosted up as social empowerment. They have been more vocal to voice their problems. Women's participation in community-based and civil society organisations has increased. They have better access to education, health service, and mobility. But, unfortunately, the stereotypic mindset to see women as subordinate, weaker being and follower has not changed notably.

In conclusion, it is seen that women empowerment process has been geared up in all sectors. But, in Marxist terms, it is still at the quantitative level, which needs to step up to position themselves for constructive intervention in the whole process of policy setting to the action based on their independent views and opinions.

Also, the gender sensitivity in the macro-level leadership of UML seems good. It shows that they have internalised the national and international commitments made by the state, in the process of setting the gender policy. But, those policies are not properly communicated at the meso level to reflect into an action plan and motivate local activists to make them as part of daily lives. This suggests that relation between leadership at the macro level to meso and micro level needs to be synchronised to perform leadership as change-agent to motivate rank and file for the effectiveness of the gender policy in action.

In addition, major policy lacking PMPD is that it fails to recognise women's work to add value in public work from home.

Women Empowerment: Putting Words into Action

Following the historical footsteps of the Communist Party of Nepal-Unified Marxist Leninist (CPN-UML), its policy, programme, and activities on women empowerment has been explained in the previous chapter. In this chapter, the nexus between UML policy, action plan, and its implementation at the local level has been analysed.

Structural Role in Taking Action

Almost all the major gender agenda raised in women's movement, such as the right to citizenship certificate to the children on mother's name as a right to descent, equal inheritance of the property, at least one-third women's participation in the party structure and state mechanism, campaign to end violence against women (VAW), affirmative action programme for capacity enhancement, etc., are addressed in the UML's party constitution, programmes, and policies.

This chapter explores the implementation status of UML's gender policy and programme into practice to empower women. I have discussed here issue-wise policies and actions taken by different levels of the UML party structure.

According to the Party constitution, the national convention is the highest policy-making body of UML. The central committee is the most powerful decision-making body between two national conventions. The major role of the central committee is to work out and translate existing policy into action. For this, the central committee is responsible for mobilising committees under it, obliging them to implement the policy decision. Rest of the committees in rank and file such as district, constituency, municipality, village development committee (VDC) and ward levels (it is in the process to change according to the federal political setup of the country) are responsible for implementing the decisions into practice. To address the research question, are studied local committees' documents as minutes and circulars thoroughly and had lively informal group discussions with the representatives of those committees (male and female both). The discussion has served to get first-hand information on those committees' successes and shortcomings in the process of implementing the policy decision.

Agenda of the Gender Equality: Discussion in Central Committee

There are four major agendas regarding gender issues in UML's policy such as descent, property, participation, to end VAW, and affirmative action. Here, it is tried to examine if those agenda are carried on in meeting as agenda, debate, and decision taken by the central committee for women's empowerment. Table 6.1 shows the issues discussed at the central committee meeting.

Table 6.1 Agenda and Decision of Central Committee Meeting (onward 2014)

Issues	*Descent*	*Property*	*Participation*	*VAW*
Policy formulation	Discussed it once in the fourth meeting (July 2015)	Never discussed this issues	Discussed how to make one-third women as a member and in committees.	Discussed it in the sixth meeting
Decision	No formal decision	NA	The sixth meeting passed the resolution to enact both of these policies.	

[CPN-UML, 2014-16 (Inter-party directives 1-5 and resolution).]

Table 6.1 shows that the policy issue on the equal right on the descent and the property rights to women could not get enough priority and importance in the agenda discussions. But it focused more on the internationally raised issues of inclusion and VAW. The possible reason may be that UML leaders are also not totally free from traditional values, dominant in Nepali society. The second reason may be that women are not included in the structure to set agenda for the meeting and supreme structure. Third, there is no effective initiation by women leadership too, for taking a unanimous and strong position on the policy-making and implementing decisions into action. Finally, women's movement close to UML itself is not clear on how to lead to enact the policy into action to make a change in gender condition and position as part of the social transformation. UML's position on different issues has been discussed in detail next.

Equal Right to Descent

Equal right on citizenship is one of the fundamental issues, which is the foundation of other rights to enjoy them. This issue has been mentioned in the very manifesto of CPN as *Sampurna Rashtriya Jiwanma Barabar Adhikari* (equal right to all sphere of national life) (Puspalal, 1949). It reiterated the issues in the Third National Convention held in 1963, stating it as 'to fight for equality for women in all walks of life' (CPN, 1963). By 1989, while the communist movement was reorganised as the CPN-Marxist Leninist (ML), it elaborated the provision and formally adopted as part of political report of the Fourth National Convention in the proposition *Rashtriya ra Samajik Jiwanka Sabai Kshetrama Mahila ra Purush Bich Samantako Guarantee Garne* (guaranteeing the equal right between women and men in all walks of national and social life) (CPN-ML, 1989b). In the Fifth National Convention as CPN-UML in 1993, the provision was reiterated (CPN-UML, 2008; CPN-UML, 2009b, and CPN-UML, 2013). While the Constitution was under the drafting process, UML's Ninth National Convention in 2014 adopted the provision in the political report that equality on descent would be guaranteed as a constitutional right (CPN-UML, 2014a; CPN-UML, 2014b). In this way, equal right to citizenship has always been at the heart of the gender issues in Nepali communist movement.

Agenda and Decision of the Central Committee

Equality in citizenship was one of the debatable issues in Constituent Assembly (both CA-I and CA-II). The issue was discussed in the fourth meeting of the Ninth Central Committee of UML in July 2015. It connected the debate and recalled series of the policy decisions in the meeting. Majority of the women took a stand and argued in favour of equal descent right. But, few senior leaders (male and female both) expressed their rigid views in line with the interim Constitution, which discriminated against women. Their basic argument was that we have open borders with neighbouring India and Tarai has a culture of cross-border marriage. Such is also the case in the northern border to Tibet/China. If we allow acquiring citizenship under mother's name, the children having Indian or Tibetan father also will acquire Nepali citizenship certificate. It may create problems relating to the issue of nation's sovereignty in the long run. Considering this a sensitive issue, the meeting did not take any formal decision on it. From the viewpoint of equality, the argument itself was ridiculous, biased and discriminatory. As a communist party, which has adopted the policy of equality since the beginning, how could it argue that having an Indian/Tibetan mother does not matter, but having an Indian/Tibetan father is a big challenge? This logic clearly spells out how deep-rooted the patriarchal attitude in the way of the thinking of the senior level decision-maker is and take away women's right in the name of sovereignty.

The undecided issue of citizenship was also discussed in the constituent assembly afterward, time and again in the process of finalising the Constitution in 2015. Some of the constituent assembly members argued in favour of equality there as well. But, the constitutional committee made a different consensus. In order to declare the Constitution, UML issued a whip to its parliamentarians to vote positively on that document by joining hands with the other major parties in the constituent assembly. The provision of Constitution 2015 categorises, 'A person whose father or mother was a citizen of Nepal at his or her birth (Article 11-2-b). It looks fine. But, the next provision in Article 11-7 says as follows:

> *Notwithstanding anything contained elsewhere in this Article, in the case of a person born from a woman who is a citizen of Nepal and married to a foreign citizen, the person may acquire the naturalized citizenship of Nepal in accordance with the Federal law if he or she has permanently resided in Nepal and has not acquired the citizenship of a foreign country.*

A woman like me experiences that the second provision clearly discriminates against women. Unless one can prove that the father is a Nepali citizen, a Nepali mother's children cannot acquire citizenship by *descent*. Reflecting on the issue of citizenship, UML agreement on the discriminatory provisions towards women's right and in favour of the males only is against the UML policy. It contradicts the very first manifesto of UML.

Inclusion is one of the issues of the current democratic movement. It does not mean only ensuring people's presence from different groups, but also entails respecting their culture. Many ethnic groups such as Meche, Rajbansi, etc., in Nepal have a matrimonial culture. But the Constitution does not respect and recognise such kind of culture-specific issue. That is still causing the problem for the Nepali women's children.

Also, those women who are living with children but whose husbands have either disappeared or died without any document to prove their relation with their children are facing serious problems to get citizen identity. Finally, those women married to foreigners (mostly in the case of India) and living back in Nepal with children caused by VAW are also facing the same problem. In this regard, let me recite a case of Rojina (pseudo name):

> *Rojina and Ram are daughter and son of a Gorkha Army personnel, born and brought up in Darjeeling. Both of them married local citizens. Later, their whole family came back to Ilam. Now, the children of Ram have got Nepali citizenship without any query. But, Rojina's 23-year-*

> *old son is facing problem simply because she had married a foreigner. The son is asking her, "If you cannot provide me citizen identity, why did you bring me to Nepal?" Is it not gender discrimination? (Rojina shared the case in the state-1 women's program in Itahari, on October 13, 2016).*

According to Article 11.2b of the Constitution of Nepal 2015, Ram did not face any problem of getting citizenship of his child, but it is problem for Rojina's child because those children having foreign fathers need to produce a paper proving that they have not acquired a citizenship of their father's country. But, the problem is that the Nepali woman's children born in Nepal would not have a birth record in their father's country. And, it is not possible to produce any paper in regard to their personal bio-data in father's country. It is humiliating for every child having Nepali mother and foreigner father. This is also a case of discrimination against the woman having cross-border marriage.

The mindset of some of the senior leaders of UML is still very conservative in regard to women. Let me share one more story here.

> *While the interim Constitution was under discussion in 2007, with reference to the Party's decision on citizenship with mother's name, I was requesting one of the senior-most leaders to adopt constitutional provision on citizenship based on equal footing. Reacting on my request, he told that I was just worried of women's right, but they (as men) were worried about the sovereignty of the nation.*

This attitude still dominant among senior leaders of UML is the reason behind the Party remaining indecisive towards equal rights to citizenship and agreeing on a discriminatory provision in the new Constitution. Being ignorant on the principle of gender policy at the stage of making decision shows that this Policy has been adopted only for public consumption suggesting that UML is in favour of equality.

Equal Right in Inheritance of Property

A property right is one of the essential issues in terms of women empowerment and gender equality. It is the part of the redistribution of economic power within the family. It recognises entitlement for women as 'half of the land' rather only saying 'half of the sky'. It is a tangible link between the family's attitude and their behaviour to indicate whether parents show equal behaviour toward daughter and son.

According to the inheritance law of USA, parents have the right to write a will that controls 'who will' and 'who will not' get their property after they die. France has a different system. Children can enjoy a maximum of three-quarters of the parents' property. The rest will go to the state. This system does not make much of a difference in these countries, because citizens older than 18 years will live independently. In case support is needed, state's social security system covers them.

The Eastern world has a different practice. During the post-Vedic era, women could own their property under the name of *stridhan* (women's property). This system was in practice in India as well for long. After going through the amendment of Hindu law in 2005, all children now get equal inheritance property rights. In the case of Muslim practices, daughters get only half of the share of property received by sons. As our reality, the land is still the major source of livelihood and a visible source of parental property for the majority of the population. Thus, right over parental property has a big meaning and importance for their children.

Internalising Nepali reality, UML's policy is in favour of the equal property right to all children. The document 'Program of Nepali Revolution' adopted by the Fourth National Convention in 1989 said *Paitrik Sampatima Chhora ra Chhoriko Saman Hak Sthapit Garne* (to establish the equal right of son and daughter on inheritance property) (CPN-ML, 1989b). This policy has been reiterated from the Fifth National Convention onward as well (CPN-UML, 1993b, 2005b, 2007b, 2008, 2009b, 2013, and 2014b). In the process of promulgating the new Constitution, it has been unanimously adopted as Article 18-5 of the Constitution 2015, which was part of the interim Constitution as well (GoN, 2007, 2015).

Agenda and Decision in the Central Committee

The issue of equal inheritance property right has been adopted without any difference of opinion in the party and constituent assembly (CA). The reason behind this might be that theoretically, UML is in favour of equality. Second, the nationwide women's movement and campaign created internal pressure on UML to adopt this policy. However, the mindset of its rank and file has not been changed enough to push this agenda in enforcement. As a result, for a decade, the issue has neither been the agenda of the meeting nor has any discussion and decision has taken to direct its rank and file to enforce the issue in action.

Socio-political Implication of Property Right

A property right is directly linked with economic empowerment. In the society like ours, where the major form of property is land as means of production, the majority of people depend on it for their livelihood in absence of other employment. Therefore, it is highly important to get a share of parental property for livelihood for a girl even for her recognition as an equal member of the natal family. Now, after having women's quota in the state mechanism, its importance has even been crucial. Let me share one of the incidents in relation to property, participation, and mindset.

> *While the Party was in the process of searching name for possible candidates in Kathmandu-2 for the election in 2014, I spelled out 'Sarita' a woman, who was born there and had already spent 15 years as a UML cadre. The senior leader of the Party immediately reacted and asked, 'Where is her marital home?' The implicit meaning of the query was that she should have gone and claimed the constituency, where her husband had a house, rather than her birthplace. It is obvious indication that she neither has parental property nor recognized as a family member (interaction with one of the senior leaders in 2013).*

The new Constitution has guaranteed women's participation in politics in federal, state and local levels (GoN, 2015). In this connection, equal property right creates meaning even to claim their constituency, based on the entitlement of land and property.

Based on all these arguments, since UML has adopted this policy already, it is crucial to go for enforcement strictly with proper inclusion of it in an action plan.

Women's Participation as Part of Empowerment

Entering the twenty-first century, many countries realised the need to strengthen women's participation in politics and set-up different policies and programmes based on the local context. Vietnamese political parties adopted the National Strategy for the Advancement of Vietnamese Women in 2010 by setting out proportional representation of women in the National Assembly and quota for different levels accompanied with a plan of action with the time frame, and focusing on leadership development from grassroots (Trung, 2013). Talking about the impact of the policy, Binh, a communist leader says that the policy helped to raise Vietnamese women's position with positive changes in education, employment and political participation, making a significant impact on the economy (Duong, 2012).

The Communist Party of Nepal-UML also reviewed its approach to bring women within its own structure, while women's participation was negligible in its structure and set policy to include at least one woman in every committee (CPN-UML, 1995). Later in 1997, UML pushed the government to adopt a bill ensuring 20 percent women's participation in locally elected bodies (GoN, 1997). It made possible for almost 40,000 women to be part of the political activities in the local level through the formal structure of the state.

Women's participation is not a new agenda for CPN in fact. It has adopted the issue of women's participation in its policy since the very beginning. Later arriving at the Fourth National Convention, the political report has addressed the issue of the participation stating *Rajnitik Kshetrama Mahilaharuko Sahabhagita Badhaune* (to increase women's active participation in politics) (CPN-ML, 1989b). This statement has been repeated in the subsequent policy documents of UML. While the Constitution of 1990 mentioned the provision of requiring a 5 per cent compulsory women candidacy

Table 6.2 Women in CPN-UML's Central Structure

Convention	*Delegates*			*Central Committee*			*National Council*			*Department Chief*		
	Total	*F*	*%*	*Total*	*F*	*%*	*Total*	*F*	*%*	*Total*	*F*	*%*
1st	78	3	3.8	17	0	0	NA					
2nd	200	NA		17	0	0						
3rd	NA	NA		17	0	0						
4th	84	3	3.57	20	0	0						
5th	799	69	8.6	43	3	7	N/A					
6th	857	121	14.2	57	4	7 1	376	13	3.46	63	0	0
7th	1010	153	15.2	67	6	9	318	16	5	22	1	4.5
8th	1818	404	22.2	116	21	18	900+	121	13+	22	1	4.5
9th	2119	424	20	184	31	16 8	NA			31	2	6.5

[CPN-UML, 1993-2015 (Department of Organization).]

for general election, UML started to make policy on quota system within the party structure (CPN-UML, 1995). By the Eighth National Convention, it came up with constitutional provision of requiring one-third women's participation's in its internal structure (CPN-UML, 2009b, Article 66-4), which has been repeated time and again in the policy documents, election manifesto and resolutions (CPN-UML 2009b, 2013, 2014a, 2014b, and 2014c). Finally, the state's constitution as well has guaranteed this in federal and state parliaments, including one woman as either chief or deputy-chief and almost 40 per cent women in local government (GoN, 2015, Articles 84-8, 92-1 and 2, 176-9, 182-2, 220-3, 222-3, and 223-3).

The data in Table 6.3 gives the impression that respect the policy of women's participation has gradually increased in UML structure. At the same time, the table shows that the adopted policy has not been fully implemented yet. It shows that UML needs to focus on membership drive as well since it is far behind to achieve one-third member in general.

Table 6.3 Women's Participation at Different Levels (June 2016)

Structure	*Total Members*	*Women Member*	*% of Women*
Membership	2,70,520	50,530	18.7
District Committees	1,331	312	23.44
Province Committee	541	121	22.37
Central Committee	184	30	16.4
Central Departments (31)	734	108	14.71
Central Secretariat	10	0	0.00
Politburo	63	6	9.52
Standing Committee	24	1	4.17

[CPN-UML, 2016 (Head Office).]

The Unified Marxist Leninist has a central secretariat as a powerful body in terms of day-to-day activities and agenda setting for the meetings of the central committee, politburo, and standing committee. It has no female members so far. Its central office has four women out of twelve staffs, which helps to create a gender-friendly environment and easy access for women visiting the office. However, most of the local offices have only one staff and are obviously populated with men.

Agenda in Central Committee Meeting

Keeping the importance of the secretariat's role in mind, the issue in the fourth meeting in July 2015 was raised to include a woman in this structure, while this was an agenda for discussion. But, there was not a collective voice even among women. As a result, we could not make it heard, while it was decided later by the standing committee, and the secretariat has no woman until now.

The issue of one-third participation within the Party was raised and discussed again in the sixth meeting in April 2016. As a result, a resolution has carried it on with a commitment to implement this in its internal structure. It had called upon the government to make the legal provisions to have a woman as either chief or deputy chief in the local election with 50 per cent of total candidates and directed its parliamentarians to play a role in this regard (CPN-UML, 2016). As a result, the Parliament adopted the law with the provision to have female candidacy either as in chief or deputy-chief in the local election (GoN, 2017). It is moving one step forward. But still, there is no provision in regard to a chair at the ward level to make 50 per cent candidates in total.

The informants were asked about the reason behind the quota system not being implemented within Party structure. They have different opinions. In the interview, women say that there are enough qualified and interested women to fulfil the quota from the central up to district level. But, lack of the will power of senior leaders in different levels and lack of women's collective action at respective levels to create collective voice are the major reasons. Men's opinions are different. They say that there are not enough qualified women to fulfil constitutional responsibility at all levels. They have different opinions on 'qualified women' as well. Women view it as constitutional provision and my women interviewees say as follows:

> *There are enough women who meet the constitutional provision for central to district level committee and women are interested as well. They opined that women should come together and take a stand that if there is no one-third seat allocation for women, they should make protest collectively and deny being part of the process. But, it is not happening. Secondly, senior women leaders need to be ready to contest in the open quotas as well. It will show women's confidence and boldness of in the process and may encourage their juniors.*

Male interviewees' opinions are different. About promoting women in the leadership position, they give more priority on seniority and experiences rather than enforcement of inclusion policy and say:

> *The Party is trying to include more women in the committee. But, there are two constraints. First, the women membership in total is not one-third. Second, even though there are enough women to include in the upper structure, they have junior standing and are less experienced in comparison to the huge number of senior and experienced male cadres. Junior cadres in the higher position and senior under them can cause humiliation for both sides.*

Both opinions seem logical to some extent. Women seem self-critical in regard to not being able to act collectively amongst themselves. Men's opinion is more aggressive and lacks respect to their own policy. But, the opinion on affirmative action is congruent, as both agree on the need to 'special package of action plan' to enroll more women as members and enhance their leadership capacity accompanied with a monitoring mechanism to put policy into action.

Participation in the Decision-making Process

To assess the gender participation in decision-making process, the trend of attending six committee meetings (from 2014 July to 2016 April), for an example of gender participation in the meeting, the women's absenteeism is 46 in against 54 per cent of men. It seems that women's presence in meeting in macro level is better than men (Figure 6.1).

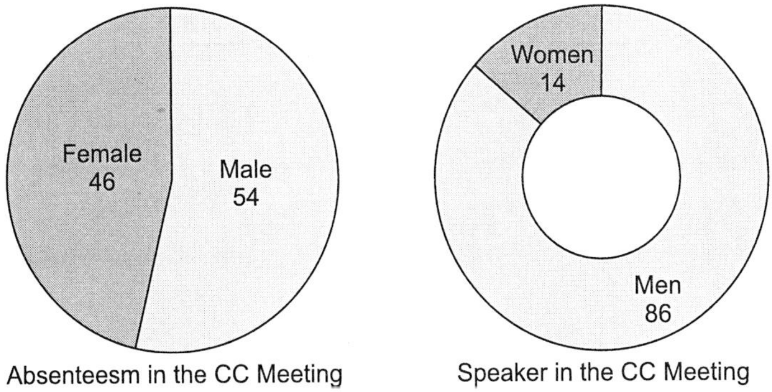

Figure 6.1 Gender Participation in Central Committee (CC) Meeting.

But, in regard to intervening the discussion, men take more opportunity (than their representation in the committee (83 per cent) as 86 per cent, while women get lesser chances. It is caused by more male in the portfolio, means gender in position make difference.

Visibility of Women Leadership

Participating in public activities and influencing the masses is essential in the Party politics. Most of the participants believe that it gives the speaker visibility and allows them to be accepted as a leader. In this regard, women as speakers in public programmes would help them to stand as leaders and change the gender perspective of the masses. Within two years period from mid-2014 to mid-2016, almost a dozen big gatherings conducted in different parts of the country on different issues. Among them, none of the mass programmes were addressed by a woman as the chief guest. Even as a guest speaker, very few women got the opportunity to address masses in the public programme. In this regard, my informant AS says as follows:

> *Ideally, the chief guest should be of a senior position. Woman hold only fifth position from the top, and can have very slim chances to be chief guest in a big gathering. Even to address as a speaker, there is*

> *no opportunity, unless local organisers sensitively invite [a] woman as one of the speakers.*

Local conference is another important event for leaders to participate in. Within the observed period, 21 districts conducted their conference. Among them, only a few districts invited women as guest speaker. But, a dozen of male leaders spoke on each of those conferences. One of the informant PG says that:

> *Generally, the organisers for the local programs invite speakers from different levels of [the] party structure, as well as mass organisations, to deliver a message of solidarity. Most of those organisation mechanisms are headed by men and whenever there is [an] invitation, they decide based on seniority in position, which has resulted in a long list of male speakers only.*

Taking both of these statements into account, interpreting with the hierarchical mindset, the male representation can be justified. These statements also reveal the reality that women are structurally denied and restricted in performing and exposing their confidence and leadership capacity. Despite the agenda of inclusion with the aspiration of social transformation, the given logic has already been rejected by people's movement 2006. This suggests that respecting people's aspiration and UML's policy on social transformation, the conventional mindset needs to be changed to follow alternative ways in practice.

Women in Party Education

Party school is the organ of UML to conduct capacity enhancing activities such as training, workshops, and seminars, especially on political ideology, Party policy and programme, Party management, and contemporary political issues among its rank and files. It is the institution to enhance knowledge and skill, and motivate its cadres to perform their role, responsibility, and duty to transform society based on equality and social justice through the inclusion of marginalised people's knowledge, skill, and experiences.

Revisiting the UML's party school activities covering a year in

2015, fifteen plus training programmes in different districts were conducted. Each programme was attended by four to five resource-persons. Among them, one woman was invited as a trainer in two places. Among the participants, there was a countable number of women (personal communication with the secretary of the Party school department, 10 June 2016). Another UML Party leader, linking with party school further says that:

> *To be a resource-person, the person should have enough political knowledge on the subject matter as well as knowledge delivery skill and confidence. We have very few women who can do that. Additionally, those women who are qualified may not be always available for the program, due to their prior commitments, which is also the problem to include more women as resource-persons. Thirdly, it depends on local organiser's choice as well. They normally propose male's name as their leader.*

Party school's activities are the real place to know local cadres' level of awareness, understanding, gender sensitivity, attitude, behavior, and potential for motivation. Its activities enrich the Party in two ways. First, the trainers' team can have the opportunity to learn from below. It helps them expand their knowledge, information, and understanding about grassroots people. This helps leaders to be empowered. Second, it works to change the cadres' attitude and perspective to accept men and women both as leaders equally. This would be the way to empower cadres by changing their gender perceptive. Keeping these points in consideration, it demands to revisit the selection process of trainers and trainees of a party school in the activities to make women visible there.

To avail enough women and qualified women to be part of the Party, women-focused programmes need to be conducted on different issues based on their interest, capacity, and Party's need. Party school may need to play a vital role in this regard. It can help to provide women in different sectors and level to implement Party policy on participation addressing both need quantity and quality.

Violence against Women

Violence against women (VAW) is one of the major and common problems of Nepali society. VAW is rampant in the society and is one of the constraints for women to come out from subordinated positions and be part of mainstream politics, economic, and social activities. Recognising the patriarchal exploitation in society, UML has responded to this agenda with policies like *mahilaharumathi bhairaheko pitrisattamak shosan-utpidanka sathai sabai prakarka shosan-utpidanharu, apaharan, bechbikhan, beshyabritti tatha samajik kupratha aadiko antya garne* (ending all kinds of injustice, kidnapping, trafficking, prostitution, abuse, and social mal-practice including the patriarchal exploitation and harassment) (CPN-UML, 1989b). The aspiration of this statement has been reiterated in every step (CPN-UML, 1993b, 1998, 2009a, and 2014a). In addition, UML has adopted a code of conduct on VAW as part of policy document of the Ninth Convention in 2014.

Violence Against Women has been realised as one of the serious issues by the state as well. Giving the emphasis on it, the interim constitution 2007 included the provision by stating 'No physical, mental or any other form of violence shall be inflicted to any woman, and such an act shall be punishable by law' (GoN, 2007, Article 20-3). Later, the Constitution 2015 has even strengthened it and carries the wording as follows:

> *No woman shall be subjected to a physical, mental, sexual, psychological or other form of violence or exploitation on grounds of religion, social, cultural tradition, and practice or on any other grounds. Such act shall be punishable by law, and the victim shall have the right to obtain compensation in accordance with law* (GoN, 2015, Article 38-3).

It shows that Nepali politics has fully endorsed the VAW as serious problem and parties are trying to seek remedial ways as one of the measures to empower women physically and mentally by providing them legal security.

Agenda and Decision in the Central Committee

The Unified Marxist Leninist has discussed VAW in central committee in 2005 and 2016 and decided 'to launch [a] campaign against VAW, harassment, abuse and mal-treatment against women' (CPN-UML, 2005b; CPN-UML, 2016). Based on these, some of the cases were registered in the Central Discipline Commission (CDC). But, CDC does not take action in the way of giving justice to the victim.

Even after the adoption of VAW Code of Conduct in 2014, it was not executed properly. Then, the issue was raised in the meeting in April 2016 linking with Code of Conduct and provision in state's constitution. It has been addressed by meeting resolutions and circulated to local committees once again to implement it.

For instance, Shusila was one of the UML members who registered a domestic violence case in CDC in 2011 and Asmita, a student, brought forward a sexual abusê case verbally in 2012. But, no action was taken on either of the cases. Shusila later went to the court and got justice. Asmita did not do anything rather just taking that incident as a lesson, engaged herself as psycho-socio counsellor to take care of other victims as a social activist.

Affirmative Action Plan as Empowerment Measure

Affirmative action is an equity measure to empower and mainstream marginalised groups for equal participation in terms of quantitative presence and empower them for qualitative intervention. Reviewing the international literature on affirmative action, Kisan (2010) has concluded three ways to increase numerical participation as quota or reservation, proportional representation, and special provision. He also mentioned that there are three methods to implement these affirmative actions, i.e. preferential, remedial, and compensatory ways (Kisan, 2010). Referring to Weisskopf (2004), Kisan has further mentioned that the policy of affirmative action may enable the beneficiary group to upgrade their professional and political capacity to mainstream them in the society, making a change towards a more unified and democratic system (Kisan, 2010).

The European Commission has stated that Quotas regulations are an important tool for giving women access to leading political positions. Mackay, Myers, and Brown (2003) mention that to achieve the intended result of equitable and dignified society, at least three components of the affirmative action including quota for quantitative promotion, training/leadership development scheme for capacity building for qualitative participation, and mentoring for attitudinal change should be architected wisely and enforced skilfully for the cause of total social transformation.

The Unified Marxist Leninist's policy of affirmative action is close to the earlier-mentioned ideas and opinions and it has included an affirmative action plan with high priority in the policy since long ago. The programme document adopted by the Fourth National Convention has included the statement as *Mahilaharuprati Rahadai Aayeko Rajniţik, Aarthik, Samajik ra Sangskritik Bived Tatha Asamanagata Hatai Saman Adhikarko Gyarentee Garna Thos Yojana ra Karyakram Banai Laagu Garne* (removing the inequality existing against women in politics, economic, social and cultural aspects and to guarantee equality, a specific programme and plan should be developed and implemented) (CPN-UML, 1989a). It has been further elaborated as *Rajnitik, Aarthik, Samajik Jeevanka Harek Khsetrama Mahilaharuko Sakriya Sahavagita Badhaudai Lagi Uniharulai Saksham Tulyaune* (to promote the active participation of women in all sphere of politics, economic and social life, their quality should be enhanced). Realising the weaknesses, the political report has mentioned that *Kamjori Hataudai Mahila Bichma Kaamlai Yojanabaddha Rupma Agadi Badhauna Bishes Dhyan Dina Abashyak Chha* (special attention is needed to conduct activities among women in plan-way) (CPN-ML, 1989b). The provision of the women-focused special programme has been mentioned repeatedly (CPN-UML, 1993a, 1993b,) It has first ever explicitly emphasized on a membership drive to achieve set target of women's participation in the document of the Eighth National Convention and has mentioned, 'We have to plan to enrol more women as party members' (CPN-UML, 2009b).

The state as well, realises the need for affirmative action to promote women's capacity to transform the society based on equality with social justice; the constitution carried the provision, as 'Women shall have the right to obtain special opportunity in education, health, employment and social security, on the basis of positive discrimination' (GoN, 2015, Article 38-5). In this way, all the documents including UML's policy and state's constitution have internalised the need for the affirmative action to empower women's leadership as well as strengthen participation as equity measures.

Agenda and Decision in the Central Committee

The Communist Party of Nepal-UML has realised and mentioned affirmative action in its policy documents time and again. To promote the implementation of the Policy, UML had already established Central Women Department (CWD) in 2004. The main objective of this is to give policy feedback to the Party on gender issues. CWD has conducted a series of activities to achieve the said objective. One of the tangible outcomes of its work is the eight-point gender agenda (CPN-UML, 2005b).

After the Eighth National Convention, CWD has been removed from the structure, keeping in mind that its work might be done by All Nepal Women Association (ANWA). But, in reality, the issue regarding special programmes to empower women within Party has neither been discussed nor activities conducted focusing on gender agenda.

Revisiting all these agendas, policy, decisions and its enforcement, the conclusion can be drawn that UML has adopted a good policy to address the women's issues. But, it has a lot of dilemma in the process of supporting with appropriate strategy and action plan to translate it into reality. In regard to citizenship right, senior leaders are just taking the policy matter for public consumption. It shows that they do not see women as equal citizens as they are. It also gives a clue to the fact that they themselves are not ready to distribute their property equally to their own children and pay adequate attention to ending VAW within the party structure, which is not solved properly. In regard to participation, only a few women have been promoted into a high public position in the state and it has double standard even within the Party. Locally, while women cadres ask for one-third seat, they say about proportionate membership. But, in the central level, women's representation has not been reflected in proportionately. Having 18.9 per cent women in total, only 16.7 in the central committee, 10 per cent in the politburo, and 4.2 per cent in standing committee is a testimony of my claim.

Local Committee as Implementing Agency: Gender Agenda in Action

Local committees are major vehicles to put words into actions in UML. There are tiers of committees in various levels from the state (formed replacing zonal committee in 2017), to wards at the bottom. Among them, some are having executive power and some are coordinating bodies. The committees having executive power can elect their own leadership from their members and decide the activities based on party policy and directives of the upper committee.

Taking the executive power of the committees into account, I selected a tier of committees as district, constituency, municipality, VDC, and ward committees. The agendas of the meetings, decisions taken to implement and circulars sent to committees under them were rigorously analyzed covering the last 2 years. Then, the informal group discussions focused on gender agenda was organised, in which representatives (male and female both) of almost all levels of the local committees participated.

Most of the issues adopted as policy and discussed in the central committee are not included as the formal agenda in the local committee meeting. Obviously, it is seen that there is no action plan to reinforce policy into practice.

Table 6.4 reflects the status of women's agenda in the meeting of UML's local committees.

Table 6.4 Local Committee as Policy Enforcement Agency

Issues	*Descent*	*Property*	*Participation*	*VAW*	*Others*
DC	Never included as formal agenda. But, many cases have been tackled practically.	Never discussed this issue	Discussed how to insist one-third women as a member, a formal decision has not been taken	Discussed as formal agenda and joined the campaign time and again	No special agenda regarding gender issue. But, joined some of the campaigns such as the celebration of 8 March, jointly with other mass organs.
Constituency committee	Never included as an agenda, but individual cases handled in a personal level.	It was discussed informally as the provision of the constitution. But no formal decision	Discussed on how to increase women member, but no formal decision	No discussion as formal agenda. But, joined the campaign following the DC directive.	
Municipal committee	Never discussed an agenda. Some cases forwarded to the municipality.	Never discussed this issue	Never discussed an agenda		
VDC Ward	Never discussed as agenda. No problem tackled yet				

[CPN-UML, 2014-16 (Minute of Meetings and Circular of the Committees).]

Equal Descent Right

Citizenship certificate on mother's name is one of the issues that is directly linked with local committees. It has not been a formal agenda in any committee yet. But, as they shared their experiences in the discussion, some of the district committee members are engaged in handling the cases brought to them. Similarly, some of them from constituency and municipality levels have handled cases individually, without making formal agenda in the committee. Many of them experienced that this is the most common and the difficult issue to facilitate with the administration. Among them, some cases have been solved successfully and some are even more complicated. The solution depends on the level of gender awareness/perspective of the bureaucrat in the related offices since the constitutional provision is not explicitly clear on it (participants communicated in the informal discussion). The lower level committees seem reluctant to include the issues in their formal agendas. They unanimously expressed their reasons that most of the time their agendas of the meeting are focused on implementing the decision sent from the upper committee as circular. The issue of the right to descent has never even had the opportunity to be a part of circular in the upper committee.

Equal Property Right

The equal property right to son and daughter has never been formal agenda in any tier of the committees. Yet, the central committee had circulated its decision a long time ago. Considering this as a very private matter of the family, unless somebody brings the problem, they think it is not needed to be discussed as agenda. In this regard, participants in the group discussion say that even women as individuals, and ANWA as a movement, have never come up with any complaint. But, on the positive side, some of them and people have started to provide an equal share of the property to both daughters and sons. For instance, BG, a district committee member is settling in parental property as an equal family member. Some others are as well practicing this according to their parents' decision, and siblings understanding, rather constitutional provision.

Women's Participation

It was found that the issue of the one-third women's participation has been discussed at almost all levels. It is directly related with a political position in the public place. Quoting the Party constitution, women delegates in conferences of almost every level raise the issue and argue for quota allocation. That is the reason it has been discussed as formal agenda and the decision has been made to implement the provision. But, putting these words into action has not been performed properly. Another fact is that as a communist party, every member should be committed to at least in a committee. But without enrolling one-third women member, it is impossible to implement this provision up to the local level.

Women in Local Committee Meetings

It was also tried to analyze the attendance at the local committee meetings and found that women's attendance is slightly lower than average attendance, which is reflected in Figure 6.2. Women's attendance at the district level is the lowest. In the rest of the committees, such as constituency, municipality, VDC and ward levels, the attendance seems comparatively better. The attendance shows it above 50 per cent.

Inquired about the reason behind the relatively better attendance is below district level BG, who is in-charge of the VDC committee and participant of the group discussion, says that most of the women in the local committees live nearby and they do not need much vehicle fare to go to the meeting. Another reason is that as locally known leaders in the committee, women can also request to manage meeting time according to their convenience to perform both domestic work and Party work. These reasons have helped women to have better attendance at the grassroots level meetings.

But, in the case of district level, there are multiple reasons behind low participation of women in political activities. SN, one of the executive members in the district committee, participating in the group discussion, mentioned that there were few reasons behind it. First, women faced financial constraint while travelling

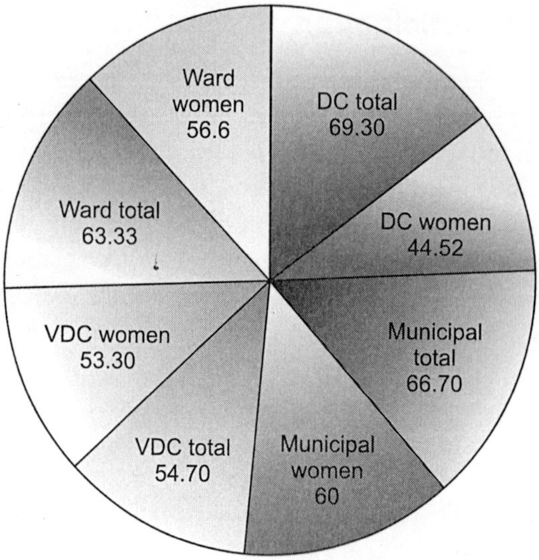

Figure 6.2 Women's Participation in Local Committees' Meeting.

to distant places. Second, the meeting time did not seem friendly to these women because of domestic responsibilities. These women had responsibilities of taking care of children and elderly people, which they could not undermine or avoid. This is thought of as the most important responsibility of women in the society. Third, they hardly understand the discourse and discussion fully in the meeting and feel isolated while having debates. Fourth, the matters of their concern are not heard. And finally, the majority of them have been promoted in the committee as part of the quota without proper ideological understanding and confidence. RG, the head of the women sector of the district committee, added her opinion and claims that the solution lies in the additional programme for women. This is important and essential to conduct, as it enhances ideological understanding and skill of women to handle the problems. Additionally, it is necessary to be more gender sensitive to be more practical in terms of gender roles, agenda setting, and time management.

Going through all these logics and opinions, as part of the remedy, UML needs to think differently with the relevant package and the programme to overcome these shortcomings and the circumstances. Equally important matters that need to be given attention are meeting times, venues, changing gender roles, etc., perceived as the inconveniences.

Violence against Women

Violence against women is a common issue for all in the context of Nepal. It has been a widely discussed in regards to the policy of UML. The district committee has discussed VAW as formal agenda and decided to be part of the campaigns against it, directing its subordinate committees to act in similar ways. Based on the directives, all the committees took part in the campaign though they did not discuss this issue as formal agenda in their own committee meeting.

One of my participants shared that there were many cases reported to the local leader, such as alcoholism, domestic violence, polygamy, etc. They settled most of those cases locally. Almost every level of the committee has been part of this process. VAW linked with citizen identity and right to property are crucial and complex. These kinds of complex cases, they refer to National Women's Commission, police cells, NGOs and some other authorities, who provide them material or mental support and legal aids. The following is the case of my informants, which I received during the group discussion:

> *A man called Dhana settled in my village by marrying a local woman. But he died after having two children. His wife, Sani, had never been to his village. She had not been introduced to her husband's family and relatives, nor did she even know any of them. Later, the children needed citizenship certificate. Nobody knew people from the children's father's side to verify that their father was a Nepali citizen. Sarita, one of the UML leaders, suggested the local party committee to support the children to get the citizenship certificate. But, the case has not been settled yet, as the problem remains that they do not have any proof that certifies their father's nationality.*

> *Ganga (pseudo name) from Kathmandu-1 suggested local UML leaders provide party membership to more women. He argued by presenting a case of Kathmandu Metropolitan City (KMC)-10 where there were 100 women and 50 men as members.*
>
> *Bimala (pseudo name), another member of UML, suggested ensuring an equal number of men/women members at the local level. Finally, the participants of the group discussion agreed that in the days to come, ANWA as a sister organization of UML could launch membership drive among women and collect the forms. Then, the forms can be processed through party committees as per its constitution.*
>
> *Shani (pseudo name), another member in the discussion, recommended that the central committee decided and circulated to all members of UML to guarantee the equal property right to all the family members. Rama (pseudo name) requested the central committee to decide not to provide tickets for those who have violated VAW code of conduct. She said this would motivate more women to join UML. The chair of the committee reminded that this has been already mentioned in the code of conduct. He further stressed that it should be taken into consideration while deciding candidates for election in the days to come.*

On the basis of the four cases mentioned earlier, the conclusion can be drawn that the UML's policy is gender-friendly. Its meetings from central to local levels need to include these policies as agenda to implement more sincerely. And timely monitoring is problem raised.

Affirmative Action Plan

As the affirmative action plan is the common issue throughout the UML's history, in the group discussion the district chair says that he raised the issues of membership drive among women and discussed in the district committee. He asked local committees to give emphasis on women when collecting membership application. But it has not been effective in action.

At the end of the group discussion, all the participating members of the local committees realised that the issues related to gender equality need to be a part of the formal agenda in the coming days. They are of the opinion that affirmative action plans should be implemented to increase women membership to fulfil the quota and enhance the capacity of new members. They also suggested imparting knowledge, skill, and experiences gained at the periphery. They further opined that mainstream leadership should be patient in hearing them carefully and changing their conventional mindset and attitudes towards women.

Gaps Between Policy and Action

Setting a vision and making policy is important but it is not enough. If the policy is not accompanied with proper strategy and action plan to implement, policy becomes meaningless. To see the impact and get timely feedback, components of monitoring and evaluation need to be part of the action plan. While going through UML's gender policy, it is found a big gap between policy and its implementation. It is a reality as big challenge. My finding is that conventional mindset is a big obstacle behind this. Because of this mindset, both the senior and the rank and file leaders do not see the children having foreigner father and mother in equal distance. Seeing a child where their Nepali father is nearer and mother is in distance is not justified. This enlightened me that gender perspective and conceptual clarity are necessary on gender issues. This needs to be discussed thoroughly in policy level prior to its implementation.

Derbyshire's (2002) claim seems relevant to be mentioned here. She says, 'too often, gender-mainstreaming policies "evaporate" before implementation and remain paper commitments only'. In regard to translating policy into action, she further adds that 'policies must include strategies and action plans with clear procedures and targets as well as designated roles and responsibilities for promotion, implementation, and monitoring'. Her analyzes enriched my understanding that equal property rights issue in UML seems to evaporate before making a decision and putting it into action. It has not been on the agenda of the meeting in UML for a decade. The root cause of this is in our society and home and hence daughters are being discriminated within the family.

Trotsky (1923) says, 'For women's emancipation, both material resources and strength of will, knowledge and effort are necessary for the process of transformation of family life'. Pointing out women's role in the social change, he further mentions that, "Every awakened woman should devote a major part of her strength and attention to the task of transforming our everyday life'. UML uses Trotsky's statement, and hence it has decided socio-economic transformation as major agenda. However, my study shows that it is not possible to achieve transformation without the active mobilisation of both women and men with a clear gender perspective. This suggests that practice should start with oneself and the family and extend to the party and the state level.

Lund (1970a) draws one great lesson to be learned from the Soviet experiences. This is that:

> *[T]he need[s] for women to be organized as women before the socialist revolution and during the socialist revolution is a must, so that they will be able to play the maximum role in the revolution to insure that their needs and aspirations are satisfied, rather than subordinated.*

Taking this aspiration in Nepali context, the inclusion of women, merely through head-count does not create the expected result. It needs enactment of a package programme as an affirmative action plan with the allocation of enough resources to make women able to stand politically, ideologically, economically, and socially as competent leaders that would lead the transformation of the society. Such affirmative action plan needs to be contextualised prior to the implementation. In the absence of the contextualised programme, UML policy remains as the document for public consumption to produce 'yes person' but not the qualified leaders to make a progressive move.

The party structures at enforcement levels are not eager enough to include party policy into its agenda to translate into action. The testimony is that almost none of the significant issues have been discussed to develop a strategic action plan for their field operation. Besides, there was a lack of the monitoring system within party system, which was found as a big challenge in terms of policy implementation. As a result, UML's policy has been the document for intellectual consumption rather than making a change in people's lives.

Reflecting the Policy Cycle

This chapter gave me the intuition that politics is the nucleus of all aspects of human life as the necessary evil, which can neither be ignored nor easily applied to transform the life of women. And, yet political parties are the vehicles on which to travel toward achieving better policy and programme to safeguard human values and social dignity of every individual. That is the reason that constituting half of the society, women need their active political involvement to address their different requirements. They need to utilise their knowledge and experiences for the benefits of them and human beings as a whole as they are the 'connected type' beings of the family and the society.

World history shows that the progressive movement to which UML is dedicated has addressed women's issues better in the past. Nepali communist movement also followed this path. But in the process of moving forward was either derailed or gotten slow. The class orientation of the communist ideology holders and the Nepali complex structure that encapsulates caste, ethnicity, religion, and topography did not match with the Marxist way and feminist values alone to fight against the patriarchy-rooted attitude and behaviour in the class society.

Out of the five women-related agendas, viz., equality in citizenship, property, participation, ending VAW and affirmative action plan, UML put only a few of them into actions. The agendas adopted by convention as a highest policy-making body are ignored in the process of making action plans. The absence of the decisive role of women in the higher position and the reluctance of the handful male leaders at the senior level (among them some are acting as a gate-keeper) are the main impediments to this. The reality reflects that even though UML has shifted the gender dimension in politics, it has not fully respected it in the course of action.

The literature says that quota for inclusive participation is a first step towards ensuring quantitative representation and qualitative change is the next step (Sadie, 2005). Ideally, UML believes Sadie's statement, but passing through a decade of setting-up 'first step', there have been no specific steps to make this agenda functional. And yet, one finds that women's numerical participation in UML has gone up. But lack of affirmative action to enhance their capacity to internalise the agenda and strategically equip them to put their words into action has not been effective enough. This demands special package programme targeting males and females differently and implementing it throughout the party structure.

Campaigning against VAW outside the party is in the priority of CPN-UML. Unfortunately, the cases within the Party have not been dealt properly. Lately, it has been adopted in the Code of Conduct. But dozens of members in the central leadership, who have violated the clause (like polygamy), have not even admitted their faults. This suggests that UML needs to be serious, committed, and proactive for developing an appropriate strategy to implement the time-bound affirmative action plan and see its systematic impact on the ground.

An equal property right is a priority for UML and has been guaranteed by the Constitution as well. Some of the members have started to practice it. This waits for women's wing of UML to act as issue raiser, to enact it in an assertive way. But equality in citizenship has been badly ignored while promulgating the Constitution. Because of this lacking, women and children have been victimised, even those who belong to UML. Some women cadres of UML have brought forward their own cases of VAW. But, the issue has not been taken seriously yet. It demands urgent attention.

The Communist Party of Nepal-UML seems clear about the policy and also about the theoretical process of policy cycle as mentioned in Figure 6.3. But, they are limited to the first stage, i.e. policy adoption. Attention is equally needed into strategy, action plan, enforcement, and monitoring which is not visible in UML leadership.

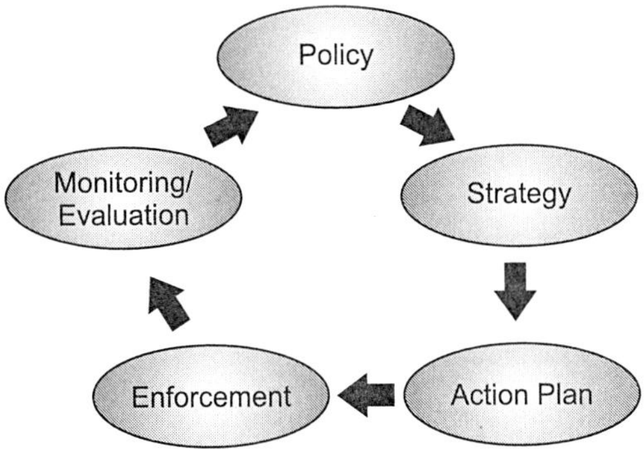

Figure 6.3 Empowerment Action Cycle.

These data enable me to come up with the understanding that only making the policy does not bring any real change. It asks for a full cycle of policy, strategy, action plan, enforcement, monitoring/evaluation, and then move to the next level of the cycle by incorporating feedback based on practical experiences, which is lacking in UML.

Finally, reflecting on this chapter from the women empowerment point of view UML's policy helped top-level women leaders to be part of the policy-making. Medium level leaders have been moved up at committee status. But, lack of enhancement of the required capacity on political clarity, confident argue with the senior leadership and skill to act, has obstructed their effective participation in the process. They are rather hesitant to intervene. Women in grassroots level have a better presence in the meeting compared to mid-level. Due to lack of the access to proper information and guidance to enact them, they are not influential enough.

Based on this information, the argument here is that quantitative participation is one aspect. To achieve the desired goals, adequate action plan of empowerment is a must. For the cause, the full cycle of policy, strategy, plan, action, and monitoring needs to be strictly followed in every level of party structures.

Situating Unified Marxist Leninist Women Leaders as Empowered Women

Empowerment nurtures leadership quality of the oppressed and the marginalised people like women. Such qualities can be manifested in different fields and aspects of their life. The intent of this chapter is to show how these empowered women leaders of today are struggling within and outside communist party of Nepal—Unified Marxist Leninist (UML).

History is the better school to learn lessons, no matter whether it is in our favour or not. The outcome of the history need not be always positive. But, the learning can be positive as preserving fact and minimising negative connotation. Every lesson needs to be understood in the context of human need and contemporary status of the socio-economic development.

Regarding situated leadership, Lave and Wenger (1991) argue that learning as it normally occurs is a function of the activity, context, and culture in which it occurs, which is called situated learning. They further say that social interaction is a critical component of situated learning as learners are involved in a 'community of practice' which embodies certain beliefs and behaviours. In the process of integration within the community, the beginner or newcomer moves from the periphery of this community to its centre and becomes more active and engaged within the culture assuming the role of an expert or old-timer. In this process, situated learning is unintentional rather than deliberate, and is called the process of 'legitimate peripheral participation' (Lave and Wenger, 1991).

Connecting Nepali women's movement within UML with the theory of situated learning, is found that women realised the social injustice and mal-practice in society and started voicing it out a century ago to forbid the inhuman practice against women like *Sati*. It was raised from the community level and was led by Yogmaya. The voice was heightened widely and effectively. This practice has been gradually moving ahead with addressing the contemporary social practice. Personal initiations to abolish Chaupudi (personal communication with Nanda on 27 November 2016), witchcraft, etc., are some of the examples of situated learning.

Brown (2013) quotes, 'Situated learning is a theoretical description of learning in a "community of practice"', which was proposed and described by Lave and Wenger (1991), and he adds that "some members will be core, long-term leaders, while others will be newcomers often with a peripheral role, at least for a time in the learning process". Brown further says learners who seek communities of enquiry do so because they have shared interests and seek to benefit from the knowledge of others who may be more experienced and knowledgeable.

Learning the community experiences is always valuable for human beings. Nepali spread over the different countries during the Rana regime from 1846 to 1951 and learned the aspiration for the liberation movement for freedom and democracy in those countries. For instance, hundreds of thousands of Nepali soldiers involved in the First and Second World War saw how people from those countries loved the freedom and been ready to sacrifice their lives for the democracy (Mazumdaru, 2014). After coming back to Nepal, they shared the experiences and motivated Nepali people to fight against Rana oligarchy for democracy. Women like Sahana and Sadhana, who were exposed to the Second World War while living in Burma with their parents, shared their experiences with other women and motivated them to be part of the democratic movement (Pandey, 2002). These were the big sources of empowerment motivating Nepali people for democracy. As a result, hundreds of women were involved in the political process during and since the establishment of democracy in 1951. These experiences say that situated learning can play a significant role to bring the peripheral people into the centre as the community of practice.

Stein (1998) says that situated learning uses cooperative and participative teaching methods as the means of acquiring knowledge. Knowledge is created or negotiated through the interactions of the learner with others and the environment. He says that the main elements of situated cognition are content, context, community, and participation.

Recalling the context and content of the Nalapani war in 1814-16, while the British were attacking the nation, it was the matter of state sovereignty and the women joined the war contextualising the situation and decided to be part of the war for the nation rather than leaving the fort. They might have realised that without a nation, none of the people could live with dignity and humanity. As a result, those women kept the strong bond of community feeling and decided to be part of the war till the end. This is the real example of situated cognition in terms patriotism and the real meaning of people with a sovereign country with dignity. This incident always inspires and empowers Nepali to live with high head in the history.

Situating Women in Unified Marxist Leninist in Equality Movement

In case of the Nepali women's movement, women gradually moved to the central role from the periphery. In the process of development of situated leadership, Nepali women followed four different ways of situated learning from a community of practices such as learning as experiences, expectational, expansional and compensatory ways, which apply in UML as well.

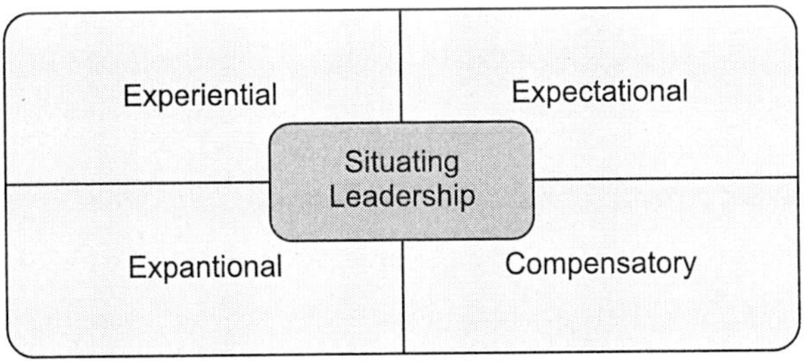

Figure 7.1 Situating Leadership in Nepali Context.

Experiential Learning: While Nepal was ruled by Rana oligarchy, hundreds of Nepali living in India took part in the 'Quit-India' movement. Dozens of them were arrested and imprisoned. These experiences inspired them to join the imitational action for the democracy in Nepal. Then, they initiated the formation of political organisations, where women were peripheral parts of the process. Some of them participated since the beginning of the formation of Nepali Congress in 1947 and the Communist Party of Nepal in 1949.

While hundreds of women were taking part in the Quit-India movement in the decade of 1950, many Nepali women who were in India like Dibya, Motidevi, etc., closely watched women's role within that agitation. They might have learnt that if Indian women could fight for their freedom and democracy, why not Nepali women? It was the situated learning of Nepali women from the experiences, which was translated into action. One of the examples of this was that while CPN was established in 1949, Motidevi became one of the founder members. Many more women took part in the democratic movement in those days back in the homeland.

Expectational Move: Women for the first time took part in the civil right movement in May 1947 and shortly formed Nepali Women Organisation (NWO). Then, they immediately led a delegation to Rana prime minister with the demand of women's education and voting rights. The then Prime Minister responded positively to their demands. Then, women got the confidence that working collectively would make it possible to achieve more on women's right based on equality. They started to move forward with expectational learning. After overthrowing Rana regime in 1951, they demanded women's inclusion in the advisory committee, candidacy in the election, etc., which were achieved one after another.

This trend is continued even now. In this regard my informant, AS shares:

> *We need to be determined by the demands based on changing time and assuming the expectation of the people in general. For instance, we collectively pushed 8 points gender agenda within the party committee in 2006, which was accepted as party agenda. Now, we are in the process to implement them in practice.*

Another informant, PA shares her latest experiences, 'While sister organizations of UML collectively came up with the code of conduct on VAW, UML's Ninth National Convention adopted it and now is in the process of enforcement.' Thus, all the sister organisations of UML having both men and women were expecting it as universalised conduct in the wider sense. These are some of the examples of the situated learning with the expectational move.

Expanded Eternal Success: Democracy provides a venue for every human being to be part of the public affairs and exposes their capability skill and knowledge learning from a community of practice. This helps to change the social perspective and accept non-conventional gender role as well. Election of Sadhana, the communist, in the municipality and Dwarika Devi, the democrat, in the Parliament helped to change the social perspective that women as well can be a leader in the state mechanism and represent people. It gave the inspiration to other women that 'If they can do, why not other women?' Experiences of the recent days are even more encouraging. Three women being in the supreme position of the state as president of the nation, speaker of the legislative parliament and chief justice of the Supreme Court has been helping to develop confidence among general people that women can be the leaders. People's opinion now a day is that it does not matter whether they are men or women in the position. Leadership quality depends on their knowledge and skill rather than gender. It is the symbol of the changed public mindset and the situation. Along with the success of some women, many others have been empowered to join public activities including politics and take responsibility confidently.

Sharing her experiences, AS says, 'The news of the women's involvement in *Jhapa Bidroha* in 1972 encouraged other women including me to join revolutionary movement.' Remembering her past, she further mentions:

> *Parijat's progressive writing encouraged many women to study extra curriculum literature and books in those days. While I completed school education, I together with a group of friends joined the Chinese Study Centre and studied many revolutionary books. That motivated us to work for working class people. We learned in the process that unless reaching the mass of the working people and involving them, revolution is not possible. Then, I became a full-time underground activist.*

It is one of the good examples that how one's success stories can be replicated and expanded to include others. Sharing her learning from the situation, PA says, 'Commitment of the oppressed people in Piskar motivated me to join the movement with deep feeling to mobilize a large number of people to liberate the oppressed class.' Another informant, Ranjana Siba (RS) states as follows:

> *During the Panchayat system, underground activist used our house as shelter, which provides me the opportunity to learn more about the oppressed live of the working people over the country, which I was seeing in my area as well. At the same time, women's life was even vulnerable in my area, what I witnessed motivated people like to join the movement.*

Another informant, Sarad Sah (SS), adds:

> *Madhesi women are much behind in the socio-political activities and we need to disseminate more information on the success stories to motivate*

> *them. Then, I started to conduct Madhesi focused activities and organized them under All Nepal National Free Student Unions (ANNFSU). It helped to bring more Madhesi women within the progressive circle.*

Listening to all of them, the eternal success needs to be expanded as sea-wave as one of the ways to bring women into the central role from peripheral locations.

Compensatory Move: Human nature is always forward-looking. Whatever they could not experience and achieve in their lives, they want to see this in the next generation. This is the general rule of the progress of human society. This attitude seems to rule the Nepali women's movement as well. Women did not have an opportunity for going to school and enter into public service including police until 1947. NWO's delegation demanded this from the government for the sake of next generation, which has been enjoyed by women in the later days. Women in movement felt the neglect of their voice by the mainstream leaders and they realised that if more women could be in the structure at once, their collective voice might be heard in the process of decision-making. Then, the movement collectively started to raise the voice to increase women's participation in the decision-making mechanism and process. As a result, Nepal's Constitution has insured mandatory participation of critical mass. These are the parts of the compensatory learning.

Some of the experiences of my informants are relevant to quote here. PG says as follows:

> *Women in the past have paved the way to move forward. The women in the new generation, who are young and educated, need to build up competence and confidence to take lead politically and socially to strengthen that.*

Sharing the ground experiences, Sarad Sah (SS) says:

> *Women during the Panchayat time were mostly acting as followers and supporters providing food, shelter, and security as junior cadres in the movement. They did not have the opportunity to expose themselves*

> *to central leadership in policy-making and enforcement. Now, the circumstances have changed and women in new generation need to learn the skill to deal with state mechanism and society to solve people's day-to-day problems. It is the necessary basic quality to be accepted as a leader in public.*

It is not only the women to opine the compensatory move, even men's experiences say that women need to make themselves ready to act upon what was not possible for the past generation to come up on the front-line leadership.

Gender Inequality: Differances versus Difference

Gender discrimination is the reality of human society all over the world. And the movement to have egalitarian society as the alternative is another reality, which is being widened day-by-day, as a common ground for both men and women. Picking up the terms of Jacques Derrida (1992), I understood that for a age, inequality remained as issues of *differances* (a French terminology) among women, i.e. murmuring within and outside with their female fellows. But in the later days, women were explicitly voicing out that the gender differences (i.e. they began to say that we are equal to men in all respects) is an issue of gender inequality and men in favour of justice are accelerating their supportive voice. In this changed context, situated learning is more valuable, which helps bring out the *differances* out and nurture the difference that was not visible in the then society. As a result of changing women's condition and position, their situated learning role shifting to centre from periphery based on experiences, expectational, expansional, and compensatory ways are making remarkable value. Their main learning in the process is that explicitly spelling out the differences rather than keeping *differances* within and let others realise the reality and change them positively.

Comparing these matters in UML's rank and file, women in the policy level have started to raise the issues systematically with alternative proposals. In Derrida's terms, they were no more *differances* but were showing their differences. For instance, women succeeded to come up with the proposal of a code of conduct on violence against women (VAW) in the Ninth Convention in 2014 and women's participation in key positions in the local election has been adopted. But, they are still in the peripheral position at the implementation level. Most of the participants in the group discussion agreed that there is no concrete proposal regarding the process to implement the gender agendas already identified and adopted by UML. They have realised that in the days to come, they have to be ready with alternative practical proposals to implement the decision based on community practice. In this saying, they were no more confined with *differances* but were visible to show their difference.

Learning Leadership

Human quality is basically acquired. It can be highly influenced by socio-cultural factors, where a person is situated and grows up. Surrounding circumstances make differences in psychology, where attitude would be deeply rooted. All these are the external factors. But, the biological factor as a gene, which transfers from one generation to another is an inherent factor, affecting the personality of every human. Without having a favourable external environment, inherent quality cannot be exposed and developed properly. But, only external factors cannot build up the quality. Leadership is one of the aspects of human quality, which has a connection with all these factors in terms of performing and acting effectively and efficiently. Presented in Figure 7.2 are the influencing forces in UML for women leaders to come out of their homes to be in the leading positions.

The discussion led me to the understating that knowledge is constructed. It depends on social circumstances as opportunity, culture, norms, values, etc. But, the capacity to observe, analyze, and extract the core values of the knowledge might be influenced by genetic factors. While talking about gender values, external factors are gendered which can be different according to community values. Internal factor as gene may as well cause some difference

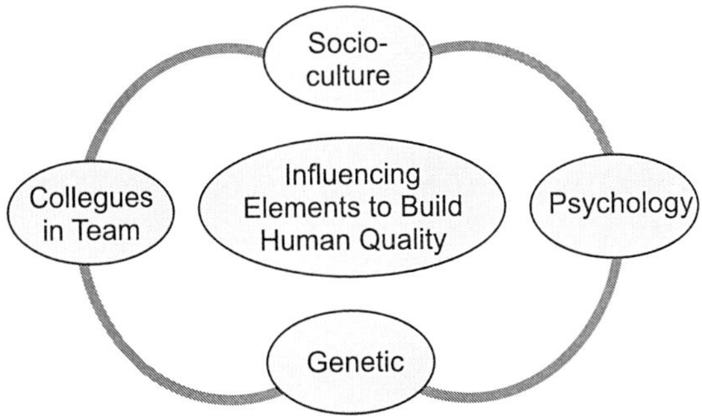

Figure 7.2 Influential Elements of Building Leadership.

in leadership quality and way of performing an action. There are some of the fundamental differences in genetic values. All these need to be taken into consideration while situating learning process and leadership quality.

Reflecting the Leadership Style

One can assume that women lived in differances and differences in their domestic life, and Nepali women's movement started from the national issue. Gradually their movement devolved as a political issue. Finally, it has got a new height focusing around the end of VAW. But the western women's movement started from the factory, home, and then went for political rights. Here the argument is that these differences in the Nepali women's movement and the movement in the West are the results of their 'situated learning' (Leve and Wenger, 1991). The expansion of the learning of Nepal and the West can be said as the effect of their 'peripheral learning' (ibid, 1991). In course of time devolved and the evolved practices met at a point where women around the world are persuading the similar agenda. UML is no exception to it, which tried to blend women's concerns and the political rights together for the egalitarian society. This is where can be claimed that Nepali women's movement and its leadership is fundamentally different from the western one to deconstruct the gendered mindset for our equal rights.

Finally, from the empowerment point of view, can be hold the knowledge that UML empowered women to be better followers, interpreting the terminology of discipline differently. It pushed women to remain skeptical rather than being creative to come up with better options of empowering more women toward the mainstream. The Party leadership failed to respect its own policy and decision for empowerment while developing the action plan. Internalising these facts and contextualising the issue of empowerment, UML needs to develop appropriate tools, having multi-dimensional approaches and apply them to promote social dignity, economic self-reliance, political competency, and morally high head of the women. These are basic components of empowerment with self-esteem and self-respect.

Findings, Discussion, Reflection, and Implication

Balanced gender participation through women's empowerment is a current international concern. The main aim of the women's empowerment movement is to change the power structure for social justice. As a response, the International Parliamentarian Union writes that women's participation has been gradually increasing (IPU, 2014). The IPU (2014) also suggests that special measures, clear strategies, and action plans help to increase women's participation in regards to power re-distribution. In the absence of this three-pronged approach, gender parity through the empowerment process will remain as a dream for generations.

Personal experience of my involvement is politics also said that change in the mindset is essential for gender balancing in the current power structure. Additionally, fixing the gendered work division and male dominance over the access and control of resources requires changed in attitude. However, a change in attitude is one part of the solution, as women need the comfortable capacity to handle responsibility called 'women empowerment'. And, as the counter half of the society, to change the way of thinking and action on the part of men is equally essential. In this background, I have presented my findings as a response to the issues presented in Chapter I which were as follows: (1) How has the Communist Party of Nepal (CPN)-Unified Marxist Leninist (UML) contributed to empowering women in Nepali democratic movement? (2) How are the CPN-UML's policies, programmes, and practices of empowering women? (3) What are the matters making differences in women's empowerment in CPN-UML?

In order to answer the first issues, first five subtopics has been drawn and answering the second issues through three subtopics. Finally, the third issues has been addressed by in four subtopics. Subsequently, eight-point reflections and seven-point possible implications have been drawn which may help to improve gender participation in politics through the process of empowerment.

Communist Party of Nepal-Unified Marxist Leninists Contribution to Women Empowerment

The Communist Party of Nepal-Unified Marxist Leninists has contributed differently in the process of women empowerment. Based on this study, have been drawn five major contributions in regard to empowering women in the process of progressing communist movement in Nepal.

1. Political Trends in Women Empowerment

Analyzing Nepali political history, there are different trends of women's empowerment process through participation (Figure 8.1). The first trend was family legacy. In this trend, women decided to show their support to their warring husbands in Nalapani which was led by Kamala. It was not connected to women's rights movement, but rather carrying on with the family legacy.

The second trend shows that women, led by Yogmaya, voiced out against cultural oppression and injustice over women and practice such as child marriage and sati. Political participation emerged as the third trend. This included women flooding the streets and demanding civil and political rights. Sahana and her colleagues braved this cornerstone step in Nepali politics in 1947.

The fourth trend showed that while male family members joined political activities, women became supporters of their activities. Dibya, Chandrakanta, Rawanta Kumari, etc., are some examples of this phenomenon. Gradually, they sought their fair share of role, respect, and finally headed towards equality in decision-making. Nona, Shailaja, Mangala, etc., continued this trend in the later days.

As a fifth trend, working women started to actively support rights-based political activists. Later, these women ventured to participate in the working class movement towards democracy. Rammaya Pode represents this trend as a supporter of incarcerated Praja-parisad activists. Nanda Nepal and her friends carried this spirit when the jute factory was closed in Biratnagar after the Rana regime was overthrown in 1951. Goma and her colleagues continued this trend to fight for democracy into the 1980s. As an extension of this trend, working-class women encouragingly participated in the people's movement of 1990 and 2006.

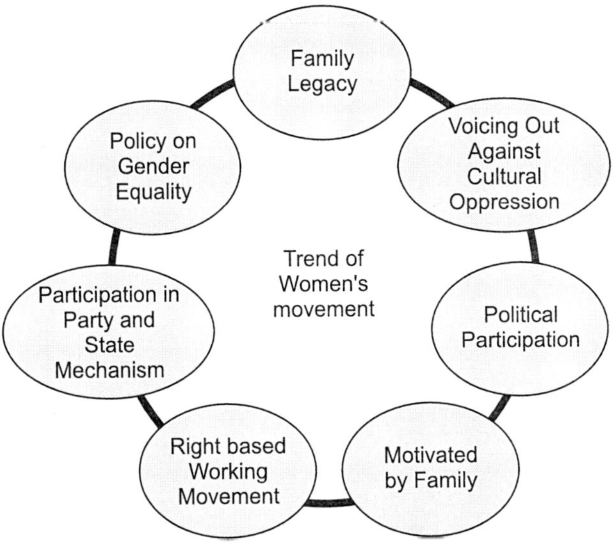

Figure 8.1 Trends of Women Empowerment in Nepal.

Note: Different trends of the women's movement are existing today as one-way or another. This was observed in women's participation and empowerment process. That is why I have linked them up in a circle.

The sixth trend evolved from the previous movements by directly involving women in *political parties and state mechanism*. This development widened women's space in political processes within the power structure. Milestones of this development include Motidevi as the founding member of CPN and Sadhana as the first female elected representative. Additionally, Dwarikadevi, Sahana, Shailaja, etc., continued this trend by being political leaders.

Finally, all these trends merged into the *mainstream gender equality* movement after 1990. After that women began to work conjointly with men as 'half of the world' in every walk of the human life. Examples of these unions include Bidya, Onsari, and Sushila who have been able to hold state positions as president, speaker, and chief justice, respectively as the first woman in those positions.

Motivating women to be part of the progressive movement within different trends (specially after the foundation of CPN) is one of the major contributions of UML towards women empowerment.

2. Women's Contribution to Democratic Movement

Human society never moves in a linear path. Nepali women movement as well has been progressing in the similar ways as moving forth and back time and again. But, stepping-up the movement with remarkable changes in policy or in practice has been defined here as stages.

Women's involvement in Nalapani cultivated the feeling of *togetherness* with men while in captivity in 1814. However, after a century, Dibya Koirala, with the motivation of her husband, produced the concept of establishing women's groups. In a real sense, Yogmaya led the collective movement for social justice with action onward 1917. This congregation morphed into political motivation, as Rawanta Kumari, Sita, Chandrakanta, etc., were involved in politics in one way or another when their family members were facing trouble in their fight with the state regime in the 1940s. It is termed this phase of the women's participation as *Kinships*.

It is found that politically motivated women, regardless of their ideology, became a part of the democratic movement under the Nepal Women Organisation after 1947 with the aspiration of *Moving the Rock*, and overcoming obstacles in front of their battleground with clear agenda such as the right to education and vote. After 1951, this Movement was divided into ideological factions.

Women like Sita, Gaura, Lila, etc., were following the Jhapa movement, led by UML at the beginning of the 1980s. Many other women joined and continued this underground movement as the progressive movement gaining momentum to consolidate it. This process established the fact that as half of the population, women's active participation is necessary to make a revolution. UML followed the aspiration of Marxist feminist perspective and conducted activities to empower women under as *Half of the Sky.* This slogan motivated a larger number of women, to take part in the people's movement in 1990.

With the restoration of multi-party democracy in 1990, women became part of state power structure and started to act by linking the outside-inside voice for gender equality in the new Constitution. While women's agenda was denied in the process of constitution drafting, women from different walks of the movement concluded that unless the male domain was denatured by women, it was not possible to shift power relations. This gave birth to the new focus on activism, i.e. *Shifting the Domain* to change the power structure. By this time, being a part of a democratic system, the women's movement started to internalise the socialist feminist perspective and they collectively reached the conclusion to follow three strategies. First, women with different political ideologies should work together in order to achieve common goals. Second, gender justice is the primary social issue and men need to be included in the change process. Third, gender equality is a political issue and should be on the agenda of political parties.

Reflecting on these three-point strategies, the women's movement came to claim their space and *Walked Side-by-Side* to attain equality in reality. As part of materialising this strategy, women's rights activists formed the Women Security Pressure Group (WSPG) under the leadership of Sahana Pradhan, as a loose network in 1991. Arriving in 2006, the collective initiation progressed to the political level and the Inter-party Women Alliance was formed again under the leadership of SahanaPradhan and with nine-points common agenda took an active part in people's movement-II in 2006 (IPWA, 2006). As a result, almost equal number of women came to the streets and fought for democracy with gender equality and social justice. As an outcome, the new Constitution (2015) has institutionalised almost all the equality agenda (except on citizenship) with the provision of affirmative actions in some areas. Figure 8.2 portrays the stages of Nepali women's movement.

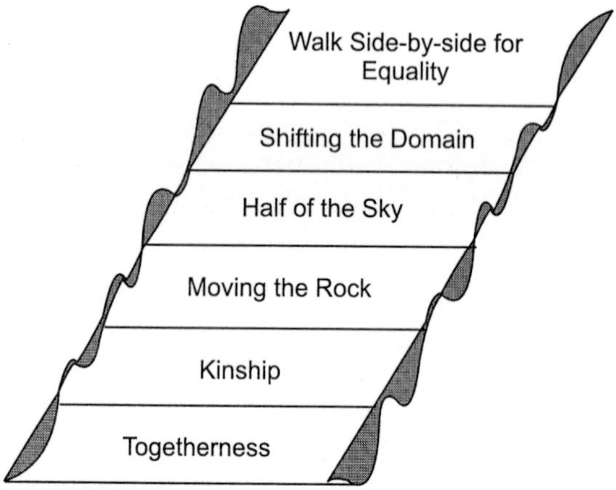

Figure 8.2 Stages of Nepali Women's Movement.

Note: The Movement did not grow in the linear form rather it went up and down in the process, which I have named as *Ukali-Orali* (zigzag) path.

Now, ensuring women's effective participation in key positions within the Party and state mechanism is a major agenda for effective and sustainable enforcement of the state policy. The *Ukali-Orali* path shows the back and forth of the Nepali women's movement. It indicates that while in togetherness some women followed individual flagship. But in the period of kinship, they slowed down their individual flagship. During the kinship, they discussed above the rock moving issues related to gender equity and empowerment. While moving to the half of the sky, some women valued the care-work equally and others continued liberation from the unproductive household chores. While some of the Nepali women were shifting the domains others were continuing their classical practice. Though equidistant in its walk, Nepali women movement remained side-by-side for gender equity. Women within UML are also passing through the *Ukali-Orali* footsteps, fuelling the process as an active change agent.

3. Policy Evolution on Women Empowerment

Based on the policy and programme, Nepali communist movement can be divided into three phases, namely, 1949 to 1960 as the first phase, 1971 to 1990 as the second phase, and 1990 onward as the third phase. CPN had adopted 'New Democracy' as its programme in 1949, as advanced by Mao. This programme was continued in the second phase as well. But, the strategy of revolution was modified, as political change can be achieved through mass mobilisation including women. The third phase of the Nepali communist movement incorporated democratic values, in 'New Democracy' and it was renamed as People's Multi-Party Democracy (PMPD). The Party was popularly known as UML. PMPD successfully changed the policy on women's empowerment (Figure 8.3).

Women in Nepali communist movement were involved since its founding phase when Motidevi took part. The CPN defined women as an integral part of the society and involved them in the movement organising them as All Nepal Women Association (ANWA), founded on 8 March 1952 with major agenda of education, property, and employment of women. They played a vital role in various movements including nation-wide peasant movement onward 1953, and *Bahdra Avagya Movement* in 1957. Women were active in Party activities as well. But, they were always regarded as 'women leaders' and not as 'leaders of CPN'; only. Sadhana was elected in Kathmandu municipality in 1953, but none of the active women were given a ticket to contest in the first general election in 1958. Based on these facts, it can be confidently said that women were mobilised as cadres but not well trusted as Party leaders in the first phase of the Nepali communist movement.

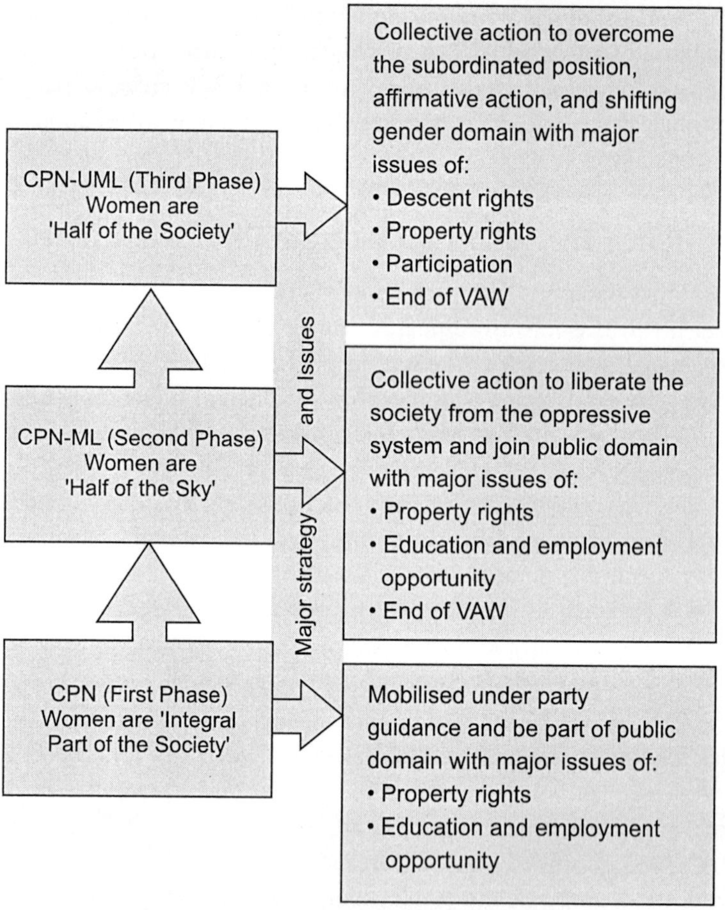

Figure 8.3 Evolution of Gender Policy in UML.

Note: Upward arrow showed the perspective change and side arrow to continue campaign on identified issues based on the set strategy.

The second phase, when UML movement was recognised as CPN-ML was started in 1971, while a radical group of young communists initiated the Jhapa movement. Women joined the Movement as well since the beginning in every front. Some of them participated in the arm-action and others supported them behind the scene by providing shelter, food and security, which was equally important and risky.

After shifting the paradigm of the Movement from armed struggle to mass mobilisation, dozens of women joined the underground movement as junior activists of the Party and continued without getting to the top decision-making body. They were consulted only about their problems, demands, and possible ways to move forward before deciding strategies on women's issues.

During the latter part of this phase, they again went through setting-up of ANWA. Considering women as half of the sky, most of the women cadres were mobilised to expand ANWA's structure all over the country with a focus on major agendas such as equal rights to property, education, employment, and ending VAW with a guarantee of social protection. In this phase as well, women did not have direct access to the decision-making process as party leaders.

The third phase of the communist movement started in 1990, which became an integral part of the multi-party democracy. UML changed its paradigm with advancing democratic values as part of its programme named PMPD.

The Communist Party of Nepal-UML came up with an affirmative action policy as additional effort to promote more women in politics and it stated that males in the family should share domestic responsibilities. Compared to the Marxist version of women liberation, this was one step forward of following the socialist feminist perspective. Adopting this policy, in UML's fifth convention in 1993, it elected women in the central policy-making body, which opened entrance for women to be part of the apex body of the party.

The All Nepal Women Association as UML's women wing had realised the importance of women's direct participation in all level of Party structure to include gender issues in policy and implement them into action. Thus, it started a campaign for one-third women participation as critical mass from 1997 and other issues such as equal rights to descent, property, ending VAW and action plan to develop women leaders as the affirmative action. ANWA vowed their readiness to shoulder a decisive role in the party and state and took lead inside the Parliament and outside among women from different parties to create joint pressure on the state and political parties. Finally, the issue of women's participation of critical mass and others has been institutionalised through the Parliament in 2006 and the Constitution of Nepal (2015) and in UML (2009). Yet, there is a wide gap in policy and practice because of patriarchal chauvinist mentality and women are not comfortably trusted as party leaders to grasp important roles within party and state mechanism.

The CPN has recognised the multi-dimensional aspects of women empowerment and included the issues such as equal participation as politics; property right and employment opportunity as the economy; education, health, issues of maternity, social security, end of VAW, etc., as part of the social aspect. Responding to the changing circumstances, the UML keeps updating its policies and agenda. While it was in the process to adopt PMPD, it has synchronised the essence of socialist feminist approach as its gender policy. It is notable that even the new Constitution of Nepal 2015, has carried the similar agendas of women's rights, where UML's gender policy makes a positive influence.

4. Agenda Setting on Women

Nepali women have been fighting collectively for justice over a century. This fight is reflected in the Nepali communist movement since the foundation of CPN in 1949. After the re-establishment of ANWA in 1981, it set-up gender agendas for equality based on the Marxist perspective, which was formally incorporated in the UML (the then CPN-ML) agenda. When the people's movement succeeded to reinstate multi-party democracy in 1990, the time was ripe for incorporating these gender agendas in state policy and law. However, these were not welcomed. Then, ANWA formally started to demand space within the structure by adopting the issues of one-third women participation as a concern, including the equal right to property, descent, end of VAW, affirmative action, reproductive right, etc., in 1997. After a decade-long campaign, the UML accepted one-third women participation in its Constitution; property, and descent right in its policy documents in 2009. The code of conduct for party member on VAW was adopted in 2014.

The three arrows down in Figure 8.4 show that Identifying the Agenda, Lobbying/Campaigning to adopt them as Policy go side-by-side and then create pressure for enforcement.

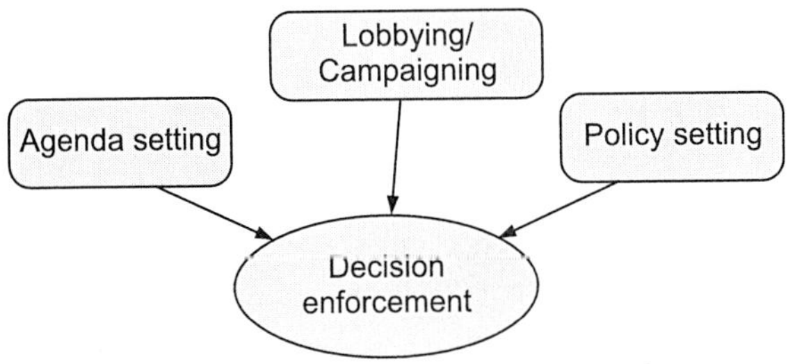

Figure 8.4 Women Role in Empowerment Process.

Additionally, women have been continuously working hard to translate those agendas into practice. These combined efforts have bolstered women's confidence. The social gender perspective is gradually changing. The new task of women in the movement is to place their efforts on the enforcement of Party policies and decisions as well as women's right stated in the state's Constitution and laws.

5. Setting-up Empowerment Modality

Participation of one-third of women as a critical mass in the state's elected bodies and in the UML structure has been constitutionally ensured. Now, it is the challenge of UML to develop an operational action plan with a result-oriented strategy. The next area of empowerment is to reach the key position in the UML leadership. The stereotypic working style such as allocation of assisting position to women making always followers rather than providing a challenging role to lead and lack of mentoring culture needs to be challenged for empowering women. In this sense, women's empowerment demands the breaking of the glass ceiling for women's vertical ascension and the breaking of the glass wall to create a working culture as the division of work, role, and image in horizontal positioning (Figure 8.5).

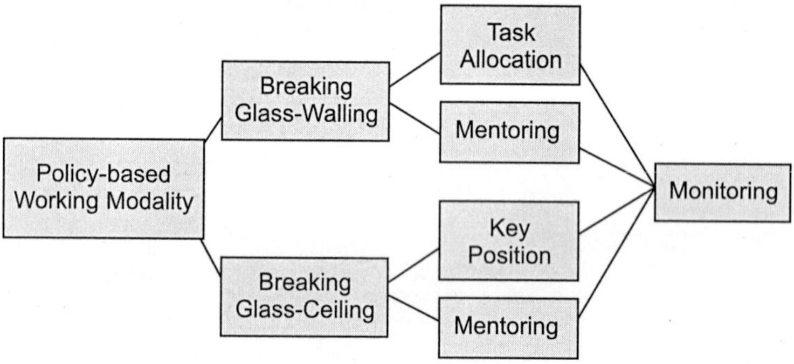

Figure 8.5 Women Empowerment Modality.

Figure 8.5 shows that gender policy based working modality needs to be focused to break the unseen barriers on the 'up and side'. It also suggests that then the women need mentoring for a while to let them be familiar with the new area of work, which can be monitored closely.

It is also diagnosed that changing the role and working modality demands the culture of the mentoring cross and within gender groups. Both of the areas need to be monitored for timely improvement in the policy and process according to need.

In summary, the CPN-UML has contributed a lot not only to set-up the gender policy but also shifting feminist dimension according to changing worldviews. Its contribution to adopt the gender agenda within the Party and the state is remarkable. The problem is that most of them are being for public consumption rather practice with the real meaning. The UML as one of the major political parties of the country, it needs to be role model oneself to reflect that policy and agendas as part of the lives in politics and society.

Communist Party of Nepal-Unified Marxist Leninist's Policy and Practice on Women Empowerment

The Policy is the basis of the strategic empowerment and its achievement in real life would be guided by the operational action plan. Psychological motivation would play a significant role to drag people in the politics. The UML's policy and practice of women empowerment has been summarised into three sub-headings. These are as follows:

1. Situational Motivation

There are many factors motivating women to join politics. Here four major situational factors are identified motivating women to join politics in the Nepali context, who were later developed as ideological consciousness and helped in the emergence of leaders.

First, women joined politics due to *novelty consciousness.* Letting women know not only about the oppression and discrimination over them, but also the possibility of liberation and to achieve better future with an example of other women in different parts of the world, especially the experiences of left movement, motivated many women (*especially young*) to join UML. For instance, those women who left school and university and joined UML in the decade of 1980s fall under this category.

Second, dozens of women have joined UML due to *sympathetic motivation.* Family members of those activists, who devoted their lives to politics and met ultimately death in the different incidents, received the sympathy of the people and Party; and this motivated them to be a part of activism. Kamala Sharma, Bisheswara Dahal,

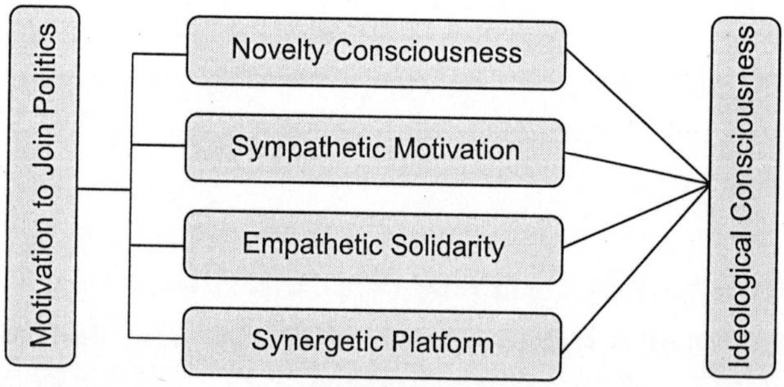

Figure 8.6 Circumstances, Motivating Women Joining the Politics.
(*Note:* Differently motivated women cadres finally became political activists with ideological consciousness through UML schooling.)

Goma Devkota, etc., fall in this category, whose husbands were killed by different place and time, but with political reasons.

The third kind of motivation is *empathetic solidarity*. Many women, after seeing the hardness of others joined the politics and became activists. In fact, the PA, one of my informants fell under this category, who was motivated after knowing the Piskar incident. The fourth category is a*synergetic platform*. Those people who knew politics but were not active in the process cause of different reasons. But, different factors pulled them into the mainstream politics again is part of the category with a synergetic platform of political ideology and enabling circumstances. Sahana and Bidya fall under this category. Both of them re-activated after the gaps of significant duration and skilfully used synergetic platform of previous political involvement and sympathy as well as empathy in relations with their husbands. Many more women have joined in politics under this category, who are in the rank and file of the UML structure. The policy and skill of UML to tap women cadres through situational motivation are one of the big assets to grow its size and height.

2. Empowerment Through Policy

The findings mentioned earlierhelped me understand that the PMPD has come up as an amalgamation of three dynamics—

Marxism as the critical theory, feminism as the principle to fight against patriarchy, and lessons learned from the international communist movement.

PMPD's gender policy came as the amalgamation of Marxism and Feminism in the process of International Communist Movement (Figure 8.7).

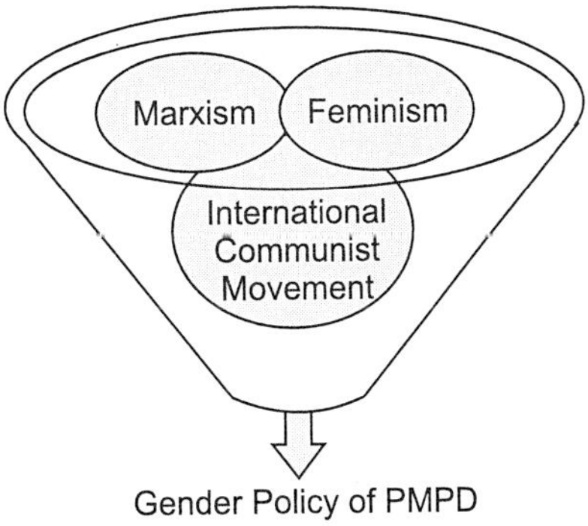

Figure 8.7 UML's Women Empowerment Policy.

The PMPD's gender policy has dreamt to attain substantive equality. The gender policy is also based on the experiences of implementing Marxism, feminism, and the changing scenario of international communist movement, which has been said by Madan Bhandari as 'constructive use of international phenomena in local context' (CPN-UML, 1993b).

Marxist philosophy says that women are politically, economically, and socially oppressed. Oppression has caused women to be dependent on men for their livelihoods and thus remain excluded from productive work. The Chinese Communist leader Mao defined women oppression differently and added patriarchy as a fourth element of constraint in regards to women's liberation. Mao set the 'Iron Girl' model to promote equality. However, this effort also could not recognise and change the reproductive role of women, enforced by tradition.

Feminism as theoretical basis challenging patriarchy has a direct relation with the power structure. The feminist movement has revealed the gender roles as socially constructed and seek to restructure society to end discrimination to achieve substantive equality in all spheres of life. In the course of moving up, arriving in the 1980s, it is called socialist feminism, which recognised the diversity within women and only changing women's roles could not lead to gender justice. This indicates that dominant male method of thinking needs to be amended as well, which can be addressed through what Paulo Freire calls 'pedagogy of oppressed'. The 'pedagogy of oppressed' arose from his blended view of Marxism and humanistic views of theism. The international communist movement also advocated this view in many ways.

Reviewing all these principles and experiences, the PMPD moved one step ahead of Mao's policy and adopted its gender policy as the 'equality between men and women in all spheres including social and national lives' (CPN-UML, 1993b). This Policy carries on the socialist feminist perspective, with the expectation that both men and women become a partner in a change in order to achieve gender equality. However, this Policy still has a fundamental shortcoming. One, the maternal role embedded naturally to women, as a biological-social responsibility has not been dealt with a clear perspective. Another significant lacking is PMPD has not recognised the care work within the private sphere as economic or productive work.

3. Empowerment Through Movement

This study has shown that the UML has adopted a *gender-friendly policy* in contemporary politics, which has been contributed by various elements as shown in Figure 8.8 which shows UML's practice to empower women.

The Unified Marxist Leninist motivated women from different corners are not necessarily linked with each other, but ultimately did contribute to empowering women.

First, the UML has integrated socialist feminist perspective in its policy. Second is the rebellion against the cultural regime

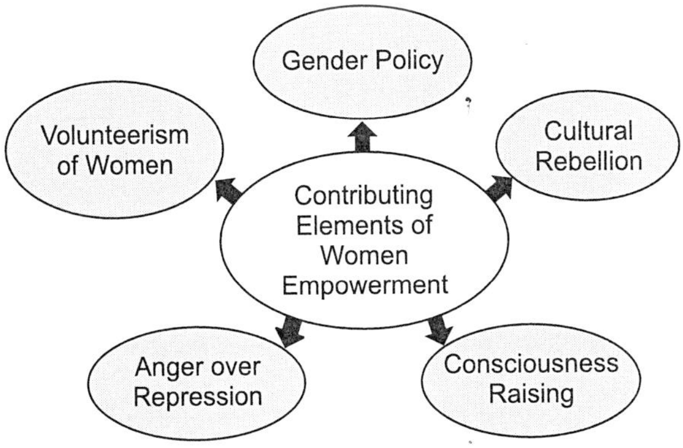

Figure 8.8 Elements, Contributing to Empower Women in the UML.

of injustice. Yogmaya voluntarily led this movement, contributing to ending the *sati*. Later in the 1980s, Kabita, one of the ANWA leaders led the path of socio-culturally restricted work for females such as ploughing-field, home-roofing, etc.

Third, UML launched a consciousness-raising campaign among women as change agent following the Marxist principle of equality and class struggle to motivate, organise, and mobilise women to be part of the working-class movement to fight for social justice.

The fourth factor is *anger over repression*. After having a multi-party system for a decade, political activists of all colour in 1951 succeeded to convey to the people democratic values. However, monarchy-imposed autocracy in 1960, which continued for three decades. In the meantime, youths and students were occasionally agitating for democracy. This turned into an uprising in 1978, where the student movement compelled the state to declare referendum. During those days, innocent people were killed in places like Chhintang and Piskar under the name of controlling people's opposition to the system. Women were raped and killed (K.C., 2005). These acts of state repression incited *Anger* especially among women and rural peasants, motivating them to organise and act collectively for justice. UML capitalised this anger to mobilise them in favour of women's right and democracy.

Finally, *volunteerism* of diverse population including men and women both, having experiences of working as over/underground; whole/part-time; mass movement, party work and social movement, professional movement, etc., contributed much to reach masses and raise their awareness and organise them to act in favour of justice, democracy, and equality for human dignity. UML was coordinating and mobilising them skilfully.

Matters Making Difference in the Communist Party of Nepal-Unified Marxist Leninist

There are different factors inherent in CPN-UML's policy and programme contributing to making difference through improving women's condition and status in the society. It is summarised into four major subtopics mentioned next. At the same time, some critical comments have been made for remedy in the days to come.

1. Quota Reservation for Inclusive Participation

There are many factors making difference in women empowerment in UML. Among them, some of the major factors have been picked up here. Different philosophies have defined women differently. The Marxist theory defines women as a group of oppressed working class and feminist theory defines them as a subordinated community by sex. Women under the communist rule could not be free from patriarchy and capitalism treated women as a commodity. International movements and our own experiences reveal that neither the communist theory nor feminist theory alone could liberate women from their oppressed positions to exercise freedom as citizen enjoying equal human dignity.

Realising this fact, UML has set quota reservation to ensure inclusion of women as the marginalised community, which has been shown in Figure 8.9.

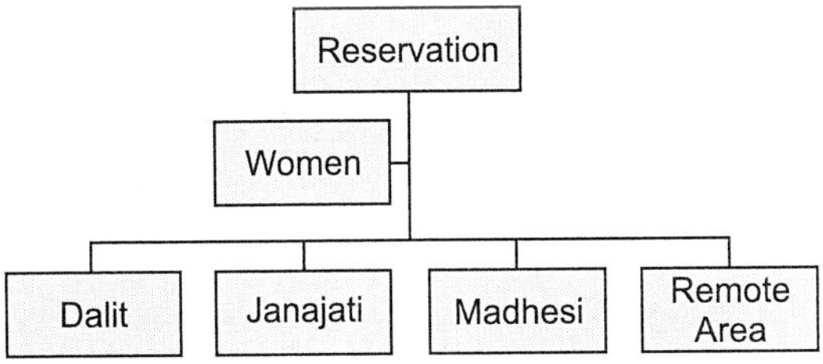

Figure 8.9 UML's Existing Quota Reservation Policy.

Note: UML has defined women as a single group above the others.

In our context, diversity is even beyond the class and gender, and women remain as an oppressed group within every category. Nepal is a country with multiple diversities, a heterogeneous society having a multi-lingual, multi-ethnic, multi-socio-cultural, and multi-religious country. Additionally, Nepal is a multi-caste society with wider topographic diversities. Taking these diversities into account, it is identified that the UML's reservation policy in defining women, as a single group is one of the major shortcomings.

This study says the quota reservation within UML needs to be revised and corrected as shown in Figure 8.10. The reality is that women are subordinated to men within each group and women need to be empowered and represented based on the social diversity to provide them equitable opportunity to share diverse knowledge, skills, and experiences widely.

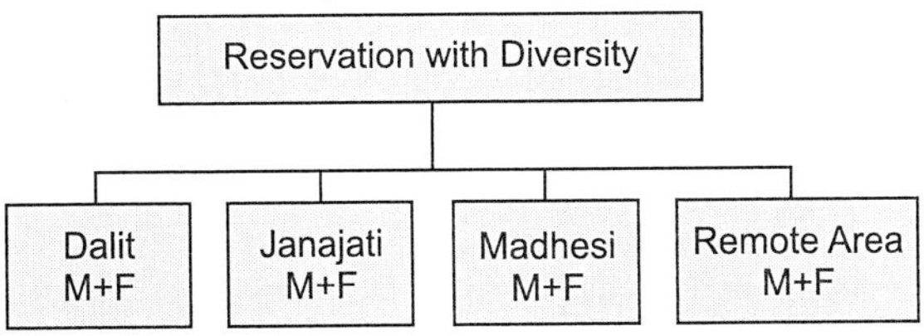

Figure 8.10 Reservation Policy Recognising Diversity + Gender.

Note: Women as equal part of all categories of diversities which indicates the need for quota reservation accordingly.

2. Affirmative Action Plan as Remedial Measures

The affirmative action plan is a widely used tool to allow the marginalised communities to catch up with the mainstream. Respecting and recognising diversity as social pride, affirmative action stands on the principle of unity among diversity to move forward towards a justice-based society. But, additionally, gender as a factor of universal discrimination needs to be emphasised explicitly. It is a theoretical groundwork to develop a strategic policy and operational plan in order to allocate enough of the relevant resources, which include budget, time, required skill, and an enabling environment within political processes.

The UML has clearly spelled out the need to have special package programme as an affirmative action policy to empower women and has started quota reservation for ensuring quantitative participation. However, a proper action plan is lacking in order to enhance the required ability and competency. My findings are outlined in Figure 8.11, with the necessary components to develop an affirmative action plan for women empowerment.

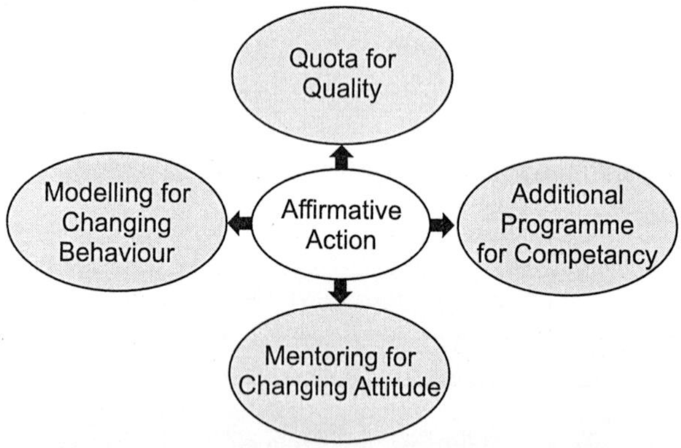

Figure 8.11 Components of Affirmative Action Plan.

Note: An affirmative action plan has different elements that work independently and make influence each other as impact.

As a companion of numerical participation, programme to enhance capacity, mentoring for changing stereotypic mind to think and commitments to act for the practical empowerment of the cadres (both as men and women), and the role-modelling would be more effective in motivating general people to follow the track. These are few essential factors to focus on the action plan:

3. Education/Training/Mentoring as a Tool for Transformation

Education does not mean only the formal one. In the political process, formal, informal, and non-formal education are equally meaningful to learn and share principles, policies, and programmes as well as to develop respect for others' socio-cultural values of various communities. It is an important instrument for widening the outlook and vision and also promoting a positive as well as progressive perspective.

This demands not only the schooling but also school to integrate the fostering lesson learned, training to explore the additional opportunities as a requirement to upgrade the skill to flow down the adopted policy and agendas to the cadres, supporters and general people for enactment. And, it also requires mentoring as one of the essential ways of developing an alternative layer of leadership to be innovative and enhancing leadership quality with changing attitude and behaviour to make politics as a part of living.

As a political activist for decades in addition to as my 4 years' experience in the constituent assembly (2008-12) and this research work in this area, it is seen that in order to be effective in political processes, every individual need to be well-equipped with five important qualities. Having conceptual clarity on their central *ideology* is the first and foremost requirement in politics. Second, one needs to have relevant facts and updated *information* in regard to the issue at hand. Third, one should have the capacity to interpret that information into *logical intervention*. Fourth, one should develop the *presentation skill* to communicate the logic effectively to the public. Fifth, and last, the person who desires to continue political activism must have a *passion* to learn it. Educating to enhance knowledge, criticality, and analytical capacity;

school beyond the schooling, training for better performance, and mentoring for sustainable leadership are the keys to add efficiency in these aspects.

There is a gap between gender policy and the educational system of UML. To narrow down this gap, the UML needs to consider at least three major areas to empower women to make better contributions in the decision-making as shown in Figure 8.12. One, in respect to Marxism as one of the guiding principles, the UML needs to seriously follow Marx's recommendation and set a special mechanism to promote women's leadership and track the issues (Munoz and Woods, 2000).

Two, the UML has adopted a good gender policy. However, it has not been properly promoted within the Party structure. In order to avoid this shortcoming, the Party's gender policy and decisions need to be included in the content of party school to enhance its members' knowledge and understanding and encourage them to apply in practical lives.

Three, women are participating in the party school activities mainly as recipients. A competent team of women educators within the Party needs to be trained and involved them as educators and mentors is essential in relation to empowerment in multiple ways—first, to promote their capacity and confidence; second, to enhance their skills; third, to make them accepted as leaders; and fourth, to promote them as a role model of change agent (Figure 8.12).

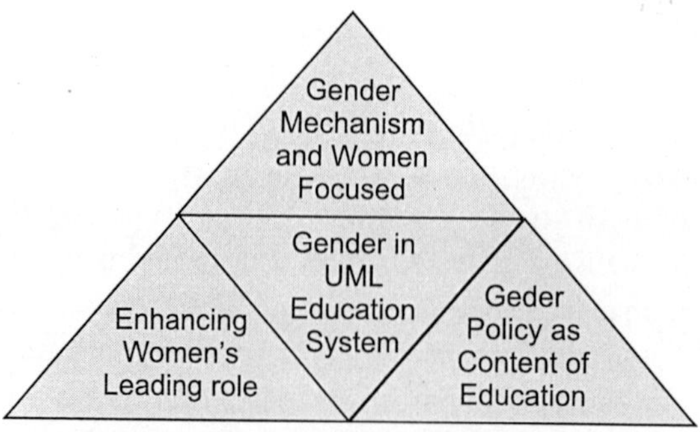

Figure 8.12 Gender Sensitivity in Party Education.

Note: Peripheral gender matters from UML's education system.

The suggested measures mentioned earlier may impact significantly to break the glass walling and glass ceiling and lead UML towards power re-distribution.

4. Incorporation of Socialist Feminism in Gender Policy

Women are equal human beings, having biologically different role than men. This fact was respected as a different capacity in the ancient era. In the post-Vedic Era, while discriminatory practices were started, women started rebelling against it. For instance, while men controlled *satdhyobadinis,*women like Gargi challenged that. Later in the modern age, women's resistance and opposition to discrimination were recognised as the Feminist Movement. In the course of moving ahead, feminism has been defined into different strands based on philosophy and perspectives. After a long journey for equality, third wave feminist movement theorised the fact that women are equal human beings, as a social group with a different biological capacity, and heterogeneities. As a result, the theory of substantive equality has been advocated rather than equality only on opportunity.

Analyzing and relating the UML policy with feminist perspectives, and going back to its agenda of equality in 1949 to the very first appeal and manifesto has followed Marxist perspective, which gives emphasis on equality. After 1979, the UML called for an equal opportunity based on Marxist feminist perspective and adopted the policy of substantive equality. In 1993, the Policy was linked with socialist feminist perspective. However, there are some gaps between the understanding and practice of gender policy, which have been shown in Figure 8.13.

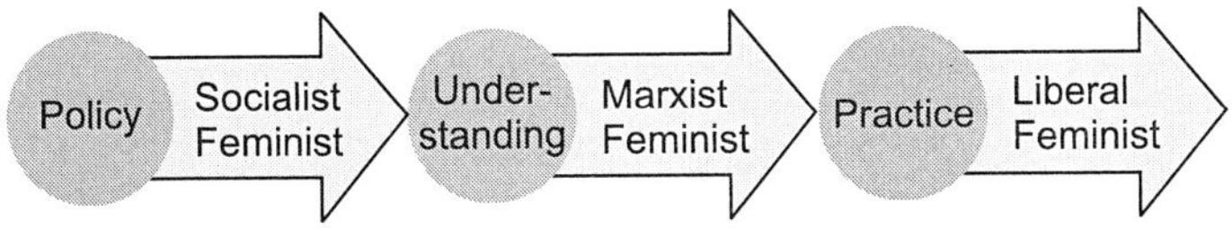

Figure 8.13 Perspective Gap in Policy, Understanding, and Practice in UML.

Majority of the UML cadres perceived women's issues theoretically in Marxist perspective and the liberal perspective when in practice. This difference in perception and practice occurred due to the lack of better knowledge on the socialist feminist perspective carried on by PMPD. That is a large political gap within UML, which needs to be reconciled.

Reflection of the Study

Being an insider of the research institution, have been able to reflect more on UML's internal facts, process and practice, which could be impossible for others. At the same time, being a colleague of the same movement, my participants could share their views and experiences openly in the process of interview and group discussion. In this way, it can be claimed that the strength of this study is that the information, opinion, and views mentioned here are much more in-depth and accurate. With this background, some of the reflections, have been highlighted here.

1. Education Plays Role in Women Empowerment

Education plays vital role in the process of setting policy and making decision. Education is linked with internalising the issues and envisioning the possible result in substance, which need both the analytical capacity and skill. Keeping eyes at the trends of Nepali women's movement, those women who had had opportunity to get education one way or another have successfully been in the movement. For instance, Yogmaya accepted Josmani sect of Hinduism, Sahana-Sadhana joined formal school, Rawanta Kumari, Dibya, etc., got political education within their families. Education like this made it possible for them to initiate decisive women's movement in one or in other way. In the later days, women like Asta, Bidya, Shusila and many others, who joined the movement onward the 1980s, got the opportunity of formal education and also the political schooling, which enabled them possible to sustain in the movement and even to be part of the campaigns to set women empowerment policy within UML and be active in the implementation process. These facts help me conclude that education is one of the essential components in the process of women empowerment and participation.

2. Determination and Stand Play Crucial Role

Education is one fact. The amalgamation of different form of education such as formal, informal and non-formal through institution, political schooling and involvement in movement made the women leaders strong, determined and decisive, in taking the agenda with logic and forward-looking attitude, which are strategically crucial to move step forward. Within UML, two actions has been realised as landmark in this regard. First, Sahana Pradhan led the eight-points gender agenda within UML central committee as member of the standing committee (CPN-UML, 2005a). For the first time, UML spent hours to discuss on gender agenda and finally adopted it, which became common gender agenda of political movement through IPWA (Appendix II). Second, Bidyadevi Bhandari led the four points motion in the Parliament in 2006 (Appendix III), which was adopted unanimously and created space, which now women are enjoying to have one-third participation here and there. These actions were possible because of their determination, stand, logical capacity, and motivating supportive masses behind/outside to give them confidence and moral support while the issues were under process.

3. Politics Influences Education System

Politic is called a necessary evil of the human society. None of the people can be out of the politics, though the level of concern and participation can be widely different. Considering this fact, I came to realise that if politics could be part of the education system, people could provide more critical view on it, to make more responsible to people. In this regard, if our education system could develop strategy to bring politician and educationist together with student of different levels to interact over the contemporary political issue, this may provide opportunity to learn and enrich both sides.

4. People's Multi-Party Democracy Needs Elaboration

While the women policy of PMPD was analysing, which was set almost two-decades ago, it is realised that it has not been further updated and elaborated to accommodate the contemporary issues and the concerns of the people. The required changes might be many more in that it is not only the policy on women empowerment, there are various other policies addressing the issues and strata of the people according to age, profession, ethnicity, topography, etc., and the state. If UML could go through the interaction with concerned groups, it might be able to enrich policy and programme to make them more effective by accommodating the voices and opinions of grassroots people and experts over the contemporary issues. This process may link it up UML and develop strong bond with broader range of the people. Their critical voice on PMPD policy may strengthen its acceptance and effectiveness, which is the aspiration of the PMPD.

5. Women Movement Passed Through *Ukali-Orali*

The nature of every movement is that it never grows upward directly. Nepali women's movement was no exception to it. It moved forward and backward and upward and downward in the process of raising the issues, achieving them, and going into actions. It has been named *Ukali-Orali*. In this process the movement drivers knew that there was a lack of proper communication of the policy and programme to the concerned group, it was not enforced at the grassroots level. This signifies that only setting a good policy does not make change happen in real life. It has been clearly seen within UML, while analyzing its women empowerment policy.

6. Unified Marxist Leninist Ignored Diversity and Followed Homogeneity in its Policy

Nepal is a diverse country and women are also the part of a diverse group. In order to respond this reality, UML needs to review its reservation policy within. In addition, diverse groups of people have different perspective, culture, and practices; which gives a clue that women have diverse interest and the issues such as right to identity, property, participation, and violence women against (VAW). In other words these issues are not common to all and the magnitudes of the problem are also different for different groups of Nepali women. But the UML did not pay attention to it. Consequently, it has advocated for the same issue for all women regardless of their lived status and the urgency. It means UML failed to identify the gender practices of the different groups of Nepali women and mainstream them as our own pride, rather than borrowing from abroad.

7. Care-work was Ignored as Productive Work

The Communist Party of Nepal-UML has adopted the socialist feminist aspiration as part of its policy on women. But, it has not recognised care work as productive work, which is being a mainstream gender agenda internationally. The United Nations, International Labour Organisation, and the International Labour movements are giving more attention to it and even allocating resources for it. Respecting those initiatives and the values of socialist feminism, it is important to review the UML policies, programmes, and practices in congruence with the international practices for care work.

Patriarchy Nurtured Systemic Marginalisation

International communist movement started to encourage women to be a part of the productive work in public sphere for their liberation, during the Marx's time. After revolution in Russia, Lenin emphasised that women's participation in political and social aspects are equally important. Arriving in Mao's time, patriarchy was identified as the aspect relating with women's subordination, which has worked as backbone of the gender discrimination. Hence, Mao tried to bring women in the forefront against males' supremacy over female. But, PMPD has agreed on Mao's idea and said that blurring the gender role is important. Based on these entire notions, I reflected in my mind that patriarchal values, norms, and practices are backing all political, economic, and socio-cultural aspect to marginalised women systematically. Delinking the patriarchy from all these aspects is important to empower women and bring them in the mainstream. Recognising care work can also contribute to this endeavour.

Implication of the Study

This study has mainly focused on the CPN-UML as one of the major political parties of the country, which is communist in philosophy with a democratic feature as part of its political aspect. UML has defined that lesson should be learned from the world communist movement and has contextualised Marxism to Nepali reality. Thus, UML is competing in the democratic process to win over people's support to rule the country.

The gender policy and programme set under the PMPD and its enforcement, have been reviewed and drawn some implications. In the following section, the issues, along with the implications for women empowerment and participation in decision-making process has been mentioned.

1. Elaborating the People's Multi-Party Democracy with Strategy and Action Plan

The gender policy under the PMPD is based on the socialist feminist perspective. The Policy needs to be accompanied by strategies and operational action plans in Specific, Measurable, Actionable, Result-oriented, and Time bound (SMART) ways. In this case, the UML's gender policy might be broadly understood and be part of the action plan within its entire structure (Figure 8.14).

2. Enforcing Gender Policy

Though the CPN-UML has a good policy, it is not properly

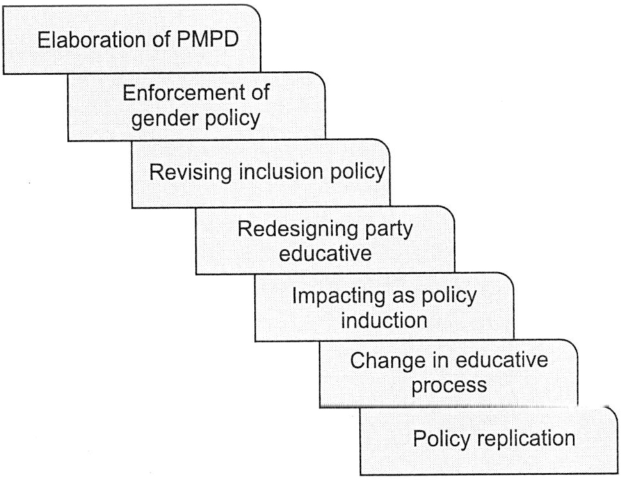

Figure 8.14 The Implication of the Study Outcome.

understood and enforced. It may be useful to set-up an appropriate mechanism to enforce the identified gender agenda and conduct relevant activities to promote the honing of leadership skills and knowledge as part of the empowerment process. If this is followed, the UML can gain competent female leadership at the different levels. This process can make a difference in the democratic exercise within the Party and outside in the society and state as well. It can add value to the UML as an agent of change that implements the party's priority policy as economic, social, and cultural transformation.

3. Revising Inclusive Policy

The Communist Party of Nepal-UML has set-up policy of inclusion to mainstream the marginalised community and has created five categories. However, the UML has missed the fact that women are not a homogenous group. They are situated at different social groups. UML may implement a correction in this regard and in the coming days to be more inclusive in terms of gender participation.

4. Redesigning Party Education

There are not enough systematic studies from a perspective of gender in CPN-UML. In this matter, this study implies that the UML's education system needs to review its educating policy in two primary ways. First, in the circumstances of increasing women's numerical participation, it may help to add female-focused activities as a special course. Second, for the effectiveness of policy into palpable action, it can motivate the education system to include gender policy as part of its content to let its cadres know and encourage enacting it. It may result to empower more women to be part of the education system as resource persons and enhancing acceptance of women's leadership with changing perceptions toward them.

Training for required skills to enhance political understanding and mentoring as an ingredient to develop new and inclusive quality leadership to avoid possible vacuum need to be made as a systemic part of the party education.

5. Impacting as Position Induction

Unless the decision-maker internalises the issues, it is not possible to make effective policy and reflect it in a programme. The study has identified both the strengths and limitations of the Party policy. It may further encourage the UML leadership to include women's issues sensitively in their activities such as task allocation, creating opportunity, mentoring, etc.

6. Change in Educative Process

Many changes from classical communist orientation to the orientation of PMPD has been found. PMPD in fact taught to be contextually accommodative. This process paves the ways for the creation of critical mass in the politics. This mass will not only be the followers of the thought. Instead, they will be critical to the ideology as Marx to the Marxists in understanding Marxism and may understand the differences in the way Lenin, Stalin, and Mao used Marxism in their own contexts. PMPD emerged in the Nepali context, while internalising Marxism in a creative way. Every organisation needs such educative process to make them lively.

7. Policy Replication

There are 164 political parties registered in national election commission in Nepal and more than 30 parties have their representatives in the Parliament (ECN, 2016). Some parties may adopt the points mentioned in this discussion to be more gender sensitive in order to enrol more women in the Party and win over women's support in the different activities of the party and society.

In addition, some of the points given next might be part of the lesson learned for other political parties and civil society organisations as well to promote women's participation and gender sensitising the movement to make a better contribution in the process of achieving substantive equality for the nation's prosperity.

Mechanism within: The women-related mechanism within the Party to initiate the issues and action is important. While UML was having the Central Women Department within during the Seventh Central Committee, its work to identify the eight-point gender agenda, later adopted by the central committee is the outcome of this. But, in the later days, though the numerical participation of women in committees has gone up, there is a lack of common mechanism within to stand collectively, because of which impact in action is not very satisfactory in UML.

Widening the collective action: In my experience, collective action within and beyond the institutions and movements is the better way to mainstream the marginalised groups and issues both. In doing so identifying common agenda and acting in coordination can make the peripheral voices heard. Nepali women's movement can be one of the good examples in this regard, even beyond the ideology.

The collective action of sister organisations of UML to adopt the Code of Conduct on VAW in 2014 is one of the good examples of a common action within. Similarly, the unanimous adoption of the parliamentary motion including the agenda of one-third women participation in 2006 is a good example of collective action beyond the ideology among broader stakeholders including mass movements and civil society.

Strong alliance within: Women within the UML family have practiced building alliance within to create pressure on top leadership to push the issues. For example signature campaign in 2009 among women and men (men in the central committee) to ensure the constitutional provision for one-third women's participation is one of the examples to learn by others as well.

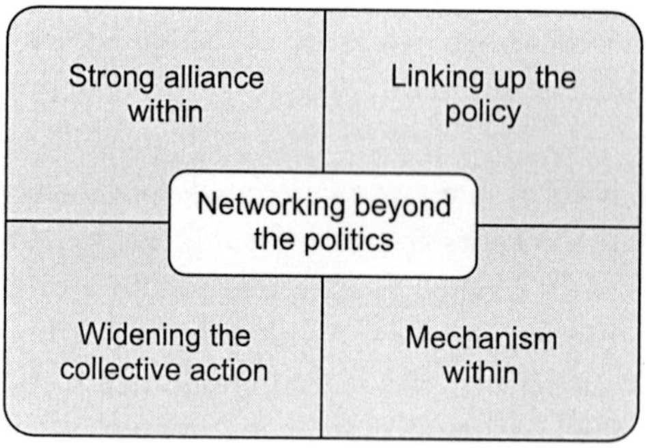

Figure 8.15 Possible Lesson Learning by Others.

Linking up the policy: The Communist Party of Nepal-UML has progressively kept changing its policy in connection with national and international commitments and contemporary gender approaches. As a result, it has gone through the liberal to Marxist to socialist feminism in its approach. Linking-up the policy in different levels has also provided logical ground to move forward to upgrade the gender policy, space to intervene in the policy-making, and push the agenda in action.

Networking beyond politics: Networking among different stakeholders, having different expertise and common goal is important. To achieve the common goals, people from different sectors such as academia, expertise, professions, civil society, and political activism can be connected into networking at different levels.

Critical Understanding of Marxism, Feminism and People's Multi-Party Democracy

Marxism focuses on economic justice to the proletariat, which has been prevailed in the Communist Manifesto (1848). Feminism, on the other hand, focuses on socio-cultural justice to the women to save them from patriarchal mindset men's subordination to them (Dorey-Stein, 2015). PMPD talks about both economic and social justice for women liberation (CPN-UML, 1993b). Analysis of all three different thoughts, I figured out some commonalities as well as differences in them.

Marxism emphasises on economic empowerment of women for their self-reliance and liberation (Marx, 1978). It says that women should be organised to free them from labour exploitation. But it does not talk about the care-work at home and patriarchy enough. Feminism, on the other hand, defines patriarchal subordination as the main obstacle of women liberation (Hanisch, 2006. It emphasises on political and socio-cultural empowerment. It believes in collective action to get rid of socio-cultural operation. Until the second wave, it was defining women as a single class, not giving enough importance to economic aspect (Friedan, 1963). But, third wave feminism includes the socialist perspective and is called as 'socialist feminism', which defines diversities within women and emphasising on multi-dimensions of empowerment including care work at home as productive work (Freedman, 2002).

People's Multi-Party Democracy talks about the gender role, patriarchy, and affirmative action to mainstream them (CPN-UML, 1993b). It emphasises on women's collective action with determination. But, it has also failed to recognise care work as productive work and silently accepted women as a single group rather responding diversities within. Figure 8.16 shows the commonalities and differences between Marxism, Feminism, and PMPD.

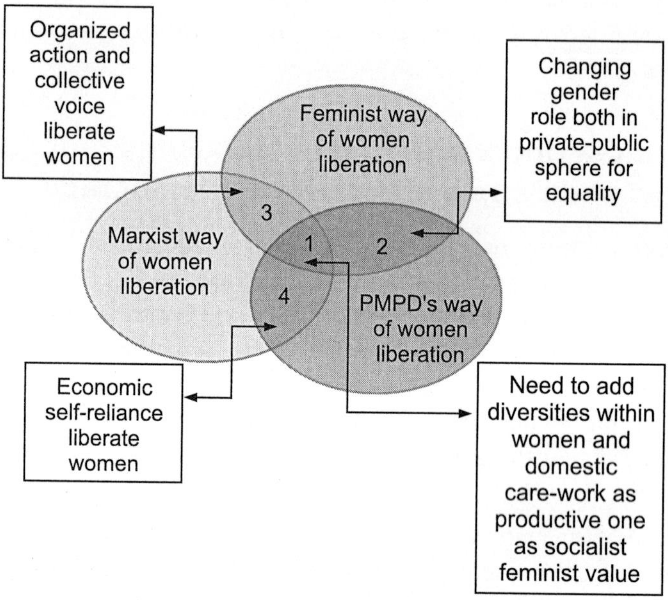

Figure 8.16 Commonalities and Differences of Marxism, Feminism and PMPD.

Based on the earlier discussion, my conclusion is that Marxism, feminism, and PMPD have a close relation. The dual commonalities are seen as overlapping areas of (2), (3) and (4) in Figure 8.16. The area (1) shows the common ground as economic empowerment of Marxism, changing socio-cultural gender construction of feminism, and shifting gender domain of PMPD with affirmative action and collective action recognised by all of three thoughts. Addition of two major socialist gender elements in this area as: (a) counting care work as productive activities; and (b) responding multiple diversities within women, may include all the necessary aspects of the women liberation, have been defined by a socialist feminist. Then, rest of the process may need to follow the empowerment action cycle mentioned in Figure 3.3, (in Chapter 3) to go for proper enforcement to achieve social transformation.

Conclusive Understanding

The findings presented in this chapter are solely based on the study of Communist Party of Nepal-Unified Marxist Leninist (CPN-UML). Qualitative research method with feminist inquiry has been followed in this study. Information has been collected through available documents, interviewing, and interaction with UML rank and files and also used my own reflectivity as Party insider. As an insider and colleagues of my informants, they shared with me their experiences, views, and opinion more openly. This is the strength of this study. And, the limitation is that it is focused solely on UML to collect the data.

Having detailed information and analysis of one of the leading parties, it might encourage the believers of other political parties as well to go through the study and do the similar study. Keeping these aspects in mind, Major findings of the study have been summarised here.

Feminism in Nepali Communism

The debate over potential energy (*Brahma/Paramatma*) and/or kinetic energy (*Atma/Jibatma/Matter/Prakriti*) first continued in Eastern philosophy for long. It was *Sankha* philosophy that explicitly accepted potential energy and the kinetic energy equal to each other. This acceptance gave birth to the idea of *Ardhanarishwar* (half man and half woman to be complete human being). Contrary to it the Hindus followed the dichotomised traditions as *Shakta* sect as female first and *Shaiva* and/or *Vaishnav* sect as a male first. These three philosophical debates are observed in Nepali society as well. But in the industrial world, the feminist movement was started in the middle of the eighteenth century with the issue of the right to suffrage at the heart of the movement. Later, when The Communist Manifesto was published in 1848 and working people started to be organised with the slogan 'workers of the world unite', women workers were also on the target to be organised. Marx was giving emphasis on women's participation in public sphere stating 'for their own liberation, women should enter into productive sphere' (Marx and Engels, 1848).

Gradually, it began to organise women workers separately to empower them before joining the mainstream organisation. As a result, the second international in 1889 adopted the motion on gender equality at the workplace as the feminist movement. Feminist movement across the borders kept continued. Symbolising that 8 March, was declared as the International Working-women Day (IWD) in 1910. In the process, the first wave of the feminist movement advocated for representing women's efforts to get the right to vote, property, divorce, receive alimony and child support, and manage their own bodies. The 'second wave' of the feminist movement tried to obtain equal access to higher education in all fields and freedom from any kinds of discrimination in their workplace. The 'third wave' of the feminist movement began with an explosion of multiple, diverse perspectives within women. It had a close nexus with the socialist feminist perspective.

Reflecting over the earlier mentioned feminist waves and linking them with UML policy, it is found that: (1) first phase of the communist movement of Nepal was based on formal equality; (2) the second phase dealt with Marxist feminist perspective, giving emphasis on women's participation in public sphere; (3) the third phase which started with People's Multi-party Democracy (PMPD) focused on the agendas of socialist feminism as encouraging both men and women to be equal parts in the public and private spheres. In doing so, PMPD failed to recognise domestic work as productive or economic activities.

Empowerment and Participation in Nepali Communism

The ultimate goal of the empowerment process is to expand choices in life for progressive and egalitarian society. It includes both representation and interventions as a quantitative and qualitative measurement of breadth and depth in values.

As an active multi-dimensional process empowerment helps women to realise their identity and power in all spheres of life to control over their own lives and acquire the ability to make strategic choices. Empowerment has been defined at the individual, group and societal or community levels in an interconnected way. It also covers political, economic, and socio-cultural aspects. Education that raises awareness for social transformation toward gender justice, is one of the vital aspects of the process of empowerment. The logic behind this is that wherever women have exercised political rights, they have been able to initiate changes in powerful public institutions, like legislatures, judiciary, and the security measures such as the military.

From empowerment and participation of the women, PMPD has adopted the concept of affirmative action as empowering instrument for women.

Breaking the Barrier and Moving Toward Gender Equality

Marx concluded that economic dependency is the root cause of women oppression and need to encourage them to be part of economic activities in public to be self-reliant and be organised for liberation from labour exploitation through collective actions. Following Marx, Lenin adopted an equality-based policy and programme to empower women to be part of politics, economy as well as social activities to liberate them from all forms of exploitation and discrimination (Trosky, 1970). But it could not deconstruct the socially constructed women's role and social attitude.

Mao Tse Tung (1940) defines women as half of the sky and termed patriarchy as one of the additional exploitative measures over women. So, he championed for affirmative action to expand women's domain. But, even that failed to address the reproductive gender roles shouldered by women.

Burrowing the experiences of the three communist leaders, Madan Bhandari set gender policy in PMPD to empower women in the public domain calling men to be equal parts in the private domain and to share reproductive gender roles equally. He also followed Mao's affirmative action plans to promote women's participation for changed patriarchal norms and values and liberate women from their subordinated roles.

Under the PMPD policy, UML has empowered women politically through a quota system and increased their numerical participation in different fields (CPN-UML, 2014a). But, PMPD has talked about the special package programme, which could include the activities to strengthen women's competency, ways for mentoring to change the gendered attitude and promote modelling to change behaviour within private and public sphere including UML itself, is lacking. This lacking has caused ineffective to root out a patriarchal way of thinking and practice as well as valuing the role differently. As a result, economically, it has not valued care work as productive work as social feminists argue for.

Based on the set policy, UML has correctly identified the gender issues and taken decisions in macro level. But, they have not been properly communicated to meso and micro level, which are responsible for their implementation. It shows that UML has limited in policy setting and decision-making, and also is lacking proper strategy, action plan, mentoring, monitoring and evaluation before going through another round of changes in the policies. UML also needs to break gender glass ceiling and glass walling within the Party.

Stepping-up the Women's Movement Towards Equality

Women's movement in Nepal has completed a century, since Yogmaya initiated a collective action against socio-cultural oppression over women in 1917 with the aspiration of *togetherness*. After formation of Praja-parisad in the 1940s, women from families and relatives helped the political activists as a form of *kinship*. Inspired by the political movement in neighbouring countries and oligarchy oppression within, women came on the streets in 1947 with political demands and form their own organisation with the aspiration of *moving the rock,* an obstacle on the way. However, there was a long silence after this until the 1980s. Women started to be reorganised from 1981 defining them as *half of the sky*. This strategy worked for them widely, which resulted in high participation in the people's movement in 1990 and they started to *shift the domain* from private to public under the name of liberation. But, realising the necessary participation in all level and sphere of lives to achieve equality in real sense, women's movement stepped-up with the spirit of *walk side-by-side* to make change in perspective and practice both with better effectiveness, 2006 onwards. In this way, Nepali women's movement is escalating with notable achievements though it is not moving always in linear form, but taking path as forth and back time and again, which I have named *Ukali-Orali* of the women's movement.

Motivational Elements

In the process of modernising the society, practice in one part of the world gives impact to other parts. It has happened in the women's movement as well. Most of the policy changes happen through international commitment of the state such as ratification of the United Nations and International Labour Organization (ILO) conventions. In the way Marx was also expanded and/ or challenged for his economic determinism. Neo-Marxists and non-Marxists saw flaws in Marx's deterministic class concept (Au, 2006). Radical feminists regarded male as class to oppress women, cultural feminist made mainstream culture as class (Maynard, 1995; Ghodsee, 2004). This paved the road to communist movement in general and UML in particular to understand women and address them from different standpoint. National contexts such as opportunity to participate in education for raising awareness by realising women's self-identity and dignity, employment to facilitate economic empowerment, oppressive nature of state with people agitating against the rulers, etc., have also played role to motivate women to be a part of communist movement. In addition, novelty consciousness, sympathetic motivation, empathetic solidarity, and synergetic platform also enabled women to advocate for change in their life and society at large.

Sustaining the Change Envisaged in the Set Policy

Communist movements of the world and in Nepal instigated many changes in women's life. But to sustain the changes remained yet questionable at least in the case of UML. In order to address this question, UML needs to make some correction in its policy and programmes. First, it has system of Party schooling to educate its rank and files including women. Schooling confines people to a particular path but school opens them for multiple avenues for their choices, which is one of the aspirations of PMPD. If UML could provide school (avenue) even on the issue of women empowerment, it will make women critical, which is lacking in this party. Second, training limits participants to do a specific task in a specific way; trainings on the other hand give options for them to develop leadership in broader ways. In the process of preparing to implement women empowerment policy, specially changing gender role of men and women both in private and public venues, trainings are needed, which are not yet planned properly. Third, the policy of inclusion considering women as a single group does not match with diversities within women that exist in the society. In other words, it does not carry on the core value of PMPD. Fourth, the UML's affirmative action plan limited on quota does not empower women as a whole, instead it provides some space for limited number of women for a definite period, unless it accompanied with additional package programmes to strengthen competency and confidence to take lead in different areas of human society. Fifth, few women have been promoted in non-traditional positions and work as part of breaking the gender glass ceiling and glass walls as good initiatives. To make it sustainable, effective and efficient enough, acceptability of new ways of thinking and working are necessary in all level within UML and outside in the state mechanism. And finally, the proper synchronisation between policy, understanding, and practices is the major thing, to be taken into consideration while enhancing public reliability in politics and the political party. Searching closely the women empowerment part within UML is still weak. It has given me the feeling that it might have happened in the other areas as well. If these aspects are not corrected in time, UML may be derailed from reaching the destination envisaged in PMPD.

Going Beyond

Two major sources have been used to generation data. One, from the field and second from the experience of UML cadre as well as the leader who has been working as activist. In both the occasions, a lot of insight has been dug out in the process of study. The filed data and my reflection confirmed that PMPD has carried on good gender policy; it needs to be elaborated with effective strategy and action plan to implement them properly. Cadres reflection also says there are shortcomings in the UML's schooling, which need to be converted into critical school to provide space for rank and file to use their innovative ideas and perspectives to change their contexts. This will also lead women leaders to be effective in their constitutionally awarded new position and policy. This process may lead to policy induction to them as well.

While talking about women's lobbying and campaigning, there are various lessons that can be learned by the UML as insiders and other political parties as outsiders. They can learn the following: (1) different mechanisms to address gender and empowerment issues; (2) collective action within; (3) alliance making beyond their political ideologies; and (4) broader networking to create pressure for progressive change. The reason is that most of the positive outcomes in the past have been achieved through the collective action of political parties of different ideologies and institutions of different orientations.

Recently CPN-UML and CPN-MC have started the process to have coalition/integrated/merged to form CPN. This suggests that someday there can be a single communist party through merger/integration of all the left forces to form a strong left power. In this polarised political system as well, this study will be helpful to raise women's issues, reflect upon the prevailing policies, programmes, and implementation strategies to empower women for gender justice. This will be equally helpful for the integrated/merged party with democratic values to make this study as a benchmark to review their women empowerment programme for gender equity.

Finally, this study implies that students of different political faiths can be encouraged to examine their parties' policies, strategies, and programmes critically and come up with alternative thoughts to make their leaders capable to ensure gender equity. It also implies Party schooling to promote critical school culture where new ideas and perspectives will be celebrated in place of schooling as UML has these days.

It can be expected that the formal education institution will also imply the idea that I came up with this study to encourage the thoughts what Mao once said, 'Letting a hundred flowers blossom and a hundred schools of thought contend is the policy for promoting progress in the arts and the sciences and a flourishing socialist culture in our land' (Mao, 1957). It is not sure how much this though could be used in his communist party that time. But, in Nepali context, UML and the integrated left can apply it under PMPD and this study might help to go through practicing in the day to come.

For the proper implementation of women empowerment policy to attain the set goal, CPN-UML needs to review its policy and its enactment carefully. If it could use even the issues raised in this study, this may help its effective implementation. In addition, people believing in other political parties as well can use relevant part of this study as a lesson learnt to eradicate patriarchal mindset against women's oppression.

Task Ahead

This study has identified some areas, which PMPD has not addressed properly yet. The three areas mentioned next can be taken for further study.

Care Work as Productive Work: Considering care-work in private sphere as productive work and counting its contribution to gross domestic production (GDP) is one of the essential issues. The feminist movement has raised this issue as male chauvinism. This issue has also been recognised by the United Nations. But, there are no established indicators to measure it. Therefore, it might be one of the areas for further study. In doing this, the researcher can identify the nature of care work and give monitory value to it. This can be done by reviewing average salary of the people who do similar work in public place (such as cooking, housekeeping, child rearing, nursing elderly and disabled, etc). S/he also can recognise it as the area of employment. Counting the time spent on care work its monitory value can be calculated. S/he also can think of the time spent by the illiterates to the highly professional people, who spend time in care work. Keeping these ideas in mind one can do research and find out the contribution of care work in national GDP. Also, s/he can come up with a composite index to measure women's contribution that equals to the productive work.

Diversity Based Women Empowerment: Nepali society is diverse in nature. With these diversities, there are mindsets towards women. These mindsets and the form of patriarchy envisaged in each diversity and the required form of empowerment needs to be explored. This study can come up with the feminism of Nepali taste and character

Politics as Part of Education System: Politics is part of the human society. And yet the majority of the people might not be interested to participate in it as party cadres and leaders. In this situation, the research can be undertaken to find out the ways to make people of different walks of life as critical mass who will be able to review, among many other factors, political ideologies, leaders' contribution, policies, programmes, and implementation strategies taken.

Postscript

Nepal is moving forward with additional achievement narrowing down the gender gap in the state mechanism as well as in civic society movement. Proper enforcement and implementation of the new constitution can foster the process, since the constitution has addressed and guaranteed most of the issues related to gender equality, raised by women's movement in the country. As the first step of the enforcement of the constitution, three tiers of the elections have been completed in 2017. New government has been formed with the solid majority; has inspired people with expectation of political stability. In the election campaign, all the political parties have expressed their commitment of proper enforcement of the constitution keeping in top priority. New government has also given the slogan of "Prosperous Nepal and Happy Nepali" keeping economic and social transformation at the utmost priority. It is a good start to move forward.

Election Under Federalism

As the first step of the enforcement of constitution, Nepal has gone through the three tiers of election as local, provincial and federal parliament in 2017. In that process, women's participation in the elected body has been geared up. Fulfilling the constitutional provision of insuring one-third women participation in provincial and federal parliament and 40 percent in local level, 41.1 per cent women have been elected as a result. The summary of the election result has been shown in Table P1.

Table P1 Summary of the Election Result, 2017

S.No.	*Level of Elected Mechanism*	*Women*	*Men*	*Total*
1.	Members of Lower House	90	185	275
2.	Members of Upper House	22	37	59
3.	Members of Provinces	189	361	550
4.	Local Governance bodies *(including chief and deputy chief)*	731	775	1506
5.	Elected member at local level	14352	20689	35041
		15384 (41.1%)	22047 (58.9%)	37431

(ECN, 2017.)

Local Election: Local election took place in Nepal after 20 years. It was third local election after multiparty democracy achieved in 1990 and first election after federal republic Nepal with having constitutional right as government. The constitution has guaranteed 2 women including 1 from Dalit community out of five members in each ward (GoN, 2015). Facilitating the provision more progressively, the act relating with local election has guaranteed that one of the candidate from each party should be woman in the two posts as chief and deputy chief in the local government as municipalities and village councils (GoN, 2017).

Based on the legal provision,out of 753 local governments, women have been elected as Mayor of the Municipalities and Chair of the Village Council and 714 Deputy-mayor and Deputy-chair. Following the constitutional provision, 14352 women including 6567 Dalit women have been elected in the ward level. It is a huge change in comparison to past; only 136 women were elected in first election in 1994 and 20 percent in second election in 1997. As executive post, only one woman was elected in the first and 17 in the second election out of 3999 local bodies.

The major drawback seen in the recent held election is that most of the women are elected in deputy post. But, it is not the assisting post this time like before. Constitution has clearly given the right to deputy chief to be the chair of the justice committee provision (GoN, 2015, Article 217). It is important indeed in the Nepali context, where governance and violence are the major problem in order to achieve the said objective of "Prosperous Nepal and happy Nepali".

Table P2 Party-wise representation in local election

Local election 2017								
Party	*Chief*	*Dy. chief*	*Ward chair*	*Open member*	*Open Women*	*Dalit Women*	*Total*	*Per cent*
UML	294	331	2559	5458	2777	2680	14099	40.2
NC	266	223	2287	4423	2156	2101	11456	32.7
MC	105	112	1103	2056	1035	1030	5441	15.5
SSFN	34	32	262	540	290	281	1439	4.1
RJPN	30	37	194	437	211	214	1123	3.2
Other	24	18	337	570	273	261	1483	4.2
Total	753	753	6742	13484	6742	6567	35041	100

SSFN–Sanghiyasamajbadi Forum, NRJPN–Rastriya Janata Party, Nepal
(ECN, 2017.)

CPN-UML has become largest party in the local election with securing 40.2 percent of total seat alone. Nepali Congress and CPN (MC) have secured second and third position.

To coordinate and monitoring the municipalities and village council work, there are 77 district coordination committee (DCC). Among them, UML has won Coordinator in 41 district followed by 20 by NC and 8 by CPN-MC. Among the DCC coordinator, only two are women as Seeta Sundas in Syangja and Tseiring Lhamu Gurung in Mustang representing UML. As the constructional provision of having one candidate out of coordinator and deputy coordinator (GoN, 2015), under the name of alliances, women have lost even the deputy position in DCC. Total of 47 women have been elected in deputy position and 30 positions taken by men under the name of being candidate from different parties. It is tactical move guided by patriarchy to abandon women in the position.

Table P3 Party-wise Gender Representation in DCC

Parties	*Party-wise Gender Representation in DCC*					
	Chief of District coordination committee			*Dy. Chief of District coordination committee*		
	M	*F*	*Total*	*M*	*F*	*Total*
CPN-UML	39	2	41	6	30	36
NC	20	0	20	6	10	16
MC	8	0	8	11	6	17
SSF	2	0	2	5	0	5
RJP	4	0	4	1	0	1
Others	2	0	2	1	1	2
Total	75	2	77	30	47	77

(ENC & Media, 2017.)

Federal and Provincial Election: Nepal has turned into federal structure from unitary system after institutionalised Federal Democratic Republic Nepal in 2015 through new constitution. As first step of the enforcement of the federalism, first election for provincial and federal parliament was held in December 2017. As per constitutional provision women's participation should be at least one-third of provincial parliamentarian (Articles, 176-9) and one out of the speaker and the deputy speaker (Articles, 182-2) should be women from each party, 189 women have been elected in seven provinces, which is 34.36 per cent. All the seven provinces have elected women as deputy speaker.

Based on the constitutional provision to insure one-third women participation (Articles, 84-8), 112 women have been elected in total as composition of 90 women in the house of representative and 22 in the national assembly. Most of the women have been elected under the system of proportional representative, since none of the party was likely to provide constituency to go first part the post (FPTP). There were only 21 candidates out of 165 constituencies from three major parties such as 5, 5 and 8 from UML, NC and MC respectively. As result only 6 women as 2 from UML, 3 from

Maoist and one independent won the election under FPTP. None of the woman elected from NC. Rest of the women parliamentarian were come from PR list.

Table P4 Party-wise gender desegregated data of Federal parliament

Parties	*Party-wide Representation in Parliament*							
	House Representative				*Provincial Parliament*			
	FPTP	*PR*	*Total*	*Women*	*FPTP*	*PR*	*Total*	*Women*
CPN-UML	80	41	121	41	168	75	243	81
NC	23	40	63	21	41	72	113	48
MC	36	17	53	18	73	35	108	36
SSF	10	7	17	8	24	13	37	13
RJP	11	5	16	6	16	12	28	10
Others	5	0	5	1	8	13	21	1
Total	165	110	275	95	330	220	550	189

(ECN & Media, 2017.)

Women in the Government: After the election, new government has been formed. Securing support of almost two-third comfortable majority to run full tenure government, almost two decade long hung parliament and system of fragility of coalition government has been ended. In regards to executive, the constitutional provision said that council of government should be formed based on inclusive principle (76-9). Since, there is no gender quota, federal government has only two cabinet ministers and two state ministers (who is not allow to be part of cabinet meeting) out of 22 members in cabinet. It has been happened caused by no insuring quota in the law.

Similarly, there are seven provincial governments. Among them, four provinces are led by UML, 2 led by MC and 1 led by coalition of SSFN and RJPN. Among them none of the province has woman as chief minister and three provinces do not have even a single woman in cabinet. This scenario shows that unless having legal compulsion, to inclusion of women in the state mechanisms is not possible yet. It is the attitudinal problem. It remains among decision makers in all level.

Table P5 Gender Disaggregated data of Federal and Provincial Government

State	*Women in Government*	
	Cabinet	*Woman*
Federal level	22	4
Province-1	5	0
Province-2	7	(1)state minister
Province-3	7	0
Province-4	7	1
Province-5	6	1
Province-6	7	1
Province-7	7	2

(Secretariat of provincial parliament, May 2018.)

Status of Major Gender Issues

Violence against women is one of the priority agenda to move forward. Some of the cases has been responded by laws such as Chaupudhi (do and don't during menstruation) and polygamy, which will come into enforcement from middle of August, this year. But, the criminal cases such as rape and attempt to rape are being reported almost everyday in the media. There is law, but it is not functioning well. According to registered cases in police, during last three years, 674 girls below 10 years were raped (Sapkota, 2018). The registered case in women rehabilitation center (WOREC) was 235 during the first two months of the year 2018. Among them, 30 cases were raped and 11 were attempted rape. It means every another day one woman is being raped and majority of them are girls. According to safe houses runner, the most difficult and risky problem is to rehabilitate the raped victims in their own community. Because of social stigma, neither family nor community accept them easily. Finally, the victim could not over come the feeling of guilty and most of the cases end at suicide. Except sexual crime, physical and mental violence are rampant. One of the recent cases of the deputy chief of the village council, who is the chief of the justice committee in the village council as well, was badly beaten up by husband and went for police case.

It is being real challenge for the women's movement, whole society and the state to move toward prosperity. Because, prosperity is not only linked with economic matter, but also humanising the socio-cultural values, norms and behaviour of all. All these are guided by way of thinking and attitude.

Property right is another issues. The civil code has guaranteed equal inheritance property right for all children. Enactment of this provision will start from this year. The achievers of this right are new generation and providers are parents. Now, the ball in the court of parents to do justice to their own children.

Finally, in regard of the decent right, still the children of single mother and children having foreign father is not easy. New constitution has opened little hole to facilitate it. But, it is still not very easy. For instance, centre for investigative journalism, Nepal has reported that court has given verdict to state and asked to provide citizenship, but the official is lingering (Adhikari, 2018). It may require more clarity in legal provision.

Reflection of the Scenario

Constitutionally, women have achieved a lot in Nepal. It has secure better position even in the list of women participation in the world. Among the 48 countries, securing 30 percent women participation in parliament as per Beijing declaration in 1995 (UN, 1995), Nepal secured 37th position (IPU, 2017). Cause of the constitutional and legal provision to insuring quota, women's participation have been increased in the elected bodies. But, wherever it has not been clearly spelled out, still the political leaders as top decision makers from the federal to local level do not dare to promote women in the public position. Tangible example of this is the composition of federal and provincial cabinets. It shows that there is a lot to work on changing way of thinking and gender attitude among political leaders as decision maker.

Not only men, even women are not promoting women. For example, nine women have been elected in deputy speaker/chair in the parliaments, but not of them have nominated women as their personal secretary and in secretariat. Unless changing the patriarchal mind set, it is not possible to promote women in the public position. It is not only the issues of men and women, but recognition and confident on women's capacity.

Communist parties are the one to motivate women to be part of the public sphere. Now, left-alliance is the largest political force in the state and has formed government in the federal and provinces. But, they did not show their confident to elect single woman as chief minister and minister in the federal government as proportionate of women's participation in parliament. Provincial government seems even worse. To fulfil the legal quota, all women are allocated deputy position in federal and provincial parliament. It has signalled that women's movement still need to take radical step jointly, to change gender attitude of the political leaders including both male and female.

Finally, women have been confident on political matter and are able to vow and voice out for political rights. But, in terms of exercising those right and expand visibility in the society, they need to focus on technical matter on how to strategies the matter and be tactical to publicise their work as role model as change agent.

Violence against women is getting serious. Even the school is not safe for girls and house for all women. To tackle the issues, not only increasing punishment through changing legal provision, state need to give attention on moral education as part of curriculum. Political and civil society movement need to take this issue seriously and civil education needs to start in family and community as well. In conclusion, changing gender attitude with moral values and social norms, the society may more forward to achieve equality and social justice in practice as part of human lives.

Appendices

Appendix I

The Declaration Made by Parliament on 18 May 2006.

प्रतिनिधि सभाको घोषणा, २०६३

शान्तिपूर्ण संयुक्त जनआन्दोलनमा नेपाली जनताले गरेको बलिदान, जीवन-उत्सर्ग र सहभागिताप्रति उच्च सम्मान गर्दै,

स्वतन्त्र र सार्वभौमसत्ता सम्पन्न नेपालको राज्यशक्तिको स्रोत जनता रहेको र नेपाली जनताले केही समयअघि शान्तिपूर्ण संयुक्त जनआन्दोलनद्वारा सार्वभौमसत्ता र राज्यशक्तिको स्रोत जनता मात्र भएको सत्यलाई स्थापित गर्ने उत्कट अभिलाषा प्रकट गरेको तथ्यलाई ध्यानमा राख्दै,

शान्तिपूर्ण संयुक्त जनआन्दोलनमा सात राजनीतिक दलको मार्गचित्र र सातदल-नेकपा - माओवादी) बीचको बाह्र बुँदे समझदारी अनुरुप नेपाली जनताले संविधानसभामार्फत् नयाँ संविधान निर्माण गरी लोकतन्त्र, राज्यको पुनसंरचना सहित समावेशी राज्यव्यवस्था र दिगो शान्ति स्थापना गर्न दिएको जनादेशलाई पूरा गर्ने संकल्प गर्दै,

मुलुकको राष्ट्रिय अखण्डता, अविभाज्यता एवं राष्ट्रिय एकतालाई सुदृढ गर्न सार्वभौम नेपाली जनताको गहन जिम्मेवारीलाई आत्मसात गर्दै,

"राज्यशक्तिको स्रोत नेपाली जनता भएको र नेपालको सार्वभोमसत्ता एवं राजकीय सत्ता नेपाली जनतामा नै निहित रहेको तथ्यलाई हृदयङ्गम गर्दै वर्तमान जनआन्दोलनमार्फत अभिव्यक्त भएको जनभावना एवं आन्दोलनरत सात राजनीतिक दलको गठबन्धनको मार्गचित्रका आधारमा मुलुकमा जारी हिंसात्मक द्वन्द्व लगायत समग्र समस्याहरुको समाधान गर्न" २०६३ वैशाख ११ गतेको राजाको घोषणामा जनआन्दोलनको बलमा स्थापित प्रतिनिधिसभा सार्वभौम अधिकार सम्पन्न रहेको स्वीकार गरिएको,

२०४६ सालको जनआन्दोलनका उपलब्धिहरुलाई रक्षा गर्दै वर्तमान जनआन्दोलनका उपलब्धिहरुलाई संस्थागत गरी निरंकुश राजतन्त्रको अन्त्य र पूर्ण लोकतन्त्र स्थापनाको दिशामा अग्रसर हुने जिम्मेवारी ग्रहण गर्न अर्को संवैधानिक व्यवस्था नभएसम्म सम्पूर्ण अधिकारहरु प्रयोग गर्नका लागि यो प्रतिनिधिसभा सार्वभौमसत्ता सम्पन्न भएको घोषणा गर्दछ, र राज्यशक्ति यही प्रतिनिधिसभा मार्फत् प्रयोग हुने भएकोले देहायको घोषणा गर्दछ-

१. व्यवस्थापिकाका सम्बन्धमा

१.१ नेपालको व्यवस्थापिका सम्बन्धी सम्पूर्ण अधिकार प्रतिनिधिसभाद्वारा प्रयोग गरिनेछ । कानून निर्माण गर्ने प्रक्रिया प्रतिनिधिसभाले निर्धारण गरेबमोजिम हुनेछ ।

१.२ संविधानसभाको मागमा अघि बढ्ने प्रक्रिया प्रतिनिधिसभाले आवश्यकता अनुसार निर्धारण गर्नेछ।

१.३ प्रतिनिधिसभाको अधिवेशनको आह्वान र अन्त्य देहाय बमोजिम हुनेछ -

(क) प्रधानमन्त्रीबाट अधिवेशनको आह्वान र प्रधानमन्त्रीको सिफारिशमा सभामुखबाट अधिवेशनको समापन गरिनेछ।

(ख) प्रतिनिधिसभाको अधिवेशन चालु नरहेको वा बैठक स्थगित भएको अवस्थामा अधिवेशन वा बैठक बोलाउन वाञ्छनीय छ भनी प्रतिनिधिसभाको तत्काल कायम रहेको सम्पूर्ण सदस्य संख्याको एक चौथाई सदस्यहरुले सभामुखसमक्ष समावेदन गरेमा सभामुखले त्यस्तो अधिवेशन वा बैठक पन्ध्र दिनभित्र बस्ने गरी मिति र समय तोक्नुपर्नेछ।

१.४ प्रतिनिधिसभाले प्रतिनिधिसभा नियमावली बनाई लागू गर्नेछ।

२. कार्यकारिणीका सम्बन्धमा

२.१ नेपाल राज्यको सम्पूर्ण कार्यकारिणी अधिकार मन्त्रिपरिषद्मा निहित रहनेछ। "श्री ५ को सरकार" लाई अब उप्रान्त "नेपाल सरकार" भनिनेछ।

२.२ प्रतिनिधिसभा सदस्य नरहेका व्यक्ति पनि मन्त्रिपरिषद्मा मनोनित हुन सक्नेछन्।

२.३ मन्त्रिपरिषद् प्रतिनिधिसभाप्रति उत्तरदायी रहनेछ। मन्त्रिपरिषद् र मन्त्रीहरु सामूहिक रुपमा र आफ्नो मन्त्रालयको कामका लागि व्यक्तिगत रुपमा समेत प्रतिनिधिसभाप्रति उत्तरदायी रहनेछन्। प्रशासन, सेना, प्रहरी लगायत सम्पूर्ण कार्यकारी अंगहरु प्रतिनिधिसभाप्रति उत्तरदायी सरकारको मातहतमा रहनेछन्।

२.४ सरकारको कार्यविभाजन र कार्यसम्पादन नियमावली मन्त्रिपरिषद्बाट पारित गरी प्रतिनिधिसभामा प्रस्तुत गरिनेछ।

३. सेनाका सम्बन्धमा

३.१ "शाही नेपाली सेना" को नाम परिवर्तन गरी "नेपाली सेना" रहनेछ।

३.२ राष्ट्रिय सुरक्षा परिषद् सम्बन्धी विद्यमान व्यवस्था खारेज गरिएको छ। नेपाली सेनाको नियन्त्रण, प्रयोग र परिचालन गर्न प्रधानमन्त्रीको अध्यक्षतामा एक राष्ट्रिय सुरक्षा परिषद् रहनेछ।

३.३ नेपाली सेनाको प्रधान सेनापतिको नियुक्ति मन्त्रिपरिषद्ले गर्नेछ।

३.४ सेनाको परमाधिपति सम्बन्धी विद्यमान व्यवस्था खारेज गरिएको छ।

३.५ सेना परिचालन सम्बन्धी मन्त्रिपरिषद्को निर्णय ३० (तीस) दिनभित्र प्रतिनिधिसभाले तोकेको विशेष समितिमा प्रस्तुत भई अनुमोदन हुनुपर्नेछ।

३.६ नेपाली सेनाको संगठन समावेशी र राष्ट्रिय स्वरुपको हुनेछ।

४. राजपरिषद्का सम्बन्धमा

राजपरिषद्को विद्यमान व्यवस्था खारेज गरिएको छ। त्यसले गर्दै आएका आवश्यक काम प्रतिनिधिसभाले व्यवस्था गरे बमोजिम हुनेछ।

५. राजदरवार सम्बन्धमा

५.१ राजगद्दी उत्तराधिकार सम्बन्धी कानून वनाउने, संशोधन गर्ने र खारेज गर्ने अधिकार प्रतिनिधिसभामा रहनेछ।

५.२ श्री ५ को खर्च र सुविधा प्रतिनिधिसभाको निर्णय बमोजिम हुनेछ।

५.३ श्री ५ को निजी सम्पत्ति र आयमाथि कानून बमोजिम कर लाग्नेछ।

५.४ श्री ५ वाट भए गरेका कामहरुका बारेमा प्रतिनिधिसभा र अदालतमा प्रश्न उठाउन सकिनेछ।

५.५ विद्यमान राजप्रासाद सेवालाई निजामती सेवाको अंग वनाइने छ।

५.६ राजदरवारको सुरक्षा प्रवन्ध मन्त्रिपरिषद्ले व्यवस्था गरे बमोजिम हुनेछ।

६. मुलुकमा रहेको नागरिकताको समस्यालाई सिघ्र समाधान गरिने छ।

७. प्रचलनमा रहेको "राष्ट्रिय गान" लाई वैकल्पिक व्यवस्था गरी परिवर्तन गरिनेछ।

८. नेपाल धर्म निरपेक्ष राज्य हुनेछ।

९. विविध

(क) राज्यका सवै अंग र निकायले यसै प्रतिनिधिसभाबाट अधिकार पाएको सम्झी यस प्रति निष्ठावान रही सवैले आफ्नो अधिकार प्रयोग गर्नुपर्नेछ।

(ख) तोकिएका सार्वजनिक पद धारण गर्ने पदाधिकारीहरुले प्रतिनिधिसभाबाट तोकिएको ढांचामा तोकिएको शपथ लिने छन्। शपथ लिन इन्कार गर्ने अधिकारी पदमुक्त हुनेछन्।

(ग) यस घोषणासंग बाझिने नेपाल अधिराज्यको संविधान २०४७ र प्रचालित अन्य कानूनका व्यवस्थाहरु बाझिएको हदसम्म अमान्य हुनेछन्।

(घ) यो घोषणाको कार्यान्वयनमा आइपर्ने कुनैपनि बाधा अड्काउ प्रतिनिधिसभाले निर्णय गरी फुकाउन सक्नेछ।

(ङ) उपरोक्त खण्ड (ग) र (घ) को प्रयोजनका लागि प्रतिनिधिसभामा एक समिति रहनेछ।

***

Appendix II

9 Points Gender Agenda of IPWA Adopted on 8, March 2006.

परिच्छेद - २

५. सञ्जालका उद्देश्यहरु

अन्तर पार्टी महिला सञ्जालले आफ्नो लक्ष्य प्राप्तिका लागि प्राथमिकताका साझा विषयहरुको किटानी र अन्य साझा सवालहरु पहिल्याउने र त्यसको लागि आ–आफ्नो पार्टी र राष्ट्रिय स्तरमा नै त्यस्ता नीति निर्माण गरी प्रभावकारी कार्यान्वयनका लागि संयुक्त प्रयास र अभियानहरु सञ्चालन गर्नेछ। अन्तर पार्टी महिला सञ्जालको गठन गर्ने दौरानमा तत्कालीन साझा उद्देश्यहरुको निर्धारण निम्न अनुसार तय गरिएको छ।

१. संघीय लोकतान्त्रिक गणतन्त्र, दिगो, शान्ति र मानव अधिकारको स्थापना गर्ने।

२. आमाको नामबाट प्राप्त हुने नागरिकतामा भएका कानूनी असमानताहरु हटाउने।

३. राजनीतिक पार्टी, राज्यसंरचना लगायत सम्पूर्ण क्षेत्रमा जनसंख्याको आधारमा महिलाको समान प्रतिनिधित्व सुनिश्चित गर्ने।

४ प्रजनन्, स्वास्थ्य र यस सम्वन्धी अधिकारको व्यवस्था गर्ने।

५. द्वन्द्व प्रभावित महिलाहरुको मानव अधिकारको संरक्षण, सुरक्षा र पुनर्स्थपनाको व्यवस्था गर्ने।

६. महिला हिंसा, दुर्व्यवहार, कुरीति र कुप्रथा विरुद्ध अभियान सञ्चालन गर्ने।

७ सकरात्मक विभेदका कार्यक्रमहरु लागु गर्ने।

८ शिक्षा, रोजगारी, सामाजिक सुरक्षा, क्षेत्रीय सन्तुलन र समावेसी-करणको प्रत्याभुती गराउने।

९. महिला विरुद्ध हुने सबै प्रकारका भेदभाव उन्मुलन सम्बन्धी सन्धी, महासन्धीको प्रभावकारी कार्यान्वयन र पूर्णपालनाको लागि पहल गर्ने।

Appendix III

The Motion on Women Rights Adopted by Parliament on 30 May 2006.

श्री महासचिव,
संसद सचिवालय ।

देहायको जरुरी सार्वजनिक महत्वको विषयमाथि छलफल गर्न सूचना दिएको छु :-

<u>जरुरी सार्वजनिक महत्वको प्रस्ताव</u>

आमा वा बाबु मध्ये कसैको नामबाट पनि सन्तानले नागरिकता पाउन सक्ने कुराको ग्यारेन्टी गर्न, समानुपातिक सहभागिताको लक्ष्यमा पुग्ने कुरालाई ध्यानमा राखि हाललाई कम्तीमा एक तिहाइ महिलालाई राज्यका सबै संरचनामा सहभागिताको ग्यारेन्टी गर्ने, त्यस्तै विभेदकारी कानूनको खारेजी गर्न र महिला प्रति हुने गरेका हिंसाको अन्त्य गर्न जरुरी भएकोले यो जरुरी सार्वजनिक महत्वको प्रस्ताव पेश गरेको छु ।

<u>छलफल गर्नु पर्नाको कारण :-</u>

समान नागरिकको हैसियतले महिलाहरुको समान स्थान हासिल गर्न अत्यावश्यक भएकोले ।

<u>प्रस्तावक</u>
हस्ताक्षर :-
नाम, थर :- श्रीमती विद्यादेवी भण्डारी
क्रम संख्या :-
मिति :-

<u>समर्थक</u>

१. हस्ताक्षर :-
नाम, थर :- कमला पन्त
क्रम संख्या :-
मिति :-

२. हस्ताक्षर :-
नाम, थर :- नारायणप्रकाश साँउद
क्रम संख्या :-
मिति :-

३. हस्ताक्षर :-
नाम, थर :- [illegible]
क्रम संख्या :-
मिति :-

Appendix IV

List of the Seven Parties as Member of Left Front

Communist Party of Nepal (Marxist-Leninist)
Communist Party of Nepal (Marxist)
Communist Party of Nepal (Manandhar)
Communist Party of Nepal (Barma)
Communist Party of Nepal (Amatya)
Nepal Peasant Workers' Party
Communist Party of Nepal (Fourth Convention)

Appendix V

12-point understanding reached between the Seven Political Parties and Nepal Communist Party (Maoists).

The struggle between absolute monarchy and democracy running for a long time in Nepal has now been reached in a very grave and new turn. It has become the need of today to establish peace by resolving the 10-year old armed conflict through a forward-looking political outlet. Therefore, it has become an inevitable need to implement the concept of full democracy through a forward-looking restructuring of the state to resolve the problems related to class, cast, gender, region and so on of all sectors including the political, economic, social and cultural, by bringing the autocratic monarchy to an end and establishing full democracy. We hereby disclose that in the existence of aforesaid context and reference in the country, the following understanding has been reached between the Seven Political Parties within the parliament and the CPN (Maoists) through holding talks in different manners.

The points reached in understanding

1. The democracy, peace, prosperity, social advancement and an independent, sovereign Nepal is the principal wish of all Nepali people in the country today. We are fully agreed that the autocratic monarchy is the main hurdle for this. We have a clear opinion that the peace, progress and prosperity in the country is not possible until and full democracy is established by bringing the absolute monarchy to an end. Therefore, an understanding has been reached to establish full democracy by bringing the autocratic monarchy to an end through creating a storm of nation-wide democratic movement of all the forces against autocratic monarchy by focusing their assault against the autocratic monarchy from their respective positions.
2. The agitating Seven Political Parties are fully committed to the fact that the existing conflict in the country can be resolved

and the sovereignty and the state powers can completely be established in people only by establishing full democracy by restoring the parliament through the force of agitation and forming an power full-party Government by its decision, negotiating with the Maoists, and on the basis of agreement, holding the election of constituent assembly. The CPN (Maoists) has the view and commitment that the aforesaid goal can be achieved by holding a national political conference of the agitating democratic forces, and through its decision, forming an Interim Government and holding the election of constituent assembly. On the issue of this procedural agenda, an understanding has been made to continue dialogue and seek for a common agreement between the agitating Seven Political Parties and the CPN (Maoists). It has been agreed that the force of people's movement is the only alternative to achieve this goal.

3. The country, today, demands the establishment of a permanent peace along with a positive resolution of the armed conflict. We are, therefore, firmly committed to establish a permanent peace by bringing the existing armed conflict in the country to an end through a forward-looking political outlet of the establishment of the full democracy by ending the autocratic monarchy and holding an election of the constituent assembly that would come on the basis of aforesaid procedure. The CPN (Maoists) expresses its commitment to move forward in the new peaceful political stream through this process. In this very context, an understanding has been made to keep the Maoists armed force and the Royal Army under the United Nations or a reliable international supervision during the process of the election of constituent assembly after the end of the autocratic monarchy, to accomplish the election in a free and fair manner and to accept the result of the election. We also expect for the involvement of a reliable international community even in the process of negotiation.
4. Making public its commitment, institutional in a clear manner, towards the democratic norms and values like the

competitive multiparty system of governance, civil liberties, fundamental rights, human tights, principle of rule of law, etc., the CPN (Maoists) has expressed its commitment to move forward its activities accordingly.

5. The CPN (Maoists) has expressed its commitment to create an environment to allow the people and the leaders and workers of the political parties, who are displaced during the course of armed conflict, to return and stay with dignity in their respective places, to return their homes, land and property that was seized in an unjust manner and to allow them to carry out the political activities without any hindrance.
6. Making a self-assessment and a self-criticism of the past mistakes and weaknesses, the CPN (Maoists) has expressed its commitment for not allowing the mistakes and weaknesses to be committed in future.
7. Making a self-assessment towards the mistakes and weaknesses committed while staying in the Government and parliament in the past, the seven political parties have expressed their commitment for not repeating such mistakes and weaknesses now onwards.
8. The commitment has been made to fully respect the norms and values of the human rights and to move forward on the basis of them, and to respect the press freedom in the context of moving the peace process ahead.
9. As the announcement of the election of municipality is pushed forward for an ill-motive of deluding the people and the international community and of giving continuity to the autocratic and illegitimate rule of the King, and the rumour of the election of the parliament are a crafty ploy, announcing to boycott it actively in our own respective way, the general public are appealed to make such elections a failure.
10. The people and their representative political parties are the real guardians of nationality. Therefore, we are firmly committed towards the protection of the independence, sovereignty and the geographical integrity and the national unity of the country. It is our common obligation to maintain friendly

relations based on the principle of peaceful co-existence with all countries of the world and a good-neighborhood relationship with neighboring countries, especially with India and China. But, we request all the patriotic peoples to remain cautious against the false attempt of the King and the monarchists to create confusion in the patriotic people by projecting the illusory the fake ('Mandale') nationalism to prolong the autocratic and illegitimate rule of the King and to raise question mark over the patriotism of the political parties, and we appeal to the international powers and the communities to support the democratic movement against the autocratic monarchy in Nepal in every possible way.

11. We heartily invite the civil society, professional organizations, various wings of parties, people of all communities and regions, the press community, intellectuals all the Nepali people to make the Movement succeed by actively participating in the peaceful People's Movement launched on the basis of these understandings reached by keeping the democracy, peace, prosperity, forward-looking social transformation and the independence, sovereignty, and dignity of the country in centre.
12. Regarding the inappropriate conducts that took place among the parties in the past, a common commitment has been expressed to investigate the incidents raised objection and asked for the investigation by any party and take action over the guilty one if found and make informed publicly. An understanding has been made to resolve the problems if emerged among the parties now onwards through the dialogue by discussing in the concerned level or in the leadership level.

22 November 2005

Appendix VI

List of Pro-people Elected Representative in Panchayat

MPs of Rastriya Panchayat Election (1985)

1. Jhapa	Dron Acharya (Winner)
2. Ilam	Nobalkemi Rai (Winner)
3. Chitawan	Jagrit Prasad Bhetuwal (Winner)
4. Kaski	Somnath Pyasi (Winner)
5. Kathmandu	Padmaratna Tuladhar (Winner)

Elected Representative in Local Election (1986)

District President of Panchayat of Dhading

1. Dhading	Rajendra Pandey

Deputy President of District Panchayat

1. Jhapa	Puspa Pokhrel
2. Ilam	Bhakta Lamichhane
3. Chitawan	Hari Pun
4. Dang	Rammanhi Sharma
5. Palpa	Yadab Rayamajhi
6. Dolakha	Wangchhe Sherpa
7. Tehrathum	Khagendra Sitaula
8. Arghakhachi	Gunanidhi Bhusal

Women Representative in Villege Panchayat

1. Ganga Dangi,	Vice chair of Itahara Panchayat, Morang
2. Bhanu Rijal,	Vice-chair of Champadevi Panchayat, Kathmandu

Appendix VII

27 Points Criticism of UML on Constitution of Nepal 1990.

1. Art-3, Sovereignty should be on Nepali people
2. Art-4.1, Removal of 'Hindu' word
3. Art-6, All language should have equal status and Nepali language should be official working language.
4. Art-7.3, national doctrine impression should be changed
5. Chapter-3, in fundamental right, remove the wording 'Offence against state and Violence action'
6. Art-17, regarding property right should be based on concept of welfare state. Regarding land reform, the limitation should be set. Constitutional provision should be set regarding nationalization of the land above the limit. Workers should have full control over on their labor and production.
7. Chapter-5, regarding monarchy, Art-27.2, 'Monarchy' as nationality and symbol of national unity should be replaced by 'multiparty democracy and democratic constitution'.
8. Art-27.3, protector of the constitution should be people and Monarchy, political party and every individual should respect the constitution.
9. Art-28.1 and 2, should be deleted.
10. Art-29, provision in regard to cannot make law to reduce expenses of monarch and his family should be deleted. And, the word 'Shree panch' should also be deleted from this article.
11. Art-30, the provision of 'the income and private property of royal family would be tax free' should be deleted.
12. Art-30, definition of Royal Family should be mentioned clearly in separate article.
13. Art-31, this article should be corrected with 'Monarch's activities according to constitution could be debated in court'.
14. Chapter-6, the provision of Rajparisad' should be deleted.
15. Art-40, Monarch should be detached from executive power

and rest of the things he should do with the consensus and suggestion of council of ministers.

16. Art-41.6, should add 'if the motion of impeachment against him passed by legislation'.
17. In the case of dissolution of parliament, the provision of 'if the acting prime minister would be died before holding election, with recommendation of upper house, monarch should nominate next prime minister' should be clearly added.
18. Art-61.1, Restriction on debate in parliament about kind should be abolished.
19. Art-73.2, the provision regarding 'monarch's pre-consensus on bill of constitution amendment' should be deleted.
20. Art-77.1, regarding ordinance, the working, 'in case of monarch dissatisfaction or he does not realize need' should be deleted.
21. Art 82.1 and 84.1, 'the work to be done through monarch' should be deleted. Th wording in Art-86 and 87 as 'monarch's self-concise, satisfaction and consensus' should be deleted.
22. Chapter-18, Art-122.8, in the case of emergency, their right to remedy as Art-23 should not be withheld.
23. Art-125, the provision of 'National security committee' is not needed. Because, the right to mobilize military-force is right of executive and it should be fully under council of ministers.
24. Art-129, 'power to remove difficulties' should be done with recommendation of prime minister.
25. Art-133, all the laws contradiction with constitution should be repealed immediate after enforcement of constitution.
26. The wording 'His Majesty Government' should be replaced by 'Nepal Government', 'Royal army' by 'Nepal army' and all the 'Royal' word in connection with 'public enterprises and authority' should be replaced.
27. If in the case of monarch would act against constitution, the provision to table and debate on impeachment should be part of the constitution.

(Unofficial translation as aspiration)

Appendix VIII

List of 16-point Suggestion on Gender Equality Submitted by ANWA to Constitution Drafting Commission (1990).

भरीका नारीहरूको मागलाई दृष्टिगत गरी भावी संविधानमा नारीहरूको हक अधिकारको संवैधानिक सुनिश्चित गर्न नारी स्वतन्त्रता सम्बन्धी अन्तर्राष्ट्रिय सम्झौता, मानव अधिकार सम्बन्धी भएका संयुक्त राष्ट्र संघीय घोषणा पत्रहरू तथा नेपालका नारीहरूको वर्तमान दयनिय कमजोर अवस्थालाई मूल्यांकन गरी निम्न लिखितअनुसारका नारीहरूका हक अधिकारको संवैधानिक संरक्षण र सुनिश्चितता प्रदान गर्नु पर्दछ।

सार्वभौमिकता सम्बन्धमा–

१) सार्वभौम सत्ताको श्रोत जनता हुन तसर्थ सार्वभौम सत्ता जनतामा निहित हुनु पर्दछ।

२) संकटकालीन अधिकार संसदलाई मात्र हुनु पर्दछ र त्यस्तो संकटकालीन अवस्था विद्यमान भएको घोषणा गर्ने अवस्थाको पनि संविधानमा नै परिभाषित गरिनु पर्दछ। निम्न २ अवस्था विद्यमान भएका संकटकालीन अवस्थाको घोषणा संसदको २/३ वहुमतको अनुमोदनमा गर्नु पर्दछ र संसद नवसेको समयमा मन्त्री परिषदले त्यस्तो अवस्था बिद्यमान भएको भए सङ्कटकालीन अवस्था घोषणा गरी ७ दिन भित्र संसदबाट अनुमोदन गराउनु पर्दछ र परिभाषित अवस्था निम्न हुनु पर्दछ:–

(क) देशमा वाहिरी आक्रमण भएमा।

(ख) गृह युद्धको समय तथा सांप्रदायीक दङ्गाले गर्दा देशको सार्वभौम सत्ता नै विखण्डित हुने अवस्था भएमा।

मौलिक हक सम्बन्धमा–

३) भावी संविधानमा नारी र पुरुषको समान अधिकारको स्पष्ट रूपमा व्यवस्था गरिनु पर्दछ। नेपालको सम्विधान २०१९ मा "कानूनको समान संरक्षणका हकदार हुने छन्" भन्ने उल्लेख गरी धर्म, वर्ण लिङ्ग, जात जाती कुनै आधारमा भेदभाव गरिंछैन भनिएको भएता पनि छोरीले पैतृक सम्पत्ति नपाउने अवस्था हुंदा छोरा, आमा बाबु, स्वास्नी दाजु भाइले मात्र पाउने कानूनी प्रावधान भएको हुंदा त्यस्तो सम्विधानसंग वाझिएको कानूनको प्रयोग भई नारी र पुरुषका बीचमा असमानता भई भेदभाव भएको स्पष्ट छ। तसर्थ भावि सम्विधानमा स्पष्ट रूपमा नारीले पनि पुरुष सरह (छोरीले पनि छोरा सरह) बराबर पैतृक सम्पत्तिमा अधिकारको दावि गर्ने संपत्तिक अधिकारको संवैधानिक निश्चितता गरी समानताको अधिकारलाई कानूनको अगाडि सबै समान (Equality to all before law) भन्ने स्पष्ट शब्द प्रयोग गरी समानताको अधिकारको संवैधानिक निश्चितता गरिनु पर्दछ।

४) नेपालमा नारीहरू कमजोर र पिछडिएको कारण प्रमुख रूपमा शिक्षाको कमि नै हो भन्ने बारेमा दुइमत हुन सक्दैन। तसर्थ नारीहरूको उत्थान गर्न संवैधानिक रूपमा नै अनिवार्य शिक्षाको व्यवस्था गरी माध्यामिक तहसम्म नारीहरूलाई निशुल्क अध्ययन गराउने तथा उच्च शिक्षा अध्ययनको लागि उचित अवसरहरू प्रदान गर्ने व्यवस्था गराई अनिवार्य शिक्षा नदिने अभिभावक दण्डनीय बनाउने व्यवस्थाको समेत संवैधानिक निश्चितता गरिनु पर्दछ।

५) नेपाली नारीसंग विवाह भएको विदेशी नागरिकले पनि विवाह भएको उचित कानूनी प्रक्रिया पुरा गरी ५ वर्ष भित्र नेपाली नागरिकता दिइने व्यवस्था गरिनु पर्दछ।

६) भावि सम्विधानमा २ सदनात्मक संसदको व्यवस्था गरिनु पर्ने र माथिल्लो सदनमा तल्लो सदनमा जित्ने पार्टीहरूले समानुपातिक आधारमा मनोनयन गर्ने त्यसरी मनोनित गरिएका जम्मा सदस्य संख्याको ५० % स्थान नारीहरूको लागि मात्र निश्चित गरिनु पर्दछ।

) समाजमा नारी सहभागितालाई संवैधानिक अङ्गहरूमा महिलाहरूको उचित प्रतिनिधित्व हुने व्यवस्था संविधानमानै निश्चित गरिनु पर्दछ।

८) नारीहरूको सामाजिक सुरक्षाको स्पष्ट ग्यारेण्टीको व्यवस्था गरिनु पर्दछ।

९) नेपाली नारीहरूको अवस्था आर्थिक स्वावलम्वन नभएको कारणले गर्दा माथि उठ्न नसकेको हुंदा नारीलाई आर्थिक रूपबाट स्वावलम्बन बनाउने विषयमा भावि सम्विधानमा स्पष्ट रूपमा निश्चित गरिनु पर्दछ।

१०) नारी वर्गलाई छिटो छरितो र सुलभ न्याय प्रदान गर्नको लागि पारिवारिक अदालत (Family Court) को व्यवस्था सम्विधानमा नै गरिनु पर्दछ।

११) सम्वैधानिक रूपमा नै महिलाको सुरक्षाको गोपनियता सम्बन्धी (Right to privaly) को व्यवस्था गरिनु पर्दछ।

१२) नाबालकहरूले अनिवार्य ममता संरक्षण तथा पालनपोषणको व्यवस्था गरिनु पर्दछ।

१३) महिलाहरू समाजको सबै क्षेत्रमा पिछडिएका हुंदा पुरुष सरह प्रतिस्पर्धा गर्न सकिरहेको छैन। तसर्थ समाजका सबै क्षेत्रमा महिलाहरूलाई विशेष व्यवस्था गरी उनीहरूको लागि आवश्यक व्यवस्था गरिनु पर्दछ।

१४) मानव अधिकारको वाहाली संरक्षण र सम्वर्धन गर्नु संविधानको प्रमुख लक्ष्य हुने हुंदा भावि संविधानमा नागरिकका नागरिक तथा मौलिक हक अधिकारका संरक्षणको निश्चित हुनु पर्दछ। जसमा मानव अधिकार सम्बन्धी विश्व व्यापी घोषणा पत्र १९४८, संयुक्त राष्ट्रसंघिय आर्थिक, सामाजिक तथा सांस्कृतिक सम्बन्धी घोषणा पत्र १९६६ र संयुक्त राष्ट्र सम्बन्धी संघीय नागरिक तथा राजनैतिक अधिकार इच्छाधित उल्लेख १९६६ मा उल्लेख गरिएका मानव अधिकार सम्बन्धी व्यवस्थालाई अवलम्वन गरी मौलिक हकको निश्चितता गरिनु पर्दछ।

१५) सबै धर्मलाई धार्मिक स्वतन्त्रता हुनु पर्दछ तर लोभ, लालचा,दवाव अनुचित प्रभाव पारी वा गरी धर्म परिवर्तन गर्न नपाउने व्यवस्था गरिनु पर्दछ।

१६) स्वतन्त्र न्यायपालिका हुनु पर्दछ। □

Appendix IX

Inventory of the Women Mentioned in the Study

1. **Astalaxmi Shakya:** Astalaxmi shakya is a Kathmandu born woman from higher business class, came in touch with progressive movement through Chinese Study Center in 1970s. She became whole-time underground activist for year, 1978 to 1990. She was elected as chair of ANWA chair in 1989. After democracy, she was elected as a parliamentarian and nominated as minister time and again. Presently, she is vice-chair of UML.
2. **Balkumari Thapa:** Balkumari Thapa is a woman activist having peasant background. She is one of the UML activist, who joined UML in 1980s. Basically, she was providing shelter for underground leaders and organisng women locally until 1990. In the process, she was empowered and became part of womem movement. Her house was used for the venue of first women's gathering of UML in 1980.
3. **Belimaiya Ghale:** Belimaiya Ghale is one of the UML's young activist grown up through trade union movement onward 2000. Later, she become UML cadre and presently working in Katmandu ditrict committee of UML and central secretary of GEFONT.
4. **Bidyadevi Bhandari:** Bidyadevi Bhandari is widow of late leader of UML's Madan Bhandari. She was student activist in 1980s before marrying with Bhandari. After marriage, she joined ANWA and sidelinig after 1990. After the assasination of Madan, she stood from his constituency. After owning that parliamentary election of Kathmandu, re-entered in active politics. Then, she became parliamentarian and minister time and again. She was elected as chair of ANWA 1997 and UML vice-chair in 2008. Both post was assuming until 1015. Presently, she is president of Nepal onward October 2015.
5. **Bijaya Ghimire:** Bijaya Ghimire was underground activist of UML in 1980s decade. Later, she became ANWA leader

and now engaging with family responsibility. She is locally active in UML's politics.

6. **Bisheswara Dahal:** Bisheswara Dahal is a widow of Ramnath Dahal, who was killed in Shukhani. Later, she became an ANWA leader and parlimentarian. Precently, she is advisor of the UML.
7. **Chandrakanta Malla:** Chandrakanta Malla was sister of late martyr Dhasarathchand, who started women school in 1940s. That school was used as the venue for the women to empower them politically.
8. **Chayadevi Parajuli:** Chayadevi Parajuli was an activist of Nepali Congress. Regardless of her old age, she was very active for democracy after snatching the power by Gyanendra in 2004.
9. **Dati Bhoteni:** Dati Bhoteni was a peasant activist from Solukhumbu in 1960s. She was strong fighter agasint local feudal for social justice. That is why, while she was on the way back to home from Kathmandu, was killed in the remote area of Solukhumbu.
10. **Dibya Koirala:** Dibya Koirala was the wife of Krishana Prasad Koirala and mother of BP Koirala. She wasa first woman to initiate women organisation in 1920s. She had requested wife of 'Rana' primier to preside, putting herself as secretary in 1916. Rather materialising the thing, she was exiled with family in India. While, Nepali Congress was founding, she was involved since the conceptualising process. Later in 1947, she was arrested in connection with worker's movement in Biratnagar.
11. **Dulalni Bajai:** Dulalni Bajai was a local woman activist from Ilam. She was active in the anti-feudal activism in 1960s.
12. **Dwarikadevi Thakurani:** Dwarikadevi Thakurani was a first woman parliamentarian and minister of Nepal, elected in 1958 from Nepali Congress from Dadeldhura.
13. **Ganga Dangi:** Ganga Dangi was pro-people elected vice chair of VDC from UML in 1987. She was re-elected in the same post after multiparty system as well. She was ANWA leader

from then and became UML center committee member in 2009. Currently, she is member of parliament representing UML.

14. **Gaura Prasain:** Gaura Prasain was a woman activist since the Jhapa Bidorna in 1972. She was prisoned for three years. After released, she again joined UML and became ANWA leader. Currently, she is alterntice politburo of UML and member of parliament.
15. **Goma Devkota:** Goma Devekota is a widow of Rhisi Devkota Adaj, who was killed by Bhiman by state in 1980. Then, she joined UML as underground activist. Later, she became parliamentarian. Recently, she is the chair of ANWA and central committee member of UML.
16. **Goma Timalsina:** Goma Timalsina was working in Heatauda Textiel Industry and joined trade union in 1980s. She continued trade union and joined ANWA and UML in the later day. Presently, she is member of senior trade unionist alliance of GEFONT.
17. **Hisila Yami:** Hisila Yami was an architect by profession and senior leader of CPN (Maoist) during the arm-struggle started in 1996. Later, she was elected as parliamentarian and became minister time and again. Presently, she is with Naya Shakti.
18. **Indira Acharya:** Indira Acharya was of the four women arrested in Biratnagar worker's movement in 1947. She was Nepali Congress activist and mother of Shailaja Acharya.
19. **Ishwari Acharya:** Ishwari Acharya was UML's underground activist active in 1980s. Later, she joined teaching procession and became a supporter of UML.
20. **Jaya Ghimire:** Jaya Ghimire was an underground activist of UML in 1980s. Later, she became student leader in 1979. Since the restablishement of ANWA, she is one of the central leaders of it. She was member of CA-I. Presently, she is central committee member of UML and vice chair of ANWA.
21. **Kabita Paudel:** Kabita Paudel is one of the rebellion women, who became UML's cadres since the 1970s. She was local

activist of ANWA and challenged the tradition, doing by restricted work for women. Later, she become writer.

22. **Kamala Amatya:** Kamala Amatya is an UML activist, joined since 1980s. She was teacher by profession and became a leader of ANWA, who was one of the shelter provider of the UML underground leaders.
23. **Kamala Sharma:** Kamala Sharma is a widow of Rhisi Sharma from Surkhet, who was killed in during the election campaign of CA-I. Later, Kamala stood in that constituency and won the parliamentary seat. Now, she is working as district leader of UML.
24. **Laxmi Gyawali:** Laxmi Gyawali is engaging locally now, was one of the key activist of UML during 1990s. She was student leader before joining underground movement. She was one of three women delegates of the UML's 4th convention in 1989. After 1990, she is involving as local activities with taking care of family as well.
25. **Laxmi Karki:** Laxmi Karki was one of the icon rebellion of the UML's student leader during the people's movement in 1990. She was elected as secretary of ANWA from second conference in 1991. In the later days, she has been involved in NGO activism.
26. **Lila Kattel:** Lila Kattel is one of the three women activist of Jhapa Bidroha, involved since the beginning. She was active in the party work for a decades and passed away by transportation accident in 1982.
27. **Mangaladevi Singh:** Magngaladevi Singh was founder president of Nepal Women Organisation (NWO) and later became a leader of Nepali Congress. She was wife of the supreme leader of NC Ganeshman Singh.
28. **Meena Acharya:** Meena Acharya is one of the prominent woman economist, who is feminist sholar and inspiration of almost all Nepali women activist. She is the daughter of ex-prime minister, late Talka Prasad Acharya. Presently, she is advisor of the president of the country.

29. **Meena Paudel:** Meena Paudel is active in NGO sector as gender expert. She was one of the icon of the people movement in 1990, who was chair of Nursing Associal of Nepal that time. Ideologically, she was UML activist that time.
30. **Menaka Pokhrel:** Menaka Pokhrel is an university professor now. She was an underground activist of UML, grown up through student movement. Later, she become leader of the ANWA.
31. **Motidevi Shrestha:** Motidevi Shrestha was one of the founder member of CPN in 1949 and remained supporter of the communist movement for her entire life.
32. **Nalini Upadhyaya:** Nalini Upadhyaya was an activist of Nepali Congress. She was one of the four arrested women in Biratnagar worker's movement in 1947 and prisoned in Dhankuta for sometime.
33. **Namita-Sunita:** Namita-Sunita were two young girls as siblings, went to visit Pokhara after their SLC examination. But, both of their death bodies were found in Seti river after raped and murdered in 1981.
34. **Nanda Nepal:** Nanda Nepal was one of the woman worker in Biratnagar Jute mill. She staged 27 days long fast to death strike with demand of opening the closed factory. The movement was ended with success.
35. **Nona Koirala:** Nona Koirala was one of the prominent woman leader of NC. She was arrested in Biratnagar worker's movement in 1947 and prisoned in Dhankuta. Later days, she was one of the influencial member of the NC until her death.
36. **Onsari Gharti:** Onsari Gharti is currently speaker of the house of representative. She was one of the Maoist combatants, who opened the fire in 1996. Later, she became parliamentarian and minister as leader of CPN (MC).
37. **Pabitra Kharel:** Pabitra Kharel is active in UML and social activities in Jhapa. She was the one leading to celebrate IWD in 1981 among general people in Jhapa. She was underground activist in 1990s and became ANWA leader as well.

38. **Pamfa Bhusal:** Pamfa Bhusal is one of the leaders of CPN (MC). She joined student movement in 1980s and kept involvement continuously. She has been parliamentarian and minister in the past. Currently, she is spokesperson of CPN (MC).
39. **Purnashova Chitrakar:** Purnashova Chitrakar is more active in NGO movement and keeping the connection with UML as well. She was actively participating in UML activities in 1980s as semi-undrground activist and was elected as general secretary from ANWA in 1989. She is married with one of the senior leader of UML.
40. **Radha Gyawali:** Radha Gyawali is one of the UML leaders. She was secretary of the ANWA, while it was re-stablished in 1981. She joined underground movement for some years. She assumed post of parliamentarian and minister. Now, she is divorcee, vice-chair of ANWA and politburo member of UML.
41. **Radhadevi Paudel:** Radhadevi Paudel was a worker rebellion in 1951, who staged 27 days fasting in Jute mill together with Nanada Nepal.
42. **Ramkumari Jhakri:** Ramkumari Jhakri is a young leader of UML. She was elected as first woman chair of UML's student wing. She was one of the icon of the people's movement in 2006. Now, she is central committee member of UML.
43. **Rammaya Podę:** Rammaya Pode was one of the sanitary worker, working in the Singahadarbar, while the great martyrs of the country were kept therebefore death sentencing them. She was supporting them as messanger.
44. **Ratna Gurung:** Ratna Gurung is one of the UML activists from Kathmandu. She was parliamentarian and currently member of Kathmandu chapter of UML and central committee of ANWA.
45. **Ravilaxmi Chitrakar:** Ravilaxmi Chitrakar is university professor. She was one of the prominent activist of UML in 1980s. She was inspiring leader among women, was given name as 'iron lady'. But, after 1990, while her husband

became overground leader assuming different position in UML and state, she dissapeared from political scene.

46. **Rawanta Kumari Acharya:** Rawanta Kumari Acharya was wife of Tanka Prasad Acharya. While, her husband was in prison, she braved different activities to support him. Later, she started woman activism as well.
47. **Sadhana Pradhan:** Sadhana Pradhan was first elected woman represented of the country. She first arrested in 1947, while joined the street rally demanding civil right. Then, she became active of CPN. After 1960, she started career as school teacher and took care of family, while her husband Manamohan Adhikari was in prison.
48. **Sahana Pradhan:** Sahana Pradhan was an prominent leader of UML. She first arrested in 1947, while joined the street rally demanding civil right. Then, she became active in CPN. After 1960, she joined profession as university teacher. While her husband died in 1980, she became active again. She was chair of the left-front in 1990 movement. Then became politburo member of UML and chair of ANWA. She assumed minister and parlimentarian poisiton time and again. She was well accepted leaders of the women movement as whole too.
49. **Sarita Neupane:** Sarita Neupane is one of the UML's young activist, ground up from student field. Recently, she is member of ANWA central committee and UML Kathmandu chapter.
50. **Shailaja Acharya:** Shailaja Acharya was a prominent leader of Nepali Congress. She braved to protest Panchayat, while the then king was celebrating 'democracy day' on military theatre in 1960. She became parliamentarian, deputy prime-minsiter and deputy president of the Nepali Congress. But, later days of her life was very pitiful.
51. **Shanta Manavi:** Shanta Manavi is an UML activist. She was a child-widow and left the country after having untolerable torture. After getting in touch with CPN in India, came back to Nepal and join UML as underground movement. She became coordinator of the ANWA, while it was re-stablished in 1981. Later, she was working as central leader of UML

and became parliamentarian and minsiter as well. Currently, she is member of the parliament and advisory committee in UML.

52. **Shanti Adhikari:** Shanti Adhikari is an activist of UML. She was parlimentarian in 2008. Now, she is member of UML Kathmandu chapter and central committee member of ANWA.
53. **Sharada Lama:** Sharada Lama was a one of the brave trade union activists in 1980s, while she was working in Balaju industrial area. She was the one providing first shelter to Astalaxmi, while she left house to be underground activist of UML. Later days, she is out of the activism.
54. **Shova Kunwar:** Shova Kunwar is in teaching profression now. She was one of the activist joined Jhapa Bidroha. After mass level arrest of major leaders and activists of Jhapa Bidroha, she was leading the Jhapa chapter of UML. After being arrest time and again, she became underground activist for few years.
55. **Shusila Acharya:** Shusila Acharya is supporing as local activist of UML. She joined underground movement, while she was studying in secondary school and continued until 1990. Then, she was asked to work different district. Later after having family, she is pushed back from the frontline activism.
56. **Shusila Karki:** Shusila Karki is one of the prominent woman. She is the first woman chief justice of the country. She is an aspiration of Nepali women as honest, dignified, logical and self-esteemed of this era.
57. **Shusila Kharel:** Shusila Kharel is local activist of UML now. She joined UML as underground activist in early 1980s and prisonned for few years. During the time, she lost family and party contact both. Then, she married with one of the police personal, to whom she met in prison. Later, she went back to Jhapa and basically spending time to take care of family.
58. **Shusila Shrestha:** Shusila Shrestha is running private school since last almost two decades. She quited university and joined

underground movement in early1990s and spent there about a decade. After multiparty democracy, she was vice-chair of ANWA. While her husband started to occupy better position in the state and party, she sideline from mainstream politics and started private school. After that, she is in and out of the UML time and again. Now, she is out of UML.

59. **Sita Khadka:** Sita Khadka is in the another party. She joined the party activities since the Jhapa Incident as one of the key woman leaders of the UML until 1990. Now, she is with one of the splinter group. She is ex-parliamentarian and minister.

60. **Snehalata Shrestha:** Snehalata Shrestha is one of the founder of NWO in 1947 after her released from the custody of civil right movement. She was one of the activists of communist party since the beginning. After 1960, she never been the part of the formal structure of CPN. But, she always remains supporter of communist movement. After 1990, she is in close contact with UML.

61. **Sulochana Manandhar:** Sulochana Manandhar is one of the member of Nepal Pragya Pratisthan. She was very active in Kathmandu during the decade of 1990s as organiser among working masses. After multi-party democracy, she lost the spirit of mass activism and become pragya.

62. **Swasti Bajracharya:** Swasti Bajracharya is a teacher by profession. She was deputy coordinator, while ANWA was re-stablished in 1981. She was semi-underground activist of UML in Kathmandu. She became the founder coordinator of GEFONT women department after 1990. She is not very active in politics now.

63. **Yogmaya Neupane:** Yogmaya Neupane was an brave woman, who initiated women's collective agitation from Bhojpur. She was child-widow. Challenging the tradition, she got widow marriage. Later, she became rebellion against inhuman cultural oppression over human being. She is one of the icon of the Nepali women's movement.

References

Acharya, M. (n.d.). *Approaches to Development and Gender: An Impact in Nepal's Policies.* Kathmandu: Tanka Prasad Acharya Memorial Foundation.

Acker, S. (1995). Carry on caring: The work of women teachers. *British Journal of Sociology of Education,* 16(1), 21–36.

Adhikari, K. (2018). *Adalatcdojuhari, amakonammanagarikatadeu* (Court said to CDO to provide citizenship with mother name), http://cijnepal.org.np/03/ 2018–02–13

Adhikari, S. (2059). *Nepali congressko Itihas* [History of Nepali Congress]. Kathmandu: Bhunipuran Prakashan.

ANWA (1982). *Mahilamukti*-2 [Women Liberation, Vol. 2]. Kathmandu: Mahilamukti Prakashan.

ANWA (1985). *Mahilamukti*-3 [Women Liberation, Vol. 3]. Kathmandu: Mahilamukti Prakashan.

ANWA (1991). *Mahilamukti*-5 [Women Liberation, Vol. 5]. Kathmandu: Mahilamukti Prakashan.

ANWA (1998). *Mahilamukti*-7 [Women Liberation, Vol. 7]. Kathmandu: Mahilamukti Prakashan.

ANWA (1991). *Organizational Report Adopted by the Second National Conference.* Kathmandu: Author.

ANWA (1996). *Organizational Report Adopted by the Second National Conference.* Kathmandu: Author.

Arnstein, S.R. (1969). A ladder of citizen participation. *Journal of the American Planning Association,* 35(4), 216–224.

Au, W. (2006). Against economic determinism: Revisiting the roots of Neo-Marxism in critical educational theory. *Journal for Critical Education Policy Studies,* 4(2), 11–35.

Basnet, M. (1996). *Nepalko Prajatantrik Janaandolanma Mahila Bargako Bhumika* [Women role in Nepalese democratic movement]. Kathmandu: Veraiti printers.

Basnet, P. (2009). *Nepali Congressko Itihaskoprarup* [History of Nepali Congress]. Kathmandu: Banglamukhi Offset Press.

Bass, B.M. (1985). *Leadership and Performance Beyond Expectations.* New York, NY: Free Press.

Brandy, C.C. (2007). *Gender, Atitudes and Perceptions of Workplace Incivility.* Cambridge, MA: Harvard University Press.

Brady, H.E., Verba, S. and Schlozman, K.L. (1995). Beyond SES: A resource model of political participation. *American Political Science Review,* 89(2), 271–294.

Bedacht, M. (1925*). The little red library (No. 3: Principle of Communist, Engel's First Draft of Communist Manifesto.* Chicago: The daily workers publishing.

Beech, I. (1999). Bracketing in research: A typology. *Qualitative Health Research,* 6(3), 20–29.

Bloor, M. and Wood, F. (2006). *Keywords in Qualitative Methods: A Vocabulary of Research Concepts.* London: Sage Publications.

Blunden, A. (n.d.). *The Minutes of the Communist International* 1864–1966. Retrieved from https://www.marxists.org/archive/marx/iwma/documents/minutes/

Booth, H., Creamer, D., Davis, S., Dobbin, D, Kaufman, R. and Klass, T. (1972). *Socialist Feminism: A Strategy for the Women's Movement.* Chicago: Women's Liberation Union Hyde Park Chapter. Retrieved from http://www.historyisaweapon.com/defcon1/chisocfem.html

Bradshaw, J. (2013). *The Women's Liberation Movement: Europe and North America.* Retrieved from https://books.google.com.np/books?isbn=1483160823

Boserup, E., Tan, S.F. and Toulmin, C. (2013). *Woman's Role in Economic Development.* New York, NY: Routledge.

Brooks, A. (2006). *Feminist Standpoint Epistemology: Building Knowledge and Empowerment Through Women's Lived Experiences*. London: Sage.

Brown, T. (2013). *Situated Learning Theory of Lave and Wenger*. Retrieved from https://www.scribd.com/document/317953247/Situated-Learning-Review

Burns, D. (1994). *The Politics of Decentralization*. London: Macmillan.

Burns, J. (1978). *Leadership*. New York, NY: Harper and Row.

Burns, N. and Grove, S.K. (2003). *Understanding Nursing Research* (3rd ed.). Philadelphia: Saunders Company.

Butler, J. (1990). *Gender trouble: Feminism and the Subversion of Identity*. London: Routledge.

Butler, J. (1999). *Gender trouble: Feminism and the Subversion of Identity*. London: Routledge.

Central Bureau of Statistics, National Planning Commission Secretariat, Government of Nepal (CBS) (2008). *National Labour Force Survey: Statistical Report*. Kathmandu: Author.

Central Bureau of Statistics. (2011). *Preliminary Report of Population Census* 2011. Kathmandu: Author.

Central Bureau of Statistics. (2017). *Statistical Pockate Book of Nepal*. Kathmandu: Author.

Chatterjee, M. (2004). *Feminism and Women's Humna Rights* (Vol. II). Jaipur: Aabiskar Publishers.

Chitrakar, P.S. (1980). *Antarrastriya Mahila Diwasko Samkshipta Itihas* (Brief history of IWD). Kathmandu: Mahilamukti Prakashan.

Chitrakar, P.S. (1991). *Anter-rastriyasramikmahiladiwasko bare* (On International working-women day-March, 8). Kathmandu: ANWA.

Chitrakar, P.S. (1991). Jana-andolanma Mahilaharuko sahavagita ra anemasagh (Women's participation in people's movement and ANWA). *Mahilamukti,* 5, 5–8.

Chowdhary, N. (1994). Women in politics. *Empowerment: A Journal of Women for Women,* 1, 21–42.

Claassen, R.L. and Highton, B. (2009). Policy polarization among party elites and the significance of political awareness in the mass public. *Political Research Quarterly,* 62(3), 538–551.

Clancey, W.J. (1995) A tutorial on situated learning. in J. Self. (Ed.), *Proceedings of the international conference on computers and education (Taiwan)*, (pp. 49–70). Charlottesville, VA: AACE.

Clark, H., Chandler, J. and Barry, J. (1999). Gender and managerialism. In P. Fogelberg, J. Hearn, L. Husuand and T. Mankkinen (eds.), *Hard work in the academy*. Helsinki: Helsinki University Press.

Coleman, M., Haiyan, Q. and Yanping, L. (1998). Women in educational management in China: Experience in Shaanxi province. *Compare*, 28(2), 141–154.

Conley, J.M. and O'Barr, W.M. (2002). *Back to the trobriands: The enduring influence of Malinowski's crime and custom in savage society*. Retrieved from http://www.jstor.org/stable/829058

Cornwall, A. and Goetz, A.M. (2005). Democratizing democracy. *Feminist Perspectives, Democratization*, 12(5), 783–800. Retrieved from https://assets.publishing.service.gov.uk/media/57a08c7040f0b652dd001322/democratizing_democracy.pdf

CPN (1949). *Nepal Communist partyko ghosanaptra: Chhaniyaka rachanaharu, Bhag*-1 (Manifesto of Communist Party of Nepal, selected work of Puspalal, vol. 1). Kathmandu: Madan-Asrit Smriti Praisthan.

CPN-ML (1978). *Apani-3, Communist Party of Nepal, Marxist-Leninist* (CPN-ML). Kathmandu: Author.

CPN-ML (1980). *Apani* 4, *Central committee of CPN-ML Feb.* 16, 1980. Kathmandu: Author.

CPN-ML (1980). *Apani* 9, *Central committee of CPN-ML, Oct.* 14, 1980. Kathmandu: Author.

CPN-ML (1985). *Apani.* 20, *Central committee of CPN-ML, June,* 22, 1985. Kathmandu: Author.

CPN-ML (1987). *Apani.* 25, *Central committee of CPN-ML*. Kathmandu: Author.

CPN-ML (1987). *Apani-23, Central committee of CPN-ML*. Kathmandu: Author.

CPN-ML (1989a). *Constitution of CPN-ML adopted by* 4th *national congress of CPN-ML*. Siraha: Author.

CPN-ML (1989b). *Political report adopted by* 4th *national congress of CPN-ML*. Siraha: Author.

CPN-ML (1989c). *Sangathanatmak Prastab* (Organisational Proposal) adopted by 4th national congress of CPN-ML. Siraha: Author.

CPN-ML (1990). 27 *points of criticism and support on Constitution of Nepal*-1990, *Central Committee of CPN-ML*. Kathmandu: Author.

CPN-UML (1991). *Election manifesto*. Kathmandu: Author.

CPN-UML (1993a). *Neplikrantiko karyakram: Janatako bahudaliya janabad* [Program of the Nepali revolution: People's multi-party democracy]. Kathmandu: Author.

CPN-UML (1993b). *Sangathanatmak prastab* (Organisatinal proposal). Kathmandu: Author.

CPN-UML (1994). *Election manifesto, general election*. Kathmandu: Author.

CPN-UML (1995). *Second national council meeting* (Report p. 44. Kathmandu: Author.

CPN-UML (1996). *Rastriya parisadko tesro baithakko rajnitik pratibedan* (Political report adopted by 3rd council meeting (Feb, 1995). Kathmandu: Nawayug Cooperative Press.

CPN-UML (1998). *Political report adopted by* 6th *national congress of CPN-UML*. Kathmandu: Nawayug Cooperative Press.

CPN-UML (2003a). *Pratibadan (Report), adopted by* 4th *meeting of central committee of CPN-UML*. Kathmandu: Nawayug Cooperative Press.

CPN-UML (2003b). *Third national council meeting* (Report). Kathmandu: Author.

CPN-UML (2005a). *Apani-* 11 (Intra Party Corcular). Kathmandu: Author.

CPN-UML (2005b). *Apani*-12 (Intra Party Corcular). Kathmandu: Author.

CPN-UML (2007a). *Aparni*-20 (Intra Party Corcular). Kathmandu: Author.

CPN-UML (2007b). *Sambidhanko Lagi Prashikshan Samagri* (Taining material on constitution). Kathmandu: Nawayug Cooperative Press.

CPN-UML (2008). *Election manifesto, constituent assembly* . Kathmandu: Nawayug Cooperative Press.

CPN-UML (2009a). *Constitution of CPN-UML 3rd amendment, art.* 38 *and* 66–4. Kathmandu: Nawayug Cooperative Press.

CPN-UML (2009b). *Political report adopted by 8th national congress of CPN-UML.* Kathmandu: Nawayug Cooperative Press.

CPN-UML (2012). *Rajya punasangrachasambandhi pratibedan-* 2068 (Report on state re-structuring). Kathmandu: Nawayug Cooperative Press.

CPN-UML (2013). *Sambidhansabha: Gathandekhi bighatansamma Swetapatra* (Constituent assembly from the beginning to end: Whitepaper). Kathmandu: Nawayug Cooperative Press.

CPN-UML (2014a). *Constitution of CPN-UML* (4th amendment, adopted by 9th national convention). Kathmandu: Nawayug Cooperative Press.

CPN-UML (2014b). *Political report* (adopted by 9th National Convention of CPN-UML). Kathmandu: Nawayug Cooperative Press.

CPN-UML (2016). *Resolution of sixth central committee, adopted on April,* 17, 2016. Kathmandu: Author.

Creswell, J.W. (2007). *Qualitative inquiry and research design: Choosing among five approaches* (2nd ed.). Thousand Oaks: Sage.

Cultural Feminism. (n.d.). Retrieved from http://shodhganga.inflibnet.ac.in/bitstream/10603/3852/8/08_chapter%202.pdf

De Laine, M. (2000). *Fieldwork, participation and practice.* London: Sage.

Denzin, N.K. (1989). *The research act* (3rd ed.). NJ: Prentice Hall.

Derbyshire, H.S. (2002). *Gender manual: A practical guide for development policy makers and practitioners.* Development Division DFID, UK

Dhungana, S. (1998). Mahila andolanko itihas: 2017 samma (History of Nepalese women's movement upto 1960). *Mahilamukti,* 7, 20–25.

Dikshit, M.M. (2010). *Shree: Shashwatnari* [Eternal women]. Lalitpur: Sajha Prakashan.

Dorey-Stein, C. (2015). *A brief history: Three waves feminism, progressive women's leadership*. Retrieved from https://www.progressivewomensleadership.com/a-brief-history-the-three-waves-of-feminism/

Duke, J. (2010). The dynamics of women participation in democratic politics and sustainable development in Africa. *Journal of Sustainable Development in Africa*, 12(4), 83–95.

Duong, C. (2012). *Modernization theory and women's political representation: A case study of Vietnam.* Retrieved from https://ruor.uottawa.ca/bitstream/10393/22853/1/Duong_Cathy_2012_researchpaper.pdf

Echols, A. (1989.). *Daring to be bad, radical feminism in America,* 1967–1975. Minneapolis: Univeristy of Minnesora Press.

ECN (2008). *Election commission of Nepal.* Retrieved from http://www.election.gov.np/election/np/ca-election-2008–136.html

ECN (2014). *Election commission of Nepal.* Retrieved from http://election.gov.np/CA2070/CAResults/reportBody.php?selectedMenu1=1andrand=1384967216

ECN (2016). *Election commission of Nepal.* Retrieved from http://www.election.gov.np/ecn/uploads/userfiles/1642073.03.12.pdf

ECN (2017). The Result of election, Election commission of Nepal, Retrieved from http://result.election.gov.np

Edward, L.G., Giacomo, A.M.P. and Shleifer, A. (2007). Why does democracy need education? *Journal of Economic Growth,* 12(2), 77–99.

EU (2005). *Women in decision-making position.* Belgium: Author.

Evetts, J. (1994). *Becoming a secondary head-teacher*. London: Longman.

Farooqi, M.I.H. (2011). *Status of women in Islamic societies: Past and present.* Retrieved from http://www.countercurrents.org/farooqi090311.htm

Feminism: Basic principles. Retrieved from http://www.colorado.edu/Sociology/Mayer/Contemporary%20

Feminist theory in education, encyclopaedia of the social and cultural foundations of education. Retrieved from http://www.armchairpatriot.

com/Encyclopedias/Encyclopedia%20of%20the%20Social%20and%20Cultural%20Foundations%20of%20Education.pdf

Fink, D. (1992). *Agrarian women: Wives and mothers in rural Nebraska,* 1880–1940. North Carolina: UNC Press Books.

Franke, K. M. (1987). *Theorizing yes: An essay on feminism, law and desire.* Columbia: Columbia University.

Freedman, E.B. (2002). *No turning back: The history of feminism and the future of women.* New York, NY: Ballantine Books.

Freeman, M., Demarrais, K., Preissle, J., Roulston, K. and Pierre, E.S. (2007). Standards of evidence in qualitative research: An incitement to discourse. *Educational Researcher,* 36, 25–32.

Friedan, F. (1963). *The feminine mystique: Myth or reality?*. London: Penguin Group.

Friedrich, C.J. (1961). Political leadership and the problem of charismatic power. *The Journal of Politics,* 23, 3–24.

Frye, M. (1993). *Some reflections on separatism and power.* New York, NY: Routhledge.

Gautam, R. (1990). *Nepalko prajatantrik andolanma Nepal praja-parisadko bhumika* [Role of Nepal Praja-parisad in Nepalese democratic movement]. Kathmandu: Author.

Geoffrey, M.V. (2005). The overreach of political education and liberalism's philosopher. *Democrat, Polity,* 37(3), 389–408.

Gibb, C.A. (1954). *Leadership: Handbook of social psychology.* Cambridge: Addison-Wesley.

Ghodsee, K. (2004). Feminism-by-design: emerging capitalisms, cultural feminism and women's nongovernmental organizations in postsocialist Eastern Europe. *Signs: Journal of Women in Culture and Society,* 29(3), 727–753.

Goetz, P.J. (2003). The effects of bilingualism on theory of mind development. *Bilingualism: Language and Cognition,* 6(1), 1–15.

Goleman, D. (2000). Leadership that gets results. *Harvard Business Review,* 78(2), 4–17.

Government of Nepal. (1951). *Interim constitution of Nepal.* Kathmandu: Author.

Government of Nepal. (1963). *Muluki Ain*-2020 [Civil Code-1963]. Kathmandu: Author.

Government of Nepal. (1990). *Constitution of Nepal, art.* 114. Kathmandu: Author.

Government of Nepal. (1997). *Sthaniya Swayatta Sarkar*-2055 (Local Autonomous Government Act, art. 7). Kathmandu: Author.

Government of Nepal. (2002). *Tenth Firfth year plan,* National Planning Commission Secretariat, . Kathmandu: Author.

Government of Nepal. (2006). *Declaration of parliament (May,* 18*).* Kathmandu: Author.

Government of Nepal. (2006). *Declaration of parliament (May,* 30*).* Kathmandu: Author.

Government of Nepal. (2006). *Report of parliamentarian secretariat (*2006–2*).* Kathmandu: Author.

Government of Nepal. (2007). *Interim constitution of Nepal.* Kathmandu: Author.

Government of Nepal. (2008). *Constituent assembly secretariat.* Kathmandu: Author.

Government of Nepal. (2009). *Report of the PMO.* Kathmandu: Author.

Government of Nepal. (2011). *Report of the PMO.* Kathmandu: Author.

Government of Nepal. (2012). *Report of the PMO.* Kathmandu: Author.

Government of Nepal. (2015). Constitution *of Nepal.* Kathmandu: Author.

Government of Nepal. (2015). *Report of the PMO.* Kathmandu: Author.

Government of Nepal. (2017). Act related with local election. Kathmandu: Author.

Greenleaf, R.K. (1996). *On Becoming a Servant-leader.* San Francisco: Josey-Bass Publishers.

Grey, M. (2012). *The nature of Women's Political Leadership: Women MPs in the Parliament of Victoria.* Retrieved from www.womenaustralia.info/leaders/sti/pdfs/27_Grey.pdf

Gudorf, C. (1998). *Who says the Church Can't Change*?. Retrieved from http://www.uscatholic.org/1998/07/change.htm

Gunter, H. (2001). Critical approaches to leadership in education. *Journal of Educational Enquiry*, 2(2), 94–108.

Gurmai, Z. (2010). *Social Democracy and Gender Equality, Qriseeu-2: The next, wave of emancipation.* Retrieved from http://www.feps-europe.eu/assets/884e1d9f-6148–400a-a616–11502b732ee8/2010_07.pdf

Haig, B. (1999). Feminist research methodology. In J. P. Keeves and G. Lakomski (eds.), *Issues in Educational Research* (pp. 222–231). Oxford: Elsevier Science.

Hambleton, R. (1997). *New Perspectives on Local Governance: Reviewing the Research Evidence.* New York, NY: Joseph Rowntree Foundation.

Hamill, C. and Sinclair, H. (2010). Bracketing practical considerations in Husserlian phenomenological research. *Nurse Research* 17(2), 16–24.

Hammersley, M. (1990). An evaluation of two studies of gender imbalance in classroom interaction. *British Educational Research Journal*, 16(2), 125–143.

Hanisch, C. (2006). *The personal is political by Carol.* Retrieved from http://www.transart.org/wp-content/uploads/group-documents/56/1362346911–PersonalisPol.pdf

Harding, S. (1993). *Rethinking Standpoint Epistemology: What is Strong Objectivity, Feminist Epistemologies.* Routledge: Elizabeth Potter.

Harris, A., Leithwood, K., Day, C., Sammons, P. and Hopkins, D. (2007). Distributed leadership and organisational change: Reviewing the evidence. *Journal of Educational Change,* 8, 337–347.

Hart, C., Jones, K. and Bains, M. (1997). *Do the people want power? The Social Responsibilities of Empowering Communities.* Contested Communities: Experiences, policies, struggles. Bristol: The Policy Press.

Henderson, J. (2004). Tradition and the status of women in the Catholic Church. *Australian Journal of Theology.* Retrieved from http://aejt.com.au/__data/assets/pdf_file/0006/395682/AEJT_2.18_Henderson_Tradition_and_the_Status_of_Women.pdf

Himali Prakashan Paritwar (1984). *Piskar Daman ra pratirodhko byatha* [Piskar: Soreness of suppression and resistance]. Baranasi: Janata Press.

Hochschild, A. (2003). *A very short summary of socialist feminist theory and practice, the second shift.* https://www.marxists.org/archive/marx/works/download/pdf/Manifesto.pdf

Huntington, S. (1991). *The third wave: Democratization in the late twentieth century.* Norman: University of Oklahoma Press.

Husserl, E. (1931). *Ideas: A general introduction to pure phenomenology.* London

IPU (1997). 161st *session of the Inter-parliamentary council, Cairo (Egypt), inter-parliamentary union.* Geneva: Author.

IPU (2010). *Women in politics.* Inter-Parliamentary Union and the United Nations Division for the Advancement of Women, France.

IPU (2011). *A global review of good practice.* Gender-Sensitive Parliament, Inter-Parliamentary Union, Geneva, Switzerland.

IPU (2014). *Atlas of electoral gender quotas.* http://www.ipu.org/pdf/publications/atlas-en.pdf

IPU (2017). *Atlas of electoral gender quotas.* http://www.ipu.org/pdf/publications/atlas-en.pdf

IPWA. (2006). *Nirdeshika* [Inter party Women Alliance]. Kathmandu: Author.

Joll, J. (n.d.). *The minute of the second international,* 1889–1914. Retrieved from http://platypus1917.org/wp-content/uploads/2015/12/James_Joll_The_Second_International_1889–1914.pdf

Joshi, S.K. (2008). *Violence against women in Nepal: An overview the free library.* Retrieved from http://www.thefreelibrary.com/Violence Against Women in Nepal—An Overview- a01073875052

K.C., S. (2005). *Collection of historical documents, 1963–1993* (part. 2). Kathmandu: Pairavi Prakashan.

K.C., S. (1999). *History of the communist movement in Nepal, 1949–1962.* Kathmandu: Bidhaythi Pustak Bhandar.

K.C., S. (2009). *History of the Communist movement in Nepal, 1993–2008* (vol.3). Kathmandu: Bidhaythi Pustak Bhandar.

K.C., S. (2014). *History of the Communist movement in Nepal, 1963–1992* (2nd Ed Vol. 2). Kathmandu: Bidhaythi Pustak Bhandar.

Kabeer, N. (2001). *Resources, agency, achievements* (discussing women's empowerment, 17). Retrieved from http://www.sida.se/globalassets/publications/import/pdf/sv/discussing-womens-empowerment---theory-and-practice.pdf#page=19

Kaplan, T. (1985). On the socialist origins of international women's day. *Feminist Studies*, 11(1), 163–171. Retrieved from https://libcom.org/files/International%20Women's%20Day.pdf

Kaundinyayan, A.B. (2006). *Baidik Dharmashastra Ra Sampattima Mahilako Adhikar-2063* [Vedic religion and women's property right]. Lalitpur: Sajha Prakashan.

Kinchloe, J.L. and McLaren, P. (2000). *Key works in critical pedagogy.* London: Sense Publishers.

Kisan, Y. B. (2010). *Dalitra Sakaratmak Upaya* [Untouchable and affirmative action]. Kathmandu: ActionAid.

Kollointai, A. (1920). *International women's day*. Retrieved from https://libcom.org/files/International%20Women's%20Day%20–%20Alexandra%20Kollontai.pdf

Kumbhare, A.R. (2009). *Women of India: Their status since the Vedic times*. New York, NY: iUnivesrse.

Kunwar, R.R. and Kunwar, D.B. (2014). *Nalapanikanayak Beer Balabhadra Kunwar* [Leader of Nalapani war–Birbhalabhadra Kunwar]. Kathmandu: Rastriyabivuti Beer Balalbhadra Kunwar-pratisthan.

Kunwar, R.R. (2014). *Birbalabhadra, eitihasikupanyas* [Birbalabhadra, historical noble]. Kathmandu: Sunrise Graphic Design.

Kunwar, T.N. (2008). *Balabhadra Kunwarko Biratako Gatha* [Story of bravery of Balabhadra Kunwar]. Kathmandu: Bhalabhadra Kunwar Smriti Pratisthan.

Kurland, R. (n.d.). *American for a Fair Change, Opportunity Through Affirmative Action*. Washington DC.

Lamsa, A.M. and Sintonen, T. (2001). A discursive approach to understanding women leaders in working life. *Ethical Leadership and Accountability*, 34(3), 255–267.

Lave, J. and Wenger, E. (1991). *Situated Learning: Legitimate Peripheral Participation*. Cambridge: Cambridge University Press.

Lawrence, A. (2006). No personal motive?: Volunteers, biodiversity and the false dichotomies of participation. *Ethics, Place and Environment*, 9, 279–298.

Lenin, V.I. (1921). *Lenin's Collected Works* (Vol. 32). Moscow: Progress Publishers.

Lenin, V.I. (1922). *Lenin's Collected Works* (Vol. 33, 2nd Ed.). Moscow: Progress Publishers.

Lenin, V.I. (2011). *Collected Works* (Vol. 23). Moscow: Progressive Publishers.

Lewin, K. (1939). *Lewin's Leadership Styles*. Retrieved from http://changingminds.org/disciplines/leadership/styles/lewin_style.htm

Li, Yuhui (2000). Women's movement and change of women's status in China. *Journal of International Women's Studies,* 1(1), 30–40. Retrieved from http://vc.bridgew.edu/jiws/vol1/iss1/3

Lorber, J. (n.d.). *The variety of feminisms and their contribution to gender equality*. Retrieved from http://diglib.bis.unioldenburg.de/pub/unireden/ur97/kap1.pdf

Lovenduski, J. and Norris, P. (1993). *Gender and Party Politics*. London: Sage Publication.

Lund, C. (1970). *Leon Trotsky, Women and the Family*. New York, NY: Pathfinder Press.

Lund, C. (1970). *Women and the Family*. New York, NY: Pathfinder Press.

Madison, D.S. (2005). *Critical ethnography: Method, ethics and performance*. Thousand Oaks: Sage.

Mainali, R.K. (2016). *Jhapa Sangharsadekhi Singhadarbarsamme* (Jhapa movement to Singadarbar. *Nawayug,* 26, 3.

Malla, M.B. (2011). *Political Socialization of Women in Nepal*. New Delhi: Adroit Publishers.

MAMF. (1999). *People's Multi-party Democracy* (policy papers). Kathmandu: Nawayug Cooperative Press.

Manusmriti: The Laws of Manu. (n.d.). Retrieved from https://vedpuran.files.wordpress.com/2013/04/manusmriti.pdf

Mao, T.T. (1940). *On New Democracy* (Trans., K. Sangraula, 1990). Kathmandu: Pragati Prakashan.

Mao, T.T. (1955). *Introductory note to women have gone to the labour front.* Retrieved from https://www.marxists.org/reference/archive/mao/works/red-book/ch31.htm

Mao, T.T. (1957). *Selected Works of Mao Tse-tung* (Vol. 7). Retrieved from http://www.historycentral.com/asia/MaoSays.html

Marx, K. and Engels, F. (1848). *Manifesto of communist party.* Retrieved from https://www.marxists.org/archive/marx/works/download/pdf/Manifesto.pdf

Marx, K. and Engels, F. (1848). *Communist Manifesto* (Trans. Krishnadas, 1993). Kathmandu: Pairabiprakashan.

Marx, K. (1866). Marxism and the emancipation of women. Retrieved from http://www.marxist.com/marxism-feminism-emancipation-women080300.htm

Marx, K. (1978). *Women and Comminism, Selection from the Writings of Karl Marx, Frederick Engels, V.I. Lenin, Joseph Stalin, Mao Tsetung.* New Delhi: New Book Centre.

Mascuilli, J., Molchanov, M.A. and Knight, W.A. (2009). *Political Leadership in Context.* Retrieved from http://www.ashgate.com/isbn/9780754671824

Maynard, M. (1995). Beyond the big three: The development of feminist theory into the 1990s. *Women's History Review,* 4(3), 259–281.

Mazumdaru, S. (2014). *Gurkhas: Nepalese Warriors in World War I.* Retrieved from http://www.dw.com/en/gurkhas-nepalese-warriors-in-world-war-i/a-17632181

Menon, M.E. (2011). *Leadership Theory and Educational Outcomes: The Case of Distributed and Transformational Leadership*. Cyprus: Department of Education, University of Cyprus.

Megharaja, B. (2014). Women empowerment: A challenge of 21st century. *International Journal of Management, IT and Engineering,* 4(2), 78–92.

Michelle, T.K. (2006). Non-formal education, political participation and democracy: Findings from Senegal. *Political Behavior,* 28(1), 1–31.

Mill, J.S. (1869). *The Subjection of Women.* Retrieved from http://www.constitution.org/jsm/women.htm

Millet, K. (1970). *Sexual Politics.* New York, NY: First Illinois.

Misra, D. (2003). *Nepalko Prajatantrik Bikaskram Ra Kathmandu Upatyakako Nirwachan* [Development process of democracy in Nepal and Election of Kathmandu valley]. Kathmandu: Hissi upset printing press.

Moghadam, V.M. (2008). *Democracy and Women's Rights: Reflections on the Middle East and North Africa, Sociology and Women's Studies.* Purdue University, West Lafayette, USA.

Muñoz, A. and Woods, A. (n.d.). *Marxism and the Emancipation of Women.* Retrieved from http://www.marxist.com/marxism-feminism-emancipation-women080300.htm

Myriad. (2006). *Citizenship Norms and Political Participation in America: The Good News is ... the Bad News is Wrong.* Washington, DC: The Center for Democracy and Civil Society Georgetown University.

Narang, U. (2012). Self help group: An effective approach to women empowerment in India. *International Journal of Social Science and Interdisciplinary Research,* 1(8), 1–7.

NC. (2012). *Nepali Congressko Bidhan* (Constitution of Nepali Congress). Kathmandu: Author.

Nepal Pragya Pratisthan (2010). *Nepali brihat shabdakosh* (97th ed.). Kathmandu: Pragya Chhapakhana.

Nepal, G.M. (1995). *Nepalkomahabharat* [The Mahabharata, 2nd ed.]. Kathmandu: Sajhaprakashan.

Nepal, G.M. (1999). *Nepal Nirupan.* Kathmandu: Nepal Pragya Prtisthan.

Nepal, G.M. (2000). *Samajik Andolanki Agrani Tatha Kavi Yogmaya Nepal Adhyayan Kendra.* Kathmandu: Author.

Nijsten, N. (2011). Some things we need for a feminist revolution. *Interface: A Journal for and About Social Movements,* 3(2), 214–225.

Nye, J.S. (2008). *Recovering American Leadership Survival: Global Politics and Strategy.* Retrieved from http://www.tandfonline.com/loi/tsur20

Odumeru, J.A. and Ogbonna, I.G. (2013). Transformational vs. transactional leadership theories: Evidence in literature. *International Review of Management and Business Research,* 2(2), 355.

Paley, J. (1997). Husserl, phenomenology and Nursing. *Journal of Advanced Nursing,* 26(1), 187–193.

Panday, P.K. (2008). Representative without participation: Quotas for women in Bangladesh. *International Political Science Review,* 29(4), 489–512.

Pandey, B. (2002). *Women Participation in Nepalese Labor Movement.* Kathmandu: GEFONT.

Pandey, B. (2006). *Ajaka Yuba-Bidhyarthi Volika Saksham Janashakti* (Today's youth and student: Tomorrow's capable human-resource). Kathmandu: GEFONT.

Parliamentary Archives (1866). *Votes for Women: The* 1866 *suffrage petition.* Retrieved from https://www.parliament.uk/business/committees/committees-a-z/commons-select/petitions-committee/petition-of-the-month/votes-for-women-the-1866–suffrage-petition/

Paudel, K. (2016). *Kadagharikoyatra* [Travelling through thorny grove, 4th ed.]. Kathmandu: Safal Printing Press.

Pokhrel, R.C. (1984). *Prajatantrakamahansenani BP Koirala* [Fighter of the democracy—B.P. Koirala]. Kathmandu: Bhattaraibandhu Prakashan.

Pounder, J.S. and Coleman, M. (2002). Women better leaders than men?: In general and educational management, it still all depends. *Leadership and Organization Development Journal,* 23(3), 122–133.

Prasain, G. (2016). JhapaSangharsadekhi singhadarbarsamme [Jhapa movement of Singadarbar]. *Nawayug,* 26(3), 54.

Prabhupad. (1971). *Spiritual Communism.* Retrieved from http://www.prabhupada-krishna.co.uk/spiritual_communism.htm

Priyadarshini. (n.d.). *Rig Vedic Society.* Retrieved from http://www.historydiscussion.net/history-of-india/rig-vedic-society-study-notes/2362.

Puspalal. (1949). *Nepal Communist Partyko Ghosanaptra-Chhaniyaka Rachanaharu* (Bhag-1) [Manifesto of communist party of Nepal, selected work of Puspalal, vol. 1]. Kathmandu: Madan-Asrit Smriti Praisthan.

Puspalal. (1996). *Nepalma Communist andolanko samshipta itihas* [Brief history of Communist movement in Nepal]. Kathmandu: Puspalal Memorial Foundation.

Ramanujachari. (n.d.). *Yajñavalkya Smriti: Dharma teachings of Yajñavalkya.* Retrieved from http://www.srimatham.com/uploads/5/5/4/9/5549439/yajnavalkya_smrti_abridged.pdf

Rampton, M. (2015). *Four Waves of Feminism.* Center for Gender Equity Pacific University. Retrieved from https://www.pacificu.edu/about-us/news-events/four-waves-feminism

Rathgeber, E. (1989). *WID, WAD, GAD: Trends in research and practice.* Ottawa: International Development Research Centre.

Reddy, K.V. (2010). Working class in 'Quit India' movement Madras Presidency, 1942. *Indian Historical Review,* 37(2), 275–289.

Redstockings. (1969). *Redstockings Manifesto.* Retrieved from http://www.redstockings.org/

Resolution of second international socialist conference of women, 1910. Retrieved from https://archive.org/details/InternationalSocialistCongress1910

Second International Conference

Rey, C. (2005). Gender, women and leadership. *Agenda,* 19(65), 4–11.

Ridd, R. and Callway, H. 1986). *Caught up in Conflict: Women's Response to Political Strife.* London: Macmillan.

Riley, N.E. (1999). Challenging demography: Contributions from feminist. *Sociological Forum,* 14(3), 369–397.

Roberto, M.A. (2009). *The Art of Critical Decision Making.* Virginia: The teaching company.

Roza, V, Beatriz, L. and Roza G. G. (2011). *Gender and Political Parties: Far from Parity, International Institute for Democracy and Electoral Assistance.* (International IDEA) and Inter-American Development Bank, USA.

Rubin, H.J. and Rubin, I.S. (2005). *Qualitative Interviewing: The Art of Hearing Data.* Thousand Oaks: Sage Publication.

Sadie, Y. (2005). Women in political decision-making in the SADC region. *Agenda*, 19(65), 17–31.

Saldana, J. (2014). *Thinking Qualitatively: Methods of Mind*. London: Sage Publications.

Sapkota, J. (2018). Foolharuko Byatha (problem of flowers), retrieved from https://www.kantipurdaily.com/feature/2018/04/07/152306673929725225.html

Sarmiento, M.N. (2003). Gender studies in Cuba: Methodological approaches, 1974–2001. *Gender and Society*, 17(1), 7–32.

Schnackenburg, R. (1995). *The Attitude of Jesus Toward Women and the Family*. Retrieved from http://www.ewtn.com/library/FAMILY/ATJESUS.TXT

Seager, J. (1997). *The State of Women in the World Atlas*. Penguin: Pennsylvania State University.

Selected Works of Mao Tse-tung. (1957). Retrieved from https://www.marxists.org/reference/archive/mao/selected-works/volume-7/pubnote.htm

Shakeshaft, C. (2006). Gender and educational management. In C. Skelton, B. Francis and L. Smulyan (Eds.), *The Sage Handbook of Gender and Education*. Thousand Oaks: Sage Publication.

Sharma, B.C. (1965). *Nepalko Itihasik Rup-Rekha* [Historical structure of Nepal, 2nd ed.]. Banarasi: Krishnakumari.

Sharma, J.L. (2000). *Samajik Andolanki Agrani Tatha Kavi Yogmaya*, Kathmandu: Nepal Adhyayan Kendra.

Sharma, J.L. (1963). *Josmani Santa Parampara Ra Sahitya*. Kathmandu: Sajha Prakashan.

Shreshtha, S. (2013). *Sahana Pradhan: Smritika Jhyalbata* [Sahana Pradhan: Through window of memory]. Kathmandu: Swapna Batika Publication.

Shrestha, S. (2013). *Sahashi Ra Nidar Mahila: Dati Bhoteni* [Courageou and brave woman: Dati Sherpa]. Kathmandu: Motidevi memorial Centeer: Nawayug Cooperative Press.

SIC-ICWC. (n.d.). *History and theory of feminism*. Retrieved from http://www.gender.cawater-info.net/knowledge_base/rubricator/feminism_e.htm

Simon, B. (2005). *German Socialism and the "Woman Question"*. Retrieved from http://www.workersliberty.org/node/5031

Singh, M.D. (1994). *Nari Sangharsaka Pailaharu* (Foot-steps of women struggle). Kathmandu: Sewa Printing Press.

Snye, J. (2008). *Global Politics and Strategy: Recovering American Leadership Survival.* London: Routledge.

Spears, L.C. (Ed.). (1995). *Reflections on Leadership: How Robert K. Greenleaf's Theory of Servant-Leadership Influenced Today's Top Management Thinkers.* New York, NY: John Wiley.

Spillane, J.P., Hunt, B. and Healy, K. (2008). *Managing and leading elementary schools: Attending to the formal and informal organisation.* Paper presented at The Annual Meeting of the European Educational Research Association, Gottenburg, Sweden.

Staff. (2010). *Seneca Falls Convention Begins, A+E Networks.* Retrieve from http://www.history.com/this-day-in-history/seneca-falls-convention-begins

Stein, D. (1998). *Situated Learning in Adult Education.* Retrieved from http://www.ericdigests.org/1998–3/adult-education.html

Stoker, G. (1997). *Local political participation in new perspectives on local governance.* New York, NY: Joseph Rowntree Foundation.

Stoner-Weiss, K. and Bunce, V., McFaul, M.(Eds.). (2009). *Democracy and authoritarianism in the postcommunist world.* Cambridge: Cambridge University Press.

Suarez, M. (1995). *Commitment to the Future, Regional Action Plan* (Beijing report). Asia and Pacific, NGO Forum Suneeta Adar.

Thapa, S. (1990). *May, Diwaskasarimanaidaichha? May, Diwaskosamkshiptaitihas* (How to celebrate May, day? Brief history of May, day). Kathmandu: INSEC.

The Minute Book of the General Council of the International Working Men's Association. (1866). Retrieved from http://www.marxists.org/history/international/iwma/documents/minutes

The Minute of the Second International, 1889–1914. Retrieved from http://hiaw.org/defcon6/iwma/documents/minutes/index.html

The Minutes of the Communist International 1864–1966. Retrieved from http://hiaw.org/defcon6/iwma/documents/minutes/index.html

Theory/Feminist%20Theory_files/frame.htm

The Puranas: A Compact, English-only Version of the Major 18 Puranas in One Document (2002). Retrieved from http://www.vcscsd.org/content/balabhavan/18–Puranas.pdf

Thayer-Bacon, B.J. and Turner, G.M. (2007). What feminist inquiry contributes to philosophy and the philosophy of education: A symposium. *Educational Theory,* 57(3), 297–306.

Timsina, M., Kunwar, L., Bhandari, L. and Bhattarai, K. (2000). *Samajik Andolanki Agranitathakabi Yogmaya*. Kathmandu: Nepal Adhyayan Kendra.

Trotsky, L. (1923). *A Letter to a Moscow Women Worker's Celebration and Rally.* Moscow: Pravda, Intercontinental Press.

True, J., Niner, S., Parashar, S. and George, N. (2012). *Women's Political Participation in Asia and the Pacific*. Social Science Research Council: Conflict Prevention and Peace Forum. Retrieved from http://artsonline. monash. edu. au.

Trotsky, L. (1925). *To Build Socialism Means to Emancipate Women and Protect Mothers, Leon Trotsky, Women and the Family*. New York, NY: Pathfinder Press.

Trotsky, L. (1970). *Leon Trotsky: Women and the Family*. New York, NY: Pathfinder Press.

Tucker, M.L., McCarthy, A.M. and Jones, M.C. (1999). Women and men politicians: Are some of the best leaders dissatisfied? *Leadership and Organisation Evelopment Journal,* 20(6), 285–290.

Tumbahamfe, S. (2009). *Nepalma Mahila Aandolan* (Women's movement in Nepal). Biratnagar: Bani Prakashan.

Trung, P.T. (2013). Are women's rights human rights? A view on women's political participation in Vietnam. *International Journal of Development and Sustainability*, 2(1), 1–8.

United Nations. (1948). *Universal Declaration of Human Rights*. New York, NY: United Nations.

United Nations. (1979). *Convention on Elimination of All Form of Discrimination Against Women*. New York, NY: United Nations.

United Nations. (1990). *Women Empowerment and Economic Development, Economic and Social Council*. New York, NY: United Nations.

United Nations. (1995). *Beijing Platform for Action*. New York, NY: Author.

United Nations. (1996). *Report of the Fourth World Conference on Women Beijing*, 4–15 September, 1995, United Nations, New York.

United Nations. (2005). *Report of the Expert Group*. Division for the Advancement of Women, Department of Economic and Social Affairs. New York, NY: United Nations.

United Nations. (2012). *Empowerment: What it mean to you?, Department of Economic and Social Affairs, Devision of Economic and Development Policy*. Retrieved from http://www.un.org/esa/socdev/ngo/outreachmaterials/empowerment-booklet.pdf

Upadhyaya, G. P. (1997). *Nepalko Prajatantrik Itihas-Sandarva* [Democratic history of Nepal: A consequinces]. Kathmandu: Ratna Pustak Bhandar.

Usha. (1989). *Nepali Mahila Andolan: Chhoto Charcha* [History of Nepalese women's movement: Brief history. *Mahilamukti* (vol.4). Kathmandu: Mahilamuktiprakashan.

Verba, S. and Norman, N. (1972). *Participation in America*. New York, NY: Harper and Row.

Verba, S., Schlozman, K.L. and Brady, H. (1995). *Voice and Equality: Civic Voluntarism in American Politics*. Cambridge: Harvard University Press.

Wagle, N. (2016). *Jhapa Sangharsadekhi Singhadarbarsamma* (Jhapa movement to Singadarbar). *Nawayug*, 26(3), 65

Wall, C., Glenn, S., Mitchinson, S. and Poole, H. (2005). Using a reflective diary to develop bracketing skills during a phenomenological investigation. *Nurse Researcher*, 11(4), 20–29.

Walter, M.A. (1989). *Feminism and the Marxist Movement.* New York, NY: Pathfinder Printing.

Weber, M. (1958). The three types of legitimate rule. *Berkeley Publications in Society and Institutions*, 4(1), 1–11.

Weisskopf, T.E. (2004). *Affirmative Action in the United States and India: A Comparative Perspective.* London: Routledge.

Westen, M. (1994). Literacy education and gender: The case of Honduras, functional literacy. *Theoretical Issues and Educational Implication*, 257–277.

White, M.I. (2000). Leadership that gets results. *Harvard Business Review.* Retrieved from https://hbr.org/2000/03/leadership-that-gets-results

Wikander, U., Kessler-Harris, A. and Lewis, J. E. (1995*). Protecting women: Labor Legislation in Europe, the United States and Australia 1880–1920.* Chicago: University of Illinois Press.

Wu, C.L. (2003). Psycho-political correlates of political efficacy: The case of the 1994. *Journal of Black Studies,* 33(6), 729–760.

Yihong, J. (2006). *Rethinking the 'Iron Girls': Gender and Labour During the Chinese Cultural Revolution* (K.E. Manning and L. Chu, Trans.). New York, NY: Blackwell Publishing.

Yingyi, M. (2009). The Chinese women's movement: From state control to independent global participation. *Bi-Annual Journal of Women for Women International,* 7(1), 1–13.

Zhou, J. (2013). Keys to women's liberation in communist China: An historical overview. *Journal of International Women's Studies*, 5(1), 67–77.

Index